And The Winner Is …

By
Michael V. Regan

This is a work of fiction. Names, characters, businesses, places, events and incidents are either the products of the author's imagination or used in a fictitious manner. Any resemblance to actual persons, living or dead, or actual events is purely coincidental.

CHAPTER ONE—Arrival

They were sitting in a chain restaurant at Simon Bolivar Airport drinking coffee, waiting for the arrival of a plane from Miami.

"Braga's work," the Colonel said. "Our visitor doesn't need to know anything about that. Agreed?" Braga was Dr. Vitorino Braga, professor of Marine Archaeology at the University of Lisbon whose presence in Venezuela was officially explained as "doing some government work."

"Or the *diario*. Or the list," he added. Elise looked up from her phone's screen and rolled her pretty eyes, eyes that had required more and more attention to remain pretty as the years had passed.

"Relax, Ferdie," she said, using a nickname she knew he hated. "I know what to discuss and not discuss. And, he is not *our* visitor. He is *my* visitor." She was pleased to see that Colonel Fernando Bautiste's face had reddened. She was not pleased to see the dead look in his eyes.

"Either way, <u>don't</u> discuss," the Colonel said with finality. She swallowed. He waited for her answer.

"Ferdie, don't worry," she said with less confidence than before. "I need the money as much as you do." She reached for her cup, but didn't raise it.

"Stop calling me that and, no, you do not need the money as much as I do. I need the money to survive and move forward. You just need the money to what? Pay for your little crap house?" His eyes challenged her to defy him. Her face reddened reflecting a rising emotion.

"Wrong, *Ferdie*," she emphasized trying hard to appear unafraid. "I need the money to be happy. That's all.

3

Simple, isn't it? Happy." She gazed into his dark eyes. "How is Braga's work going anyway?" she asked changing the subject. "I thought you said he would finish today." As he had said, to Bautiste the money was necessary for survival. His cartel deal was not working out.

Bautiste gazed out the glass wall at the flight line and considered how he should answer.

Braga, the old academic, squinted at the laptop display. The afternoon sun was reflected in the flat screen. Braga was disturbed by the data. He shook his head, looked around and immediately located his most trusted diver.

"Angelo, recheck Area 5. I don't think the they spent enough time there." Angelo was standing in the water up to his knees. He knew they had spent plenty of time there. He was, however, devoted to the project leader.

"Yes, Doctor. But I am certain there was nothing. Fourteen boxes would be hard to miss, yes?" Angelo slid his diving mask off his forehead and over his face. He bit down on his breathing apparatus and waded back out into the water.

Vitorino Braga, PhD. at that moment was not "doing some government work". He was working though. In fact he was perspiring heavily, not just from his efforts and not just because of the relentless Caribbean sun. Braga was getting nervous. He had promised his patrons results by this night and he needed their patronage to perform one of the greatest salvage coups every attempted. On the beach he directed his team of recovery experts, reviewing the settings on their equipment and assigning them to the jobs that needed to be done. He was puzzled that the team hadn't found anything yet. He agreed with Angelo. Fourteen boxes would be hard to miss, and he was afraid that his secret sponsors, not understanding the complexities of the recovery process, might withdraw their funding. Or worse.

4

Braga's team had begun by dividing the area around the shipwreck into a search grid. Divers working in pairs had searched the sandy bottom for two days. And they hadn't found anything of interest.

A month ago Braga's network of worldwide followers had solved the puzzle of the journal entry, a simple list of last names and first initials. "The captain's tears" were salt water and the fourteen boxes of gold, silver, and jewels were located in the salt water. He had been confident that it was going to be just a matter of days before the fourteen boxes were found. Now it had been nearly six weeks since the puzzle had been cracked. Braga was proud that his network of former students and colleagues had ultimately found the answer, but he couldn't understand why the search was taking so long. He did feel vindicated though. Ever since his arrival in Venezuela, he had always suspected that there was more to the submerged wreck than just an interesting history.

Braga was present on the beach and in charge because it was Braga, summoned to the beach by the Venezuelan government, who had identified the sunken hulk as the *Little Ranger* and Braga who had recognized the significance of the ship's presence in Venezuelan waters.

"*Monsieur* Wilson," Braga said calling to the barefoot and diminutive Frenchman who was standing close by frowning over the latest reports, "when will the Navy ship be here?" The little man was miserable in the island heat.

"*Professeur,*" Wilson said using Braga's formal title, "I believe they are scheduled to be here in one week." The Frenchman and his colleague, Mlle. Rideau, were not privy to the concept of secret sponsors. They believed that the Venezuelan government was the backer of this latest diving effort. This was not true. They also believed that the Venezuelan government was the exclusive partner of the French and this was true.

Renee Rideau, ignoring that her black hair was soaked by her own perspiration, studied the most recent photos.

"JJ," she called to Wilson, "these are the best yet. The drone is fantastic, isn't it?" Wilson shifted his attention from the schedule of the French navy to his fellow countrywoman.

Colonel Bautiste brought the coffee to his lips, realized it had gone cold, and set the cup down. He knew that no appeal to Elise's sensitivities would be effective so he decided to be more direct.

He was going to say something about what a good team they made, thought better of it, and, instead, said, "I may have a use for this American, *your* visitor, so keep him happy. Please." She smiled sweetly.

Bautiste ignored her and studied the Arrival announcements. She had already noticed the time, but Bautiste spoke first. "Let's go and meet your American friend."

The "friend" was Alex Browning. He was father to Connie and Joanne, brother to Brother Terry (it gave rise to awkward explanations from time to time), and uncertain abecedarian regarding, what had been up until this day, a virtual romance with Elise.

Alex Browning was sixty-seven years old; well over six feet tall, blue-eyed and white-haired. An unbiased observer might say he was in good shape, but Alex felt differently. His blood pressure required monitoring and medicating and his weight was, if not a serious concern, at least a small embarrassment. After a career as a defense industry software engineer (Navigation and Guidance software was his specialty), he had recently retired and, pending a suitable period of waffling and against his brother's advice, had agreed to this trip to Venezuela.

"You're sure you have room for me?" Alex had asked. It wasn't that he doubted Elise. Alex, normally a confident person, was strangely nervous that he might be an inconvenience to her. They had been discussing his upcoming trip from his home in California to hers in Venezuela.

"I have space for you, *bebe*," she had assured him pacing the small living room of her one bedroom house. "Are you a person who worries? How is it called? I can't remember." She was teasing and he knew it.

"It's called a worrywart. I think," Alex answered putting his beer bottle to his lips and realizing it was empty, added, "and, no, I'm not." He set the empty bottle down on his kitchen counter, a counter he had cleaned at least twice a week over the last two years. Those were the first two years of his retirement and he had put himself on a rigorous schedule of cleaning/maintaining his home and developing unsuccessful computer games. "At least I don't think so. I guess I'm just being cautious, for both of us," he added. "It's been a long time, fifteen years, since Mary died and I haven't dated that much." This was, Alex knew, an exaggeration. He had hardly dated at all.

"I am sorry for Mary." Elise had known Alex's wife a long time ago, but barely remembered her. "This won't be dating," Elise had said as she had smoothed an imagined wrinkle in a colorful duvet. "We are two adults. You will be visiting me. I will show you my island. We will have a good time. How many years since I see you?" Alex knew without having to think about it.

"Thirty-four," he said a little too quickly and then added, "I think."

"A long time." Elise surveyed her home. She tried to imagine how Alex could fit in there for a month.

That conversation took place in early January, just after New Year's Day, and Alex's trip was planned for late

7

February, a trip that would cause him immeasurable loss and immense gain.

A little drunk on airline Bloody Marys, Alex was mentally reviewing the January conversation before he stepped off the plane in Venezuela.

Oddly, Alex felt valued this day. He smiled to himself. A widower for fifteen lonely years, Alex had finally accepted the offer, Elise Diaz' offer. He had known Elise years ago and, although married to Mary, he had been tempted to pursue an inappropriate relationship with the young attractive Venezuelan. Nothing had happened, but she had left a lasting impression on him like a high water mark on a building after a long ago flood. Social media was the means by which Alex had reconnected with Elise. She had politely pushed him off at first, but he had persisted until she unexpectedly relented and extended an invitation. Clear of the stream of disembarking passengers, Alex pulled out his iPhone and opened the Messages app.

Five people were keeping their various digital devices, tablets, phones and computers, close as they anticipated Alex's message. Two of the devices belonged to sisters, Connie and Joanne Browning. They lived in Philadelphia, Pennsylvania. Since the two lived in separate parts of Philly, Connie IM'ed her younger sister. "U c tha msg?" She knew her sister would be as relieved as she was. The answer arrived: "Ya."

Connie, Caroline Browning, was taller than her younger sister. Besides long limbs, she had dark blonde hair and a heart-shaped face that was framed by that hair. When the message arrived that Monday night, she was at home. Home was a large first floor apartment, a one-bedroom with an open plan. She had an impressive workspace installed in one area with several flat-screens on the wall and a premium sound system. She was a "techie", a Twenty-First century geek, one of the rare women who made up the low percentage of females in the tech industry. Men found her to be a pretty young woman. She was in excellent physical condition and, at twenty-seven years, was a rising star in the field of software security. She had gambled early in her academic and professional careers that the relatively unexploited software vulnerabilities, which existed in Apple's many products, would not go unexploited forever. She believed that the worldwide hacker community would eventually tire of attacking the Windows operating system. Therefore, as a grad (and even as an undergrad), she had concentrated on exposing, reporting and developing fixes for the Cupertino, California company's software weaknesses. Apple, while not exactly loving her, appreciated and supported her work. Hackers, it seemed, were more and more attracted to the challenge of cracking Apple software. Connie was able to profitably operate her own software security company.

Joanne Browning was two years younger than her sister Connie. She had dark hair, appeared slight of build, though those in her kick boxing class soon learned that her build belied an iron frame and a will to match. When her father's message arrived, she, like her older sister, was home. Home for Jo, as she was known, was her second story apartment in an upscale area of Philadelphia. It was also an open plan with the bedroom on an upper level. She was a gifted software developer and a body builder. Almost antithetical to her body type, she possessed impressive reflexes and was an accomplished sand volleyball player. Unlike Connie, she was easy going and difficult to agitate. Although she had been heavily recruited out of college, she had no desire to work at a large company like Facebook or Google. She enjoyed the close social aspect of working at small software start-ups where her colleagues were as gifted as she. The risk/reward ratio of working at a start-up was not only acceptable but was attractive to a twenty-five year old programmer. She had yet to strike it rich, but was making a comfortable living. She was also expanding her knowledge exponentially.

Bautiste and Elise Diaz standing in the international arrival area at Simon Bolivar Airport (listed as in Caracas, but actually located in Maiquetía, Venezuela, 12 miles outside of Caracas) also separately viewed Alex's message, Elise by plan, Bautiste by malfeasance.

Colonel Fernando Bautiste of the Venezuelan National Police was a small, neat man, attributes that often led those who came up against him to, with great regret, regard him lightly. He customarily wore the dark blue uniform of his office, but tonight he was dressed casually in slacks and a loose white shirt. Bautiste was the top lawman for Nueva Esparta, the smallest of twenty-three governed districts that made up the country of Venezuela. Nueva Esparta included Margarita Island, the largest island off the northeast Venezuelan coast. Margarita Island was where Bautiste maintained his headquarters and his home.

As the top law on the Island and as a confidante of President Hugo Chavez, Colonel Bautiste was one of the most powerful men in the Latin American country. He deprecatingly spoke of himself as "just a policeman". Tonight Colonel Bautiste was not acting in his official policeman capacity. He was there as a longtime friend and sometimes co-conspirator of his companion.

Colonel Bautiste's companion, Elisabeth Diaz, known to her friends as Elise, was a petite and striking two-time divorcee who, at the age of fifty-two, still turned heads. This evening she wore an expensive bright sheath. It was short and strapless and showed off her dark skin tones. Her shoes with heels designed to display the shape of her ankles and calves were made of the softest leather. Having studied abroad, she was fluent in English, Spanish, French, and Portuguese. She had returned to Venezuela as an educated young woman, thanks to doting parents, where she had begun to work her way up a Chavez-led government career ladder. Her climb included a stint as a law officer until she became the Communications Director for Nueva Esparta.

This position gave her final approval over all press releases intended for public consumption.

Elise had a sweet face and stunning smile. Her looks, as is sometimes the case, were the direct opposite of her nature. Narcissistic and a natural schemer, she was adept at manipulating others, mostly men, into serving her needs. She maintained a Facebook account. Her Facebook pictures didn't capture the hardness around her slanted brown eyes.

Another recipient of Alex's message was his younger brother, Brother Terrence Browning, F.S.C. Brother Terrence with his large frame, black robe and full white beard was an intimidating figure around the La Salle University campus where he was assigned. In fact, he was an intimidating figure everywhere in the city, whether mingling with Philadelphia society or at an alumni function representing the University's endowment fund. He was the Provost at the university, a position akin to Senior Vice President at a corporation. He was working late that night and was in his well-appointed office at La Salle when he read Alex's message. He was angry at the content, but, then, these days, it seemed he was usually angry. "Shit and effing shit," he declared to the empty room. "He never effing listens to me." As a Catholic, he would have to confess this outburst. He was angry with that, too. His assistant in the outer office just rolled her eyes.

In the late 1960's Brother Terrence had been a young undergraduate, a member of the religious community which lived in a 1920's era mansion located in Elkins Park, a suburb to the north of Philadelphia. To Terrence's horror, three years after his graduation that mansion, along with the forty-plus acre estate, was sold to a Philadelphia developer. The developer promptly razed all the estate's buildings and replaced them with upscale housing, suburban crap, as Brother Terrence saw it. The sale was driven by a community decision by the young undergraduates. To a man they felt that their living conditions were shameful. The group voted to move from the luxurious estate of the suburbs to a humble home in the city, closer to the "people". Brother

11

Terrence was the only sibling of Alex and uncle to Connie and Joanne.

Inside the Simon Bolivar Airport with his carry-on slung over his shoulder, Alex Browning had stepped out of the flow of bodies and pulled out his iPhone, thinking for the umpteenth time that he was so glad he had taken his daughters' advice and dumped his Blackberry. The small Blackberry display had gotten to be too much of a challenge to his unaided eyes and he hated the rigmarole of retrieving, donning, and storing his glasses just for a quick read. Also, as an engineer, he loved the fact that everything worked on the iPhone – and worked well. (Ironically, when actually making phone calls, the speakerphone seemed kind of tinny or, maybe, his hearing was going the way of his eyesight.) Anyway, clicking on the green messaging app icon, he had sent a group message. It read: "Hey guys. Just landed in Venezuela. Will update AOAIC. Don't miss you-yet. ;-)". He knew that Elise, his daughters, and his brother would be glad for the update. He had no idea that Fernando Bautiste had intruded. He could have emailed everyone, but he found that texting was more convenient. He also appreciated the brevity of messaging.

Alex put away his iPhone and looked around him. With a wry smile and a deep breath, he shook his head. As other passengers flowed around him, he rubbed his forehead, reviewing the circumstances that had brought him here. He was a widower. Fifteen years ago, Hodgkin's disease had suddenly taken Mary. On Monday she had felt "weird" and went in to get checked. She was just forty and thought maybe it was early menopause. The doctor ordered a bunch of tests, sent her home and, on Wednesday, made his diagnosis. That same day, weak and confused, she was admitted to the hospital. Alex could barely keep up with the events as, on Thursday, she died. His wife of twenty-one years, best friend and mother of little Connie and Joanne was gone. After that, his "wiring" frazzled, his spirit broken and lacking clear direction, he spent the next decade and a half concentrating on his career and raising his teenage daughters, seeing them both graduate high school and college. He also had become a cranky bachelor and a loner. Then, a year ago, on a whim and at his daughters' urging and with their help, he had set up a Facebook page. He had earlier tried online dating, but hated the very idea of it. Facebook, Connie explained, wasn't about dating. It was just about being available to old friends.

Facebook, wisely or not, made it easy to seek out those people who, over time, had been dropped off on the shoulders of life's road. Alex had postponed his Facebook search for Elise many times. For one thing, he felt disloyal to Mary's memory. Also, unsure exactly how Facebook worked, he feared that Elise might be notified that he was searching for her profile. When he found hers and read her Facebook status, twice divorced and financially independent, he had decided to send a message to Elisabeth Diaz, and so that and a resolve to introduce more living into his life put him on his journey.

Alex had contacted Elise with a Facebook friend request and they began a direct message exchange that could best be characterized as "catching up." Elise had over five hundred Facebook friends (Alex had eight) and Alex was flattered that she not only remembered him, but also was attentive to his thoughts and ideas. He was a little surprised that her English skills apparently hadn't degraded. In any event, when communicating with everyone else, she posted in Spanish. So when he put one of Elise's shouted Facebook posts into Google Translate, it had touched his heart:

"*QUIERO ALGUIEN REAL!!! BASTA DE TANTA VIRTUALIDAD....OLER....TOCAR....ABRAZAR A UN TELEFONO, UNA COMPUTADORA???? NOOO!!!*"

He had genuinely felt sorry for her. Over the last fifteen years, in many darker moments, he had needed a hug himself. After a number of email exchanges, Skype video calls and a couple of $100.00 cell phone bills, they agreed that he should come down to her country for an extended stay.

The Simon Bolivar Airport ("CCS" in airline notation) terminal was modern, steel and glass. Putting his concerns over Elise aside, he was beginning to feel the excitement he had always felt when, whether for business or pleasure, he had arrived at a foreign destination. He took in the noise, the smells, and the semi-organized chaos of his fellow travelers dealing with the bureaucracy present in every international airport. "This may work", he thought to himself shouldering his carry-on.

Having claimed his large checked bag, he adjusted his carry-on and wheeled the big bag up to the Passport Control officer.

"Where you will be staying while you are in our country?" Alex was appreciative anytime anyone tried to use another language, although the man's body odor and halitosis detracted from the experience.

"Porlamar," Alex answered. "On Margarita Island," he added rapidly and, he was sure, needlessly. Settle down, he urged himself.

Alex had named the largest city on the island and the hub of commerce. Once a sleepy fishing village, the construction of the Santiago Mariño Caribbean International Airport transformed Porlamar into a busy Caribbean tourist destination. Unfortunately, along with the tourists came the petty criminals who preyed on them. There were also the not-so-petty criminals. Porlamar, due to the continuing crackdown on the Columbian drug cartels, became a natural transit city for the drug trade headed for the U.S. and Europe. Porlamar was also a base for small time drug producers, living well off "crumbs" that fell from the Columbian dining table. More troubling than the drug trade, however, was that Porlamar was a transit city for human trafficking in slaves from Brazil and Columbia. Men and children were trafficked for free labor and women for sex.

"You go there about the sheep?" the officer was suddenly alert at the mention of Margarita Island. He was tapping Alex's passport and studying his face. "Tourists are not permitted in that area of Margarita Island," he pointed out. "You cannot go there."

"Sheep?" Alex asked and then realized what was being asked, though he had no idea why. "Oh, no," he said, "What ship?"

"The reason for your travel?" the officer demanded, eyeing Alex skeptically. A supervisor seemed to be drifting over toward them.

"Just visiting an old friend," Alex tried to explain with the least amount of information. This either satisfied the man or he felt he had completed his responsibilities. In any event, the officer stamped his passport, welcomed him to Venezuela, and gestured for the next person in line. He said something to the supervisor who drifted away.

Alex moved over to the next line. When it came his turn, the customs officer motioned him forward. Thankfully, he seemed to embrace the principles of personal hygiene more completely than his colleague.

"*Abrir una,*" he said indicating the large bag. Alex unlocked the large suitcase and opened it.

He barely noticed the Venezuelan official pawing through its contents. The officer appeared hassled. Alex let his carry-on slip off his shoulder to the floor. It contained his Kindle, laptop, chargers, cables, and a variety of thumb drives loaded with software tools and utilities.

He was most concerned about the laptop. If the official asked him to boot it up, the officer would see the usual desktop icons for innocuous applications such as email, folders of photos, text files, and some games and music. Clicking an icon would open a suitable program as expected. This was all "cyber-theater", however. It wasn't that the real contents of the drive had to be hidden. In fact, they were fairly innocent. It was just that Alex objected to strangers snooping on his musical tastes (mostly Oldies and Folk), financial statements (this was just embarrassing), and his emails. A program called Truecrypt, which Joanne had recommended, encrypted and hid the real contents of the hard drive. Alex knew that an expert wouldn't be fooled. For one thing, the fake desktop applications couldn't account for the amount of memory being used on the hard drive. But it would pass casual inspection. As it turned out, it didn't matter.

The official closed the bag and motioned impatiently for the next passenger in line. With a muttered "*Gracias*", Alex picked up the carry-on, grabbed the handle of the rolling bag, and moved out of the Customs area following the line of passengers. She saw him first.

"*Hola, amore*," she called out with a big smile as soon as he rounded the last corner. She was waiting right there, the first of the greeters. They embraced and he let himself get lost in the smell of her hair (and that perfume!) and pressed her soft woman-weight to his own body.

He kissed Elise on the mouth, sensed they were blocking others and moved her deftly toward the wall.

"Finally," he said holding her and then, at arms' length, admiring her. She was tanned. "God, you look great, "he said. He noticed that she looked a little older and heavier than he imagined she would. Her online pictures were apparently not that recent or had been selected for what they didn't show. It was in the lines around her mouth and eyes, he realized. Also, the airport's fluorescent lighting was not kind. Probably not kind to me either, he thought.

"I am old, no?" she stated with a smile, a shrug of her shoulders and her palms lifted upwards.

"Me too," he laughed patting the paunch which, to his embarrassment, had slowly developed over time. He cradled her face and felt an unexpected excitement. "It's good to see you." She smiled brightly at this. He kissed her again then and, this time, she returned the kiss.

"So," he said putting his arm around her shoulders, "Where to?"

"The local terminal is this way," she pointed. "It's not far. You will see." She took his hand and held his arm in place. "The plane to Porlamar leaves in forty-five minutes. The flight is thirty minutes. So we'll be at my apartment by (she checked her watch) twelve-thirty. Are you tired? Is that ok?"

"Sure. That's fine," he answered. "I'm fine. Looking forward to unwinding, that's all. It's been a long day." At this point he sensed a presence hovering at the edge of their space. She stepped out of Alex's half-embrace.

"Fernando," she said addressing Bautiste who, Alex noted, was a neatly but casually dressed middle-aged man. He was a head shorter than Alex. He also was very tan.

"This is Alex." She beckoned Bautiste closer. "Alex, this is my very good friend on Margarita, Fernando," she said taking Fernando's forearm and pulling him closer. "Ferdie volunteered to help in case there are any problems with your arrival."

Alex extended his hand. "Fernando, thank you. Or is it 'Ferdie'? That's very kind," he said looking directly into the man's unreadable eyes. Alex shook Fernando's hand and it was warm and dry. Fernando's expression remained distant. "I've had no problems so far," Alex said and patted the pocket containing his passport and ticket with his free hand. They broke off the handshake awkwardly.

"*Salud*," Fernando said without warmth, but without antagonism either. "It's 'Fernando'. Not 'Ferdie'," he emphasized. Alex took in the man's aristocratic face. The eyes were brown and intelligent. His hands, despite his small stature, were large and strong. He had a white scar on his left cheek, but his most noticeable feature was the small

17

brush moustache. Alex nodded once, a slight bow wondering how much English Fernando understood.

As if he were reading Alex's mind, Fernando said, "Let's go," with barely any accent. He turned to the exit Elise had pointed out earlier and took the lead without looking back. Alex adjusted the weight of the bag on his shoulder and regripped the handle of the rolling suitcase as he followed the others out.

When they left the international terminal and its air-conditioning, Alex was hit by the warm, humid Venezuelan air. It was the first time he had been outdoors since leaving the Dallas-Fort Worth airport. Almost immediately, the sweat formed on his forehead and beneath his shirt, along his spine. Elise fired off some rapid Spanish in Fernando's direction. Alex understood and spoke rudimentary Spanish, which included a lot of curse words learned while working odd jobs during his pursuit of his engineering degree. He couldn't follow what Elise was saying, however.

The domestic terminal, he could see, was just across a well lit but busy airport roadway. Fernando pulled a small wallet from his pocket and held it high over his head as he entered traffic. Immediately, cars slowed and then stopped -- one car a little too closely. Fernando glared at the car's driver as Alex and Elise followed him across the gap in headlights. As he maneuvered his bags over the road, Alex couldn't tell what Fernando was displaying, but he assumed it was some sort of badge.

"Is he with the authorities?" Alex asked Elise as they gained the far curb. He was breathing through his mouth from the effort.

"On Margarita, I *am* the authority," Fernando said over his shoulder as he entered the domestic terminal. Elise nudged Alex and just rolled her eyes. As they approached the check-in counter, Alex noticed that Fernando hadn't put his little wallet away.

"Your ticket," Fernando said holding out his empty hand. Alex handed over his one-way ticket to Porlamar. He watched as Fernando added it to the two tickets he was already holding. He spoke briefly to the attractive clerk at the ticket counter and the clerk caught the attention of a man loitering nearby. The man and Fernando had a short conversation. The man then spoke to the clerk. Three boarding passes were issued and handed over.

"What was that all about?" Alex asked Fernando as they made their way to the gate.

"I arranged for us all to sit together," Fernando answered. "They are happy to accommodate us. Here." Fernando handed over one of the boarding passes. Alex inspected it and noticed that he had been upgraded to first class. He waved it at Fernando.

"Nice," he said, "thank you." He saluted Fernando with the pass. Fernando shrugged. Alex's bag was efficiently checked and the claim check handed over.

"We board first," Fernando announced and began to walk toward their gate. Alex and Elise followed him.

"He is an important man on our island," Elise explained with half-mocking admiration. "He is like our-- *como se dice?* -- Chief of police, but more."

"I figured that out," Alex said smiling. "He seems to have some authority here on the mainland, too. I mean the way he handled that traffic. Correct?" Alex asked.

"Yes," Elise confirmed. "Some of the police in Venezuela are national. They have authority anywhere in the country. They are responsible to President Chavez directly. Fernando is one of those." Alex examined Fernando with new respect.

"And he's a good friend of yours?" Alex asked.

"He is. He was a good friend of my second husband, Daniel. *Como se dice* -- Ex-husband," she amended. "Daniel

19

no longer lives in Venezuela. I will tell you about it later," she said. "When Fernando is your friend, he can make life on our island a little easier," she added entering the plane's cabin.

They arrived at their row, which had three seats, and Fernando had already claimed the one next to the window. Elise moved into the middle as Alex stowed his bag of electronics in the overhead bin. He was glad to be free of the weight. He sat in the aisle seat, thinking that he might be able to stretch his legs a little once they were under way. In spite of the first class roominess, his knees could have used a few more inches.

Drinks were offered and Alex ordered a Bloody Mary as the other passengers began to board. Fernando ordered a premium Scotch and Elise ordered a glass of Merlot.

"To Venezuela," Alex toasted once the drinks were served. Fernando and Elise raised their glasses. The aircraft sped down the runway and bumped slightly as they became airborne. They quickly gained altitude into the Caribbean night sky. Alex reclined his seat back and enjoyed the renewal of a Bloody Mary buzz.

***

Years ago, as a young college student, Elise had had dark hair, a dazzling smile, an incredible body, and self-confidence beyond her twenty-two years. She had caught his eye at a time when Mary was pregnant with Connie. Elise was a foreign student from Venezuela, a Communications major at Arizona State University where Alex was teaching English as Second Language. Elise, though not his responsibility, charmed Alex into helping her polish her undergraduate assignments. Alex was appalled at her lack of English skills, though he couldn't help but be amazed at her determination. He was forty years old at the time, yet he often turned into a stammering fool when she was near. She was clearly aware of the effect she had on him. Fortunately for Alex's marriage, it was one of those situations where a potential tryst would never be realized due to the lack of a

20

mutually convenient time and place. Although, nothing occurred between them, Alex (1) never forgot Elise and her perfume and (2) on the wise advice of his brother Terry, never told Mary. After Connie was born, Alex gave up teaching and pursued an Electrical Engineering degree to better support his wife and daughter. Joanne was born two years later and his EE degree was awarded a year after that. A new career in the well-paying defense industry was launched and the family moved to California where they were happy and prosperous.

**

"What is 'AOAIC'?" Elise was holding her phone.

Alex's eyes popped open at the question and pulled his seat back upright. "Sorry," he said. "It's kind of shorthand for 'As often as I can.' Like 'LOL.'" She tilted her head back to show she understood.

"So," Alex said leaning forward in his seat so he could address both of them, "what's going on about a ship? I was asked about it at Customs today."

Elise looked at Fernando and lightly elbowed him. "What were you asked?" she said to Alex.

"It was more like a warning: 'Don't try to go there. No foreigners can go there.' Like that."

"It's not important. That Customs guy was being a jerk. Just some research," Fernando said and gulped the rest of his Scotch. He caught the attention of the flight attendant and ordered another. They passed the rest of the flight talking about inconsequential things.

What about Fernando, Alex asked himself? That bit with the badge seemed a little much. Maybe that's how they do things down here. You don't know. Give it time. Just don't trust anybody yet. You don't really know these people. Even Elise. You've lived long enough to know one thing – trust no one until they've earned it.

You're just a little overwhelmed right now he told himself. Get a drink, get something to eat, get some rest, get some... He smiled over at Elise, who smiled back. You'll feel better in the morning. He tossed back the last of his Bloody Mary. It was watery from the melted ice.

***

He certainly had had his doubts over the last month as he made preparations for this trip– arranging web access to everyone and everything important. Freshly retired, he had a small savings after paying off his mortgage and was ready to live off a combined pension/Social Security income that equaled maybe sixty per cent of his previous salary. He knew he could be one unforeseen expense away from financial disaster. But, he was sure that those were the new realities for most retired "boomers". A month's commitment didn't seem too bad back when he was sitting in his comfortable home in California.

"Dad," Connie who'd come to visit had said, "I'm glad you're doing this. So is Jo." They were having a beer, lounging in the upstairs TV room exactly a week ago, Connie visiting from Philadelphia. An NBA late season game was on, Dallas Mavericks/Boston Celtics. "I mean, we know Mom's been gone a long time. We know you have no need to feel guilty. We think you really owe yourself this chance, a chance at a relationship." At this, Alex had held up his hand, even though, he had always encouraged his daughters to speak frankly with him.

"I agree with you and Jo, Con. I've thought it through and it's something I think I want to try," he explained. "I should just get off my ass," he said exasperated. "I don't know how the relationship part will develop or even if it will develop, but it's only a month and, if nothing else, it should be an adventure, right?" He would look back on that and just shake his head.

He took a deep swallow of beer. "Maybe an awesome adventure. Living on a Caribbean island could be

22

pretty cool, don't you think?" His daughter tilted her head noncommittally.

"Well, I guess you'll find out," Connie pointed out. "Venezuela doesn't have the greatest reputation for warmly welcoming all things American lately," she added referring to the socialist government installed there by Hugo Chavez, an, if not avowed, at least a subtle enemy of the United States. They turned their attention to the game for a while.

"Anyway," Alex said, "I'll stay in touch through email and tweets. It's not like I'm dropping off the face of the earth."

"Well, start with letting us know that you arrived ok. And keep it up by letting us know how you're doing."

"I'll tweet, text, or email as often as I can. Probably use Twitter. Don't worry about it," Alex insisted. "I've been around."

***

Alex, indeed, had been around. In fact, as a young man, the same age that Connie was now, Alex had taken a job in a different oil-rich country, although that was before marriage and a family.

So Alex had assured Connie that he was aware of and sensitive to Venezuelan politics and had no intention of even expressing an opinion. They had watched the rest of the game and the Mavericks lost 93-88.

***

As the commuter plane banked and lost altitude on their final approach to Santiago Mariño Caribbean International Airport in Porlamar, Alex watched as the darkness of the sea was replaced by dimly lit outlying airport buildings and eventually runway lights. The landing was smooth and they disembarked using the folding stairs incorporated into the small plane's door. Alex stood in the doorway briefly and took in the fresh air and the night sights and sounds of Margarita Island. Palm trees close by rattled

23

in the night breeze. The air was warm and clean. He moved down the steps and felt unaccountably happy.

Inside the bright terminal, a sloppily dressed airport official was seated on a stool with rolled up sleeves and his hairy elbows on the counter. It wasn't obvious what his function was exactly. His eyes were red and his cheeks were stubbled. Clearly, night duty at Porlamar's airport was not very demanding. He began to lazily wave Alex and Elise through his checkpoint. As soon as he noticed Fernando coming behind them though, he made a big show of raising his palm, standing, and scrutinizing the couple. He pretended not to see Fernando.

"Your documents," he said in Spanish, holding out his hand. Fernando stepped forward.

"*Jefe*," the official said, feigning surprise. "What a pleasure to see you here. These are your friends?" He indicated Alex and Elise. "*Bienvenido a Porlamar*," he said with two little bows.

Fernando directed some rapid Spanish in his direction and the man began to tuck in his shirttail and fix his shirtsleeves. The trio moved off to claim Alex's big bag. Elise smiled at Alex and said, "Welcome to Porlamar."

As Alex was about to collect his bag, Fernando excused himself saying he had other commitments. He left the two alone. With his computer bag over his left shoulder and the handle of his rolling bag in his left hand, Alex put his right arm around Elise's waist. "Let's go," he said.

They walked through the airport parking lot and Elise chattered brightly. She explained that there was going to be a big welcoming party the next night. Inwardly Alex cringed at the thought. In true geek fashion, he didn't enjoy mingling socially. In fact, he had developed a sort of social anxiety over the last five years.

24

He had felt comfortable at work and at home. That was it. Otherwise, his pulse would begin to race if he had to deal with unfamiliar social situations.

"On this island," Elise explained as they arrived at her little white Ford, "there are many parties all the time." In fact, as he would learn, Elise's social circle on Margarita Island loved any excuse for a party.

CHAPTER TWO — The Party

Elise lived on the east side of Porlamar and, as she drove, Alex took advantage of the opportunity to look out and experience a portion of the city. Even at this hour a lot of people lined the streets. The traffic was light, but slow, and the sidewalks were crowded and at unpredictable places the crowds spilled out into the streets. Alex liked the liveliness. It reminded him of vacation spots he had visited, Cabo, for example. Maybe that's the trick he thought, think of this as a month-long vacation.

With the Ford's rolled down windows, he was able to smell sea air and -- some sort of meat and onions frying. His stomach grumbled with hunger.

"Are you hungry, cutey?" Elise asked as if she had read his mind.

"I am," he nodded. "Want to stop and get something to eat?"

"At this time, in this season, it's not possible. All of the restaurants will be filled with tourists. I will fix a meal when we get to my house. All right?"

"Perfect," he said. "Are you a good cook?" he teased. She glanced over from her driving, saw that he wasn't serious and lightly punched his arm.

"What do you think?" He laughed and turned to look out at Porlamar.

The faded sign for Elise's development was in English and said "Land's End Resort -- A Five Star Development". It boasted one, two, and three bedroom villas. It also announced communal pools, bars, and restaurants—a residential dream.

Elise's part of the dream was a one-bedroom, a "type C" in Land's End's terminology which meant that it was a modest one-bedroom abode of four hundred thirty square feet, hardly a villa. It was set on a small lot in a cluster of identical dwellings. When she bought the house it had met her two non-negotiable requirements: that it be set in a diverse, multi-lingual neighborhood and that it have access to a good beach. At that time, she was pleased that the development was being marketed almost exclusively in Europe, Canada, and the United States. Also, the beach was good; unfortunately, the access was not. The beach was at the bottom of a twenty-foot sheer drop. The developer's plan had been to construct stairs to accommodate beach-goers, eventually.

So, a few years ago when prices were at their peak and property values seemed to increase by twenty percent every year, Elise had decided to give up her Porlamar apartment and become a homeowner once again. Elise and her second husband, Daniel, had owned a large villa in Caracas, but had lost it when Daniel ran into legal trouble. She financed over six hundred thousand Bolivars for her new house, about one hundred fifty-five thousand U.S. dollars. She had put twenty percent down.

Less than a year later, the developer abandoned the "dream", cashed in, and moved to California, USA. Venezuela's economy, especially that portion which depended on tourist spending, had crashed following the economies of the West. The project had been taken over by a new owner who was working with the Ministry of Tourism to reshape and rescale the "dream". As a consequence, new construction, what little there was, was being offered at drastically reduced prices and the residences were being marketed to mainland Venezuelans as vacation homes. The beach access stairs had yet to be started.

Alex, of course, was aware of none of this. All he could see by the Ford's headlights was that Land's End's streets were newly poured concrete irregularly lit by temporary lights powered by sagging wires mounted on wooden poles propped up by two-by-fours. The sea air held the smell of new construction, freshly cut wood. Elise explained all this to Alex.

"So my house is not worth what I paid for it and the new buyers here have been from the big cities of Venezuela. The construction, as you see, goes slowly. Broken promises," she summed up.

Elise parked the car in front of her neat bungalow, which was illuminated by the Ford's headlights. As Alex lifted his carry-on and rolled his suitcase up to Elise's front door unseen waves broke on a nearby beach.

Inside, as he set down his bags, Alex first impression was that the house was cramped. It was more of a beach cottage than a house. A large padded bench seat dominated the main living space. The seat was covered with a brightly colored duvet. There was a small coffee table and an end table with a shaded lamp. A sort of privacy screen depicting a beach mosaic divided this space from the small kitchen area. The kitchen held the usual appliances, although these were not full scale. There was a sink along the wall to the left of the screen. Set in the upper half of the wall directly opposite the privacy screen was a large glass-louvered window. The remaining wall wasn't a wall but a breakfast counter with two stools facing into the kitchen. On the counter was a laptop. Alex imagined that this was where Elise had sat when they had communicated and left messages for each other over the past year and a half.

"This is nice," Alex gestured including the visible space. "Cozy," he affirmed. She smiled at the compliment.

"It's not too small?" She walked into the kitchen area and looked around at her neat little home trying to see it through his eyes.

"Not at all. It's perfect for you. Don't you think?" Alex had no idea if she was happy here, but he understood self-doubt. "Can I help?" Elise was moving things around in the kitchen.

"No, sweetie, I'm ok.   I'm just going to make something simple."

Alex retrieved his own laptop from his carry-on and, as Elise was poking around in the undersized refrigerator, asked, "Do you mind if I use your Wi-Fi then? I'd like to email my daughters."

"Go ahead," she said, "but it's sometimes slow." She got busy making sandwiches and opened a bottle of wine.

Sitting beside each other at her kitchen counter, they ate the sandwiches and drank the wine. He noticed that Elise was a woman who enjoyed her wine. He had previously checked his email and composed a brief message for Connie and Jo announcing that he was now safely in Porlamar.

When they finished the meal, he asked where the bathroom was. It was small and was filled with a collection of feminine products with which Alex was acquainted from his years of marriage. He washed his hands and face and dried them on a towel that was still damp from a previous use. As he stood at the sink, he stared at his reflection in the mirror and blew his hair off his forehead.

After Mary's death, Alex had only dated a few times. Using several popular Internet sites, he was unfortunately and invariably disappointed. It seemed that most of the women who used those sites were predominantly skilled at misrepresenting themselves and their goals. Once, Alex met a successful pediatrician, who had never been married. She described herself as a "former evening wear model". Alex eventually discovered the reality: she was divorced and had an eating disorder. Before those revelations, however, Alex found that, as they were cuddling, her body was so angular it was like sleeping with a bicycle. Eventually, he just stopped dating.

When he rejoined Elise, she had cleaned up their plates and poured more wine. They took their wine glasses to the duvet-covered seat. Alex took a sip of wine and then put down his glass. She put down her glass and they reached for each other and suddenly kissed with passion. In

29

Alex's mind, she was still the twenty year old for whom he had briefly lusted. They continued to embrace as she led him stumbling to her bedroom. They made love on her big bed enjoying each other's bodies. They were both experienced lovers.

Afterwards, no words were spoken, caresses were exchanged, and they napped in each other's arms. Alex slept deeply. He was exhausted after his long day of travel. When they awoke it was around four in the morning with rain beating noisily on the roof and windows. She got up and showered and then he did. When he found her in the kitchen, she was cooking another meal for him.

"This is a local sort of fish," she explained. "And this is a wine sauce that my mother taught me to make." She let him take a sip of the sauce from a proffered spoon.

"Mmm," he said smacking his lips. "What're those?" He pointed to a stack of what looked like flatbread.

"Those are called *arepas*. They are the Venezuelan version of tortillas. We have them on the side." Alex didn't even consider that it was unusual fare for the time of morning. He was ravenous and ate with a huge appetite. She apologized for the food. He could see no reason to apologize and told her so with distorted speech as his cheeks were full of food.

"This is great," he said mopping up the remaining sauce. "You were right, you're a great cook." She smiled at that. There was more wine with the meal and, although the hour dictated coffee, they both drank the wine. The rain had ended and they sat close to each other. A late-February breeze carried pre-dawn sounds through the window's open louvers. They began to talk.

Elise began by telling him of her two marriages and one son, Jaime. She and her first husband, Liam, had lived and worked in Caracas when she had Jaime. Liam, it turned out, had eventually wanted to emigrate from Caracas to Miami in the USA. It was 1999 and, as a successful electronics businessman, Liam didn't trust the socialist leanings of the newly elected Chavez.

"I told him I didn't want to go. I told him that I loved him and I loved my homeland. So, after much discussion, we agreed to split up after fifteen years," she said with a shrug. "Then I was overwhelmed with the responsibility of raising a teenager by myself," Elise said. She explained that she met and married her second husband, Daniel, more as a matter of convenience than of love. He was wealthy, a successful import/export businessman and she wanted financial security for herself and Jaime.

"We divorced after five years when he got into some legal trouble." Elise characterized the trouble as a false accusation by "some Columbians". She said that Daniel hadn't been able to defend himself given Venezuela's political climate and so he had fled to Europe leaving her some cash and an uncertain future.

"So any chance Daniel's trouble involved the drug trade?" Alex asked.

"Why do you ask that?" Elise studied Alex's face.

"Just that you mentioned Columbians. In the U.S. that's almost always synonymous with the drug business. No offense. I didn't mean to accuse your ex."

Alex went on to explain that he had read that, after the U.S-led crackdown on the Columbian cartels, Venezuela had become a surrogate conduit for Columbian drugs moving north to the U.S. and Europe. Hugo Chavez during his second term as President and after many years of cooperation with the Drug Enforcement Agency suddenly reversed policy and severed ties with the U.S. He had ordered all DEA agents to leave Venezuela. He announced to the world press that he suspected that the U.S. agents were spying.

"I know that people in the U.S. thought it all sounded kind of crazy and, to tell the truth, the media just painted him as a nut," Alex said.

31

"Well it is true that Chavez accused the United States of not doing enough to curtail the use of drugs there," Elise agreed, "but that doesn't make him insane, right? Chavez' argument was that if there were no demand, the supplier cartels would disappear. You have to admit he had a point, right?"

"Personally, yeah. I agree," Alex said, "but I also saw reports that, after Chavez' about face, corrupt elements of the Venezuelan military and police were facilitating the movement of drugs."

"I heard that too," she said, "but I also heard that the government denied that, pointing to Venezuela's record as a drug-enforcing nation."

"It's not easy to know what's true, is it?" Alex asked. Elise agreed as they sat listening to the early morning sounds.

Anyway, Elise explained, amid the "they said-they said", Daniel, fearing and anticipating a prosecution, fled the country. She was single again, but this time she had resolved not to remarry. She sobbed as she told Alex that her son, just turned twenty years old, was hit head on by a truck while riding the motor scooter she had given him for his birthday. He was killed instantly. The driver of the truck had been drunk. She refused to press charges. After that, she sought solitude and moved to Margarita Island.

As Alex listened, he was surprised at her resilience. When he had known her back in Arizona she had seemed spoiled, acutely aware of her beauty and a bit of a flirt, someone who was largely superficial. After what she had been through, he wouldn't have been surprised if she had slipped into a destructive self-pity. Maybe that's what her drinking is about, he thought. He had noticed that she was rarely without a glass of something alcoholic. Her story left him with a measure of admiration for her. He would learn, almost too late, that most of her story was untrue, a manipulative mixture of fact and fiction.

32

As she drew quiet, he told her of his own relationship with Mary. He tried to explain how he had struggled to deal with Mary's death. He described in funny detail his Internet dating experiences. He spoke with obvious pride of his own daughters. He was enormously grateful as she pressed him for details. He held nothing back in explaining the marital mistakes he had made. She made him tell how he had gotten out of teaching and into the computer field. He described how he had gone to night classes after working all day as a technical writer. It was difficult to convey the "whiplash" he felt going from teaching English to learning circuitry and software.

"After I was awarded my Electrical Engineering degree, I wanted to work for one of the big computer companies, which unfortunately meant I would have to give up my hopes of reestablishing my East Coast roots and look to a company in the West," he told her.

"I applied to various Silicon Valley companies. I had concentrated my technical studies on software development and wanted to join a company in the forefront of what I was sure was an exploding field. You follow me?" She assured him that she understood. "So I abandoned my hope that I could find a job on the East Coast. I found that the companies I really wanted to work for were almost exclusively concentrated in central California. It seemed tha the Venture Capitalists, you know, those guys with money who funded the Silicon Valley startups, somehow were able to insist that those new companies headquarter in California."

Alex explained that he wound up making a geographical compromise by taking a job as a software developer with a big technical company in southern California.

They talked until well past dawn. He had never been this open to a woman since Mary died. By morning's full light he thought they were friends in the deep sense where each knew that one could trust (and was trusted by) the other. This was a rare thing for him. Alex also had discovered something else. He   wasn't in love with Elise.

33

At the same hour, Bautiste was already on his cell phone as he sipped his first coffee.

"So what does it look like?" he asked.

"Promising. Maybe something big, but too early to tell until we complete the graphic profile."

"When will you finish?"

"Today, certainly by tonight. This equipment is not the best. But, as I said it looks good."

"All right. Keep me informed."

Bautiste turned the phone off. He knew the equipment wasn't the best. They kept telling him that, but it was all he could afford to get the job done. Some hard people wanted their money repaid and, right now, this was his best hope of being able to pay them.

Alex and Elise slept again and awoke around noon. Since she was attending to household chores and making last minute arrangements for his welcoming party that night, she chased him out and told him to go for a walk. In the early afternoon heat, dressed in a Dallas Mavericks tee shirt and cargo shorts, he followed the shoreline and ended up by the port of Porlamar. He found a café and sat at an outdoor table. He ordered an icy cold bottle of Zulia, a Venezuelan beer, and was enjoying it and the sunshine when a shadow fell over him.

"*Bienvenido a mi restaurante,*" a man said. His voice was deep. Alex, looking up, noticed three things about the man: that he was black, that his round face matched his belly, and that the man's left arm ended in a stump just beyond his elbow.

Alex said, "*Gracias.*" The big man was pulling up a chair from an adjacent table. "Speak any English?" Alex asked with an eyebrow raised in hope. He knew his Spanish was rudimentary and that he wasn't ready to rely on it for social conversations.

"A little," the man rumbled in unaccented English obviously joking. "I'm John Magrew." He extended his right hand. "People call me 'Mack'. Mind if I join ya?"

The man didn't wait for an answer and lowered his big frame into the chair. His outsized body barely fit the molded white plastic. Alex didn't know it but this was a ritual for Magrew –to join new customers to his restaurant, spend a little time with them and try to gain them as repeat customers.

"Please," Alex said leaning forward. "I'm Alex Browning, by the way." They shook hands and Magrew ordered the waitress to bring two beers. She said something in Spanish and laughed.

"You a fan?" Magrew asked pointing to the Mavs tee.

"It's like this," Alex started, "I'm a fan of the sport. Love the action/reaction aspects – athleticism and thinking one step ahead. Know what I mean? I see in basketball what the rest of the world sees in soccer – *futbol*." He used the universally accepted pronunciation. "Make any sense?"

"Yeah, nicely put. Never thought about it before, but that's what I like about hoops, too."

"You American?" Mack nodded his affirmation. "So college or pros? Which is best to watch for you?"

"Mostly I follow the NBA, but I catch college whenever I can. It's easier with the Internet now. Who's your team? The Mavs?"

"Not really," Alex said. "They don't play enough D for me. Maybe it's just the NBA product though – glorifies scoring."

"Agreed," Magrew said. "How long have you been here?" Magrew asked. He could tell from Alex's pale complexion that the answer was "not long".

"Just got in last night, from southern California. How about you?"

"Well, you guessed it. I'm American. Been here a little longer than you, though," Magrew joked. "More like thirty years. Not many *Norte Americanos* come to our island all the way down here," he said as the beers arrived. "What brings you to paradise?" he asked. Alex couldn't tell it but Magrew's "antenna" was up. Magrew was instinctively wary of anyone from the U.S.

"Long story," Alex said. Alex gave Magrew a highly edited version: retired for a couple of years, reconnect with old friend, learning how to live with less.

"Well, congratulations on the retirement and reconnection," Magrew offered lifting his bottle in salute. "And welcome. You hungry? How about some lunch?"

"I could go for something," Alex said. "What's good here?" Alex looked around at the nearly empty restaurant.

"Everything," Magrew answered patting his ample belly. He explained that it was well past the lunch hour for the locals and this was normally siesta time. He motioned for the waitress who was lounging nearby.

Magrew asked the waitress to bring them *nibs* and stuffed *arepas*, the ubiquitous corn tortillas, to munch on. He studied Alex. He was starting to like this fellow American. In his experience, the Americans who visited Margarita Island were basically rich assholes. Clearly Alex was neither. And, Mack found, they shared a sports fan connection, especially basketball.

Alex thought the snacks were delicious. The *nibs* were spicy nuts and went well with the cold beer. The *arepas* were, as Alex was finding out, a staple at most meals. The stuffing made them kind of like quesadillas but better. As they ate, Magrew explained how he was originally from Albuquerque but had been in Venezuela for the last thirty years. The first part was untrue.

They discussed their respective marital statuses, Alex as widower and Magrew as cohabiter with his Venezuelan common law wife and business partner, Maria, who it turned out, was the "waitress", "cook", "accountant" and "cleaning crew" for the restaurant. Magrew introduced her but she spoke very little English so the conversation was brief before she drifted off. Alex told of his daughters and Magrew said he and Maria had had no children. Alex explained that before retirement he had been a software guy. He asked if Magrew had always been a restaurateur.

"No, no," Magrew said in a way that made Alex realize he wanted to clarify. "Came down in eighty-two to work the oil fields." This was not exactly why he came to Venezuela, as Alex would later find out. "Enjoyed that work and was doing well until this happened," Magrew said. He held up his left arm to better display the stump.

"Yikes. What happened?" Alex asked with his mouth full.

"I was working on a rig one day. I was a rough neck. Had no real skills, but was working on it. I was spinning the pipe when the chain caught me. Lost my concentration for just a second and then 'whap'. Gone."

Magrew went on to explain that, in the Eighties, Venezuelan oil companies performed most of Venezuela's oil production. So an American working in the oil fields had to be working for a Venezuelan company. The catch was that the American had to possess a skill that wasn't held by a Venezuelan. Magrew was more ambitious than his fellow workers, national or expatriate. He developed his skill, slant drilling, and a relatively new method at that time for reaching previously unreachable oil deposits. The most famous, if not notorious, focus on slant drilling was when Iraq accused Kuwait of using the method to reach across their border and tap into Iraq's vast Rumeila oil fields. Iraq invaded Kuwait as a consequence which led to the U.S. war on Iraq called "Desert Storm". Venezuela used slant drilling to develop offshore oil and, of course, in areas where it was not feasible to drill vertically.

In fact, Magrew told Alex, he was slant drilling when his moment of inattention occurred. He was well compensated by the Venezuelan company for his lost limb and would have continued his career in petroleum except that, by then, his skill at "slanting" was not that unique anymore. So he took his financial windfall, got out of the oil business, and put money down on two purchases: the café and a slurry barge. Under Magrew's management, both were moneymaking enterprises.

Magrew asked Alex if he was familiar with the concept of a slurry barge.

"Not a clue," Alex admitted so Mack elucidated. Magrew's slurry barge, he explained to Alex, was British made and easily handled by a one- or two-man crew. It had a catamaran design with the slurry tank in the center. Magrew used his contacts in the oil fields to drum up business and business was steady. Magrew's slurry business consisted of regularly visiting seaside drilling sites, pumping out their slurry ponds (the slurry, also known as drilling mud, would eventually become unusable due to contaminants), and then dumping the used slurry out at sea. The dumped slurry would disperse and settle on the ocean bottom. Through his slurry business, Magrew could earn enough to make the monthly payments on the barge and still have a small profit. The café, with Maria's help, also paid for itself.

"I guess computers are a little safer, though", he mused scratching the stub of his arm.

"Agreed," Alex nodded tipping the neck of his beer bottle in Magrew's direction.

They started talking about sports and slipped easily into the masculine back and forth of comparing their favorite NFL and NBA teams. The talk moved to other subjects and they discovered that they had a mutual passion for chess. They agreed to get together for beer and a game or two. The possibility of an evening game came up.

To excuse himself, Alex mentioned the welcoming party planned for that night. It was going to be held at Fernando's house.

"That's for you?" Magrew asked making the connection. "Hah, we already turned Elise and Fernando down on that one. I'll call Fernando and tell him I changed my mind."

"Good. At least I'll know someone at the party who speaks English."

"Almost all of Elise's friends speak English," Magrew explained. "You'll see." They said their good-byes and Alex paid and left.

Alex made his way back to Elise's house and they got ready for the party.

After Alex left, Magrew went quickly (as quickly as his bulk allowed), to the tiny office at the back of the café and made two phone calls. The first was to Cor Delaney, a drilling buddy of thirty years, originally from Louisiana and the most tied-in friend Mack had. The other was to Manny Velez, fellow slurry barge competitor and second most tied-in friend. He was looking for any information on the newly arrived American. For thirty years, Mack had had to always be careful around Americans. Neither friend could offer anything on Alex. They could only confirm his arrival was recent and that, apparently, Alex Browning was just what he claimed to be.

Elise drove her little car to the party. Fernando's "house" turned out to be a six thousand square foot villa. It was built on two acres of beautifully landscaped gardens enclosed by high walls and hedges. It had four bedrooms and five bathrooms Elise explained. It was located in the hills above Porlamar where it enjoyed every available breeze.

Music was playing in the background as they entered through the carved wooden doors of the front entrance. The early arrivals were gathered on the back terrace and Alex and Elise joined them.

The terrace was covered to provide shade during the day. Several ceiling fans swirled slowly. The terrace, tiled in glazed terra cotta, overlooked a glistening pool. Palms were in abundance. A thick wooden railing painted aquamarine surrounded the terrace. There were lounges and chairs with deep brightly colored cushions. There was a bar, which was very well stocked.   Alex noticed his favorite bourbon, Woodford Reserve, was present. Dressed in the Venezuelan version of a white long-sleeved guayabera and lightweight slacks, Fernando was playing bartender. He greeted Alex and Elise and began the introductions, emphasizing to everyone that Alex was the guest of honor.

"Juan Martinez," a slight man with thin slick-downed hair said formally. He had a limp handshake, which Alex tried not to notice.

"Juan is the -- *como se dice 'Curador'*?" Fernando looked at the small group for help.

"Curator", someone said.

"Juan is the Curator of our Museum," Fernando said. He turned to the next person.

"This is Mack Magrew and his Maria." Alex told Fernando that they had already met so Fernando moved on.

"And Erin Rosen," Fernando indicated a tall woman who was embracing Elise.

She was taller than Elise and was wearing an orange top and white shorts which showed off her tan. Alex noted the shapely legs and the curve of her small waist. Her hair was dark and long. As she turned to take Alex's hand she extended hers while still conversing with Elise. Her arm was brown and her fingers were slim. She turned to look Alex full in the face. He estimated she was between thirty and thirty five years old. When she smiled, Alex noted the white teeth, slight dimple in the right cheek but not the left, blue slanted eyes reflecting good humor, and full lips. If she were a model or a beauty pageant contestant, Alex thought, her nose would be considered a defect. It was large for her face and had a pronounced bump as if it had once been broken and poorly set.

For a moment, Alex couldn't think of what he was supposed to do. Fortunately for him and others his age certain actions have been performed so many times that thought isn't necessary. Reflex takes over and this happened to Alex.

"Alex Browning," he said taking the tall woman's hand. His voice sounded strange even to himself. His throat didn't seem to be working, as it should. Fernando looked up from his bar tending. He met Elise's eyes with amusement.

"Let me give you my welcome to our island," Erin said smiling. Her voice was deep and rich. She had emphasized the "my" in her last sentence. "Elise and I, we are best friends. She has told me so much about you." She took his shoulders in her hands and pulled him close. She smelled of soap and some light perfume. Her breasts brushed his chest as she kissed one cheek and then the other.

Somewhere inside Alex witty ripostes were being generated. He just couldn't bring them out. She let him go and stared into his eyes.

"Elise was right," she said, "you are very handsome. She calls you her 'handsome gringo'," she teased. Alex exhaled and realized he hadn't been breathing. He smiled into her eyes, some control returning.

"I could argue with her, but that would be so impolite," Alex said with a smile. Erin laughed.

"Let's get a drink," he suggested past the lump in his throat. They turned toward the bar and Fernando.

"Can I try some of your bourbon?" Alex asked. Fernando poured him a generous amount.

"I serve the first one," Fernando said, "then you serve yourself." He smiled and turned to Erin. "You too," he told her and walked off to tend to some new arrivals.

Erin retrieved her glass of wine as Elise joined them.

41

"So you have met?" she said. "Was I right?" This was directed to Erin.

"A handsome gringo," Erin agreed smiling. "And tall," she added. "I like that."

"And good *en la cama*," Elise said laughing bawdily with Erin.

"All right," Alex said as he took a sip, "stop embarrassing me. I'm starting to feel like the new kid in high school." He sipped his drink. "Tell me who those people are." He gazed toward the latest couple to arrive. They were both young.

"That is Ramon Goncalvez and Julia Martinez," Erin said.

"Julia is Mr. Martinez's—*sobrina*?" she asked Elise. Elise had lost the word too.

"The daughter of his brother," Elise said to Alex, "how is it called?"

"Niece," Alex said. "Family relationships are hard in other languages, aren't they?" The women agreed.

"Julia is Juan Martinez's niece," Erin continued, "and she works with Ramon. They are writers for our local newspaper, *La Hora*."

"Reporters?" Alex asked.

"Yes," Elise said. More people were arriving and joining the growing crowd on the terrace.

"Here comes Father Victor," Erin said with something in her voice that Alex couldn't immediately identify. Alex turned to see a priest in black trousers and short-sleeved black shirt with Roman collar approaching. He had white hair around his bald pate. His lips were moving as if he were silently praying.

Alex was one of a generation who, growing up, crossed the street when someone approached them engaged in an imaginary conversation. With the advent of Bluetooth technology, however, it became difficult to distinguish the insane from the merely rude.

Alex as a former Catholic had a knee-jerk respect for clergymen. He made the mistake of making eye contact with the priest.

"I am Father Victor Emmanuel," the priest said to Alex. Alex shook the offered hand. It was soft and clammy. "You are the American, yes?"

"Alex Browning, Father," Alex said. Alex waited for one of the women to say something and then realized they had left him. The silence was growing awkward so Alex asked, "Does everyone on this island speak English?"

The priest's lips began to move soundlessly. He blinked his brown eyes twice and then said, "Yes. It is a common language for speaking with the tourists. Our tourists come from all the European countries. Plus I have served a parish in Los Angeles, California. In America," he added unnecessarily. His lips continued to move after he finished speaking like a badly dubbed movie.

At this point Juan Martinez walked up and rescued Alex with the excuse he had to ask him a software question. Alex begged the priest's pardon and drifted off with Martinez. He caught Elise and Erin laughing at him from the terrace steps.

"Elise sent me to get you," Juan said rather shyly. "That priest is a little crazy."

"He's unusual," Alex agreed.

Juan Martinez and Alex rejoined Elise and Erin. The women apologized to Alex for leaving him alone with the priest. Since they were still laughing, Alex didn't take their apology very seriously.

The two young reporters joined the quartet and the whole group moved to some chairs by the pool. The pool lights were on and their glow gave the faces a bluish tint.

"*Tio*, you should tell Alex about the wreck and the *diario*," Julia Martinez urged. "It's an interesting story," she assured Alex. The old man shifted uncomfortably in his cushioned chair and stared at the pool water avoiding the eyes of the group. It was Elise who spoke.

"Alex isn't interested in some old history. This is a party. We..." she addressed the circle. Julia's reporter sense was alerted.

"Old history? Really? I think it's important history. Don't you agree, Ramon?" Ramon was caught off guard by the question and Alex could see that he wasn't sure what to say.

"Well, I hope I have a chance to visit it, but meanwhile, I'd like to hear about the Museum," Alex said directing this comment at the Curator as he edged forward in his chair. The old man brightened at the attention from the stranger. He started by explaining that he was indeed the Curator of the Museum, the Museum Nueva Cadiz in La Asuncion, the capitol of Nueva Esparta.

Alex liked the old man's self-deprecating manner as he described the museum and its contents. Alex couldn't help but notice that Elise tried to steer the conversation in a different direction whenever the subject of the Curator's work with the *diario* came up. The group chatted about inconsequential things for a while and then the subject of the press arose.

"How is the press in America?" Ramon Goncalvez asked of Alex. Alex wasn't sure what he meant and said so.

"I mean is it free? Is it -- *Como se dice 'preciso'*?" he asked the group.

"Accurate," was the answer supplied by the group.

"Is it accurate?" Ramon posed.

"It is free," Alex acknowledged. "But I would say that it isn't always accurate."

"Is that because of the freedom?" It was Julia who asked. She leaned toward a government-run press.

"Boy, tough question," Alex admitted, taking a sip of his drink. "Here's my opinion and, it's only my opinion." Alex went on to explain that he thought freedom had nothing to do with it and that, recently, the lack of accuracy could be attributed mostly to the pressure of being the first to break a story in the digital age. "And, by 'recently', I mean in the last ten to fifteen years."

"That's not recent," Ramon observed and then added, "no offense." Alex laughed.

"None taken. You're way younger than me. Let me point out that when you're my age, fifteen years ago is pretty recent." Elise rubbed his forearm as the others laughed. "Anyway, maybe some of you know a person who's been the subject of a news story, and I'll bet if you do, those people complained that the media made a bunch of mistakes." They all nodded agreement and stories were exchanged relating misreporting of facts from age, employment and even spousal information.

"Exactly," Alex said. "When my brother got promoted at his University the article in the local paper, and this was in a big city, got his name wrong and even described my daughters as his nephews. So bad." Alex shook his head. "Why do you two think there are so many mistakes?" He addressed the two young reporters. They looked at each other.

"You said it before," Julia answered, "the rush to be first. At school they taught us to check our facts with five sources. You can't do that today." Alex raised his finger.

"Well, two things. First, why not? And second, this kind of bad reporting was going on in the '70s. It's not new."

They all laughed as Julia threw up her hands in surrender. "There is one bright spot today, though," Alex added.

"What is it?" Julia asked.

"Social media. Social media has made it possible for anyone to challenge what they think are reported inaccuracies. And they can do it immediately."

"Inaccuracy is sometimes a problem," Julia Martinez admitted. "Reporters, we, have a responsibility to be accurate. Let me ask about something else, though," she said. "What about press bias in America?" Alex thought to himself - this is a party? He went ahead and answered as well as he could.

"Well sure bias exists in the American media," Alex said. "It always existed, but years ago I think most cities, regardless of size, had more than one outlet to deliver the news and ideas. Back then newspapers were those outlets. Maybe radio, too. So, in any city, one paper or radio station could be liberal and the other could be conservative." Elise yawned and Ramon laughed as she apologized.

Alex smiled and went on to say that, although American media currently used slogans like "Coverage You Can Count On" and "Fair and Balanced", the pressure to get ratings forced media outlets to attract eyes and ears even if it meant showing bias. Otherwise, readership and viewership would turn away, ratings would slump, and advertising revenue would dry up.

"So the free press in a capitalist country is not so free?" Ramon concluded. Alex could see that he wasn't being critical, just surprised.

"That's one way to put it, I guess," Alex agreed. "Like you said, not so free. As long as making money drives the news channels, there's going to be competition for those eyes and ears. Maybe at the cost of free expression?

"But what about you guys?" Alex said indicating the two reporters. "How is the press here? Any big stories on Margarita Island?" He was half-teasing.

"*Drogas*," Julia answered solemnly. "Drugs. And sometimes human trafficking. These are our problems. The criminal gangs are powerful and secret."

"And organized," added Ramon. "Everyone knows the gangs are here and operating, but the members are difficult to identify. Believe me, we," he indicated Julia, "have investigated. It's not like Mexico, though," he shook his head. "Thanks to God."

"Meaning the violence?" Alex looked from one to the other. "That stuff is out of control. I mean what are all the beheadings and executions supposed to accomplish?"

"Right," Ramon confirmed. "The police and the military here, though, somehow seem to have that under control."

"Tourists are safe," Julia said touching Alex's knee. "The gangs do not bother you, them. Maybe only the little criminals bother the tourists." Ramon nodded in agreement. "But that's not all. One story which is curious," Julia added, "is the story of the boat wrecked on one of our beaches. It's..." Elise interrupted.

"Not that interesting to our guest, don't you think?" she inserted. Julia directed her gaze downward and the conversation meandered to more innocent topics.

The group broke up soon after as Alex went to freshen his drink and Elise and Erin wandered off.

Alex found Elise and Erin sitting in Fernando's living room toward the front of the house. Alex joined them and Elise asked Alex if he was having a good time. He was assuring her that he was when loud cursing broke out in the area of the terrace. Elise got up and said, "That's Fernando!" She looked upset as she headed for the terrace.

"Don't you want to see what's happening?" Erin asked.

"I've seen drunks before," Alex said with a shrug.

Alone with Erin and encouraged by his second bourbon, he asked her about herself. She was born in Israel. Her parents had died when she was young, something to do with contaminated medication. She said that she didn't understand what it was. She was brought to the U.S. by her aunt and uncle who were from New York and was raised by them on New York's Long Island. Her uncle, a lawyer, sued the pharmaceutical company on her behalf, won and invested the settlement for her. She had been living off the small annuity since she was twenty-one. She had been enrolled at Columbia University in New York where she had met a Venezuelan graduate student. He was handsome and ten years older, but she thought that she loved him. They graduated, married and moved to Caracas. By that time she had multiple citizenships, Israeli, U.S. and Venezuelan. Sadly it turned out that her new husband had neglected to divorce his first wife. This meant that, in a Catholic country like Venezuela, she had to have her marriage annulled. Elise, who had been just an acquaintance at that time, had given her emotional support. She and Elise had been best friends ever since. Elise learned to speak Spanish like a native. Her English was as good as her Spanish.

"And that is who I am," she concluded, her palms uplifted in a simple gesture.

"Thanks for telling me," Alex said and he tried to convey his sincerity. He had been genuinely touched by her story. "I'm sure Elise is lucky to have a good friend like you."

"No, I am the lucky one," Erin returned.

A group composed of Ramon, Julia, and Magrew with his wife joined Alex and Erin just then. They were talking about Fernando and they switched to English for Alex's benefit.

"Fernando just found out that an investment he made fell through," Magrew said. "He threw a fit. Sounds like it was going to be a big deal. Elise may have had some money in it, too," Magrew directed this last remark at Alex.

"Listen, I'll go to see how they're doing. I'll let you know what I find out," Alex said to the group. He took Erin's hand and squeezed it and then went off to look for Elise and Fernando.

He found them on the grass below the terrace. They looked up as he approached.

Going down the stairs, he said, "I heard you had some bad news." This was directed at Fernando. "I'm sorry. And can I say something else?" Fernando nodded and gestured to proceed.

"I'm going to be here for a month. Maybe more," he looked at Elise who smiled. "I was told that you had an investment that went wrong?" Fernando nodded. "I have had that experience myself. If it's an investment that you still believe in, there are ways to keep your money working. And you can reduce your risk. There are such men who are called Venture Capitalists, VCs. They make their money by investing. I could help you contact such men and we'll see what happens."

"I have apologized to my other guests for my outburst," Fernando said, "and so I apologize to you too-- as Elise's friend and my guest." He gave a short bow.

"It's understandable," Alex said. "No need to apologize to me. Let's just solve the problem. It's what I'm good at."

"You are right, Alejandro. Thank you." Fernando had insisted on using his Spanish name.

Fernando was already imagining how the American could help him solve his problem. He would speak to Elise about it.

CHAPTER THREE—Margarita

It was after midnight when Alex and Elise had left Fernando's villa. The party had been still going on. Alex guessed that, based on the reactions of the other guests, outbursts were not uncommon in Elise's circle of friends and were no reason to end festivities. During the drive home they talked for a while about Fernando's disappointment. Alex asked for the details of Fernando's "investment", using Magrew's word. He was contemplating the feasibility of using a VC. He wanted to know how much Fernando had risked. Elise said not to worry and that Fernando would be ok.

"I'm in trouble, though," she added. When Alex asked what she was talking about, she sighed and said, "This will take some time." She drove down a dimly lit neighborhood street lined by vacant houses and parked the car at the end of a road that looked over a moonlit beach. Endless rows of small waves lit by the three-quarter moon frothed and died on the sand below as she told Alex a story.

"Those who weren't born here can't understand this area of the world, the Caribbean." She shifted in her seat so she could see Alex's dimly lit face. "We have always been, how do you say, people of opportunity?"

"Right. Opportunists."

"That's it. Some say it's because of our ancestors, the first settlers here. Explorers, yes, but when you consider, they were actually just men looking for an easy way to get rich. It's who we are today. It's who I am too. But to understand me, us, you must first understand the history." Elise recounted the history.

***

Christopher Columbus is believed to be the first European to arrive at Margarita Island around 1498. The

50

friendly native islanders welcomed Columbus and his men. Columbus initially thought that the island had little to recommend it until the islanders were helpful and unlucky enough to call attention to the fact that the island's waters abounded in pearls. This was wealth enough to give the Spaniards a reason to claim the island for the Crown. As the centuries passed and their wealth accumulated the colonizing Spaniards had to fortify their most important settlements against a developing scourge, pirate attacks. The pirates of the Caribbean were no movie characters. They were greedy, lawless, merciless, and, above all, ruthless.

Bartholomew Roberts was born in 1682 in Wales. His name was originally John Roberts, and his father was thought to be George Roberts. It's not clear why Roberts changed his name from John to Bartholomew, but it was not unusual for a pirate to adopt an alias. He may have chosen that name after the well-known buccaneer Bartholomew Sharp. He is thought to have gone to sea when he was thirteen.

By 1721, Roberts had become an accomplished sea raider and he and his men had practically brought maritime shipping in the West Indies to a standstill. Seeking more rewarding waters, the pirate crew set sail for West Africa. By late April of that year, Roberts and his ships were off the Cape Verde islands. There it was discovered that one ship, the *Royal Fortune*, was leaky. It had to be abandoned. The *Royal Fortune*'s crew transferred to another ship, the *Sea King*, which was then, rechristened the *Royal Fortune*. The new *Royal Fortune* accompanied by the small pirate fleet arrived off the Guinea coast in early June, near the mouth of the Senegal River. Two French merchant ships, one of ten guns and one of sixteen guns, foolishly sailed too near. The French tried to flee but their abilities were no match for the sailing skills of Roberts' men. Both ships were captured. One, the *Comte de Toulouse*, was renamed the *Ranger*, while the other was named the *Little Ranger*. The *Little Ranger* from then on became Roberts' storage and supply ship.

The next year, on February 5, 1722 a British Royal Navy ship, the HMS *Swallow*, commanded by a Captain

Ogle, was patrolling the waters off West Africa when they came upon the *Royal Fortune*, the *Ranger* and the *Little Ranger*. The *Swallow* was a "fourth-rate", a term used by the Royal Navy to describe a ship mounted with from forty-six to sixty guns.   The pirates were performing routine maintenance on their three ships. In the first of what was to become a series of unlucky events for the pirates, the *Swallow* veered to avoid a sandbar. This maneuver caught the attention of the pirates and apparently made them think that she was a fleeing merchant ship. The *Ranger*, the ship most prepared to sail, took off in pursuit. Captain Ogle realized what was happening and ordered his ship out to sea. The pursuit lasted almost a day, when, finally, the *Swallow* came about. The captain of the *Ranger* was confused and supposed the *Swallow* was about to surrender. Instead, the British ship opened her gun ports and a brief one-sided engagement began. The *Ranger's* sixteen guns were outmatched by the "fourth-rate". Ten of the *Ranger's* pirates were killed on the first volley and the *Ranger's* captain had his leg shot off by a cannon ball. The *Ranger* and its surviving crew surrendered and were captured.

Four days later, the *Swallow* returned to Cape Lopez to look for the remaining pirates. This time the "fourth-rate" was armed with information also. The captured pirates had provided a bounty of details regarding Roberts' armament, cargo and treasure, and his likely tactics. Ogle found the balance of Roberts' men still there. At first, the pirates thought that the approaching ship was the *Ranger* returning, but a sharp-eyed boy recognized the *Swallow* for what it was and gave the alarm. Roberts, breakfasting in the shade, ordered the *Royal Fortune* to set sail.

Roberts' plan was to sail past the *Swallow*, which meant exposing the *Royal Fortune* to one broadside. Once past, Roberts felt they would have a good chance of escaping. Unfortunately, the *Royal Fortune's* helmsman failed to keep a tight course, and Ogle, who was prepared for Roberts' maneuver regardless, was able to approach and deliver a second broadside. Captain Roberts was struck in the throat by grapeshot while he stood on the deck. The effect was decapitation. However, before his body could be captured by Ogle, Roberts' wish to be buried at sea was fulfilled by his crew, who weighed his body (and head) down, wrapped the corpse in a sail, and threw it overboard. It was never found.

Captain Ogle, who had taken possession of the lesser loot from the *Ranger* and then the *Royal Fortune*, missed out on the treasure that Roberts' had stored on the *Little Ranger*. By the time Ogle and his men turned their attention to the *Little Ranger* it had gone.

Several weeks following the defeat of Bartholomew Roberts, Captain Ogle had sailed across the Atlantic and was in Port Royal when he received a report that the *Little Ranger* had been seen sailing south of Aruba in the Lesser Antilles.

***

"So that is the background," Elise said. "But that was not the end of the *Little Ranger*. To understand the rest of the story you will have to meet Vitorino Braga. Doctor Vitorino Braga of Portugal."

"Who's that?"

"He is the man who I hope made a mistake."

While Alex and Elise sat in her parked car and as he said good-bye to the last of his guests, Fernando received an unwelcome phone call. The caller was one of the few men Fernando feared. This man was owed eighty thousand dollars, ten thousand for each kilo of cocaine Fernando had accepted on consignment. The man had been made aware of Fernando's outburst at the party and the reason for it. The man now wanted to know how Fernando was going to pay for the eight kilos of cocaine.

The man's name was Pablo Rodriguez. Behind his back, his colleagues in the drug trade referred to him as *El Sordito*. Rodriguez didn't really have a hearing problem. However, since he processed information more slowly than his fellows, he had the habit of asking for statements to be repeated. He was five feet four inches tall, but had dead eyes, which chilled.

Rodriguez, like most of the emerging Venezuelan drug criminals, was merely a Columbian cartel employee, a facilitator for moving Columbian cocaine headed for the United States and Europe. He provided a service to the Columbian cartels. Venezuela produced no drugs and the Columbian cartels' traditional shipping routes had been shut down due to a global effort by law enforcement. Therefore, the partnership was a natural fit.

The problem for Venezuelan smugglers like Rodriguez was that international drug enforcement had slowly become aware of them. With growing frequency, Venezuelans attempting to move drugs were being arrested and their shipments seized. Colonel Fernando Bautiste, on the other hand, had successfully developed a unique smuggling method that allowed him to get rich over the last seven years. He and his subordinates identified European women travelling alone, befriended them, and requested that each woman take a "package of food" back to a "relative" living in the European country. It was a low volume distribution model, but was almost one hundred percent effective.

The model was not working out on the North American continent however. Few North Americans, more Canadians than Americans, vacationed on Margarita Island and so the pool of suitable tourists was tiny. Fernando had been forced to use Venezuelans to transport his drugs destined for North America. Arrests and package seizures in the U.S. were almost guaranteed. In fact, it was just such an arrest and seizure that had accounted for the loss of the first four kilos of Fernando's consignment from *El Sordito*. A Venezuelan "mule" named Sammi LaFell was pulled aside at New York's LaGuardia airport, searched, and arrested while carrying a body belt stuffed with cocaine. Fernando had now lost forty thousand dollars worth of cocaine without realizing one bolivar in return. He knew that, if he could successfully deliver the remaining four kilos to the U.S., he could, at least, break even. His relationship with Rodriguez was one of mutual need: the criminal had product that he couldn't smuggle and the lawman had the means to smuggle but no product.

Bautiste learned that the way the drug "business" worked was that the drug producers sold the drug distributors *puro*, which was pure unadulterated cocaine. The drug distributors smuggled the *puro* to the destination and turned it over to local drug distributors. The local drug distributors then mixed the *puro* with other, mostly harmless, chemicals, which increased the volume of product available for sale, but diluted the cocaine content. On the street, five percent cocaine content was not unknown, but fifty percent was more common. Thus Fernando's remaining four kilos, if diluted, could eventually be retailed as eight kilos. He could break even on his "investment".

Though no one knew it, Fernando was already a multi-millionaire and could have paid *El Sordito* in cash. He had, however, a different vision and a different financial plan. He had been promoted to Colonel seven years before. His predecessor, Colonel Raul Sanchez, hated Margarita Island, the beaches, the ocean, the fish, and the fishermen. Upon retirement, Sanchez immediately settled on a ranch in the Venezuelan state of Guárico far from the coastline and lived there happily. He had presided over Nueva Esparta fairly honestly during his tenure. Fernando, on the other hand, saw opportunities for profit everywhere when he was promoted. At the end of seven years, after skimming, conniving, bullying, threatening and bargaining, Fernando had the equivalent of ten million dollars in several numbered Swiss accounts. By his reckoning, though, this was only half of what he needed to leave government service and live the life of complete debauchery he saw as the greatest benefit of wealth.

As Alex fidgeted in the passenger seat, he was fascinated as Elise explained about the *Little Ranger* and how it had been Fernando who had been responsible for securing the wreck site. In the beginning, the wreck was merely a curiosity to everyone who visited the area, and somewhat of a danger to the local fishermen. Colonel Bautiste used his authority to establish safe limits to the activity around the *Little Ranger* and to bring in academics from Caracas to give their opinions. The professors all agreed that the ship was old, perhaps old enough to have historical significance. They also agreed that Venezuela should bring in an expert to determine the ship's identity and its story. Fernando, Elise went on, with proper government permission, hired Dr. Vitorino Braga, a Portuguese expert from the University of Lisbon. Braga, it turned out, was outstanding at his job.

In fact, as Braga arrived and went to work, the local press easily discovered and reported that he was one of the world's foremost authorities on Spanish Main era shipwrecks and had been hired by the Venezuelan government to assemble and lead a team of researchers whose job was to identify and investigate the partially exposed wreck of an old and large wooden ship. The article went on to say that the wreck was sunken in shallow water off the northern coast of Margarita Island. It had been exposed by the wind and wave action of a hurricane designated "Felix". Hurricanes as strong as Felix were rare in that part of the Caribbean and the effect on Margarita Island was profound. Less rare was the phenomenon of wind and wave action that revealed the wooden wreck. Around the world, shifting sands moved by powerful tides would bury wrecks sunk just offshore and, then, storms would redraw the shoreline and scour away the sands and expose the hulks.

As interest in the wreck grew and the all media sought to satisfy the public's curiosity, it was reported that Braga's team was able to accomplish the first part of their task rather quickly: identify the wreck. Using artifacts recovered from the wreck site, the ship was discovered to be the remains of the *Little Ranger*. Further, Braga's researchers doggedly pursued the second part of their task: investigate the *Little Ranger* and fill in her story. They determined that the *Little Ranger* originally sailed as a French merchant ship. Their research showed that it had been captured by pirates, renamed the *Little Ranger*, and sailed off by them. It met its end in the early eighteenth century.   The ship turned out to be one of Captain Bartholomew Roberts' pirate fleet, the infamous Black Bart.

Just as the press' interest in the *Little Ranger* began to wane it was discovered that there was an old book, which could be linked to the wreck. "The book" was actually an old leather-bound journal, which had been on display in the museum in La Asuncion, the capitol of Nueva Esparta, since 1915.   Before that it had been in the possession of a prosperous fishing family from the Island city of Juangriego, northwest of La Asuncion. This family, it was reported, was descended from the early Guaiqueria inhabitants of Margarita Island and the book had been in their family for many generations.   In 1915 the family befriended an American archaeologist performing research related to the pre-Columbian inhabitants on Margarita Island.   The Heye Foundation out of New York was funding the archaeologist, Samuel Ballecer.   Realizing the significance of the journal and appalled at its condition, Ballecer convinced the family to donate it to the local Museum so that it could be properly preserved.   Since then, the journal had been a part of the Museum's permanent collection. It had been restored as well as the museum's resources allowed and was displayed in a glass case, completely unremarkable and mostly unnoticed over the years until Dr. Braga had a chance conversation with Dr. Juan Martinez, the museum's curator.

At Venezuela's expense, Braga had brought in the necessary equipment and personnel and had set to work using his worldwide contacts to determine that the ship had last sailed as the *Little Ranger* and had originally been known as the *Comte de Toulouse*. This last bit of information was important because it meant that the French government, according to maritime law, had to be notified and engaged as the legitimate owners of the wreck. Elise explained that this had to do with treaties. Anyway, the important part, she said, was not the French, but the fact that the *Little Ranger* had been a pirate ship.

"What?" Alex said coming alert. Her story along with the bourbon and the late hour had caused his attention to drift.

"Yes," she said, "a pirate ship. And that was not the interesting part." She went on to say that a brief meeting between Braga and Juan Martinez led to an exciting discovery.

"When Juan heard the name *Little Ranger*, he told Braga about the journal."

"What journal?" Alex asked.

Elise explained that the Museum in La Asuncion where Juan was the Curator had on exhibit an old leather-bound journal and had had it on display for almost one hundred years. Martinez told Braga that the name *Little Ranger* was inscribed on its spine. Martinez also told Braga that, to his knowledge, no one had ever examined the book, certainly not recently.

Martinez, with Braga's help, investigated all the pages. Only several adjoining pages contained anything.

"What did they contain?" asked Alex. Elise pulled out her cell phone and pushed a few buttons.

"This," she said handing him the phone. On the screen was text and, as Alex scrolled down, the text read:

Morgan, W

Akers, H

Tibbett, M

Elgin, B

Smith, R

Smyth, L

Thoth, G

Ance, P

Rogers, P

Teppers, G

Atkins, A

Trinkle, B

Taylor, G

Howell, T

Earl, P

Burke, N

Irwin, S

Gordon, L

Brown, R

Lawson, M

Aston, P

Cobb, C

Kucker, B

Revelle, C

Odell, J

Connelly, A

Keating, D

Grubb, N

Oglethorpe, J

Thomas, R

Hill, E

Edwards, K

Pritchard, M

Arab, M

Tomberlin, R

Hinds, S

Thomas, N

Herford, A

Eddington, B

Stanford, W

Underhill, P

Nicholls, T

Tyndall, U

Anglin, C

Kent, V

Ellerman, R

Sand, G

Guy, H

Orthman, E

Anderson, T

Nutt, L

Ulster, M

Mann, G

Bridges, B

Evans, L

Roberts, K

Ongle, C

Fagan, A

Phillips, W

Applewhite, C

Corey, D

Edwards, M

Sayers, A

Enlow, C

Quarles, C

Underwood, P

Ahern, T

Lytle, M

Teague, T

Osborn, B

Thompson, L

Hurt, S

England, W

Christian, M

Aycox, C

Pruitt, L

Tolson, B

Ainge, C

Ipock, B

Newman, W

Sterling, P

Yancey, K

Engels, J

Abel, C

Richards, Q

Stewart, E

Tender, M

Hoare, T

Ewell, C

Rusk, A

Eason, G

Tell, P

Harkins, T

Easton, L

York, T

Leeds, P

Ingram, W

English, D

Fields, G

Owens, K

Udall, B

Rich, D

Tercey, M

Eller, G

Eastfield, R

Nicely, W

Blackwell, N

Oxley, P

Xu, F

Enders, W

Stack, H

Orr, T

Finlay, M

Grant, H

O'Neill, L

Long, C

David, S

Sanders, Y

Ivey, C

Lancer, M

Verge, C

Elmore, N

Ragland, T

Axel, P

Nells, D

Daniels, O

Johnson, S

Euler, J

Williams, J

Eton, P

Lively, G

Stuckey, R

Banfield, W

Otter, L

Upton, J

Newsome, E

Tootle, R

Young, S

Grey, T

Olson, M

Dell, N

Bean, C

Loper, T

Ericson, K

Salisbury, M

Sampley, C

Usher, H

Scarsdale, T

Alba, E

Leeds, P

Longfellow, F

"What is this?" Alex asked holding up the cell phone with the long list of names.

"It is the entry from the journal, the diary," Elise answered as if it were obvious.

"What's with the list of names? Who are these people?" Elise shrugged. "Where did the diary come from?" Alex asked with growing frustration. "How did that family of fishermen get it?"

"It must have belonged to a crew member from the ship, the *Little Ranger*. He probably gave it to them. Or they found it. Who knows?"

"So how is any of this trouble for you?" asked Alex coming back to the start of their conversation. Elise, reluctantly, admitted that when the link was made between the *Little Ranger* and the journal's list, Fernando, Braga, Martinez and she let their collective imagination turn toward a discussion of what the list might mean. It was generally agreed that the list was the names of the *Little Ranger's* crew. The list was too long to be the names of an active crew for a ship the size of the *Little Ranger*, so Braga posited that it was perhaps a list of Black Bart's entire pirate band. The others agreed that this was reasonable, but Elise had asked why they would maintain such a list. Again it was Braga who made a sensible guess. He thought that the names were a sort of payroll list, no amounts given, but just the names of those who were owed. The group considered then that there must have existed some payroll, something to be divided among those on the list. Braga told the others he would not rule out the possibility that the payroll would be in the form of treasure. This fired their imaginations even more. In his lawful capacity, Fernando took absolute control over the information. Only Fernando, Martinez, Braga, and Elise knew about the journal entry.

"How did you get involved?" Alex asked.

It turned out that money, funding that would not be reported to the Venezuelan government accountants, was needed to pay for a discreet survey of the wreck site. The purpose of the survey was to locate any payroll/treasure that had accompanied the *Little Ranger* to Venezuela. Fernando knew that Elise was sitting on some money from her second divorce and offered Elise the opportunity to "invest".

"You were on a treasure hunt," Alex said incredulously. Elise nodded and traced the steering wheel with her hands. She said that the group had decided that there had to be something of value at the wreck site. She went on to say that Braga had called Fernando a few hours ago to report that the site survey was complete and that there was nothing found, no treasure. Elise's "investment" was gone as was Fernando's.

"That's why Fernando was so upset at the party," she explained.

"How much did <u>you</u> lose?" asked Alex.

"Twenty thousand U.S." Elise said. She watched for his reaction.

"It's a lot," Alex said nodding, "but not a disaster, right?" She tilted her head noncommittally.

"There's more you're not telling me?" She agreed that there was. She only had had ten thousand, so she had arranged to borrow the rest. Her excitement about the treasure had clouded her judgment she confessed. She had taken out a loan using her house as security. She told him she could lose the house if the money was not repaid within ninety days.

If Alex had the statistical data available, he would have realized that Elise's gamble, while understandable, was ridiculous. There were, at the time, over fifty active salvage companies in the Western hemisphere alone. These fifty plus companies competed for the wrecks that had been lost over the years. The number of these wrecks was huge. The percentage of these wrecks that transported a salvageable cargo was deemed to be around twenty percent. This was still a very large number of salvageable ships. However, the odds of finding a valuable cargo were estimated to be about the same as those of the New York Knicks winning the NBA title in 2010.

"So that is my problem," she said. Alex thought that this was not an investment opportunity. It was a crazy form of gambling where only long shots were available for wagers. He reviewed his own financial status to see if he could help her out with a loan. He decided that, if she asked, he could.

Elise changed the subject as she started the car. She asked Alex what he thought of everyone at the party.

"I like your friends." Alex answered honestly. "Good group."

"And what about Erin?" Elise asked glancing over. Alex sensed trouble and knew the best way to avoid it.

"She is attractive and interesting," he stated simply and truthfully.

"You seemed interested a little in Erin." Elise didn't seem either enthused or distressed over this prospect. Alex could have agreed, but he felt like he didn't want to give Elise anything else to worry about.

"As I said she's very attractive," Alex began.

"You said she was very interesting," Elise corrected.

"I said 'interesting'. Ok. She's both. But, two things:" Alex said, "one, I'm here because of you. Two, I'm monogamous— I can only be interested in one woman at a time." Alex knew that this was more of an aspiration, some men realized the goal and some did not. Elise seemed satisfied with the answer, though. They drove on in silence.

When Alex and Elise entered her house, they both went straight to her bedroom. They shared the bathroom, washing and brushing, and then headed to bed. They cuddled for a while without speaking and then, as Elise realized Alex's arousal, they made love.

Alex and Elise slept late that Wednesday and it was already early afternoon when they went out to drive around Porlamar.

Despite the fact that La Asuncion was the capitol, Porlamar had become the business hub of the island with shops, restaurants and nightlife supported by the tourists. It had been a duty-free port since 1973.

Shopping, Elise explained, was good. "Alcohol is very popular because of the low price," she told him. She parked the little car on a boutique-lined avenue so that they could stroll along with the tourists.

"Everything is available in these shops, but the price is not so good," she told Alex as they walked hand in hand. "The good price is found in Conejeros," she said naming the most popular shopping area. "We will go there some time."

Alex was impressed with Porlamar's international flavor. English could be heard everywhere. Elise explained that Porlamar and, on a larger scale, all of Margarita Island had ambitions to be big tourist attractions like the better known cruise ship stops on the Caribbean circuit. Unfortunately, Margarita did not have the port facilities required by the big cruise lines and was too far south for the smaller lines, so it depended on air traffic to bring the tourists.

As they walked, Alex enjoyed the ocean air and the cooling breezes. This is paradise, he thought to himself. He enjoyed Elise's company. She didn't seem to have any worries today. They entered a shop selling colorful beach towels. Alex turned over the price tag and did the conversion from bolivars to dollars.

"Expensive," Alex said to her. Especially since the quality isn't that good, he thought to himself. He held up the towel and noticed that it was only printed on one side. It was also thin.

"Conejeros has better prices. This place is for the tourists," she said. "Also there is Sambil Mall where is the cinema and bingo. And   good prices."

"Bingo? Bingo is Spanish?" She nodded.

They went back out on the sidewalk.

"What smells so good?" Alex asked. The sea air seemed to give him a constant appetite. Or maybe it's all the walking, he thought.

"Empanada," Elise said. "Want some?" She explained that the favorite food of the tourists (and young Venezuelans with little cash) were the empanadas, corn flour dough stuffed with meat or fish, cheese, fried plantains or black beans or any combination. Empanadas were fried in oil or lard. Heart attack food, Alex thought to himself.

"No wonder it smells so good," Alex said.

"You can get classic *cazón* empanada. It is filled with small shark. Or you can get the *pabellón*, which has *carne mechada, caraotas negras, platano frito* and white cheese all in one. We usually eat them for breakfast." From her enthusiastic description, Alex sensed that she was hungry too. They hadn't eaten at her apartment before they left.

"Well, we haven't had breakfast yet, so let's get empanadas for our breakfast," he suggested happily. They sat at a small table on the sidewalk and ate their pastries, which were served with hot sauce. As before, Alex drank beer with the meal.

When they had finished, Alex paid and they spent the next hour walking around, visiting the port of Porlamar and the ferry terminal. Alex brought up their conversation about the diary from the night before and said he wanted to see La Asuncion and Juan's Museum. Elise had reached the point where she felt that she had exhausted the most interesting points of Porlamar so they returned to her car and drove the fifteen minutes to La Asuncion in her small Ford.

As they drove Elise explained that La Asuncion was the capital of Nueva Esparta. Besides government employees and politicians, it was home to many artists and intellectuals. The downtown architecture was a well-

69

preserved collection of buildings from Venezuela's colonial era. The town had been fortified against attack shortly after being established and the fortress remains were still in evidence.

"I work in that building," Elise indicated a large building in a complex on the left as she drove. The highway was wide and modern.

"What is it you do there again?" Alex asked. "I know you told me but I'm not sure I understand exactly." Elise steered left-handed as she fished a business card out of her bag. She handed it to Alex. It was in Spanish. Alex worked out her title.

"Communications Director of National Police, Nueva Esparta State, right?" Alex asked.

"Yes," she said, "like a public speaker."

"Spokesperson?" Alex guessed.

"Exactly," she agreed.

They parked in a plaza near the Museum Nueva Cadiz and walked to the museum. Alex liked the feel of this city, too. It was less touristy than Porlamar. Palms were everywhere. Although, five miles inland, the fresh smell of the ocean prevailed.

"This is Plaza Bolivar", Elise said as they entered a lush park. They continued toward Calle Independencia and Elise pointed out the Cathedral.

"It is one of the oldest churches in Venezuela," Elise told him. "They started to build it in 1570 and finish it in 1617. Do you go to church?" she asked.

"*No mas*," he said. It was an unintentional wordplay and he instantly realized and regretted it. He didn't think she noticed it. He expanded, "No, I don't go anymore. I haven't for years. Do you?"

"Every Sunday," she said with a small show of piety. Alex wanted to explain that he didn't attend church regularly because he was no longer a fan of organized religion. He didn't strictly consider himself an atheist, but it was too subtle of a distinction to make with limited vocabulary and sentence structure. He let it go.

He had always found it ridiculous that those who professed atheism would loudly protest against someone else's symbols of faith. These were the people who made a stink when crosses were displayed in government buildings or Nativity scenes were put up on government property. If you don't believe, then why care was Alex's opinion. Don't make atheism your religion he thought. His brother Terry, as a religious person, would argue that belief was a gift-- you had received Faith or you didn't. Alex thought religion met some basic human need and organized religion was the inevitable consequence of a combination of man's societal drive and some weird desire to codify.

"There is the Museum," Elise pointed out. It was a big two-story white stucco building with a red-tiled roof. It sat on a corner and had balconies overlooking Calle Independencia, a main thoroughfare in La Asuncion. The front doors were open as were the balcony doors above.

"This building used to be a jail," Elise said, "and before that it was the Spanish Government building for Margarita when we were a colony." Alex tried to imagine the streets as they were then, travelled by Spanish grandees on horseback. This is just a cool place, he thought to himself.

"It's really in great shape," he said as they approached the front doors. "And I like how well cared for everything is." The streets and sidewalks were immaculate.

The museum itself had a shady yard full of palm trees. It was, as Alex noted, beautifully restored. Once inside, a visitor found several exhibits: artifacts from Ancient Nueva Cadiz, an impressive plaster model of Margarita Island, a permanent art exhibit by modern painters and sculptors, and a collection of pre-Columbian artifacts. The museum was also, Alex noted, empty of visitors.

Juan Martinez, the diminutive Curator, appeared out of a side room. He was wearing a stained work apron. "Welcome, bienvenidos, my friends," he said with outstretched arms. "I am so happy you came." He kissed Elise on both cheeks and then took Alex's hand and pumped it. He seemed please beyond reason to see them. He offered them refreshments and a tour.

The Museum consisted of just a few rooms on both floors. Not a very big jail, thought Alex. Each of the rooms contained either modern sculptures and paintings or centuries-old artifacts or both. The old articles defined the Island's history and they ranged from faded clothing to rusted tools, some of whose purpose was hard to guess. To Alex it was a little disappointing as museums went.

"I told him about the *diario*," Elise told Juan.

"Ah," he said, "you told him everything?" He looked at Alex.

"Everything important," she said, "Besides, what matter now? Where is the book?" Although Elise had invested in the book's contents, she had yet to see it.

"Come," he beckoned, "I'll show you." He led them through a set of double doors, across another room, and then turned left into a third room. The leather-bound journal from 1722 was on a pedestal in its own glass case. The case was off to the side with a typed white card. This was the book that had suggested the existence of pirate wealth. Senor Martinez, ever the science nerd, explained how he used the journal's construction to establish its provenance.

He explained that the pages were ruled sheets, not printed. "Like a schoolboy's notebook," he said. The journal's front and back covers were pasteboard. Alex could sense that Elise was bored and was not surprised when she seized the first opportunity to drift away. Alex found the Curator's   explanation   interesting.

72

The Curator told him that using pasteboard instead of wood was an advanced technique for the bookbinders of the eighteenth century. The pasteboards were sewn to the sheets. The leather covering the pasteboard and spine was of one piece. So the journal was clearly of eighteenth century origin. "Unfortunately, it was not in good condition," Martinez lamented.

He went on to explain that the temperatures and humidity found on Margarita Island were not conducive to preserving objects made of organic materials such as cotton and leather. The fact that the journal had avoided total destruction over the three hundred intervening years was mostly a testament to the fortunate choice of storage the owners gave it, keeping it wrapped in palm leaves.

"When I try to open this book, it was so tight that I thought it had somehow become something solid. Our Ministry of Culture give me advice so I got it open a little and, over time, separated the pages. We use some harmless chemicals. All the pages were blank, except for a few. Do you know what was on those pages?" Martinez asked Alex enjoying his little lecture. Alex shook his head.

"The owner's name was there, John Spence. Also a date, 10-5-1722, and a long list of names."

"The pirate crew?" Alex asked.

"That is correct," Martinez said. "You know the list?"

"I've seen a copy. Elise had the text on her cell phone," Alex explained.

"This book," Martinez pointed at the display and shifted back into technical mode, "is a good example of why it is difficult to determine the date of manufacture. Take the bindings for instance." They stared at the exhibit as if they expected it to come alive. Martinez went into more detail explaining that the sewing cords of the binding were stitched in. He pointed out that this was more like eighteenth century bindings than a later period. But the cords were made of leather, which was more like earlier bindings. Also, there was

73

no endpaper, which was also like earlier constructions. Alex was not arguing. He didn't care how it was made. He was more interested in seeing Spence's writing.

The Curator told Alex that he could not let him handle the book. This disappointed Alex. Martinez offered to show the Museum's copy of the text. Alex's disappointment vanished.

"That would be great," he told the Curator enthusiastically. Martinez disappeared for a few minutes and returned with a piece of paper. He handed it over. Alex's disappointment returned. The "copy" was just a printed version of the text Alex had seen on Elise's phone. In fact, it matched name for name as near as he could tell.

"I've seen this, *Senor*," Alex told Martinez.

"What?" Dr. Vitorino Braga joined them as he caught the last sentence. Martinez beamed at Braga. "Dr. Braga," he said with a smile. "What a surprise!" He introduced Alex and addressed Braga by his academic title.

"Call me Rinni," Braga told Alex. "Everyone does."

"Do you know who Dr. Braga is?" Martinez asked.

"No," Alex said amused at the Curator's excitement, "tell me."

Martinez, with the near adoration of a student for a teacher, told Alex how Dr. Vitorino Braga was part archaeologist, part historian, part forensic scientist, and part engineer. He was from the University of Lisbon and had a worldwide support network of professional contacts. As a provenance specialist, Fernando had hired him. He was an expert on Spanish Main era shipwrecks. He had successfully established the identity and ownership of Fernando's wreck. This was the most difficult part of his job and the most important. He had, after identifying the wreck and with Fernando's permission, advised the French government of their need to be involved. This was a legal obligation agreed to by all nations who had adopted the Salvage Laws of the sea. He also was the one who tied the obscure journal displayed in this little museum to the wreck of the *Little Ranger*. Through all of this Braga stood listening humbly.

"Doctor Braga, er, Rinni, tell him what you discovered. It's amazing," Martinez encouraged the Portuguese professor.

"It's not so amazing," Braga said blushing, "it is just science my friend."

Braga began by giving some background on the *Little Ranger* and how it came to be in Venezuela. He explained that in late 1720 a pirate named Bartholomew Roberts, a.k.a Black Bart, was terrorizing Spanish and Portuguese shipping in the Caribbean. During this time, one of the ships that were captured by Black Bart's crew was the *Greyhound*. The *Greyhound's* chief mate, James Skyrme, joined the pirates and would later become captain of another of Black Bart's ships. Also during this time, Roberts captured the Governor of Martinique and promptly hanged him from the yardarm of his flagship, the *Royal Fortune* just to make a point. Almost a year later, due to the nearly continuous raiding, Caribbean shipping had nearly come to a standstill.

"Two important things happened that year," Braga explained. "One: after several successful months of raiding in the western Caribbean including a single haul of forty thousand gold moidores and a jewel encrusted cross intended for the Portuguese king, Roberts sailed off in pursuit of another fat prize leaving his second in charge of the loot in a ship called the *Rover*. Roberts got stuck in unfavorable winds and when he returned the *Rover* was gone along with the loot."

"Apparently, pirates were not very trustworthy," Braga injected with a smile. "Anyway, the second thing was that, after Caribbean shipping had nearly ceased as I said, Roberts moved his activity to the west coast of Africa intending to take up the slave trade."

"One thing you need to understand," Braga said, "is that pirates changed ships in those days like you and I

75

change our socks. As soon as a ship became unseaworthy, they usually didn't repair it. They simply stole a new one and rechristened it using the old name. This happened in Africa. The *Royal Fortune* became leaky, a ship named the *Sea King* was captured and was renamed the *Royal Fortune*. There would be more *Royal Fortunes*," Braga added.

"Somewhere off the coast of Africa the newly named *Royal Fortune* was noticed and chased by two French ships, the *Comte de Toulouse* with ten guns and the *Notre Dame* with sixteen guns. The crew of the new *Royal Fortune* proved to be better sailors than the French and they captured both ships. Roberts renamed the larger prize the *Ranger* and renamed the other the *Little Ranger*." Alex was enjoying the tale and the skilled telling by the mild-mannered professor. He wanted to ask questions but didn't want to interrupt.

"So now we have our ship, the *Little Ranger*, off the west coast of Africa," Braga went on. "James Skyrme of the *Greyhound* became captain of the *Little Ranger* and this ship became a sort of store ship for Roberts' band of pirates."

"The pirates apparently had abandoned their plans for the slave trade and instead raided other shipping, seizing the money destined for the purchase of slaves. This lucrative raiding continued until early 1722. Then, bad luck and bad decisions doomed the pirates." Braga shook his head in sympathy.

"What happened?" Alex asked. He liked this quiet academic.

"A British warship happened," Braga answered, "the *HMS Swallow*. British warships were feared more than any other. The *Swallow* came upon the three pirate ships and, for some reason, maneuvered to avoid them. Maybe the British thought they were still a couple of French ships. James Skyrme, who was now for some reason captaining the *Ranger*, gave the order to pursue. The *Royal Fortune* and the *Little Ranger* did not take up the chase. By the time the *Ranger* pulled alongside the *Swallow* Skyrme realized his mistake, but it was too late. The pirates and the *Ranger* were no match for the British navy and the *Swallow*. Skyrme was killed and his crew were all killed or captured. The *Ranger* was now in British hands."

"It is not clear why, but the *Swallow* did not go immediately after the other two pirate ships. Maybe she was damaged and had to be repaired. Almost a week later, though, the *Swallow* retraced her course and again came upon the *Royal Fortune*, the *Little Ranger*, and another ship, a newly captured *Neptune* which had been under the command of a Captain Tom Hill." He took a breath. "This story is getting long." Braga said, "Should I go on?"

"Absolutely," Alex said, "don't stop now."

"All right," Braga agreed, "so the *Swallow* was facing three ships. Against good judgment, Roberts in the *Royal Fortune* ordered the crew to run for it right past the side of the *Swallow*. Predictably, Roberts, along with a number of his crew, were killed by the *Swallow's* broadsides."

"Now a strange thing," Braga said, "the records say that the captain of the *Swallow* claims to have been unable to prevent the *Little Ranger* from sailing away. Remember the *Little Ranger* had been assigned to carry all Black Bart's stolen treasure. It had sailed off with Captain Hill at the helm, the former Captain of the *Neptune*. Apparently, the *Little Ranger* sailed across the Atlantic and was seen in Port Royal, Jamaica in the spring of 1722. So it seems that Black Bart's treasure ended up in the hands of Captain Tom Hill and the crew of the *Little Ranger.*"

"Somehow, the ship found her final resting place to be off the shore of our island." It was Elise. She had rejoined them unnoticed.

"How did you know the wreck was the *Little Ranger?*" Alex asked of the professor.

"Well, we at first did not know that," Braga said. "We recovered items which were inscribed with '*Comte de Toulouse*'. It took a lot of research and email from people all over the world to uncover the *Little Ranger's* story. This happened little by little and took almost eight months."

"Did you ever think that the items might just be stolen from the '*Toulouse*' ship?" Alex asked. "That seems like a reasonable possibility given the integrity of the people involved." Braga smiled enjoying the intellectual challenge.

"Of course, the items were just the beginning, the first thread in unraveling the story." Braga went on, "Once we had a hint and moved certain equipment in place, we could determine the exact size and shape, number of cannons, and so forth. Each little piece came together to confirm the ship's identity and history. It's interesting, is it not?"

"Very interesting," Alex agreed. "So there might really have been a treasure?"

"Almost certainly there was," Braga said, "but remember that three hundred years have passed. The most likely scene is that the original pirate crew and Captain Hill made off with everything. Maybe to spend it in Jamaica on rum and women."

"That would be too bad, but what about the journal list? It seems to imply that what's his name, Spence, was keeping accounts due for the pirates." Alex asked.

"Well, the list in the journal could have been written and intended to be left behind maybe for the crew of the *Royal Fortune*. Who knows? Maybe Hill's crew including Spence left some of the loot behind and made off with the rest or maybe they had already spent it all."

"How did the *Little Ranger* remain undiscovered for all that time?" Alex asked, "and so close to the shore?"

"As for the *Little Ranger* remaining undisturbed that is explainable with more history," Braga said. "First, understand that this area of the Caribbean where we are now is hardly ever touched by hurricanes. That is important. However, in 2007 something unusual occurred."

Braga went on to explain that he had researched that very issue. He discovered that the records showed that in the late summer of that year, as happened every year, a tropical disturbance developed off the coast of Africa and began tracking westward. Initially it was invisible to the weather-watching satellites. Feeding off the warm water, however, the disturbance began to rotate and developed, a week later, into a recognizable tropical depression. It continued to gain energy. It was still slowly moving westward. In four more days it had the full attention of Hurricane Hunters. In what seemed like no time it was a major hurricane. Then it was quickly upgraded to a strong Category 5 storm, one of the most powerful ever seen. It was named Hurricane Felix and Felix's path took it through the southern Caribbean. Although it did not directly strike the island, Felix's effect on Margarita Island was profound. Extremely strong winds and currents, ten-foot waves, and one dead were the final results. This was just from incidental contact, a mere brush. Felix went on to strike Central America without much weakening, resulting in many more deaths and incredible damage.

As for Venezuela, the beaches on the north side of Margarita Island were rearranged so that they were unrecognizable to those who had lived and worked there all their lives.

"Even the sea bottom was shifted by the action of those strong waves," Braga said. "The water is not very deep there, maybe one meter. Anyway, the *Little Ranger* was once again exposed."

"What do you mean 'once again'?" Alex asked. Braga explained that wind and waves cyclically revealed and covered shipwrecks. This was the routine of the sea.

"So," Martinez jumped in, "Colonel Bautiste recognized the importance of the wreck and brought Rinni here. Rinni pulled all of the information together."

Most importantly, Martinez pointed out, Braga had unfortunately helped Fernando come to the conclusion that there was sunken treasure on the wreck. This was based on the journal list and the history of the *Little Ranger*. All four looked toward the glass case. As Martinez concluded, Braga's cell phone rang. He excused himself to take the call.

Martinez, thinking he and Braga had monopolized Alex's time, apologized if they had been boring. Alex assured him he had not been bored at all, but said that he and Elise should be getting back to Porlamar. They left Martinez with the promise that they would revisit Museum Nueva Cadiz soon. Alex suddenly recalled what he and Martinez had been discussing when Dr. Braga had arrived.

"*Senor* Martinez, if the journal's list was, somehow, transcribed incorrectly, well, the difference could be significant." The man dipped his head in agreement, but said nothing. "Could you photocopy the original pages?" Alex asked.

"It's not possible," the Curator said shaking his head, "for two reasons." He explained that the old book could not be exposed to the bright light of a photocopier environment. This was following museum protocol as dictated by the Ministry of Culture. No document of museum quality could be so exposed. Secondly, even if the exposure could be permitted, the binding of the book was so old and tight that it could not be opened any wider than the angle a person could separate two adjacent fingers. Martinez demonstrated with his right hand. He said that he and Braga had used an automotive inspection mirror to read and record the names.

"How about a photo?" Alex asked, "Without a flash? Maybe with a cell phone camera?" Martinez thought for a moment and said that he would inquire.

Alex exchanged phone numbers with the Curator and left the museum after Martinez showed them the Island's model out on the patio. Braga had not returned. Alex was impressed by the model's detail and got a good idea of the topography of Margarita Island.

They took their leave and headed back to Porlamar. Leaving La Asuncion, Elise pointed out the white "La

Columna de Matasiete" standing on a cactus-covered hillside, a reminder of the victory of the Republicans over the Spaniards in 1817.

After returning to Porlamar, they by lucky happenstance met Rinni Braga coming out of a drugstore. The three made hasty dinner plans and, before Alex could mention his concern over the accuracy of the transcription of the journal entry, Braga went on his way. As they walked along, Elise explained again how Fernando had hired Braga.

CHAPTER FOUR – Dry Run

While the others were at the Museum Nueva Cadiz, Colonel Fernando Bautiste had spent the day gathering several items. He had bought a used hard shell suitcase; a box of heavy-duty freezer bags, a plastic scoop, a paper filter mask of the kind used everywhere, a utility knife, glue, and a spray bottle of Armani <u>Code</u> cologne. When his shopping was finished and the purchases secure in the trunk of his Mercedes, he returned to his office in La Asuncion, told his assistant, Sergeant Garcia, he was not to be disturbed, and sat at his desk to think.

With the arrest of LaFell and the disappointment of the *Little Ranger, El Sordito* had wanted to know how Fernando was going to pay for the eight kilos of cocaine.

"I have an American," was Fernando's answer.

His career began as a humble patrolman in the poorer neighborhoods of Caracas. He quickly learned, as did his superiors, that his special talent was in handling cases of domestic abuse. Other patrolmen dreaded these calls because of the unpredictable and sometimes horrific circumstances. Young Bautiste reared in an abusive household himself, waded in to each situation and took control in no uncertain terms. If a cowardly father or husband was stupidly or drunkenly (or both) uncooperative, Bautiste's method was to move the offender to a separate room and break the bones of a hand or two with his patrolman's baton. The suddenly cooperative and sober person was then told to reform or the patrolman would be back. Bautiste found he was promoted to Corporal and then Sergeant. At this level, the policeman abandoned brutality in favor of intelligence. He made the effort to learn the criminal mind and methods from serial killer to thief to organized crime. Also at this level, the policeman was reassigned to a wealthy neighborhood in northern Caracas. Here he saw what money could provide and he was newly motivated. It was as a Sergeant that he began to apply his newly gained criminal knowledge and to cultivate the friendship and patronage of the wealthy.

When one of those wealthy people, Senor Valdez, asked Sergeant Bautiste to discreetly investigate several arsons in the neighborhood, Fernando gathered evidence that, as Valdez suspected, it was Valdez's adult son who was setting the fires. Rather than officially document the evidence, Fernando took it to Senor Valdez who pleaded with the Sergeant to allow the father to arrange for the son to receive the treatment he needed. The Sergeant agreed and destroyed the evidence. Shortly, thereafter, Sergeant Fernando Bautiste received a phone call from a government official who asked him to please hold for Hugo Chavez. It turned out that Senor Valdez was well connected and a personal friend of the President. The President warmly thanked the Sergeant for helping his friend and that seemed to be that as far as Fernando was concerned. At least until the Sergeant's commander summoned him to inform him that he had been promoted to Lieutenant. From then on, as someone deemed to be *cooperativa* and under the special notice of the President, promotions to Captain, Major, and Colonel came to Bautiste unusually quickly. His assignments improved steadily also. As before, Fernando watched and learned. He especially studied how the Generals and top politicians smoothly and confidently maneuvered to reach and retain power. Fernando couldn't decide whether these people learned their persuasive skills on their way up or were born with them. In any event, they all had one thing in common: they were master manipulators. Fernando had been determined to become one of them. He noticed that these powerful people also reserved the option of violence as a last resort when faced with recalcitrance. Of course, when needed, the violence was delivered, not by the powerful, but by surrogates who served loyally and without question. So Major Bautiste had discovered and added to his staff Sergeant David Garcia, a short but immensely powerful bull of a man. Sergeant Garcia, known on the force as *El Martillo* (the Hammer), had proven to be the perfect surrogate for the Major. When a rich slumlord in the Major's district had refused a local politician's request to suspend evictions of families behind on their rent, the politician asked the Major to

83

investigate if some law were being broken. The Major could find no applicable law so he attempted to reason with the wealthy landholder. Bautiste had argued in a friendly way that late payment was better than no payment. The evictions were shortsighted, the Major reasoned. The man had only laughed at the Major. Bautiste had naively failed to realize that the landlord's scheme was to replace the evicted with renters who would pay a higher rent. For years, he had been getting rich employing this method. The politician, more concerned with losing voters than with the welfare of the poor, was chagrined at the Major's report and let him know it. Bautiste had offered to try once more. He turned *El Martillo* loose on the man. The Hammer made it clear that a change in rental contracts was non-negotiable. The man laughed at the Sergeant. It was the last articulate sound his mouth made for many months. The Hammer had brought with him a – hammer, a heavy framing hammer. He swung it suddenly at the laughing mouth and smashed jaw, lips and teeth with a single powerful blow. The next swing further shattered the man's mandible. The Hammer gripped the man's head with powerful hands and forced him to focus his tear-filled eyes. The man agreed to new rental contracts. Sergeant Garcia asked the man if he was left-handed or right-handed. Being right-handed, the Sergeant brought the hammer down and crushed the left hand. The man could still sign contracts.

Bautiste concluded his reverie in less than an hour. He was quick to adjust to changing circumstances and had already made up his mind that Braga, his team, and the *Little Ranger* would become no longer Venezuelan responsibility, but French responsibility. He was sure that the French government would agree to raise and recover the *Little Ranger* and return it to French soil. Bautiste knew that Braga would be tasked by the French with finding the least expensive way of accomplishing this with all deference to avoiding damage. He summoned Sergeant Garcia to make the arrangements through the appropriate government agencies.

Bautiste also made his mind up. He would approach that American with a proposition.

Alex and Elise had felt closer after their outing. Alex looked at her more fondly and saw the woman who had attracted him so many years ago. For her part, she liked how Alex handled himself among her friends and on her island. She found him shy, which she usually disliked in men, but Alex was shy without being daunted. They made love that afternoon and got ready for their dinner with Braga.

It was around eight when they arrived at the *Punto Criollo*, a centrally located restaurant in Porlamar. Braga was already there and had claimed a table for four far from the kitchen. Regardless, the overall decibel level made conversation difficult. Alex, on Elise's recommendation and with Braga's encouragement, ordered *pasticho Venezelano*, a Venezuelan take on traditional lasagna. They drank wine and talked about their backgrounds. Alex was surprised at Braga's interest in his patchwork educational background. Alex was explaining his interest in language's when he remembered the question he meant to ask Braga at the Museum.

"Dr. Braga, er, Rinni, how was the journal message transcribed?"

"I don't know what you mean, *Alejandro*." Alex explained that he was concerned over the fidelity of the transcription that he was shown compared to the content of the original message. Elise saw the point he was making.

"A small mistake might make a big difference," she pointed out. "It happens all the time." Braga nodded pensively and stroked his gray beard.

"I think you are right," he agreed. "I will speak to Senor Martinez and see if there is some way you, Alejandro, can view the *diario*."

Alex enjoyed the meal and, even more, the conversation. When Braga returned to the story of the *Little Ranger* and Bartholomew Roberts, Elise asked him to explain why he thought the wreck had been transporting treasure and

85

what he thought the treasure was. Braga opined that the treasure would have been gold coins or other pirate loot that would be easy to transport and could have easily been used to purchase African slaves who would be brought west to work on Caribbean plantations. Braga explained that by the early 18th century, pirates were opportunistic beyond mere thievery and operated as entrepreneurs expanding their activities well beyond shipping raids.

Changing the subject, Braga said that during the afternoon and in light of the failure to find anything resembling treasure, the Venezuelan and French governments had quickly reached a new agreement. Now it was the responsibility of the French to raise and recover the *Little Ranger*, its artifacts, and return everything to French soil. Braga, as a French contractor, was tasked with finding the most efficient way of accomplishing this.

"You know, the French were as disappointed as anyone when no treasure was found," Braga said. Alex and Elise were surprised at this and said so. They thought that the established economy of a major European nation would be unaffected by something as whimsical as "pirate treasure."

Braga shrugged. He pointed out that the global economy was truly unhealthy and the French, though not as bad off as the "PIIGS" nations, were no exception. Braga said that the French were not happy with the prospect of incurring a substantial cost with no prospect of gain in recovering the *Little Ranger*. He told Alex and Elise that he privately believed the French were hoping to return the *Little Ranger* to France and put her on display so that she could generate some revenue. Two archaeologists, a man and a woman, had been dispatched to coordinate the recovery of the *Little Ranger* and her contents. Alex asked if there were any intrinsic value in the wreck. The answer was probably not much, just to scientists. Alex asked if Braga knew what the biggest financial recovery at sea was. Rinni told them the story of the "*Black Swan*". He warned that the story also illustrated the legal tangles involved with recovery at sea.

Starting in March 2007, a Florida-based company, Odyssey, Inc., discovered and salvaged in the Atlantic Ocean the contents of a shipwreck located well off the coast of Portugal using a remote-controlled submarine. They estimated the haul's value at about $500 million almost all of which was in Spanish coins. But, when the company filed a salvage claim in Tampa, the Spanish government objected, arguing that the loot came from a Spanish military ship, the *Mercedes*, which was carrying coins from South America to southern Spain in 1804. The *Mercedes* was recorded as sunk during a battle with British warships.

Odyssey announced that the ship they found was the "*Black Swan*," an obvious alias for a Colonial-period wreck located in the Atlantic. Odyssey reported that the site yielded a quantity of silver coins weighing more than 17 tons, hundreds of gold coins, gold ornaments, and other artifacts. Odyssey, in keeping with good archaeological practice, had performed an extensive photographic survey of the "*Black Swan*" site.

Braga explained that, in a move that was sure to antagonize the Spanish government, the coins and artifacts were secretly loaded aboard a leased airliner in Gibraltar and legally imported into the United States in keeping with U.S. law. Odyssey brought the artifacts under the jurisdiction of the U.S. District Court by filing the necessary paperwork. This procedure allowed any legitimate claimant with an interest in the property to make a claim.

The Spanish government filed a formal claim to the treasure alleging that the coins were originally from the *Nuestra Señora de las Mer*cedes, a Spanish naval vessel which sunk in 1804. Spain claimed that it was entitled to all of the coins and that the treasure was outside the jurisdiction of the U.S. Court under the Foreign Sovereign Immunities Act. Regardless of the fact that the Spanish had not conclusively proven the recovered cargo came from the *Mercedes*, Odyssey presented evidence to the court (including the ship's manifest) that purported to show that regardless the primary purpose of the *Mercedes'* last voyage was commercial in nature rather than military and the vast majority of coins on board were owned by private merchants, not by Spain. Alex began to appreciate the professor's disclaimer that maritime law was complex.

Odyssey's claim initially had the full support of the U.S. government. The United States, however, filed an amicus brief in the case changing its position in support of Spain. The U.S. government justified its reversal by re-interpreting the language in the Sunken Military Craft Act which allowed government owned vessels even on commercial missions to enjoy sovereign immunity.

"The U.S. government obviously wanted something from Spain in return," Braga pointed out. "Who knows what it was, but this was frustrating to Odyssey. These issues can get very tricky."

How tricky was illustrated, Braga said, by the salvage case of the *R.M.S. Titanic*.

"Look at what happened there," he said. Once the wreck of the *Titanic* was located, the U.S. basically ran the salvage effort, although the ship was found in international waters and was of British origin. The R.M.S. Titanic Maritime Memorial Act claimed that these arrangements were because the ship had "major national and international cultural and historical significance" and merited "appropriate international protection."

Odyssey and the "*Black Swan*" had received no such consideration. Without conducting a hearing, the district court in Florida sided with Spain and ruled that the treasure should all be turned over to Spain. The case was on appeal.

"What about the *Little* Ranger? How did the French and Venezuelan governments decide who owned all the stuff associated with the *Little Ranger*?" asked Alex. They were by now enjoying coffee and Calvados.

"Well, Colonel Bautiste had the power to negotiate for Venezuela and the two French marine archaeologists negotiated for France," Braga said. He went on to explain that ever since the wreck site survey had come up empty,

Caracas had been adamant in turning over responsibility and disengaging from any salvage claims and activities. The French were pretty much on their own.

"How'd the law get so complicated?" Alex asked. "What ever happened to 'finders keepers'?"

"Now you are talking about ancient Roman laws that evolved over thousands of years," Braga laughed. "'Treasure trove' it's called. These are interesting subjects, but for another day. I should be going." He took a final draining sip of his Calvados. "Elise, you must bring Alex to the site, yes?" Braga said getting up to pay.

"I will," Elise agreed. "We will see you soon at Playa Madrid." Alex and Elise said their good byes and signaled for more coffee.

Fernando, who had just missed Braga, found Elise and Alex having their coffee. He was a little drunk. He joined them and was overtly hostile with Alex. He managed, in fact, to be offensive to both of them. He referred to the *Little Ranger* as Braga's slave ship. Alex amicably tried to explain, as much as he had understood from Braga, that the ship itself was not to transport slaves, just the money needed to buy them. Bartholomew Roberts had other ships to carry the slaves. Fernando acted too drunk to care and Elise gave him a strange look.

Fernando pressed Alex on his opinion about slaves and slavery. Alex had no opinion other than that they were abominations and said so. He tried to change the subject. Fernando offered that slavery was only a business in this world that Alex had entered. Fernando drunkenly explained that modern slaves were not for plantations and that a young girl or woman worth a small fortune could easily disappear in the Caribbean, turn up drugged in some Arabian Gulf state, and profits would be made, big profits. Alex again tried to change the subject, but Fernando slyly winked. Elise fired off rapid Spanish and got up to leave. Fernando agreed to give Alex a ride home, but insisted on one more round before they left.

"She doesn't like talk of human trading," Bautiste slurred. He flagged the passing waitress and ordered more coffee and Calvados. Alex tried to protest, but Bautiste would have none of it. "Her friend's daughter, she stood for at the Baptism, *como se dice*?" Bautiste asked.

"You mean 'goddaughter'," Alex guessed, confused.

"That's it."

Bautiste went on to explain that Elise's goddaughter, Monica, had disappeared at the age of eighteen. Monica had turned eighteen in March, but had waited until the school year was finished before making a casino vacation to Aruba with several of her friends. After a night of casino gambling and drinking, she had vanished while returning to her hotel alone. Elise believed that human traffickers abducted her. Bautiste had tried to light a fire under the Dutch investigative forces, but they had been ground down by the affair of an American girl who disappeared in 2005, and were defensive to their maximum capability. The investigation resulted in a conclusion of death by drowning, although a body had never been recovered.

"I think Elise is correct. Monica is a sex slave somewhere," said Bautiste as he stared into his coffee.

"That's horrible," Alex said, "I hope you didn't tell her that." This was the reaction Bautiste had wanted.

"This trafficking is a bad business," Bautiste said glumly staring at his coffee. He looked up at Alex. "As bad as the drug trafficking," he said.

"Are you kidding?" Alex asked incredulously. "There's no comparison!"

"What do you mean?" Fernando asked. He signaled the waiter to bring two more Calvados.

"Well, for one thing using drugs is a choice! People don't choose to be slaves," Alex said with passion. He was speaking as the father of two daughters who

"What about those who supply the drugs?" This confused Alex.

It went like that back and forth as Fernando led Alex toward an alcohol-fueled paradigm whereby the "business" of drugs looked harmless and victimless in comparison to human trafficking. By the end of the conversation Fernando made his proposal.

"So, an American, I believe, could travel without suspicion, especially, someone without a criminal history. You would, of course, travel with no drugs. And, I would pay you for your time. Let us say five thousand dollars US?"

Alex raised his eyebrows. "Really? Tell me what you have in mind."

"It would be a sort of test," Fernando said. "Someone else would actually carry the drugs at a later time. Unless you wanted to."

Fernando explained that he was thinking of using a large suitcase with a secret compartment. It would be packed with the usual garments and accessories that a traveler would need for a short trip to Miami. The compartment would be filled with blank pages of printer paper to simulate the drug weight. If Alex could hand off the innocuous bag without raising any alarms then Fernando would be satisfied that he had found a "safe" method of smuggling.

"You know," Alex felt the need to point out, "I am against drugs. I believe it's a personal choice, but I think people are making a bad choice when they do drugs."

"Ok," Fernando shrugged. "Will you do it?"

"Since it's just a test," Alex said, "yes, but only to help out Elise. I feel like she was really counting on some profit out of the *Little Ranger* treasure: and not for five thousand. I want ten."

"Good," Fernando said pleased. "I must go now. I have arrangements to make. Today is Wednesday. Can you travel on Sunday?"

Alex made the trip from Porlamar/Caracas to Miami on Sunday March 3 as agreed. He was calm and this surprised him a little. He imagined that he would be nervous going through Customs in Miami, but he reminded himself that he was doing nothing illegal and that, according to his personal experience, drug enforcement people were less than impressive.

His personal experience was gained before Connie was born. He and Mary had been returning to the U.S. from a trip to Mexico when, before allowing the passengers to deplane, the flight attendant had introduced a gentleman and woman as agents looking for a volunteer. Alex had shrugged at Mary and raised his hand. The couple was delighted to have someone cooperate and explained their dilemma. They were training drug-sniffing dogs.

In the past, they had always had a member of the flight crew participate in the training, which consisted of concealing a small amount of heroin, marijuana or cocaine on the crewmember. The person would then walk off the plane with the other passengers and the dog would, if all went well, point out that there were drugs in the vicinity. After a few months, false positives began to occur. The agents began to realize that the dogs had missed the point of their training: they were dutifully identifying members of the flight crew.

The male agent placed a small plastic baggie of black heroin in Alex's left sock and then let him and Mary walk off the plane with the other passengers. The dog had no reaction to Alex, the agents ended the exercise and thanked Alex and Mary for their cooperation, and the dog and agents began to walk off.

"Don't you want your heroin back?" Alex called after them. He concluded that the dog wasn't the only member of the team who needed additional training.

The Miami International was bustling as usual. Alex retrieved Colonel Bautiste's large suitcase without incident and approached the U.S. Customs agent.

92

"Anything to declare?" the bored agent asked. Alex reminded himself that he was doing nothing illegal. He assured the woman that he had nothing to declare. The woman welcomed him home and waved Alex through. He proceeded.

Alex arrived on the sidewalk outside the terminal. This day Miami had no cooling breezes as those found on Margarita. The air was sweltering with both temperature and humidity in the nineties. Fernando had told Alex what he should do when he arrived and he followed his instructions. He leaned against the terminal wall with the large bag at his side. He sweated while he waited for a man in a red shirt to appear.

Fernando had said: "It will be easy. A man wearing a red shirt will bring a bag like this one. He will stand by you for a short time. Then he will leave with the bag you brought. You take the other bag to the hotel. Stay overnight; have a good time. Come back the next day. It's simple, yes? Understand?"

Alex had assured him that he did indeed understand. He had said little, which Fernando interpreted as acceptance of his instructions.

As Alex waited a skinny middle-aged man in a red golf shirt made his way in Alex's direction. Alex didn't know it, but the man's name was George Volek. Volek was a lieutenant in the extended Miami crime organization. He walked up to Alex's side and set down the large bag he was carrying. He did nothing to acknowledge Alex's presence, pulled a phone from the pocket of his cargo shorts, and, pushing a few buttons, studied the display. Appearing satisfied, he picked up Alex's bag and walked off. Alex mopped sweat from his forehead and controlled the impulse to look after the man in the red shirt. Alex, of course had no idea that two men watching from a van parked nearby had digitally recorded the bag switch.

Alex retrieved the Volek bag and stepped to the curb to hail a taxi. Fernando had explained that the contents of Volek's bag would be identical to the contents of the original bag. So Alex would have everything he would need for an overnight stay in Miami.

Alex gave the driver the address of a modern hotel on Miami's South Beach. He wasn't sure what kind of room Fernando had reserved for him, but he wasn't worried. He could change rooms if he didn't like Fernando's choice.

Alex needn't have worried. Fernando's choice was excellent and had been prepaid. Alex had a view of the ocean and beach from a comfortable twelfth floor glassed-in balcony. The "room" itself was a suite with separate sleeping, living, and dining areas. Alex smiled to himself as he picked up the phone to order room service. He ordered a Cuban sandwich and a bottle of Woodford Reserve. He pulled out his iPhone and hooked up the charger. He was going to need a full charge for the conversations he was about to have.

Alex's first call was to Connie. Connie was surprised to hear her Dad's voice so soon and said so.

"Yeah," Alex said, "things haven't exactly been going the way I thought." He described his time in Venezuela and as the story began to unfold Connie realized that this was going to take a while. She asked Alex to pause while she poured herself a glass of wine and got comfortable.

"Go ahead," Connie urged. Alex felt relief in speaking to his daughter. He trusted his daughters like no others. He spoke about the *Little Ranger* and lastly about the list in the journal. He told Connie his feelings for Elise. He got to the part that brought him to Miami.

"So I need you to do something for me," Alex said. "In my stuff stored with you is a box that has my old Daytimers. They're in plastic file boxes. Can you find the one for like April 1979?" Connie said it would take a couple of minutes so they continued to talk about Margarita Island while Connie searched.

"By the way, it's paradise," Alex said, "unbelievably beautiful. And the weather is fantastic. You should see my tan. And, I've lost a little weight."

"Send me a picture," Connie said. And then, as she located the correct box, "Ok. I got it." Alex told Connie to pull out the little booklet for April.

"I can't remember the date. Just flip through each page. There will be a business card for the FBI."

"Got it," Connie said. Alex asked Connie to read the name and phone number. Connie did, Agent Peter Simmons, and asked what was going on.

Alex, sipping his bourbon, explained about the two identical suitcases.

"Holy shit, Dad," Connie exclaimed.

"I think I've got it under control. Don't worry. I'm covering myself. That's what I needed the phone number for. Which reminds me. It's nearly four o'clock in California right now. Let me go and I'll call you later. I want to try and catch Simmons before he leaves work."

They said their good-byes and disconnected.

Alex was pretty sure that Pete Simmons would remember him. Alex was indirectly responsible for making Agent Simmons into the more important *SAIC* Simmons.

In August of 1979 a group of Muslim men studying English as a Second Language in California asked permission of their Director to miss classes for one day. The reason offered was that there was an important meeting of "student leaders" in Kansas City. A certain FBI Agent Peter Simmons who was, honestly, on a fishing expedition had previously contacted the Director of the English Language School, not sure of exactly what he was looking for. The Director was impressed with Simmons' discretion, though. Simmons was mainly interested in a heavy-set student, older than the others, Abolghassem Sadegh. Simmons' most important goal was to obtain Sadegh's photograph. The

Director agreed to do what he could. When the students proposed taking a group photo with the Director, the Director requested his own print of the photo. The print, not a copy (it *was* 1979) was snail-mailed to Agent Simmons at his office in Riverside, CA with a piece of scotch tape and an arrow marking the rough-looking Sadegh.

When the students requested their leave, the Director alerted Agent Simmons who passed along the information to the Bureau's field office in Kansas City. The meeting in Kansas City turned out to be a revolutionary planning session, a move to organize (but mostly control) thousands of young Muslims studying in the United States. Also, a shocking event was being planned at the session and the FBI regional office was stunned at the audacity. The Kansas City field office credited young Agent Peter Simmons in California for sounding the alarm when they submitted their report to Washington. Kansas City had turned out to be an intelligence bonanza. Very little was known about a planned Islamic regime even though the "revolution" was months old.

When Washington received the "KC Report", as it came to be known, fear and excitement circulated in equal parts within the halls of the J. Edgar Hoover building. The excitement was due to the realization that the Bureau had scored a huge intelligence coup. The fear was due to the possibility that the information was incorrect. Over the next several months, Washington requested clarification from Kansas City; Kansas City clarified, and more clarifications were requested. The cycle ended on November 4, 1979 when "students" overran the U.S. Embassy in Tehran, Iran and clarification became moot.

As the "KC Report" was made public, careers were advanced in Kansas City, others were quashed in D.C., and one career in California was particularly improved. From then on, for Agent Peter Simmons the name of Alex Browning, the Director of the English Language School in California, was always remembered with affection. Regardless, the two men had not been in contact with each other for thirty years. So it was with mild surprise that, late on an early March afternoon, after much transferring, SAIC Simmons received the phone call from the former English Language School Director.

"Alex Browning here," Alex began, "Remember me?" he asked hoping.

"Absolutely," said Simmons with warmth. This made Alex relax. "What have you been up to? Holy fuck. It's been a while."

Alex gave Simmons the bare bones version of the last three decades of his life. Simmons made the appropriate sounds at the right places.

"How about you?" Alex asked. "I'm kind of surprised to find you in the same place."

Simmons briefly recounted his own career, which had included two stints in D.C.

"My wife hated Washington and couldn't wait to get out. I jumped on the first opportunity to move back here even though it's a desk job. So now I don't chase bad guys," he summed up, "I send the young out to do it." Alex laughed.

"That's the way it should be. Anyway," Alex said, "got a minute? I need a favor."

"Sure," Simmons said without hesitation. " What do you need?"

Alex explained about his trip to Venezuela, his involvement with Elise, and Fernando's strange request, including the suitcase.

"Wait. You did that?" Simmons was incredulous.

Alex suddenly felt foolish. "Anyway," he said, "I decided to pass their stupid plan on. Do you know anyone in the DEA? That's the right group, isn't it?"

Pete Simmons asked Alex to hold on while he found the name of a contact at the Drug Enforcement Agency. He gave the name and

97

number to Alex, Agent John Reynolds.

"Let me give Reynolds a heads up before you call him, ok?"

"Ok. You probably won't be able to reach me so let me give you my daughter's contact info. Her name is Connie."

"You have a daughter," Simmons commented, "congratulations."

"Two, actually. I'll tell you about them when we have more time."

Alex passed on Connie's email and IM info and they broke off the conversation awkwardly. As he set down his phone, Alex realized that he had consumed nearly half the bottle of bourbon. He barely felt any effects. He nibbled at some cold fries and redialed Connie's number.

"I'm not bothering you, am I?" Alex asked.

"No. I'm glad you called. I've been online since we hung up. Listen to what I found out." Connie was excited. She told Alex how a Portuguese academic, Dr. Braga, had identified the *Little Ranger* and had asserted that the ship had, in all probability, been transporting the finances necessary to purchase African slaves when the crew had to run for their lives from the west coast of Africa back to the Caribbean."

"Right. I know that. I met Rinni, Dr. Braga."

"Really?" she said obviously impressed. "That's cool. Well, according to the *Little Ranger's* Wiki page the fortune had never been accounted for except for a few gold pieces and Braga believed it was there with the wreck, but no luck. Braga and his support team thoroughly surveyed the wreck and Venezuela fired Braga when no treasure was found. The French government, after agreeing to take over the wreck site, hired Braga to join their team which was quartered on a research vessel moored near the wreck site."

"Wow. I didn't know all that. Things are moving fast. Actually, Braga told me that he's convinced that the most likely scenario was that the crew of the *Little Ranger* made off with whatever money there was," Alex said. "Anyway, listen and this is important. I actually called to tell you that an FBI agent, Pete Simmons, would get in touch with you with some info for me. He's helping me contact the DEA. I'm not letting this drug smuggling go."

Connie approved of this and let her father know it. She also was responsible for the germination of a thought in Alex's mind when she said, "You know, it seems to me that just because the wreck site survey came up empty doesn't mean that's the end of the story."

"What do you mean?"

"It seems that the only thing that is for sure is that the area around the wreck has been ruled out as the location of any treasure. If there is a treasure," she added, "maybe it's still in the area."

"I'll look into it more when I get back to Venezuela," Alex said.

"Is that smart? Going back, I mean," Connie said.

"I've wondered about that," Alex admitted. "I kind of feel that I don't have a choice. I feel kind of responsible for Elise, and blah, blah, blah."

When Connie advised her father to stay close to the police on Margarita Island, Alex was reminded of how little his daughter understood.

"Ok. Well, listen. I'm beat so I'm going to let you go." They promised to stay in touch and Connie agreed to bring her sister and uncle up to date as soon as she could.

Alex felt exhausted, but when he tried to sleep, sleep wouldn't come.

As Alex and Connie were having their conversation, Pete Simmons was able to get in touch with John Reynolds of

99

the Drug Enforcement Agency. Simmons explained his relationship with Alex and how Alex now had some information that would be of interest to the DEA.

"What was the name again?" Reynolds asked. To Simmons, he sounded distracted. Simmons gave him Alex's name and spelled the last name for him.

"Well, looks like your boy's in a bit of trouble," the DEA agent said after some time.

"What are you talking about?"

"There's a warrant out for him. He came in to Miami today, right?" The DEA agent went on to describe how two agents tracking a known drug distributor, a George Volek, recorded a delivery from Alex Browning to George Volek.

"That's nuts," Simmons said. "Browning's bag was empty. Just a decoy he told me. A kind of test."

"That right?" Reynolds asked. "Well, let me read you something."

Simmons listened as Reynolds, obviously reciting from a report, described the encounter between Volek and Alex, the switch of suitcases, the detention of Volek and the surreptitious search of his bag. Blocks of cocaine weighing 4.7 kilograms or 10.4 pounds were found in a false compartment. The cocaine's value was estimated to be $2.6 million. Given that one gram of cocaine can serve three people, the cocaine would affect over 14,000 users. Volek's bag was tagged with a tracking device and the drug distributor was released.

"Your boy's dirty," Reynolds concluded.

"What are you going to do?" asked Simmons audibly upset.

Reynolds answered that Alex was a small fish. The criminals were using a drug distribution model described as WA, "wide area". This meant that many points of entry were used to overwhelm the enforcement resources. This model was in contrast to one where smuggling large amounts of drugs at a single point of entry was used.

"We're not going to pick him up, if that's what you're asking," Reynolds said. "Not yet, anyway."

"Pretty sure he's clean," said Simmons beginning to doubt, "but it's your call. Let me know how it goes, ok? I think he's just in over his head."

That evening the two agents went home to their families. Alex got up early and caught the first flight back to Venezuela.

CHAPTER FIVE – The Wreck Site

Alex's redeye trip back to Margarita was less than memorable mostly because he was so lost in thought; he couldn't remember a single travel detail. The morality of illegal drugs had not been an issue for him. The excitement he felt at his tangential involvement in the drug trade was undeniable and this bothered him. His life had always been planned, calculated, and moved forward precisely. Fernando and Elise's world, Margarita, was a world of action. Action was exciting. And, Alex thought, there were no consequences. He hadn't, strictly speaking, done anything unlawful.

As Alex was transported south and struggled with his conscience, Pete Simmons' own conscience kept him awake. He slipped from his bed and his sleeping wife. The FBI agent turned on his Blackberry and pulled up the contact number Alex had given him for Connie. Despite the hour, Simmons punched in the number and pressed the call button. He didn't really expect that Alex's daughter would still be awake, but the call was answered almost immediately.

Simmons identified himself. He apologized for the late hour.

"That's all right," Connie said, "I was online anyway. What can I do for you, Mr. Simmons?" Simmons was impressed at the young woman's equilibrium. Most citizens would be rattled if they received a call from law enforcement in the middle of the night. Simmons briefly explained his background with Connie's father. He told how he felt that Alex had been responsible for kicking off his career success. He ended by saying that he considered Alex a friend.

"Wow." Connie's surprise was evident. "I never knew that." Simmons went on to describe how Alex had given him Connie's contact information.

"Which brings me to the reason for this call. Did you know your Dad was recently in Miami?"

Connie acknowledged that she did. The agent sensed wariness in the young woman's voice.

"Do you know why he was there?" Simmons made an extra effort to keep his voice friendly. He didn't want the conversation to sound like an interrogation. Connie decided to trust the agent.

"Are you talking about the suitcase switch?" Connie asked.

"That's exactly what I'm talking about," the agent agreed, "but I've come into some additional information. Will you be contacting your Dad soon?" Connie said that she could.

Pete Simmons then related what DEA agent Reynolds had told him. Connie couldn't think of anything else to say so she asked, "Are you sure?"

Simmons emphasized that Alex, as far as he was concerned, had unwittingly broken the law. The situation would have to be addressed and resolved. Simmons assured Connie that a good lawyer would have no problem getting any charges dismissed. They ended their conversation.

Connie wasn't put at ease in the least. She believed, as did her father and brother, that the U.S. legal system was a Venus flytrap. Once you were caught up in it, you became part of an impersonal process that could eventually destroy you. Connie needed advice before she spoke to her father. She would have to wait until the morning to call her uncle and sister.

Elise picked Alex up at the Porlamar airport and Alex marveled to himself at the apparent domesticity of this small interaction. Back at Elise's house, Alex unpacked as Elise

103

quizzed him on the details of his trip. Alex wasn't sure how much Elise knew. Her questions convinced him that she knew everything. He wasn't sure why Fernando would have found it advisable to compromise Elise. He made a mental note to ask him later.

When they were finally drinking beer and sitting in the March breeze coming through the open windows and her screen door, Alex asked Elise what she knew about drugs in Venezuela.

"Remember that old TV show *Hogan's Heroes*?" she asked. "I am like that Sergeant Schultz—I know nothing." Elise was disappointed at Alex's reaction to her little joke. "Ok, seriously there is some traffic, but compared to Columbia, it is nothing. And, sweetie, I agree with my president—there would be NO traffic if the Europeans and Americans did something that would control the crazy demand."

Alex was familiar with the argument and really had no sympathy or empathy with the drug-using community. To him they were a weak-willed group. They seemed to be self-pitying and were probably self-hating. They were people who had stopped taking responsibility for themselves. They were the ones who had stopped trying, the ones who expected society to give them a hand up when they hit rock bottom.

"You're right, you and Chavez," Alex said. "The users are a bigger problem than the suppliers. I agree with that. What do we have to eat? I'm starving."

Elise laid out a plate of smoked mozzarella, provolone, and capicola. She sliced bread too. Venezuela had a large Italian immigrant population and there were many markets that catered to their tastes, especially on Margarita, which tried to satisfy Italian tourists as well as all tourists from Europe. Alex ate with a good appetite. He was surprised that he was hungry after the last couple of days.

Connie made the call to her uncle Terry the following morning. She explained what Agent Simmons had told her.

"Fuck!" Brother Terry bellowed. His secretary, in the outer office, rolled her eyes. "And he went back there? What the hell is the matter with him?"

Connie could only say that she wasn't sure. She assured her uncle that she was certain her father was ignorant of the drugs, but she wasn't sure what to do.

"I'll have to check with some lawyers I know, but I'm not too sure that ignorance is a viable defense," the religious man told his niece. "Have you told Jo yet?"

"No, not yet," Connie said. "I was waiting to get your input." Her uncle smiled to himself at the geeky statement.

"Well my *input* is this—tell your father what that FBI guy told you. Tell your father I'm looking into his legal liability. Tell your father to get his ass home as soon as he can. Tell your father to stop trusting these weird strangers." The younger woman thought her uncle was finished and was ready to say good-bye, when her uncle continued. "And, Connie, find a secure way to communicate with your Dad. This guy who gave Alex the drugs is a cop. He's going to have the resources to keep a close eye on your Dad including taps. Be careful and tell your Dad to be careful."

Connie agreed to be cautious and, after thanking her uncle, they broke off. Connie called her sister next. Jo was driving to work when she answered. Her Acura ILX had a Bluetooth connection so her side of the conversation was hands free. Connie reiterated what she had told their uncle. She also relayed their uncle's assessment of the situation. She finished by telling Jo about their uncle's admonishment to be careful.

"I don't know what to do about that," Connie said.

"For email PGP is an option," Jo offered. She was referring to encryption software available to anyone for free.

PGP stood for *Pretty Good Privacy*. It required the sender and the receiver to possess a "key" which would encrypt and then decrypt the data being sent. Security professionals trusted it, but the general public found it unwieldy.

"Might be overkill. Suppose Dad's reading mail on his phone?"

"It'll still work. Ok," Jo said, "how about this? It's simple and fools almost everyone." She described an email trick that was, indeed, simple.

"That's pretty devious," Connie laughed. "I'll use it."

"Ok. Listen, I just pulled in to work. Copy me on the email to Dad and I'll talk to you later."

"You got it. Later." That ended the call and Connie, immensely relieved, sat down with her laptop, brought up Outlook and formulated the email. She made some changes under the Tools->Options menu and hit Send. Then she sent a text message to her father's phone.

Alex was charging his phone so he didn't see Connie's text right away. He checked his email while Elise was making a list of their grocery needs. After Alex had deleted offers for refrigerator water filters, upscale woolen goods, and a sale on men's wear, he was puzzled when he opened his daughter's "message." There was no message. Alex assumed that Connie had meant to attach a file but had hit "Send" before dropping in the file. He replied "???" and opened a browser window. He Googled the *Little Ranger* once again and got the same set of resulting links as before, so he Googled *Playa Madrid*, the location of the wreck. As Google returned its results, he got an email alert. It was from Connie and said, "Check your texts?" Alex got his phone from the charger and read Connie's text and, then, read it again. He thought he understood and, returning his phone to the charger, went back to Outlook and Connie's email. He Select-ed the "empty" text area in the body of the email and changed the Font Color from white to black. Connie's message appeared including the admonishment from his brother regarding trust and it infuriated Alex.

"Shit!" Alex said "that fucking bastard!" He closed the laptop.

"What's wrong, *bebe*?" Elise asked. Alex had forgotten she was close by.

"Oh. Sorry," he said. "It's -- Jo's boss, my daughter. These startup guys are unbelievable; so damn demanding. He expects his workers to come in on Saturdays now." Alex shook his head in pretend disbelief.

"But, then, she is having a chance to become rich, no?" She stood beside him and stroked his forearm.

"What? Oh, yeah. I guess. Yes. She has a chance. I don't know if it's a good chance. So, what about tomorrow?" he asked changing the subject. "What time are we leaving to see the wreck? I'm looking forward to that."

"Oh, cutey. I'm sorry. I have to work tomorrow. I already missed too much time. Is it ok if Erin takes you tomorrow? She said she would do it." Elise stuck her head forward so that her hair tumbled in her face. Alex was a little annoyed at the change in plans and was angry with Bautiste, but the hair was enough to distract him.

"No problem," he said as she snuggled into his lap.

After making love, Alex napped on Elise's couch. He had been tired after traveling and staying in a hotel and needed to recharge. When he awoke, he found that it was already dark and Elise had gone to bed. She had left him a note that there was a sandwich in the fridge and that Erin was coming by around nine in the morning. He grabbed the sandwich and a beer and opened his laptop intending to figure out two things: a suitable revenge on Fernando Bautiste for tricking him and some sense of how serious his legal troubles were now that a wider slice of U.S. law enforcement was aware of the "dry run". Instead he found that his browser still displayed the Google results for *Playa Madrid* that he had searched for earlier. The first links were just news stories about the wreck site. He began to wonder what the law was on recovering sunken treasure and was about to research it when he remembered why he had logged on.

He began by trying to get a feel for Bautiste's background and the strength of his position. He immediately discovered that Bautiste was well connected to the Chavez power structure. Alex made a face. He was impressed. Maybe Bautiste was too strong to mess with. Maybe Alex would just have to let it go and make sure that it didn't happen again. Terry was right; he shouldn't have trusted the Venezuelan cop. He had been stupid. However, he hated to just let Bautiste off. He decided to be more patient and to watch for an opportunity to sting the policeman without causing a larger problem.

Meanwhile, Alex returned to his search results. Playa Madrid didn't seem to be special. Other than being the location of the wreck, it was just another lovely Margarita beach. Alex turned his attention to what Google had to say about the legal rights of treasure hunters. It seemed simple enough — finders keepers. Well, pretty much, after negotiating with anyone else who seemed to have a claim. Alex concluded that it all came down to that one thing: negotiation. If everyone involved could be satisfied, it looked like nastiness could be avoided. There were numerous examples of successful and unsuccessful negotiations and it was hours later when Alex finally stretched out on Elise's couch and fell asleep.

Erin appeared the next morning just at nine and after Elise had gone to work. Alex was again taken by her beauty. She wore a sleeveless yellow top and dark blue shorts that fitted snugly and hid nothing of her long perfect legs. She wore sandals. Alex noted that, unlike Elise who always applied some form of facial cosmetic, Erin's attention to

108

make-up seemed minimal.   He had to remind himself that this was Elise's friend and that he was here visiting Elise.

Erin's car was an old Corolla. It had once been gray or silver, but was now faded into a nondescript color spotted with rust. It had cloth seats that smelled of old body odor and mold; there was also a strong aroma of gasoline. Alex tried not to stare at Erin's tanned legs as she worked the gas, brake, and clutch, guiding the small sedan through the Porlamar streets and onto Highway 1, north toward La Asuncion. With the windows down, conversation was difficult so Alex contented himself with the highway sights. She was a good driver and Alex found that he was relaxed and wondered why he had been annoyed at the change in plans yesterday. He began to wonder about how the wreck would actually look and if Rinni Braga had gathered any more information since Alex had last seen him.   He was still thinking about this when he realized that Erin was talking.

"What?" he asked. "Sorry." He leaned in closer to her.

"This is La Asuncion," Erin was saying, "where Elise works."   Alex didn't mention that he had been there last Tuesday.   "That is her building there."   Erin indicated a modern low building. "Elise has an important job, but she is disappointed that it doesn't pay more. Money is important to Elise."

"I got that idea," Alex agreed loudly over the noise of the airflow. "I guess government jobs pay poorly everywhere in the world. Something to do with a tradeoff between job security and wage I suppose."

Erin nodded. Alex couldn't tell if it was to show that she understood or that she agreed.

"How far is it to the beach?" Alex asked.

"To Playa Madrid? Not far; about thirty minutes. We will pass by a few small towns - El Saman, Tacarigua, Santa Ana, and some others - on the way to Juangriego on this highway. Then we will take a smaller coast road to the beach. Juangriego is important to the history of Margarita Island. Did you know?"

"No, I didn't know that. I'd like to hear about that."

"We can stop and look at the fort if you would like," Erin offered. "There is an old Spanish fort there."

"Can we look at it after we see Dr. Braga?" And Alex immediately regretted asking. Jeez, be a little spontaneous, he chided himself. You're with a beautiful woman and you're treating this like a focused business trip.

"No problem," Erin said. "We can take our lunch there. Make a picnic," she smiled. And, what a smile, Alex thought.

"That sounds great," Alex said. "I'd like that," he added sincerely. "Sorry if I sound like OC."

"Osea?" she asked puzzled.

"O. C.," he explained, "obsessive compulsive. It's always been a little problem of mine." He smiled.

"Like 'gotta do this'," she offered. "I understand. Here's Juangriego."

The town from the highway was a smaller version of Porlamar to Alex's eyes. Tourist hotels with views of Juangriego Bay were prominent. Erin turned the Corolla northeast toward Playa Madrid.

"I don't know this part of the island very well, but I like these hills over the beaches." Low hills overlooked small bays and inlets and Alex liked the combination too. The hills weren't built up much. A few huts were visible. They passed a lagoon on their right.

"I think that is called 'Laguna de Los Martires'", Erin said.

110

"Who were the 'Martyrs'?" Alex asked.

"I'm not sure, but I think they were the ones who died fighting for independence. There was a famous battle fought near here, I think. We'll check it out on our way back." She turned northwest now, following the road marker for Playa Madrid. The road was a secondary road with sand shoulders. They cleared some palm trees and the beach was before them. Alex recognized Braga standing with some other people on the beach. Some temporary signs had been erected closing the beach to tourists.

"There's Dr. Braga," Alex said exiting. A security guard appeared and started to wave them off. "Rinni," Alex called getting Braga's attention. Braga signed to the guard to let them approach.

"Alex and Erin," Braga said with obvious delight. "*Hola* and welcome." He pumped Alex's hand and gave Erin a light kiss on each cheek. "Come. I want you to meet my new employers, my French colleagues."

He led them over to a man and a woman. Alex's impression was that the man was short and the woman was heavyset. Braga introduced the man as Dr. Jean-Jacques Wilson and the woman as Dr. Renee Rideau.

"Everyone calls me JJ," Wilson told Alex and Erin taking their hands in turn. It sounded to Alex like "Gigi". His informality was in contrast to what Alex thought was a theatrical bow.

Rideau was less friendly. Her skin was glowing pink from the sun, but her fleshy hand was cold and moist. "I am Dr. Renee or just Renee," she said and then laughed for no apparent reason.

Alex and Erin completed the introductions and Braga broke in with his news.

"Just this morning, after what was revealed the night of Fernando's party, the Venezuelan government turned over

111

all responsibility and recovery effort to the French government. JJ and Renee are jointly in charge and will coordinate the work here. They have retained me to ensure that care is taken not to damage the remains of the *Little Ranger*. This is great news for the French and for the marine archaeological community." Braga was beaming.

"So everyone is in agreement that there is no truth to Bautiste's belief that there was treasure to be found?" Alex asked.

"Certainly," Wilson interjected as Rideau laughed, "there is not."

"But," Braga cautioned with a raised finger, "in these cases, one never knows. And, that reminds me, my friend. I have received a text from Curator Martinez. He has acquired the necessary approvals for you to photograph the message in the journal. He is at your disposal whenever you would like to take the picture." Alex was about to thank Rinni for his help when there was a mild commotion at the water's edge. Everyone moved there.

A couple of divers in scuba gear were reporting to the French couple. From what Alex could tell, the conversation was conducted in French, Spanish, and some English. He took advantage of the situation to look around. Alex noted, for the first time that the offshore wreck site was cordoned off by buoys and rope. He was struck by the unexpectedly small size of the demarcated rectangle. Alex also noticed that apart from a collection of small workboats gathered outside the buoys, a large, gray official-looking vessel was anchored nearby. He surmised that this was a French government ship. It was large enough to be the base of operations for Wilson and Rideau he guessed. Rinni touched Alex's shoulder bringing the American back to the moment.

"That big ship is French. It arrived a couple of weeks ago," Rinni explained, "just to take a look I think. JJ and Renee are living on it for now. Since last week, events have moved very rapidly. The Chavez government wants the wreck recovered and removed as soon as possible. All of the workers who had been working for Venezuela are now working for France." Rinni lowered his voice and added, "I'm not sure, but I think that JJ and Renee have been given a strict budget under which to operate. The French, like everyone else in this world economy, are counting their - what - francs?"

"How will that affect your work?" Alex asked also in a quiet voice.

"Honestly, I'm not sure. The French may be tempted to cut some corners, which could result in damage to the wreck if they are not careful. I will try to convince them that it would be more economic to go slowly and not make a mistake. Who knows? I hope they will accept that."

"What did the divers have to say?" Alex asked.

"Oh. They were reporting that the part of the ship not covered by sand has been burned. JJ and Renee have fear that this condition has weakened the hull and will make the recovery more risky. I explained to them that most probably the burning has made the wood more stable. Tougher. More strong." Rinni clasped the fingers of both hands together to illustrate his point. "Understand?" he asked.

"So the charring made the wood easier to raise and relocate?" Alex asked.

"Exactly," Rinni confirmed. "Come and look at these pictures." Up until now Erin had been hanging back, content to absorb the science and technology from a distance. Now she moved up to join the Portuguese expert and the American amateur.

Rinni opened a Lenovo laptop and brought up a blurry picture. Alex and Erin leaned in to get a better look. Rinni cycled the picture to the next in a sequence. This photo was clearer and of better resolution.

"Fernando arranged last year for the Venezuelan Air Force to fly over the site with a, *como se dice*, a plane with no pilot, a UAV?" Rinni asked.

"A drone," Alex and Erin said simultaneously.

"Exactly," Rinni affirmed. "See the dark shadows? That is the outline of the *Little Ranger*." Alex thought to himself that 'little' was appropriate. The old ship couldn't be larger than a large-sized yacht.

"It is mostly still buried in the sandy sea bottom," Rinni explained, sensing Alex's skepticism. "But, yes, it is not a large ship."

Alex thought back to the long list of names in the journal. If they were crewmen, they had to be past <u>and</u> present.

Despite Alex's surprise at the *Little Ranger's* lack of size, he was excited about the proximity of the wreck, the shadowy computer image, and the fact that now, being here and having all ready seen the journal, it all felt real, very real. He promised himself to take a photo of the journal list as soon as possible.

Braga was explaining to Erin that the divers had initially used magnetometers to survey the site. These devices would detect any metal in the area. They had located several 18th century cannon, a few other metal artifacts including barrel banding or hoops and some coins.

After an hour Alex and Erin left Braga to his work and strolled on the unrestricted part of the beach, which was populated by locals taking advantage of the weather to enjoy the sand and the water and to watch the foreigners working. Alex and Erin made their way to the west end where a jumble of rocks blocked their way. The waves had eroded the formation in places so that small caves had been washed into the rocks.

"Come on," Erin said taking Alex's hand and pulling him forward to the largest of the washouts. Alex pulled his hand free and, good-naturedly, said, "Later. Right now I'm starving. Didn't you say something about a picnic lunch?"

Erin pouted in an overly dramatic show of disappointment and then smiled and said, "Ok. Let's find some food for you."

They turned back and, as they turned Alex had what he later thought of as a "Shawshank" moment. He noted that a black boulder the size of a Volkswagen beetle sat in the shallow water at the end of the rock jumble. He remembered Andy's words to Red about a black rock that had no business being in the place where it was found.

"Did you ever see "The Shawshank Redemption"? Alex asked.

"Yes. I love that movie. It's one of my favorites."

"Me too. That black boulder reminded me of that scene when Red finds the metal box." Alex pointed out the boulder.

"The rock that didn't belong where it was," Erin said. Alex nodded in response. They got Braga's attention as they returned to the car and waved good-bye. Alex took one last look around at the scene and tried to imagine it, as it must have been three hundred years ago.

They arrived in Juangriego at the tail end of the traditional lunch hour so they had their choice of places to eat. Erin suggested they settle for burgers and fries. This amused Alex. He assumed she was deferring to what she saw as an American preference. This was ok with him, he decided. As they drove around, he asked her how hamburgers came to be on an island.

"Oh, we have a couple of large cattle ranches and some pig farms as well. Fresh meat is available year round and, especially, during tourist season. We don't only eat fish." She puckered her cheeks and crossed her eyes, her attempt at a fish face. Alex laughed.

They found a burger joint and Alex's mouth was watering as the food was prepared. He hadn't eaten since his nighttime sandwich.

"We can walk up the hill," Erin indicated the hill overlooking the town, "and eat up there."

"Picnic," Alex said as he paid for their food.

Erin led them up the hill to the remains of the fort of Juangriego. Alex felt all of his sixty-seven years as he hiked. Erin easily outpaced him as they climbed and Alex found himself entranced by the rhythm of her pumping buttocks as she led the way up the trail. Erin turned unexpectedly to ask Alex if he was all right and she caught him admiring her rear. She turned back to the trail with a smile.

When they reached the ruins of the fort they were confronted by a historical marker of the type found the world over, raised metal letters on a metal tablet and a bas-relief tableau depicting a portion of whatever significant event the marker was memorializing. Erin translated the marker. It explained that this site was dedicated to the memory of the famous battle of Matasiete. The battle was central (or at least had always been celebrated to be) to determining the independence of Venezuela from Spain.

"The battle wasn't really fought here. It happened near La Asuncion," Erin explained. She told Alex that all Venezuelans and, especially, *Margaritenos* celebrated the battle and observed its anniversary every year.

"When was the battle?"

"In 1817, in July. The holiday is celebrated on the last day of July."

They ate their lunch and Alex talked about his daughters. Erin was delighted at Alex's obvious pride in

116

Connie and Jo and his ability to describe them in amusing ways.

"It must be wonderful to watch your children grow into successful adults," Erin observed, "and, can you imagine how awful it must be to see them make mistakes and bad choices?"

"I can't imagine," Alex said, "I've just been lucky." Erin rolled her eyes. "My girls are unbelievable. What about you, though? How did you turn out so squared away?"

Erin laughed at this. "Squared away? What does that mean? And, I don't think you were just lucky. You and your wife obviously did the right things bringing up your children."

"Thanks for that. I guess it's never easy, but, as parents, you try to do the little things that will give your kids an edge, an advantage, like spend bonding time with them. I think, honestly though, it's them. They wind up making the right decisions. You can't take credit for that. And, since you asked, squared away means you've got it together. You make the right decisions, too." Alex smiled, a little embarrassed.

"Well, thank you for that. I'm not sure you're right about me though, but thanks." Erin leaned in and gave Alex a small kiss on the cheek. To Alex she smelled, not of perfume, but of onions and burger. Oddly, he found this more attractive. He was, again, a little embarrassed.

"So, what about you?" he asked. "What is your story? How _did_ you turn out to be so squared away?"

Erin reiterated what she had told Alex at the party. "But, seriously, I think I turned out 'squared away' mostly because I took responsibility for my own life early."

"What do you mean?" Alex asked. "I mean, I agree. People who manage their lives well are the ones who had

117

responsibility early. Give me an example. How did you manage your life early?"

"Wow. I don't know. I guess, I mean does anyone really know that they're-what did you call it- managing your life when it's going on? I think it's the people who start out with nothing, or start out in a low economic condition, and then realize that hard work is the only way they're going to improve their life. And, then, they dig in, work hard, conquer obstacles and find success." Alex was nodding vigorous agreement the whole time.

"Right," he said. "Maybe it's a competitive thing, too," he offered. Erin thought this over.

"Yes. I think that's a big part of it. I'm a competitive person. I always want to win. I hate losing at anything. Are you like that?" She was laughing.

"I am ridiculously like that," Alex said shaking his head. "I even have competitions with Connie and Jo to see who makes the best *pancakes*. Ridiculous." Alex smiled and shook his head again. Erin was laughing harder than ever.

Alex liked and trusted Erin. He became more serious and confessed his dislike for Fernando. He was reluctant to tell her about his trip to Miami, but felt that they had passed some invisible barrier, that they could talk about more subjects openly.

"What do you think about him?" Alex asked.

"Alex," Erin said, also serious, "he is a dangerous person. Do not underestimate him. He is capable of anything. And, he is very well connected, all the way to the top. And don't underestimate the Venezuelan people. There are many who would like to see a change." She lowered her voice at this last causing Alex to lean in close to hear her. She did not withdraw from his closeness.

"The top," Alex said feeling a sexual tension and making the decision to not push the moment. He leaned back relaxing, but still holding her eyes. "He behaves like he has a big brother watching over him. I kind of suspected that. Thanks. I'll be careful."

"That would be best," Erin said softly. She looked away and took in the view. The view from the fort was amazing and the weather was perfect. Alex followed her gaze toward Juangriego. He spotted a cafe on the bay and was reminded of Magrew and their agreement to play chess.

"What do you know about Magrew, the restaurant owner?" he asked only because his thoughts had tended that way.

"The one-armed black man?" she said, "Not much. He's an American. He was already in Porlamar when I arrived. He used to work for some oil company and now sometimes works for them in some kind of capacity, an independent contractor, maybe. Like I said, I don't know much." She told Alex that she had never been to Magrew's cafe, but that it was a popular tourist spot for those in search of local color.

"I met him at his place and I liked him, but, you know how sometimes you feel like people are a little off?" Alex looked to her for affirmation, didn't get it, and so went on, "Anyway I have that feeling with him. It's probably just me. I wondered what you thought."

"I've maybe spoken to him five times since I've been in Porlamar," Erin explained. "He always seemed nice. Maybe a little guarded." She brushed back her hair. "Now that I think about it, whenever the topic of conversation was the U.S. or living in the U.S., that's when he seemed guarded or cautious. I don't know," she said a little frustrated. "I don't want to label him as 'a little off' just because of that."

"Maybe because he's black?" Alex asked.

"No," Erin protested looking at Alex to see if he were serious. "Well, yes," she amended. "I guess so. There's nothing wrong with that," she asserted.

"Except that it's racist," Alex said.

"How is it racist? It's the opposite of racism." Alex could see that Erin was bothered by the thought.

"You just treated Magrew differently based on the color of his skin, his race. That's racism."

"Wrong," Erin said. "It's not racism if I treat someone better because of their race. How is that racism? Racism is persecution. What about equal opportunity, voting rights? All of that?"

Alex had spent a lot of time arguing the same points with Connie and Jo. His response was ready. "Racism isn't persecution. It can result in that, I agree. But racism is treating someone in a way that is different from how you would have treated him or her if they had been of a different race. That's what racism is." Alex could see that Erin was thinking this over as they sat side-by-side taking in the view. "And, I bet Magrew, as just one example, isn't the kind of guy who wants to be treated differently just because he's black. On the other hand, I'm also sure there are many black people who feel that they're entitled just because they're black."

"Then by your definition, they are racists," announced Erin.

"They are," Alex laughed and agreed although he thought she didn't really believe it. "Anyway," he said, "think it over and let me know what you conclude." He started to get up and clean up the remnants of their picnic.

"For now, let's change the subject," she said. "Look at *The Little Ranger* down there," she said indicating the small harbor of Playa Madrid. "What do you conclude about it? The history, I mean."

Alex was obviously considering his words carefully and she found his deliberation attractive. She was also afraid that this was becoming a problem.

120

"I think two things about the *Little Ranger*," Alex said. "First, real people sailed on that ship. That's fascinating to me. And that ship down there makes those people more real to me than ever. Second, I think that only someone very intelligent is going to figure out what happened to it after three hundred years. And," Alex smiled, "I think that you are very intelligent. Oh, and one more thing", he added, "I think that someone needs to check the list in the journal and check into the law concerning found treasure."

Alex would have blushed if he weren't almost seventy years old. Instead, he shrugged and said, "There's a lot of investigating to do. Would you like to help?"

Erin, once again, leaned in close and kissed him on the cheek. "How do you say it?" she asked, "I'm your girl." Alex was a little surprised at her apparent disloyalty to Elise, but, since he was pleased, he let it pass.

While Erin and Alex were having their picnic and conversation, Elise was on the phone with Fernando. "I think he knows", she said.

"He couldn't possibly know," Bautiste disagreed. "He would have confronted me."

"He got a message on his phone and was very angry about it. He told me some story about his daughter, but I think he knows." Elise twirled her hair around her right index finger. "One thing is for certain. He handed over the money you gave him very quickly. Perhaps, another trip would be a good idea, whether he knows or not. At least, then, we'll, er, you'll know."

Fernando was amused at Elise's point of view. He had no doubt that she was happy to be the beneficiary of the money he had paid Alex.

"You maybe right, *amore*," he said. "Perhaps another trip is in order. And soon."

At Juangriego, Alex and Erin decided to head back to Porlamar. Alex was going to offer to drive, but he then realized that he wasn't sure of the status of his driving privilege in Venezuela. He made a mental note to ask Elise about it.

During the return trip, Alex asked a question that had been on his mind since the night of Fernando's party.

"So, you know my dating status, my relationship situation. I'm not sure though that what you think you know is accurate. If you don't mind my asking, what is *your* dating situation?"

She admitted that she was not dating anyone and that, really, she wasn't attracted to the typical Venezuelan male. Too self-centered and macho, she explained. This, of course, severely limited her choices.

"I occasionally date European tourists that visit the island but there's not much of a chance for permanence in those relationships. Anyway, the important thing is I'm not unhappy," she asserted firmly gripping the wheel and ten and two.

"I'm sorry if I've upset you," Alex quickly responded. "I just wondered...." He let his thought trail off and was suddenly saddened at the moment. Like most men who found themselves in similar situations with women and, in spite of his age and experience, he was at a loss as to what to say next. "Sorry if I was being pushy. I guess I was getting too personal."

"You weren't getting too personal," Erin said simply and without a smile. "It's just that, it makes me a little sad that, at my age, that I don't have a real relationship. That's all." Alex sat up straighter in his seat.

"Don't play the age card with me woman," Alex came back with mock seriousness. "You kids need to grow up, stop your whining and...."

"Don't," Erin commanded in mock seriousness herself. "Don't *you* play the age card with me! Old man, just shut up over there and enjoy the trip," she laughed, looking over at him in the passenger seat. "Hey, I know," she said suddenly inspired, "Let's go to Playa El Aqua tomorrow and get some sun. It's so much nicer than Playa Madrid. Elise wants me to entertain you tomorrow anyway. Sorry. I know it's a shitty way for you to be treated. She has to work again."

"Sounds great," Alex said not feeling the disappointment that he thought he should have been feeling. "But can we also go to the museum? I have permission to take a picture of the journal list." He oddly felt that maybe it had some significance. He looked at Erin as she drove and the Corolla's radio played a slow song on the local radio station. "I feel like it's important." The song suddenly stopped and an announcer began to speak.

Just then Erin stiffened in the driver's seat and was obviously upset.

"What?" Alex asked thinking that he had said something wrong.

"The radio," she answered, "Chavez." She sounded stunned. "*El Comandante* is dead."

They never noticed the unmarked police car that had been following them all day.

123

CHAPTER SIX – Erin

The news of *El Comandante's* death and the reaction to it spread. Alex and Elise, in her bed, watched the coverage on her little television set that night and Elise translated when the commentary was important. Alex gathered that Venezuelans seemed equally divided in their grief and their elation. Those who grieved the most seemed to be the ones who had the least. The glad, hopeful ones were those who wanted a return to free enterprise. Nicholas Maduro, Chavez's handpicked successor, was already posturing as if he were the President. In interviews and with statements released to the press he assured the populace that all of Chavez's policies would continue. There were scattered reports of rioting and looting. These, Elise explained, were probably being minimized in a hope to maintain local peace.

"They are saying that the robbing is being done by small criminals and, uh, those who are taking advantage of the situation, local troublemakers."

"What situation?" Alex asked.

"They don't say exactly," Elise answered, "Can you move over a little? You are hurting my arm." Earlier, Alex had snuggled over, trying to maximize the physical contact between them. He moved away.

"Sure," he said. "Better?"

"Yes," she said settling. "*Besos,*" she demanded, once their new positions were established. She bent in to receive his kisses and then, abruptly, retreated. A commercial for a national electronics chain was airing as the news took a pause.

"So Erin and I are going to Playa El Agua tomorrow. She says it's a beautiful beach. Do you know it?" Alex asked. Elise yawned.

"It is nice," she said. "Now I have to sleep. The morning comes early." She rolled even further away, her back to him.

"Good night," he said and reached for the TV remote.

The next morning, Wednesday, Alex got up before Elise and made eggs and coffee. After cleaning up, showering and shaving, and packing some things for a few hours at the beach, Alex suggested that Elise take the day off and go with Erin and him.

"*Bebe*, there is too much going on at the office right now. With Chavez dead," she explained, "there is a lot of uncertainty and a lot of information that must be distributed. It's important," she assured him.

Alex hugged and kissed her and watched her walk out the door. He decided to walk the ten blocks to Erin's apartment. In spite of nine hours sleep his legs were still sore after yesterday's Playa Madrid walking and then the climbing. He had always believed that pain brought on by exercise was best addressed by more exercise. His muscles protested as he set a brisk pace in the morning warmth of the sun. He carried a backpack, which contained his beach towel and a change of clothes and sunblock and a bottle of water. After one block, he decided that it was wise to listen to his body and back off. He set a more leisurely pace.

Alex covered the distance to Erin's so that he was there before his scheduled arrival time. He was thirsty when he arrived. He knocked on her door. The door wasn't latched properly and swung in at his pressure. He went ahead and entered the apartment, closing the door behind him. He called her name.

He stepped further into the dim interior his eyes adjusting from the bright outside sunlight. He could hear water running and called her name again. He looked ahead down a small hall. The running water stopped and suddenly

125

Erin appeared nude in front of him carrying the pieces of a red bikini. Alex registered every detail without realizing it.

"The door wasn't closed," he started to say. He took in her tan lines and her perfect body in obvious admiration. Alex sensed that she was unaccountably pleased that he was studying her.

"Would you like to help?" Erin asked breathily holding up the bikini. Alex smiled broadly, said nothing, and followed her into her bedroom. There she dropped the bikini, Alex dropped his backpack and they reached out for each other.

"I didn't take my vitamin V today," Alex joked nervously.

The feel of her naked body through his clothes excited Alex in a way that he hadn't felt in many years. They kissed at first longingly and then familiarly with open mouths and active tongues. Erin pulled off Alex's t-shirt and fumbled with the button on his cargo shorts. Alex's hands meanwhile freely roamed over her smooth tan and he marveled at the softness of her skin. She guided him to her bed.

Naked, their mouths continued exploring and Alex, inches from her face, wondered at the small white scar on her forehead. A wave of tenderness came over him and he felt the blood flow harden his penis. He reached down and guided himself to her and then inside her. The pleasurable change in temperature from the cool of the room to the warmth and wetness of her hastened Alex's rhythms. He watched her face and again felt a wave of tenderness. Then, Erin did something that Alex had never experienced in his life. She locked her long tan legs around his middle and squeezed him closer to her in the heat of her own passion. Her legs pushed on his back urging him deeper inside her. His pleasure was nearly painful as his face reddened with effort. He found his release as she found hers and their two exclamations blended as two notes in harmony. They both laughed, breathing heavily.

"Viagra, my ass," Erin managed to gasp. "Wow! How old are you?" she   laughed.

"Two things," Alex said also trying to control his breathing. "One: remember that I wasn't the one who brought up ages. And, two: it's all about the motivation and, beautiful, you motivate me." He kissed her full lips, slid over and cuddled beside her.

Alex's contentment was short-lived, though, as his mind began to drift to mundane matters.

"We should go to the beach," he said with disappointment. "We're expected to have some color at the end of the day." He moved aside so that Erin could move. She didn't seem at all annoyed at his practical thoughts.

"You want to go to the museum today, too," she said. "Don't you?" They went to her bathroom together and cleaned up their love stickiness. She put on the red bikini.

Alex's first impression of Playa El Agua was that of a crowded, commercialized chaotic wide strip of sand between the sea and a line of brightly painted businesses along a concrete "boardwalk". Umbrellas were everywhere and the predominant smell was of cooking as the restaurants along the boardwalk competed for beach-goer money. The smell of cooking was underscored by the smell of suntan lotion and the ocean and Alex did not find it unpleasant. He held Erin's hand as they looked for a place to spread their towels and get some sun. It was late morning and comfortably warm.

"Seems like everyone knows about your secret beach," Alex quipped as they settled down.

"Shut up," Erin smacked his arm. "This is the most beautiful beach on Margarita. Enjoy it." She lay back and closed her eyes. He looked over at her and couldn't believe his luck. Not only was she incredibly beautiful, but also was witty and intelligent.

"I'm enjoying, I'm enjoying," he muttered stretching out and closing his own eyes. And he did enjoy the warmth of the sun, the monotonous lapping of the small, breaking waves, and the underlying din of the rest of their fellow sun-worshippers. Eventually though Alex's sunbaked thoughts were pulled to that leather-bound journal encased in glass in the museum in La Asuncion.

"Erin," he tilted his head toward her without opening his eyes, "I really want to get a picture of that journal list today. I don't know why, but it's important to me. Can you drive us up there?"

Erin reached out her left arm and stroked his sun-oiled right. She stroked it with the back of her fingernails.

"Of course. It's not far. When do you want to go?"

"Let's have lunch at one of these restaurants and then we'll go. Ok? The food smell is driving me nuts." He had goose pimples on his arm from her light caress.

As Alex and Erin enjoyed the sun at Playa El Agua, Fernando was on the phone with The Hammer. They were discussing the civil unrest.

"The little criminals are making a nuisance," The Hammer reported, "nothing more. They use *El Comandante's* death as an excuse. Nothing to be worried about."

"All right," Bautiste said, "but I don't want things to get out of hand. I hear that things on the mainland are escalating. That will not happen here," he ordered. The Hammer got the message and assured his boss that things were under control. He changed the subject.

"Surveillance reports that the American has gotten very close to Miss Rosen. I thought you would want to know." The Hammer anticipated the response.

"Why should I care?" Bautiste asked.

"Surveillance thinks that it has gone as far as sex," The Hammer answered. Bautiste sat back in his chair, considering.

"Thinks or knows?" he asked. He looked out the window at the broad boulevard below. The sun shone on the pedestrians, some who were government workers and some who were citizens who had business with the government.

"They know," asserted The Hammer, "they planted a microphone in her apartment."

Bautiste got up and walked to the window.

"Of course they do," he said. "Here's what I am thinking: the American can screw who he wants." Bautiste used a cruder word. "It's better for us. Maybe it keeps him off-balance. I don't want him thinking too clearly. At least one more trip to Miami for us, that's what I'm thinking. A half-million more, maybe a million?" The Hammer knew his boss meant US dollars. "What do you think?" The Hammer was taken aback. It was rare that anyone asked him *to think* let alone what he thought. He scratched his immense head.

"I have saved a lot as you encouraged me," he said. "A little more would not hurt." Bautiste laughed at the big man's simplicity.

"How much have you saved?"

"A little more than one million," The Hammer said, his brow furrowed as he dealt with the conversion from Bolivars to dollars. Bautiste was impressed by the amount and, since it was his nature, he immediately considered how he could make the Hammer's million his own. It was just a reflex, though. He had no intention of cheating or robbing his rough colleague. Bautiste congratulated the big man on his thrift, which flustered The Hammer enough to end the call.

"I must go," he informed his boss.

"All right. We will talk later." Bautiste broke the connection.

While that conversation was taking place, Alex and Erin were packing up at Playa El Agua. They shook sand from their towels and placed them in Alex's backpack. Alex squeezed a dollop of sunscreen onto his palm, rubbed it on his neck, which had begun to burn, and dropped the tube into the backpack. They checked the sand for anything that might have been dropped and walked to the shade of the palm-lined concrete walkway. They picked out a small restaurant whose theme was blue and sat down at one of the patio tables. A waiter appeared and took their drink orders: beer for Alex and lemonade for Erin. They sipped their drinks and perused the lunch menu.

"*Arepas* for me, with chicken," Alex announced. He felt that he had a good appetite despite the time in the sun and he ordered the Venezuelan food with which he was most familiar. He thought about comparing them to the American Hot Pocket for Erin's amusement but thought better of it. It would take too much explanation for too little laughter. Erin ordered the same, except with cheese. As they ate their lunch, they discussed photographing the journal entry and then began speculating on the laws governing found treasure. This reminded Alex, with some irritation, that he had yet to research the law and he promised himself that he would take care of it at the first opportunity.

After their lunch, they walked back to Erin's car and drove back to her apartment to shower and change. That morning's, —Alex couldn't easily put a name to it in his own mind, assignation?, romp?, connection? — whatever had not so subtly changed their relationship. He clearly knew that he felt closer to Erin now than he did to Elise. He also knew that he was uncertain about how Erin felt and knew that it was not something that he immediately felt comfortable bringing up.

Erin fixed everything, though, through a simple act, defining how she felt and how she viewed their changed relationship. She invited Alex to join her while she showered.

130

When they were ready to go to La Asunción, Alex checked that he had his iPhone. This was how he planned to photograph the journal list. Erin attempted to talk about the journal and the *Little Ranger* as they drove, but Alex felt that he didn't have much to say about the names with which he was unfamiliar. He wanted to wait until he had seen the entry as it was written before he formed an opinion.

Señor Martinez greeted Erin and Alex with genuine warmth and obvious excitement. Alex felt a great fondness for the old curator. He guessed that it had something to with the old man's devotion to his charges, the artifacts and historical gimcrack that had become his career. Alex also guessed that his own feeling of bonhomie had a lot to with the great day he and Erin were having.

"Welcome, welcome my young friends," Martinez effused. Alex smiled at this. It had been a long time since he had been grouped with the "young."

"Thank you, so much, Señor Martinez. And especially, thank you for the opportunity to photograph the journal entry," Alex said. "How have you been?"

"*Bueno*, good," the curator answered. "You won't believe what I have been able to do with the journal." His excitement was obvious.

"What have you been able to do?" Erin asked smiling. She looked affectionately at the old man.

"What have I? Ha, come you will see," and Martinez began to lead the way to the glass case. "You know, the old cover of the book was stiff and dry from all the years sitting closed?" Erin and Alex nodded that they understood.

"Well, I began to think. How can I loosen this cover without attacking its material? And I came up with a method of, *como se dice*, *masaje*?" he asked Erin.

"Massage," she answered. "You figured out a way to massage the leather cover. You were trying to make the leather soft again, right?" she said.

131

"Exactly," Martinez confirmed happily. "I massaged it with my own face oil." Erin and Alex looked at each other confused. They both thought they might have misheard the old man.

"Face oil?" Alex asked.

"*Si*," Martinez said. "We all have it on our noses, chins, *como se dice, frentes?*"

"Foreheads," Erin translated. "Ok. I get it. You softened the leather by rubbing it with your own oil." She waved her palm in front of her face.

"*Si*, yes, exactly," Martinez agreed, "ah, here we are." They arrived at the spot lit glass case and Martinez produced a small key. He unlocked and opened the hinged glass. Alex couldn't see any obvious change to the leather cover of the book despite the curator's massage. Martinez donned a pair of light latex gloves, picked up the journal and carried it to a nearby well-lit worktable.

"Watch," the old man said, as he put the book on the table and opened the journal to a ninety-degree angle. Alex was impressed; Erin less so since she wasn't at the previous museum visit.

"Good job," Alex said approvingly. He pulled out his iPhone and showed it to Martinez. "Ready when you are," he said.

"No flash, ok?" Martinez cautioned. "These light should be enough." He indicated the tracks of light above the worktable.

Alex checked that his flash was off and, in doing so, had a moment of inspiration.

"Besides taking some stills," he announced, "I'm going to shoot some video. The change in perspective may be interesting and helpful." Martinez paged the open journal to the beginning of the roll of names and held the L-shaped book on the table so it was easy for Alex to access the page. Alex took the photos that he wanted careful not to block the

132

overhead lighting. He then switched to video and shot several minutes changing the angle every so often. He checked the results on his screen and verified that everything looked ok. He knew that the work would look much better when displayed on his laptop screen and was looking forward to doing that.

They thanked the old curator for his time and his help and promised to let him know what, if anything, they discovered. As they settled in Erin's Corolla, she bent over and presented her face to be kissed. Alex kissed her and then asked, "What was that about?"

As she put the car in drive, she smiled at him and said, "I'm having a great day."

When they got back to her apartment, Alex didn't want to wait until the evening to view the pictures and video on his computer at Elise's house. Erin had a MacBook Pro and so they connected the necessary cables and imported Alex's work to her laptop. The photos were clearer than Alex had hoped for and he immediately saw several mistakes that Martinez had made in his transcription. However, and he wasn't sure why, he didn't mention the errors to Erin.

"Interesting," was all he said.

"What is?" Erin asked as she sat beside him.

"The list of names viewed this way in the actual penmanship of the writer plus the visit to Playa Madrid yesterday make a treasure's existence more possible to me. I'm not sure why. What do you think?" he asked.

"I think it's time we researched the law on who gets to keep buried treasure," she said reaching for the laptop. She entered "buried treasure" into Google and they were immediately disappointed in the links returned.

"Try 'Who gets to keep buried treasure'," Alex suggested. Erin typed in the query and this time they were rewarded with a myriad of links.

"That one," said Alex pointing to the one that was entitled "Treasure Trove". Erin clicked the link to expand the article.

They read together. The article explained that treasure trove started under the Roman emperors and continued nearly unchanged through the 16th and 17th centuries. Alex recognized that 'trove' was a derivative of the French 'trouve'. Basically, with little deviation over the centuries and widely accepted throughout civilized nations, the law said that the finder of found wealth was responsible for alerting the owner, if the owner could be identified, and had to return the found object(s). The finder could be awarded a fee or even the value of the found objects if the owner had no wish to retain them. Probing Google further, Alex found that the Abandoned Shipwreck Act enacted by the United States prohibited salvaged goods from being retained by any finder as long as the shipwreck was located in U.S. territorial waters.

Obviously, Alex realized, the Act did not apply to the *Little Ranger* because of the location and he told Erin so. Erin was confused as to why that mattered. She pointed out that there were no identifiable salvageable goods associated with the *Little Ranger* anyway.

Alex explained his thinking: there was an internationally accepted principle where found treasure was concerned. First, finders had an obligation to do their best to locate and notify the owners of the find. Second, it had become the custom of courts active in the twentieth century to award finders the antiquarian value of the treasure trove; in other words, finders were paid the museum value of the treasure trove. Any negotiations beyond the commonly accepted bounds of fair division were, of course, allowed as long as they were lawful within the jurisdictions of the negotiating parties.

"This is simple *and* complicated," Alex said shaking his head. "What do you think?"

"I think it doesn't matter. There is no, what, treasure trove? So what difference does it make about the law?" Erin was clearly frustrated.

Alex squinted into her face and said, "Well, imagine that there is treasure trove. Imagine that it's recoverable and imagine that we are the finders. Now, what do you think?"

Erin frowned. Alex was impressed once again at her intelligence and equilibrium.

"I think, in that case, that we would have to negotiate a deal with the owners as quickly as possible. And, I think that, possibly, you know something that you are not saying." She studied his reaction.

"I don't know anything for sure," Alex admitted, "but I'm starting to have some suspicions. I need to do some poking around. Can I count on your discretion?"

This wasn't the reaction she was expecting. "You can count on me," she said. She leaned over and kissed his mouth as her phone began to vibrate. The number was unfamiliar as she accepted the call.

"Ms. Rosen? This is Fernando Bautiste. I am looking for Mr. Browning. Do you know where he is? I tried Elise, but she said he had been with you. Sorry if I am intruding." Erin looked over at Alex.

"No, sorry, Fernando. Mr. Browning left an hour ago after a most pleasant day at the beach and a visit to the museum at La Asuncion. Is everything all right?"

"Erin," Bautiste said with amusement, "put Alex on." Erin's heart beat faster as she searched for another lie. Her search failed. "Hold on, Fernando," she said. "It's Fernando," she said as she handed her mobile to Alex.

"Hello?" Alex said.

"Alex, hello," Bautiste said. "How are you? How was your day? Pleasant I hope." Alex felt uncertainty rise in his throat and tried to push   it back down.

135

"My day was great, Fernando," Alex said with more conviction than he felt. "How was yours?" he asked to buy time.

"Alex, cut the shit," Bautiste admonished. "I hope you enjoyed your little fuck with Erin. But, now, we have business to discuss. Do you understand?"

Alex was flustered, angry, and confused all at once. "I understand that you're an asshole," Alex said with more courage than he felt. "Is that what you meant?" There was a silence at the other end of the connection.

"Well done, Alex," Bautiste congratulated. "You feel brave. That is good. I want you to be brave when you go to Miami again. I want you to go to Miami again." Alex was caught off guard.

"Fernando," Alex began his mind racing to frame the proper response, "fuck you." He was playing for time. He heard Fernando start to talk and cut him off. "Let me say with all honesty that you are an asshole and, in spite of that, I want to thank you for the $5000.00. I spent it all."

"Alex, you are welcome, and," Bautiste said with equanimity, "I agree. I am an asshole from your point of view. But, there is business to be conducted and more so now that the country is becoming, how do you say, restive?"

"Yeah, restive," Alex said. "And explain a couple of things to me."

"All right. What do you want to know?"

"Why do you think I'll go to Miami again?" Erin looked at him pleadingly. She was upset at the half of the conversation she could hear and didn't want him to keep antagonizing Bautiste.

"Because you need more money and because you have decided that you need a way to punish me." Alex was stunned at Bautiste's accuracy.

136

"So how will it punish you to help you?" Alex was playing for time to think. He wasn't panicked but he was confused.

"My friend," Bautiste said with a tone that conveyed humor and warmth, "you will be the one to decide the answer to that question. I will be the one to decide how to avoid your punishment. Alex, I ask you plainly. Will you go again to Miami?"

Alex, in spite of his emotions, felt himself being drawn in by Bautiste's implied challenge. Perhaps a little more competitive than the average person, Alex believed that his best response was ambiguity.

"Fernando, I am not your friend. I don't befriend assholes. But, I will say this. I will think about going to Miami again. Only think about it. I am not saying yes. I am not saying no. I am saying that I will think about it." Alex waited for Fernando's answer. After a short time, he got it. Fernando broke the connection.

"Prick," Alex said to dead air ending the call on Erin's phone.

"What did he say?" the big Sergeant asked Bautiste. They were back together in the Colonel's office at Headquarters.

"He surprised me," Bautiste admitted. "I expected him to say no and then he would have been your problem, my friend. Instead, he said he would think about it. So, we will have to wait a little. But, only a little. Our partners in Miami are depending on us."

"You're not going to do it, are you?" Erin asked taking back her phone. She obviously disapproved of the idea.

"Honestly," Alex said stroking her right thigh, "I don't know. I want to get

137

some counsel before I decide."

"Counsel? Who's going to give you counsel?" Erin asked.

"I think I'm going to ask Magrew," Alex announced.

"Why him?" Erin pressed.

"Good question," Alex admitted. "I guess it's because he's a successful businessman or, maybe, because he's been through some shit himself." Alex felt tired.

"I should get going, baby girl," he told Erin. "I'll catch up with you later." He embraced her and gave her a long and lingering kiss, which she returned.

Alex's walk back to Elise's house was uneventful in spite of the darkness. Crime was on the rise all over the country in just the short day since Chavez's death. The wind threatened rain and the atmosphere was heavy with humidity. Alex's mood was as heavy as the air. He was disturbed at his feeling of disloyalty to Elise and his sense of passion and sex with Erin. The conversation with Bautiste had made his turmoil even worse. He wanted to boot up his own laptop and study the photographed journal entry at his leisure. He wanted to get Magrew's opinion on Bautiste, too. But that would have to wait until tomorrow.

When he arrived back at the house, Elise was occupied with her tablet.

"*Hola, bebe,*" she said. "Look at your color! How was the beach? It's nice, huh?" Alex had forgotten about his morning at the beach. It seemed like a long time ago.

"It's a great beach," Alex agreed. "A little crowded, though." He instantly regretted saying it knowing that the comment would be construed as criticism.

"You have to be more social, *bebe,*" she said. She was needling him and he knew it, but he decided to let it go.

"You're right," he said. "What are you looking at?" he asked indicating her tablet. She turned the screen so that he could see. It was a picture of Chavez.

"The funeral is scheduled for the day after tomorrow," she said. "Friday. I think they are in a hurry to move forward. People need to know that there is — stableness?" she asked.

"Stability," he clarified. "Yep, that's what the people want," he added half to himself. He reached for his laptop. Elise announced that she was going to watch television in bed, but Alex barely acknowledged her.

Alex connected his phone to his laptop and synched his pictures between the two devices. His laptop's retina display was one of the highest resolution displays available and he was counting on it to determine the journal's content beyond any question. He scrolled to his pictures of the journal. The list was written in Spence's spidery penmanship:

"Morgan, W

Akers, H

Tibbett, M

Elgin, B

Smith, R

Smyth, L

Thoth, G

Ance, P

Rogers, P

Teppers, G

Atkins, A

Trinkle, B

Taylor, S

139

Howell, T

Earl, P

Burke, N

Irwin, S

Gordon, L

Berger, R

Lawson, M

Aston, P

Cobb, C

Kucker, B

Revelle, C

Odell, J

Connelly, A

Keating, D

Grubb, N

Oglethorpe, J

Thomas, R

Hill, E

Edwards, K

Pritchard, M

Arab, M

Tomberlin, R

Hinds, S

Thomas, N

Herford, A

Eddington, B

Stanford, W

Underhill, P

Nicholls, T

Tyndall, U

Anglin, C

Kent, V

Ellerman, R

Sand, G

Guy, H

Orthman, E

Anderson, T

Nutt, L

Ulster, M

Mann, G

Bridges, B

Evans, L

Roberts, K

Ongle, C

Fagan, A

Phillips, W

Applewhite, C

Corey, D

Edwards, M

Sayers, A

Enlow, C

Quarles, C

Underwood, P

Ahern, T

Lytle, M

Teague, T

Osborn, B

Thompson, L

Hurt, S

England, W

Christian, M

Aycox, C

Pruitt, L

Tolson, B

Ainge, C

Ipock, B

Newman, W

Sterling, P

Tankey, K

Engels, J

Abel, C

Richards, Q

Stewart, E

Tender, M

Hoare, T

Ewell, C

Rusk, A

Eason, G

Tell, P

Harkins, T

Easton, L

York, T

Leeds, P

Ingram, W

English, D

Fields, G

Owens, K

Udall, B

Rich, D

Tercey, M

Eller, G

Eastfield, R

Nicely, W

Blackwell, N

Oxley, P

Xu, F

Enders, W

Stack, H

Orr, T

Finlay, M

Grant, H

O'Neill, L

Long, C

David, S

Sanders, Y

Ivey, C

Lancer, M

Verge, C

Elmore, N

Ragland, T

Axel, P

Nells, D

Daniels, O

Johnson, S

Euler, J

Williams, J

Eton, P

Lively, G

Stuckey, R

Berger, R

Otter, L

Upton, J

Newsome, E

Tootle, R

Young, S

Grey, T

Olson, M

Dell, N

Bean, C

Loper, T

Ericson, K

Salisbury, M

Sampley, C

Usher, H

Scarsdale, T

Alba, E

Leeds, P

Longfellow, F"

One hundred fifty-one names that seemed to mean nothing other than that: a list of names. The original was written in Spence's hand, but, when compared to the transcription on Elise's phone, it contained marked differences in spelling: Taylor vs. Tailor, Herford vs. Hereford. These differences were the reasons Alex wanted to study the original content. He expected that mistakes were made. Apparently, Martinez had taken it upon himself to clean up Spence's spelling. Alex found this unacceptable, but of no consequence. He zoomed the photo to 150% and was mesmerized by the thought that he was looking at a man's writing from almost three hundred years ago. Some other thought was pushing into his mind, but he couldn't quite grasp it and it slipped away.

Alex realized then that he was exhausted. The combination of sun, unaccustomed exercise, and mental stimulation had taken its toll on his body and mind. He decided to call it a night. He resolved to see Keith Magrew early the next day Thursday.

In the morning Elise again had to get up early and leave for work. There had been rain the night and everything was washed fresh. Alex kissed her lightly good-bye and watched her drive away. He ate some bread with his coffee and stretched his sore legs and back as he chewed. He popped open his laptop and again looked at the photo of the message. Nothing new came to him, but the feeling of the night before that he was missing something was still there. He shut the laptop, locked up the house, and left for Magrew's cafe.

The walk to Magrew's was pleasant in the clean morning air. Alex's mild sunburn of the day before made the air seem chillier than it actually was. He made a mental note to try to stay extra hydrated that day.

Magrew's small restaurant was shuttered when he arrived and Alex noted that the time was just a little after nine. He knocked on the front door anyway. He tried to look through the barred windows, but it was impossible to see anything. As he cupped his hands around his peripheral vision, he heard a sound to his left and looked to see Magrew stepping outside.

"Mac," he called, "you got a minute?" Magrew stared for a second, instinctively hostile and caught off guard.

"Hey," he called recovering, "my chess opponent, right? Alex?" He had adjusted rapidly. He stuck out his large right hand.

146

"Sorry to catch you by surprise," Alex said taking the proffered hand, "but I wasn't sure you were here yet." Alex returned to the business at hand. "Have you got some time? I've got an issue to discuss."

Magrew looked at Alex with mock suspicion and then, realizing that Alex was not in a joking mood, said, "Sure. What's going on?"

Alex looked around at their environs without answering and this sensitized Magrew to the fact that he wished privacy.

"Let's go inside," Magrew suggested. He led the way into the dim interior of the cafe as Alex followed.

"Coffee?" Magrew offered as Alex's eyes adjusted to the difference in lighting.

"No, thanks," he said. "I had a cup at home already. Can I have a glass of water?"

"Sure," Magrew said. He got himself a large mug of coffee and a glass of water for Alex. "Now, what's going on?" he asked as they settled into a booth.

Alex took a big gulp of water, swallowed and looked at Magrew. "Remember the trip I took to Miami?" he asked. Magrew nodded sipping his coffee. Alex went on to explain how he had been manipulated by Bautiste, tricked, and paid five thousand dollars. Magrew listened with narrowing eyes. He cleared his throat.

"The guy's a fucking asshole," he asserted. Alex laughed.

"Yeah, I told him that," he said. Magrew raised his eyebrows.

"You told him that? Look at the big balls on you," Magrew joked. "But seriously, he's not someone to take lightly. The *Policia Nacional Bolivar* is not to be messed with. Elise must have given you a heads up," Magrew said. Alex drank some more water.

"Yeah. I was pissed off. Probably not smart," Alex admitted. "Which is kind of why I'm here. The asshole wants me to go back to Miami and do it again." Magrew looked at his fellow American incredulously.

"And you're considering it?" Magrew asked. Alex shrugged.

"I told him I'd think about it." Magrew got up and refilled his cup before reacting. He sat down and looked at Alex.

"There's something else, isn't there?" Magrew probed. Alex nodded, finished his water, and began to explain how he had alerted the federal authorities to the drug smuggling. Magrew didn't show it, but he was growing increasingly uncomfortable as Alex related what Pete Simmons had told him.

"So this FBI guy is going to let you do what? Act like an undercover cop? Sorry, Alex, but that doesn't sound very smart," Magrew said. Alex agreed, but he argued that cooperating with Simmons and anybody else he brought in, might go a long way toward exonerating him of blame for the first trip. Magrew thought this over.

"But you took money and spent it," Magrew said. "That doesn't sound blameless. Does it to you?" Alex admitted that it didn't. Magrew went on to describe Bautiste's reputation as a suspected drug supplier, recruiter of drug 'mules', and, with his subordinate, The Hammer, enforcer.

"The word is that he recruits young European tourists, usually girls, to carry his drugs back to their home countries. He apparently is tied in to quite a network. He also apparently tells them all what he told you: it's just a dry run, nothing illegal is taking place, it's just a test of the system." This made Alex feel worse.

"Ok," Alex said, "let's say that I agree to make one more trip. What do you see happening?" Magrew sipped his coffee as he considered his response.

"With the FBI involved, right?" Magrew said, scratching his stump. Alex nodded.

"With the proper authorities, whomever they may be, fully informed and fully engaged. What do you think would happen?" Alex asked.

"Well, I see two scenarios," Magrew began. "One, they fake arrest you and real arrest your contact. They seize the drugs and any money. They let you go and your time in Venezuela is over." Alex nodded at this.

"Or, two," Magrew continued, "they let you make the exchange, come back to Porlamar, and put a tail on your contact to follow the drug trail." Magrew smiled. "And then I have to watch your back for the whole time that you're here to make sure nobody sticks a knife in it. Since you'll be a badass drug dealer, and all." Magrew sat back. Alex laughed.

"Just call me 'Walter White'," Alex quipped.

"Who?" Magrew asked. Alex started to explain, thought better of it and let it go.

"Anyway, thanks for listening to my problems. I owe you one. Oh, and I forgot. Take a look at this." Alex produced his phone and showed Magrew the photos of the long list of names. Magrew studied them briefly and gave back the phone.

"Looks just like Martinez's copy, right?" he said.

"With a couple of differences. Small ones. Anyway, for me, the significance is that this is the actual list in the guy's actual writing. That is very cool to me."

"Ok," Magrew said, "I see your point. Kind of exciting when you put it that way." He drained his cup. "What are your plans for today?"

"I'm kind of loose. Elise is working and Erin has some errands to run. Chess later?"

Magrew agreed and Alex headed back to Elise's house.

CHAPTER SEVEN – Investigation

Alex hiked back to Elise's house. When he got there he retrieved his laptop and went back out again. He thought about going right back to Mac's place but decided that Magrew might be busy. Instead, Alex headed toward Playa El Agua, the site of his pleasant morning the day before. Because of the sudden rise in crime and the civil unrest that seemed to be erupting countrywide following Chavez's death and because of the valuable gear he was carrying in his computer bag, he was hyper-aware of his surroundings. It was then that he noticed the black sedan. He had a vague sense that the sedan had been around before, but he couldn't validate the feeling.

Alex claimed a table at a beachside eatery that boasted free Wi-Fi and ordered a crème cafe. He unpacked his laptop and logged on to the Internet. As his coffee arrived, he brought up the images of the journal list once again. He reread the names, sipped his coffee, studied the images, and tried to let his mind absorb what his eyes saw. A thought, recognition appeared at the edge of his consciousness. He was tempted to try and grab it and drag it into the light, but he relaxed and tried to let it drift in on its own. But it wouldn't come. Alex shut down the laptop and drank his coffee. When he was finished, he opened the computer again and studied the list. It didn't help. Alex scratched his chin and stared out over the sun worshippers to the sea.

Alex's relationship with his daughters had always been characterized, from his point of view, as mentor to mentees. After Mary died, he had resolved to be the go-to person in the family, the one who could be relied on to solve problems, provide solace, and dispense wisdom. So it was against his nature when on rare occasions he turned to one or both of his daughters for assistance. There had been times, of course, when Alex had needed his daughters' input/expertise, especially when he lacked the knowledge they possessed. Alex realized that this might be one of those occasions. Since Jo not only enjoyed puzzles and was also very good at solving them, Alex forwarded the photos to her email account.

Since it was Thursday, Jo was working out of her Philadelphia apartment office. She noticed Alex's email arrival, but was concentrating heavily on a piece of code and ignored it for the time being. An hour later and with great satisfaction, she completed the program and watched it pass a simple test. She leaned back and stretched her arms, legs, and spine. As she was rotating her neck muscles she remembered to check her Inbox. She opened Alex's email first.

It took her two hours of manipulating, staring, and manipulating again to solve the puzzle of the list of names and so for the second time that afternoon she stretched her body and smiled in satisfaction. She drafted an email reply and couldn't resist the opportunity to show off to her Dad. Her email was succinct.

Dad,

There is a message contained in the list. It reads:

"Mates, Start at the big black Rock. Go the Path the Sun takes.

Go a number of Paces equal to the Captain's Tears.

There they lie. Fourteen Boxes of gold, silver and jewels.

Bounty! God bless us All."

You're welcome. (The young prevail!)

Love,

Jo

She pressed, "Send" and went to the kitchen to pour herself a glass of Chardonnay.

Alex was still at the seaside restaurant when he received Jo's response. He smiled at his daughter's "digs". He appreciated that she felt the right to gloat. He also knew she wanted him to try to see how she had "cracked" the list. He brought up the photos on his laptop once again and stared at them. He alternated his staring between the photos and Jo's "solution". It took him under half an hour to see what Jo saw. Of course, having the answer at hand hastened the process quite a bit.

The message's reference to "Tears" confused Alex. He rechecked Jo's work and found a flaw. The name "Tankey, K" had been incorrectly interpreted.

The message suddenly made sense and Alex recognized not only what had led Jo astray, but why. The crossbar on the letter "T" in "Tankey" was not a straight line. It looked like a shallow dish atop the vertical bar. Alex had attended a Catholic elementary school in Pittsburgh where one of the students in his class was named Andy Pelfret. Andy and Alex were close friends and Alex noticed early that all the Pelfrets that he met were related to Andy. As Alex grew up and moved away, he found that a much more common variation on Pelfret was Pelfrey. Eventually he had realized that what must have happened was that at some time an unknown immigration official had carelessly written the "Y" for an Irish immigrant named Pelfrey, the immigrant did not protest when further officials read the name as Pelfret and the name was legally accepted.

Alex concluded that the pirate Spence had made the same sloppy mistake as the immigration official. The message actually read:

"Mates, Start at the big black Rock. Go the Path the Sun takes.

Go a number of Paces equal to the Captain's Years.

There they lie. Fourteen Boxes of gold, silver and jewels.

Bounty! God   bless us All."

He fired off a snarky email to Jo explaining the actual message, how the error happened, and touting the triumph of experience over youth.

Now Alex had to find out who captained the *Little Ranger* when it arrived on Margarita Island and when that Captain was born. He Googled the *Little Ranger* and was rewarded with a number of links. Unfortunately, most of these referred to a movie of that name from the 1930's. Alex tried a more specific search including the terms "pirate ship". This gave him more links and, especially, one that was for Bartholomew Roberts' Wikipedia page. This was the pirate Black Bart of whom Professor Braga had spoken. Alex read the article and was disappointed to find that it held no clue as to the last captain of the *Little Ranger* or as to the fate of the ship itself. The article said that Black Bart died in battle in 1722, but reported that no corpse had been found. The members of his crew who dropped his weighted body into the sea were the only witnesses to his death.

Alex ordered another crème cafe and wondered. He opened a Notepad session and began to document the facts, as he knew them. The facts were: the *Little Ranger* was last seen off the west coast of Africa in 1722, the wreck of the ship lay off the coast of Margarita Island, John Spence claimed that fourteen boxes of gold, silver and jewels existed, Black Bart was last seen off the west coast of Africa in 1722, and Black Bart was claimed to have died in battle. Alex took a drink of coffee and stared at what he had typed.

He drew a horizontal line of asterisks across the page and typed "Speculation" below the line. The speculation was: Black Bart didn't die off the west coast of Africa, Black Bart left the crew of the *Royal* Fortune to fend for themselves that day in February, Black Bart captained the *Little Ranger* and its crew back across the Atlantic, the *Little Ranger* was transporting all of the wealth the pirates had accumulated during their long months in African waters. Alex looked at his computer screen and smiled. He added one more guess: the crew of the *Little Ranger* felt the need to hide their cargo, hid it, and then disappeared when their ship sunk in

Venezuelan water. Alex saved his work and closed his computer. He paid for his coffee and went looking for Mac.

That Thursday morning Colonel Bautiste had contacted his surveillance crew via cell phone.

"What news?" he demanded.

"He took his computer to a cafe at Playa El Agua and has been there all morning and a lot of the afternoon, drinking coffee and using his computer. There is Wi-Fi there, so he could be browsing also." The young officer sitting in the black sedan knew to keep his report factual and succinct.

"*Bueno*," Bautiste said. He ended the call and turned his chair to look out his office window. He knew that, with the spike in violent crime since Tuesday, his men were wondering if following the American was the best use of police manpower, but he also knew that his men wouldn't dare question his judgment. He had reports from Caracas that roving gangs mounted on motorcycles were attacking citizens and looting stores. The gangs were armed with knives, machetes, and guns. It seemed that the death of *El Comandante* had unleashed a suppressed criminal desire to wreak havoc. The gangs were apparently of two kinds: *collectivos* who patrolled the neighborhoods and who supported the Chavistas and wanted to punish those who openly celebrated Chavez' death and those who were just common criminals and who were devoted to taking advantage of the perceived power vacuum. Colonel Bautiste had only a taste of such a problem on Margarita Island but since his men were part of a national force they could be deployed anywhere in the country where they might be needed.

Bautiste felt a small pang of guilt at his orders to follow the American, but the unrest that Caracas was experiencing had not developed much in the cities of Margarita Island. He summoned Sergeant Lopez.

"I want to start an e-surveillance on the American Browning," he declared. "I want telephone and email and I want texts and attachments. This guy spent the morning on the web and we have no idea what he was up to. I want it up by tomorrow."

The sergeant nodded and said, "I'll alert the tech guys." He was referring to the technical arm of the *Nacional Policia Bolivar* who had all of the eavesdropping capabilities of any western country.

"Anything else?" the sergeant asked.

"That's all," Bautiste said. He was irritated and the sergeant knew it. Lopez left the office.

Meanwhile, Alex found Mac Magrew cleaning up after the lunchtime crowd. Alex saw he was tremendously busy, but the American was tremendously excited about the message.

"Mac," he said, "got a minute? It's important." Magrew continued to direct his small staff to take care of restaurant minutiae.

"Kind of busy, Alex," he said. "Can it wait 'til we're ready to open for dinner?" Alex was disappointed with the response, but understood Mac's reticence. He headed for an outside table and a white plastic chair.

"No problem," he called to Mac. He sat down and pulled out his cell phone. He called Erin's number. She picked up after a number of rings.

"Hey," Alex said, "It's me. Can you talk?"

"Sure," came the answer he was hoping for, "what's up?" Alex's heartbeat, breathing, and thought process were quickened.

"I had a spare minute and wanted to let you know I had success with the journal." Alex paused, but there was no

156

reaction from Erin. "I'm going to explain it to Mac and see what he thinks."

"Good job, baby," Erin said. "Lemme know what Mac thinks. Anything else?"

"No," Alex said, "That's it. I'll catch up with you later." He hesitated. "I miss feeling you."

"Mmm," was the response. "Get here when you can." Alex hung up and ordered a beer. He was a little edgy from all the caffeine he had had and the beer, he felt, would relax him a little. He enjoyed the sun and marveled again at his good fortune to be here in this Caribbean paradise. He finished his beer as some of the other tables began to fill up with early arrivals. He watched Mac give some final directions to the wait staff and then head over to join Alex.

"Hey," Mac said settling his girth into one of the empty plastic chairs. "Thanks for waiting. What's going on? You said it was important." Mac signaled for a beer and a redo for Alex.

"I think I figured out the message," Alex said. Mac didn't seem very impressed.

"Ok," he said. "What message?"

"Fuck, Mac." Alex was frustrated. "The pirate ship, the *Little Ranger*, the journal in the museum. The French. The message. C'mon." Mac laughed.

"Settle down," he said, "I've been busy with this place. And I'm a little worried about the reports of the rioting going on in Caracas. I wouldn't want to see that happen here. I've got a business to protect." He gestured with his hand and stump.

"Rioting?" Alex questioned. "I heard last night it was protesting Chavez's guy, Maduro. Seems like people don't want an appointed President. They want to elect one. Who's Maduro anyway?"

"A Chavez insider, his vice-president, a former bus driver. He's the odds-on favorite to win the next election, though, whenever that might be," Mac said. "So what were we   talking   about?"

"The list in the journal. There's a message embedded in it," Alex said, refocusing the conversation. "I think I figured it out. Well, my daughter did. Want to know what it says?"

"Sure," Mac answered taking a pull on his newly arrived beer. "But I'm fucked if I know what you're talking about."

"Fourteen treasure chests motivate you?" Alex asked leaning forward, "gold, silver, jewels?" Mac's brow wrinkled in thought.

"You're full of shit, buddy," he said smiling. "What the hell? You're buying that pirate crap? How old are you?" Mac went on with mock incredulity.

"There were a couple of errors in Martinez's transcription, but they didn't matter it turned out." Alex rushed on to defend his growing belief in the journal. "Martinez is the museum curator in La Asuncion, remember? So I wound up photographing the list and sent it to my daughter. She figured it out. Mac," Alex said. "I'm starting to think there's something to all of this." He sat back and took a swig of beer. He felt like a lawyer who was resting a poorly presented case, but he wanted to see what Mac would do.

"Ok, so what were the errors and why are you starting to believe?" Mac toyed with his bottle rolling it between his palms.

Alex showed Mac his image of the list and explained how the "T" was misinterpreted and how Jo assumed that "tears" was probably an allusion to salt water.

"So the 'T' is actually a 'Y' and now tears are years." Alex paused. "Do you see what I mean?"

"No, I don't see," Magrew said with irritation. "What the fuck are you talking about?"

"Four things: one, the captain's years refers to how old the captain was in 1722 when the *Little Ranger* arrived in Margarita waters; two, the path the sun takes is traveling West; three, paces was a common form of measurement in the 18th century; and, four, the black rock is a rock located in a jumble of rocks at Playa Madrid. I think. I mean I saw it. It's still there." Alex had hardly breathed during his explanation and was now panting.

"Ok. Sounds simple. How old was the captain? Then you walk off the distance and start digging, right?"

"Well," Alex hesitated, "not so simple. See, I don't know how old the captain was in 1722."

"Why not? I thought everyone kept good records in those days, meticulous in fact."

"Yeah, well, they did. Except when things got sketchy. Then the records got a little messy." Alex smiled slyly. "But I have a hunch."

Mac ordered them another round and pawed at his chin. He raised his bottle when the beers arrived in a proposed toast. "To pirates," he said as they touched bottlenecks.

"I was hoping that you would help me with my investigation," Alex said.

"Why me? What about you and Elise? Can't she help? She has a lot of contacts on this island."

"Yeah," Alex started, "well things aren't going so well between us. It's difficult to explain, but I can't count on her help, let's say."

"Sorry to hear that, relationships and all that. Difficult," Mac offered awkwardly.

"Mmm," Alex agreed. "It's mostly my fault. I was hoping for something — warm and cuddly, I guess. Sex, of course, but also a connection, a bond, maybe? I don't know. Anyway, frankly, it's devolved into discussions of Viagra and grooming down there, if you know what I mean." Alex looked at Mac to see if Mac understood.

"I don't," Mac began and then, "oh fuck! Really? Wow. Wrong generation for that, I guess," he laughed. Alex was not laughing.

"Look, will you help? I feel a little overwhelmed by this stuff and you have skills and knowledge that, I think, will be useful."

"What's your hunch?"

"What?" Alex was caught off guard. Mac carried on a conversation the way he played chess.

"You said you had a hunch," Mac said, "What is it?"

"Well," Alex hesitated, suddenly doubting his feeling, "I'm not going to tell you. Right now. Maybe later. Will you help?" Alex leaned in.

"What skills and knowledge do I have?"

"What?"

"You said I had useful skills and knowledge. What were you talking about? My chess acumen?" Mac said laughing. "But seriously, what were you talking about?"

"I meant your drilling background and your knowledge of the island," Alex admitted. "I believe that if there's something to find, it's under the ground, buried somewhere."

"So that's your hunch?" Mac quizzed. Alex shook his head in disagreement.

"No, it's just a belief. I guess we've both seen enough movies and *read* enough books to realize that if

160

something is hidden for a long time, it's either buried in the ground, sunken underwater, or in a cave somewhere. That's my belief." Alex sat back and waited for the one-armed man's response.

Mac didn't get a chance to answer since, at that moment, a group of six men riding motorbikes roared up. All of the men wore bandanas over their lower faces and all brandished some sort of weapon, mostly clubs, but some knives. They dismounted their bikes and entered the patio where Mac, Alex, and some other early dinnertime diners sat. They began to threaten the restaurant's patrons.

"Fuck," Mac said and started to rise from his chair. Alex was suddenly and inexplicably angrier than he had been in years. He was gripping his beer bottle tightly by the neck and reached down to the concrete patio surface, sharply tapped the bottle's bottom on the concrete, and created a sharp weapon of jagged glass. He reached over for Mac's bottle as the big man seized the nearest thug in a one-armed bear hug.

"Let me go," the young criminal squirmed, obviously frightened and near panic. Alex moved in with his broken bottle and, without hesitation, slashed the punk's knife-wielding arm. The knife clattered to the patio as Mac lifted the disarmed young man on his hip and slammed him to the patio. The young man screamed in pain as something broke. Another young attacker moved in to help his fallen buddy. Before he could get close Alex stepped in and hurled Mac's beer bottle. Jeter couldn't have done better as the bottle smashed on the target's chest.

"Oof," was all the man said as he stared down in surprise at his beer-soaked T-shirt. Alex moved forward brandishing his broken bottle with clear resolve. The would-be defender turned and ran dropping his weapon as he fled. Mac and Alex searched for further threats, but their lack of fear was sufficiently confusing to the criminals that all of them sought out their motorcycles, remounted them, and fled. The remaining cafe customers rose and applauded the large black man and his white-haired companion. Mac and Alex waved briefly in acknowledgement. They sat back down as the cafe staff cleared the broken glass and other damage and tried to reassure their customers.

"That was fun," Mac said signaling for two beers.

"Make mine bourbon," Alex said, "if you've got it." He was breathing hard.

"Good idea," Mac said reaching over and patting Alex's forearm. "Private stock." He called a waitress over and explained what they wanted and where to get it. She nodded in understanding and left.

"Fun, huh?" Alex jibed regaining his mental equilibrium. "What the hell was that?"

"*Collectivos* most probably," Mac said, adding, "the douchebags who supported Chavez and, apparently, now think that there's no law except them. Probably looking for some 'donations'." Their drinks, with water, arrived. Mac lifted his knock glass and tipped toward Alex.

"Nice fucking job with those beer bottles," he said admiringly. "Where'd you learn that?"

"Pure instinct," Alex answered, "plus I was pissed off. Were those guys just after money? Makes no sense to me." He took a long sip of his bourbon. He had added no water to his drink.

"Well, some people need money," Mac retorted. "And, hopefully, the word will go out not to bother with Magrew's restaurant.   But can I give you a couple of pointers?" He didn't wait for Alex's answer. "Next time, don't waste effort smashing the bottle on the ground. Smash it on somebody's temple. Not here." He pointed to the middle of his forehead. "That's movie stuff. The bone is really hard there. Smash it here. On the temple." He indicated the dimple just below the hairline. He took a mouthful of bourbon and let it burn his palate and gums. His eyes watered as he said, "By the fucking way, I don't care what your hunch is, I'm

162

in. Anyone who fought like that can have whatever skills and knowledge I have at his disposal."

Alex took another sip of bourbon and felt that he was recovering from the excitement of the altercation; his heart rate was returning to normal. His own eyes watered a little. "Thanks, Mac," he said. "You fight pretty well yourself." He was referring to Mac's impressive one-armed body slam of the punk. "I think you broke something on that little guy." Alex raised his knock glass in Mac's direction.

"Thanks," Mac said. "I believe something did break. Did you hear him scream when I pounded him into the patio? Holy shit. Something broke." He raised his stump toward the sky. "Yeah, fat one-armed men rule!" Alex laughed and kept on laughing, partly out of stress being relieved and partly out of amusement.

"You are one bad dude," he said and then added, "for a fat one-armed man." Their bourbon drinking quickly subsided and, just as their excitement had rapidly peaked, it rapidly waned. They sat for a while each lost in his own thoughts.

Mac drained his glass and spoke first, "So what is this hunch of yours?"

Alex was a little buzzed from the bourbon and the whole day in general, but just a little. He hesitated as he formulated what he wanted to tell Mac.

"Well, I researched the ship and its history and its crew. The thing that struck me was that there was a battle in Africa before the *Little Ranger* showed up in the Caribbean in 1722. During that battle, the big boss, Black Bart, Bartholomew Roberts was supposedly killed. But his body was never found and the only witnesses to his death were his crew, a crew that was fanatically loyal to him." Alex paused.

"Two things," he continued, "one: I think that Black Bart was on the *Little Ranger*. That was the only ship that escaped that day. And, importantly, we know Black Bart's birthday. Second: what does it matter? Is there a big difference between 20 paces or 40 paces? With the technology we have today, can't we pinpoint a large buried mass if we know the general location? Fourteen boxes or chests should present a pretty big target, right?"

Mac thought this over. He felt that this was a chance to bring his skills and knowledge to bear. "Well, if you think about it it's not only about the length and number of the "paces", but the part about the "path the sun takes." Meaning a westerly direction and I'm using that expression "westerly direction" on purpose. In 1722, those dudes only had a rough idea of westerly direction. So, imagine an arc," he explained gaining some enthusiasm, "say a forty degree sweep. That's the idea of how accurate 'west' is going to be for those guys."

"How do you know that?" Alex asked. He held up his hands. "I'm not doubting you. Just curious."

"Oil drilling is all about placement," Mac explained. "Once the engineers determine where a well should go, the drillers better not fuck up by even a couple of feet. If the engineers say it goes there, it goes there." Alex stuck out his lower lip. Just then they heard police sirens approaching. Mac explained that the police were going to want to take statements. He suggested that they leave and take a walk along the waterfront.

"There are plenty of people here to give their take on what happened," Mac said leading them off, "and, besides, the police aren't going to do anything with the information anyway."

They walked along and the sun was pleasant in the early evening. Alex asked again about the attack. He was shaken by the sudden violence and was also trying to understand his own response to it.

"Just punks," Mac said, "trying to take advantage of the current lack of leadership. They know that the army, the national police, and the local police are all trying to figure out who's going to end up on top. Everybody looks out for number one. As soon as Chavez went to Cuba for his cancer treatment, the opposition and the loyalists started making political moves. There's a big faction here that would like to see the Socialist experiment end. The government calls us Fascists."

"'Us'?" Alex asked.

"Yeah, me too. I'm not a socialist. I worked hard, most of my life, for what I've got. I don't want to share it with some welfare bum just because they were born into a rough situation. I was born into a rough situation, too." Mac was vehement.

"What rough situation?" Alex was trying to calm the big man and, besides, he was curious about Mac's background. Instead of answering, Mac suggested that they patronize one of the waterfront cafes and have another beer.

They picked a small place that was painted blue and yellow. The beers arrived in frosty mugs and there were ice chips floating in the foam.

"Wow, that's good," Alex said after his first swallow. "You know, I've been eating and drinking so much since I got here, and I'm still losing weight. Must be all the walking I've been doing. Back home, I hardly ever walked." Alex was just chattering on, trying to fill up the conversation. Mac was silent studying his beer.

"What rough situation?" Alex quietly asked. Mac shifted his bulk and took a swallow and seemed to reach a decision.

"I grew up in Houston, mostly on the streets," he began. "My mom died when I was like two years old and my pop raised me even though he didn't have a clue of how to raise a kid and he probably didn't have any business making babies anyway." Mac went on to explain how he learned to hustle the streets and how to hustle the other kids in school. He got into trouble, but he and his dad were always able to talk themselves out of it.

"So, eventually I caught the proverbial southbound freighter, literally. I ended up in Caracas, lied about my oilfield experience, and got a job. I never heard from my dad again. What the fuck, I landed on my feet." He sipped his beer as he peered at Alex awaiting his reaction.

"Ok. Rough situation." Alex said. "Wow. That's some bullshit. And your dad never tried to contact you?"

"No, and yes, that's some bullshit. My dad fucked me and I never heard from him again. I worked the fields here in the V and never looked back. That answer all your questions?" Mac was a little defensive. The atmosphere was heavy with humidity and irony.

"Yep, that answers all my questions," Alex said. "But, what the hell?"

Mac was nonplussed. He had contemplated this moment for many years, but was not as forthcoming as Alex believed.

"I ran and here I am." Mac actually felt some relief to unburden his conscience a little. He looked at Alex.

Alex was trying to absorb all of this information.

"So what's your legal status back home?" Alex asked.

"Not sure," Mac said. "I'm probably OK. I've never tried to go back so I don't know."

"I'm glad you told me, Mac," Alex said. "I'm still shaking from those punks. Sorry." He held out his trembling right hand.

"Nothing to be sorry about." He thought back to the bourbon they had had earlier. "Let's have something stronger than beer," Mac suggested. They ordered chilled vodka and shrimp and spent the rest of the late afternoon getting slowly, but thoroughly, drunk.

The next morning, Friday March 8, Alex woke up with a headache and a thirst that no amount of water seemed to slake. Elise had already gone to work. Alex checked his phone and there were several missed calls, mostly from Mac

166

and a couple from Bautiste. Alex really didn't feel like talking to anyone and he was pretty sure that attempting speech would produce croaks rather than anything intelligible. He made coffee and used the first cup to wash down a couple of aspirin. With his second cup, he began to feel better and switched back to water. He opened his laptop and initiated a search for information that he had been wondering about since Jo had deciphered the journal message.

The information he wanted was simple: how big was an 18th century pirate chest? Alex discovered that the answer was variable, in fact, *really* variable. The smallest boxes were described to be roughly 8" wide, 4" long, and 4" deep. In other words, they were the size of a medium cigar humidor. However, a large chest was reported to be 3 feet across, 16 inches long, and 18 inches deep. Pretty big, Alex thought to himself. He tried to imagine a box that big filled with gold. The weight would be tremendous, but the Internet told him that the boxes were banded and reinforced with iron. Gold, silver, and jewels the message said. He decided that he needed to do some computations.

First he assumed the largest box. Next, silver coins would be less valuable than jewels and gold. So, to keep it simple, he figured a one ounce silver coin was an inch in diameter and 1/8" thick. So a stack of 8 coins would be one inch and 8 ounces. So 144 coins would go to the top of the box and would weigh 144 ounces. Roughly, 36 stacks repeated 16 times would be 576 stacks. So one chest could hold almost 83,000 ounces of silver.

Alex checked the market price for one ounce of silver. It wasn't that straightforward, but appeared to be around $20.00 US. That would make the value of one chest conservatively at more than $1.6 million. So fourteen boxes would be worth, conservatively, over $23.2 million. Alex blew out his breath. What if?

He made the same dimensional assumptions for gold coins. He knew he was being super-conservative since a gold coin weighing an ounce would be smaller than a silver coin. He checked the market and saw that it was around

$1300 US. Holy shit, Alex thought and his fingers trembled as he worked the calculator program. One box of all gold coins was over $107.8 million and 14 boxes would be, best case, although a conservative best case, $1.5 billion. Alex couldn't comprehend the figures. He redid the math and verified. He found that he was sweating and went to the sink for more water. He decided he needed to talk to Mac.

Alex returned Mac's calls and finally reached him as he was getting the cafe ready for the Friday lunch crowd. Alex looked out Elise's window as Mac's phone rang. It was another perfect day, sunny with a light breeze moving the tops of the palm trees. When Mac answered, Alex asked if he had some time. Mac suggested that Alex come by after the lunch serving period. Alex agreed.

Alex called Erin next and she immediately sensed his excitement. Alex said nothing about his calculations. He wanted to tell her in person. She sounded happy and relaxed and Alex was content. They agreed to meet in the late afternoon.

Next Alex called Fernando. Bautiste got right to the point.

"So, have you thought about it?" Bautiste was aggressive. Alex was annoyed.

"No. I haven't had a chance yet. Am I working against some fucking deadline?"

"I need an answer. Otherwise, I will find someone else. What can I do to convince you?" Alex found the question to be vaguely threatening.

"You can't do anything," Alex said coldly. "I'll make up my own mind. Anything else?"

"No. You can go." Fernando broke the connection before Alex had a chance to tell him to fuck off. Bautiste summoned his IT officer.

"Have you started the electronic surveillance on the American?" he demanded of the young officer.

"Yes sir. In fact, I have the first report here. It is up to date as of a few minutes ago." He handed the paper over to his boss.

"That's all," the Colonel said studying the paper and dismissing the subordinate. The report was short and to the point. Calls to Keith Magrew and Erin Rosen, the duration of the calls, and highlights of the contents. More interesting was Alex Browning's browsing activity. He had searched treasure trove, pirate chests and the trading prices of precious metals. Why? Maybe he was fantasizing about the nonexistent treasure that Braga hadn't found. Bautiste let the one page report drift to his desktop.

When Alex arrived at Mac's, the big man was just saying good-bye to the last of the lunch patrons. He noticed Alex and called him over.

"Great lunch crowd," he said tired but excited. "Must be because of those motorcycle jerks yesterday. The word is out, 'Magrew's is definitely the cool place to be'," he said. He was obviously running on.

"Congrats," Alex said. "No ill effects from yesterday?"

"Aspirin washed down with a Bloody Mary, extra hot sauce, took care of me. How about you?"

"Super-hydration and aspirin," Alex admitted. "Hey, do you have a minute? I kind of want to show you something, some figures."

"Sure," Mac said not even guessing what figures Alex was referring to.

Alex had brought along his laptop and moved over next to Mac so that they could share the screen. He pointed out the search links and explained what he had found. Mac immediately noted a discrepancy in Alex's math.

"You based all of your calculations on the assumption that the boxes are of the large size. What about the smallest size? That would be the most conservative result," Mac pointed out. Alex was impressed again with Mac's analytic capability.

"Fuck, you're right," Alex said frustrated with himself. "Crap, I thought I was being conservative. Let me refigure." Alex brought up the laptop's calculator application. He had recorded the dimensions of all the boxes, and figured the small box volume, calculated the ratio, and then used it. "All right. I've refigured," he said, "Worst case, a little less than a half mil, best case two mil. Not bad. But, what do you think? One point five billion? Even if it turns out to be a couple of million, it's still a lot of money, right?"

"Right," Mac agreed. "But forget about that for now. What about where to look for the boxes? We should concentrate on that, don't ya think?"

Alex couldn't argue with Mac's logic. It turned out that Mac owned a Jeep Grand Cherokee, not too new but not too old, beginning to show the effects of being driven in a humid island atmosphere. Mac asked Sonia to handle the after lunch chores. The men loaded the Jeep with some of Mac's equipment from the oil field days and made the drive to the vicinity of Playa Madrid in less than an hour. They actually arrived on a road that was to the west of and overlooking the beach. They exited the Jeep to stand in overgrowth, apart from a thicket of trees.

"So there's the black rock," Alex indicated the boulder below their position, a little distant and half-submerged in the gentle surf. Mac had equipment in the Jeep and he pulled it out and set it up. It was basically a surveyor's tool and Mac used it to determine the distance between their current location and the black rock. There was better technology available Mac knew, but he couldn't justify the expense to Sonia.

They needed to know whom the message referred to as the "captain". Alex's hunch that Black Bart, who was born in 1682, was the captain of the *Little Ranger* when she appeared in the waters off Margarita Island meant that the fourteen boxes were located 40 paces from the black rock following a westerly direction. The variables, as Alex needlessly pointed out, were the precise distance of a "pace" and the precise direction, "west".

Mac concentrated on what was unknown. He returned to the Jeep and pulled an old metal detector from the back. He swept the area due west and exactly 40 yards from the black rock searching for return signals from the detector. Nothing was indicated.

"Are you sure that thing is working?" Alex asked after a time. He was feeling growing frustration at the number of obstacles they faced. He trusted technology, but their operators often made mistakes. "Can you set the sensitivity to something deeper?" Alex wanted to believe that there was a possibility that the machine had not been suitably adjusted.

Mac shrugged and made some changes. The results were obvious. The meter's display pegged as if Mac had found a buried car. Alex was pleased, but then said, "Oh, shit."

"What's the matter?" Mac asked focused on the gauge and sweeping the detector.

"I forgot about those bozos," Alex said. Mac looked up to see what Alex was talking about. He saw the dark sedan.

"Who are they?" he asked shutting off the detector and shouldering it.

"I think they're Bautiste's guys. They've been following me since yesterday. At least that's when I noticed them."

Mac thought for a moment and then said, "We should leave this spot and lead them to somewhere else. Maybe a couple of other places." He put the detector back in the Jeep.

"Good thinking," Alex said getting in the passenger side. "You're better at this than I am." Mac started the Jeep and drove off. The dark sedan followed at a distance.

When the men later reported on Alex and his companion, Bautiste pressed for more details. He let the men go and stared out his office window scratching his chin. He realized he needed a shave.

CHAPTER EIGHT — Getting Rough

Alex and Mac took Bautiste's men on a merry tour of the western section of Margarita Island known as the Macanao Peninsula. As they did so, Mac wondered aloud how much of any treasure the Venezuelan government would claim. Alex explained his previous research of "treasure trove" and how the common arrangement was 90/10 in favor of the sovereign government. Mac thought this was outrageous after all the work done by the recovering party. Alex was amused at Mac's indignation and asked, "What work?"

"The work it took to find and recover the treasure. What do you think? It's nothing?" Alex just shrugged.

Afterwards, Mac dropped Alex off at Elise's house. The two men made plans to get together on the next day, Saturday. Elise was home, back from work, drinking wine and she admired Alex's new color from his entire time outdoors. In fact, Alex was feeling good about himself. He had been getting a lot of exercise since his arrival in Venezuela and was eating healthier.

Alex was also feeling guilty about his developing relationship with Erin. He didn't want to hurt Elise, and he certainly didn't want to hurt Erin. Alex and Elise spent a contented night together, although a part of his thoughts weren't in the room.

Saturday morning Alex was feeling his age. Elise had gone out early, so Alex decided to take a walk to organize his thoughts. He headed past the big casino toward the port and found himself again at Mac's cafe. Magrew was drinking coffee and reading the sports pages, mostly soccer news but some MLB coverage too. Magrew was pleased to see Alex who purposely extended his left fist for a stump-bump. Magrew laughed.

"Sit down," he said. "The PNB were here early to ask about the visit from our motorcycle friends. I told them you were magnificent and subdued four of them on your own."

"Thanks, but I think I handled five while you cowered under the patio table," Alex said.

"'Cowered'? Nice word. I like that, but I seem to remember a body slam and broken bones," Mac said. "Anyway, they didn't seem to know anything and I didn't say anything. They left a little disappointed." Alex laughed this time.

"Can I get a coffee?" Alex asked, in a good mood. The Venezuelan coffee was, as usual, strong, a little bitter and satisfying. Alex suggested that they break out the chessboard. Over chess, Magrew kept up a patter about how he had never seen a magnetometer pegged the way the meter had pegged when they were above Playa Madrid.

"Then we should start to figure out a way to dig up whatever is down there," Alex said moving his queen's knight into a threatening position.

Magrew agreed and, then, continuously wore down Alex's defense until he eventually mated him. Alex opined that he was taking it easy on Mac because of his handicap. Mac raised his stump in defiance and Alex, good-naturedly, wagged his finger in disagreement. He tapped his forehead to clarify the handicap to which he referred. Mac slapped the tabletop, laughed and started to set up the board again. Alex suggested that they switch from coffee to beer. Mac agreed only if Alex would pay the tab. They reached a compromise agreeing that the loser would pay.

As they made their opening gambits, Alex brought up the subject of how they would recover whatever was buried above Playa Madrid.

"Is there a way to dig up whatever you detected without somebody noticing?"

174

"Not with what's going on, not really," Mac answered. "I mean the bad news is you're being followed by Bautiste's dudes. What can we do? Unless you can lose them, they're going to be there."

Alex pushed a pawn. "Is there some way to dig without their knowing it? Some way to make it look like we're doing something else?" Alex asked.

"Buddy," Mac said, "there's always a way, but sometimes the cost is more than someone is willing to pay. How much are you willing to pay?" Mac looked steadily at Alex.

"I don't fucking know," Alex answered honestly. "You tell me. How big is the object your meter sensed down there?"

"Big. Bigger than I've ever seen," Mac came back. "But, let me tell you, it could be nothing: just junk; nothing of any value. I've seen that happen. This guy thinks he's found a stash of coins or lost jewelry or whatever and insists this is it. He surveys the site, keeps it secret, sneaks around and, eventually, starts digging." Mac laughed.

"And?" Alex said.

"And, guess what?" Mac asked. "Nothing. There was some junk boat parts not really buried, just kind of discarded. So it's too bad, disappointment. What the hell? He packed up and went back to work as a hotel manager." Mac shrugged and pushed his king's side bishop halfway up the board in a strong threat.

"What if your boy had found something?" Alex asked.

"What? Like if he had brought up some treasure or something? This guy wasn't one of those guys." Mac said. "Little d'bag who hoped his train or boat or whatever the cliché is had come in. He was FOS. Know what I mean?"

Alex nodded. Now he was conflicted. He began to doubt that he and Mac could pull off a recovery of whatever was buried without creating a shit storm.

"I know what ya mean," Alex lied. "We're not d'bags, though, Mac," he continued, "We have a definite place to dig. And, I believe, a specific purpose. So, let's go for it."

"Ok, bud, let's do it," Mac said. "But before we do, lemme ask you a question."

"Fine. Go for it."

Mac didn't hesitate. It was something he wondered about since he had met Alex. "What the hell'd you come here for?" Alex, reflexively, gave the stock answer, "I hooked up with Elise on Facebook and came down to see what would happen."

"Yeah, that's bullshit," Mac said. "I meant the real story. What's up with that?" Alex felt a little trapped, a little called out.

"Ok, ya got me," Alex joked weakly. "What do you want to know?"

"The truth. The background," Mac said seriously. Alex could see that he was completely serious.

"Ok." Alex swallowed the rest of his beer. "I guess you've earned the truth. It is true that Elise and I hooked up on Facebook. I had just recently retired from a thirty-year career in the defense industry and had decided that I needed to have one last swing at life before I couldn't lift the bat anymore. I'd been taking life pretty slow and quiet at the end of my career there. I was a widower. I didn't socialize much. You could probably call me a loner. Anyway, I retired pretty comfortably. I could have moved to a cabin in Alaska. Except I hate the cold. I could have moved to Key West. Except that I hate bugs. I could have stayed put and continue to live the quiet life.

176

"But, like I said, I chose to try the relationship path one more time. My daughters actually convinced me to try. They're quite the girls," Alex smiled. "And, it's not working out the way I had hoped." Mac felt Alex's sorrow and was beginning to feel bad that he had asked.

"What do you mean?"

"Elise," he started and then said, "oh fuck. I'm not going to blame her. We're just not that compatible."

"In what way?"

"Well, I guess in all the important ways," Alex said. "Take money, for example. It's not that important to me. As long as I've got enough for beer," he joked, "it's not a big deal. For Elise, though, it seems like it's everything to her. Did you know she gambled big on the *Little Ranger's* treasure? She and Fernando, both, put up thousands to fund some of Braga's work."

"I heard rumors, but it sounded irrational to me so I discounted it. They really did, huh?"

"Yeah, and now she's kind of rattled that there's not going to be an ROI. Anyway, that's one way. Another way is in the sack." Alex looked to make sure Mac was taking him seriously. "I don't think either of us finds the other attractive that way. A long time ago, there was something there, but not now. She thinks I should take Viagra."

"Well, you're not a kid," Mac observed, "plus from what I've heard, it can't hurt." He shrugged.

"Yeah, but to me it's fake shit. Chemicals making up for what nature should be providing. Sorry, but if a guy's girlfriend or whatever is unattractive, do the chemicals make her attractive?"

"Well, regardless maybe the boner makes her feel attractive," Mac said. "Just spitballing here," he added.

"Hmm. Didn't think of that. That makes some sort of twisted sense, I guess. Works out for both him and her. I guess that could be. Anyway, like I said, Elise and I aren't really connecting. On the other hand," Alex said a bit too casually, "Erin and I are."

"Are what?"

"Connecting."

"Really?" Mac said with both surprise and what Alex took as approval. "Congratulations. I don't know her well, but I hear she's a great person. And a helluva looker." Mac lifted his beer bottle in salute. Alex smiled and lifted his own bottle.

"Lemme ask you something," Alex said changing the subject, "is Bautiste dangerous?"

"He's the law," Mac answered, "but he's an asshole."

"What kind of asshole?

"The unavoidable kind," Mac said laughing. "It's a small island."

Returning to their chess game, Magrew won the second game with a strong knight attack that never let Alex get organized. Alex suggested they play a third game to break the tie. Mac laughed and started to set up the board. Alex paid for more beer.

Although it was Saturday, Colonel Bautiste was in his office and, so, the Hammer was there as well as the technical staff.

"These reports from Caracas," Bautiste said holding up a sheaf of printouts, "have they been verified? This shouldn't be happening. Protests; shortages; and Maduro is threatening to implement controls on foreign exchange."

The Hammer merely shrugged. He really didn't understand and it made him uncomfortable to hear the government criticized. The fact that the criticism came from his boss and idol somewhat ameliorated his feelings. "Maduro only does what he believes Chavez would do," he said lamely.

Bautiste eyed him with contempt at his simplicity, but said nothing. In fact, it was Sergeant Garcia's simple mind that made him a valuable tool. Bautiste sighed.

"You're right, my friend. Our acting President is following *El Comandante* even in death."

The irony of Bautiste's remarks was lost on the Sergeant.

"Now," the Colonel said dropping the bundle of reports to his desktop, "what of the American? What news?" The Sergeant pulled a small notebook from his pants pocket and consulted it.

"The American has been spending a lot of time this weekend with the black cafe owner, the one with the big belly and big lips and half an arm. The American has spent most of his nights at Mrs. Diaz's house, as usual, though he has spent some nights with Ms. Rosen. He spends his days either driving around with Magrew or playing chess with him and drinking beer." He flipped to another page. "He has spoken to Ms. Rosen by phone, but has not met her again since their day at the beach. Their conversation was friendly and uninteresting. That's it." The Sergeant closed his notebook and stored it in his pocket. He stood in silence.

"Interesting that he has not been in touch with Ms. Rosen," Bautiste said somewhat distracted. "Remember when we arrested the uncooperative thief? The one in Caracas, the one who would not admit his guilt and would not return what he stole?"

"I remember him," the Sergeant said. "He was tough and did not care about his physical safety. He laughed at you when you threatened him."

"He was tough, and uncooperative. Until you took him to visit with his wife," Bautiste mused gazing out his office window at the weekend crowds milling below. "Remember?"

"I remember. First, she was angry, then she was crying, and last she was screaming. He broke when the screaming started, but you had to be sure."

Bautiste smiled at the memory. "He returned everything. He was never able to return his wife's dignity, though. Anyway, I am wondering if Alex Browning may require similar, uh, encouragement to cooperate. Maybe the lovely Ms. Rosen can help us."

"Whatever you think," the Hammer said.

At the cafe, Alex lost his third straight game of chess to Magrew. He leaned back, stretched and raised his face to the sun.

"That'll cause wrinkles," Mac warned.

"Yeah, wouldn't want that," Alex said still facing the sun's warmth.

"Aren't you going to buy us more beer?" Mac said. "I'm thirsty."

Erin Rosen spent her Saturday tidying up her apartment and running errands such as grocery shopping and dry cleaning and gassing up her Corolla. Then she called Elise to see if she was free for lunch. Elise sounded excited at the prospect and they arranged to meet at the Marina Bay, a Porlamar landmark hotel and casino. Erin was not much of a gambler, but Elise was avid. As they walked through the

180

doors of the casino, there was a faux treasure chest filled with gold foil-wrapped chocolate "doubloons".

Elise scooped a handful into her purse. "For luck," she winked at Erin. They passed the slot machines and stopped as Elise played a couple of pulls and continued on into the hotel's dining room. Lunch was buffet style and was generally a good value since the casino subsidized it. They filled their plates and took a small table.

"So how was your time with Alex?" Elise asked as she bit off a large piece of chilled shrimp slathered in cocktail sauce.

"It was great. Didn't he tell you?" Erin's face was as blank and unreadable as one of the casino's dealers.

"He said he had a good time, but you know how men are. No details. What did you guys do?"

So Elise spent the rest of their lunch listening to Erin tell how they had visited Playa Madrid and the wreck site. She told how they visited the ruins of the fort and had a picnic. She told how, the next day, they went to Playa El Agua and took the sun.

"Yes," Elise said, "I told him I like his tan. I think he's losing some of his belly, too," she laughed. "It must be all of the exercise. It's good for him." Erin considered this.

"I agree. You should have seen him climbing the hill above Playa Madrid. He was struggling, but he seems in really good shape for someone his age. Don't you think?"

"He's in pretty good shape except for the most important exercise," Elise said with a knowing grin. She laughed.

"Uh-oh," Erin said, "problems in bed?" By way of response, Elise held out her right index finger and then bent it. She shook her head. Erin laughed.

181

"Have you tried a little extra stimulation?" she asked waving her fist in the air.

"Why should I need to do that? If he's a man, he would be hard." Elise was dismissive. Erin shrugged noncommittally.

After lunch, they reentered the casino and Elise announced that she was going to play Twenty-One. Erin excused herself, wished Elise luck, and left her friend to lose her money.

Alex and Mac were still drinking beer by the middle of the afternoon. The chess games and conversation had waned and both men appeared lost in their thoughts. Alex lifted his beer and then realized it was empty.

"I've been thinking," he announced to Mac. Mac lifted his own bottle and drained it, belching loudly. "Nice," Alex said. "And after that bit of wisdom, let's discuss what I've been thinking about. First, there's the split. From what I've been able to determine, the Venezuelan government by established international conventions is going to ask for a ninety-ten split. Ok, worst case: there's nothing to recover. Second to worst case: there's just silver and it's worth a half million, leaving fifty thousand for us after the split. So that means twenty-five for you and twenty-five for me. That's not too bad, is it?"

"Well, look. I measure all reward based on the amount of effort needed to get it. Know what I mean?" Alex smiled in assent. "So how much effort is worth a twenty-five k return?"

"Well, you've dug in the earth before. How much effort would it take to dig up whatever's there?"

"Out in the open? With no restrictions? Hardly any effort. I'd borrow a backhoe and be done in an hour." Alex nodded   in   understanding.

"Pretty good hourly rate," he said. "What if we could make the hourly rate ten times that? Then how would you do it?" Mac called a waitress over and asked for two more beers. The late afternoon was growing cooler signaling a coming change.

"Now you're talking about a different proposition," Mac said. "Meaning we would have to be sneaky, very sneaky. We'd have to not only dig without being detected, but also hide whatever we find until we could convert it to cash. That'd be tough." The beers arrived. The bottles were beaded with condensation.

"So how would you do it?" Alex pushed the issue.

Mac held the bottle up and stared at it as if it were fascinating.

"Well," he announced, "secrecy is the key. We could dig at night. The problem with that is we would need some light to work by. A light in that area would draw attention. That area off the beach has some trees, maybe enough. I'm not sure. On the other hand, if we had to dig in the daylight, I guess dawn would be the best time, fewer people about. Maybe a couple of fishermen who would be minding their own business anyway." Mac took a drink of his beer. The engineer in Alex was intrigued at the problem.

"It seems to me that the problem with starting at dawn is that we don't know how much time it would take to finish the job. We could conceivably still be working in the middle of the morning," Alex observed. "If we were still unnoticed, that would make it tough to recover and conceal whatever we found and remain unnoticed." Alex took a long draw on his bottle. "We could split the digging up over several mornings."

"Well, that's an idea," Mac said enjoying this day more than any other in recent memory.

"What about using slant drilling?" Alex asked. "Is this a situation where that would be useful? I mean if we could

183

drill from those trees above the beach, we'd have less chance of being noticed, right?"

"Be right back," Mac said by way of response. He got up and went into the dimness of the restaurant. Alex assumed he was going in to pee.

Mac returned with a large sheet of paper. Alex leaned in as Mac spread the paper on the tabletop. He produced a Sharpie.

"So," Mac began drawing simply, "here's the location off of Madrid." He drew a square. "And here's the spot where the meter went nuts." He drew a smaller square within the first. He drew a series of small circles outside of the large square. "These are the trees. Now there's no way to know precisely how deep an object is: too many variables. So, if we want to use slant drilling, how do we know what the target depth is?" He paused and looked at Alex who laughed and shrugged his shoulders.

"Ok," he said, "since geometry is involved, we need to either determine points or angles. Let's suppose that there is good concealment for us here." Alex pointed to the circles on the paper. "So let's assume that this is the closest and safest place to start drilling. Not saying that this *is* the place, just, for example. So that's the starting point. Next is the question of depth or angle. You'll have to answer that, bud." Alex took a suck of beer. "How do you know where to go? Do you start shallow and go deep or vice versa? What's the best strategy? What usually works?"

"Well," said Mac, "it's not so simple. If we were trying to hit oil, we'd have seismic maps to show us where and how deep to drill. Without that intelligence, let's make some guesses and also do some rough calculations as to the volume of the mass the metal detector sensed."

Alex searched his phone for the chest dimensions. He retrieved the smallest dimensions and calculated the volume.

"So what do you think? Multiplied by fourteen, at the smallest, we're looking for a pretty large mass."

"Wow," Mac agreed, "not bad. Ok, that should be an easy target to hit. My gut tells me to start shallow, maybe six feet. If you were a pirate, would you dig deeper than that if you didn't have to? We can always go deeper if we come up empty. The real problem is what do we do with all that mass once we bring it up? That's a lot of shit." Alex had to think that one over.

"You're right, Mac. I'm not sure what we should do. How would we, how did you put it, hide the stuff and convert it to cash? Not my expertise and not yours either," Alex pointed out.

"It would be extremely tricky without some help. I suppose, and I can't believe we're having this conversation, we could smuggle whatever we have out of the country somehow and make some sort of connection in a more sympathetic country. If you believe all the movies, there are guys around every corner looking to make some sort of shady deal."

"Seems pretty risky to me, especially since I'm being watched. I'd feel better if we could partner up with somebody who knows more about this than we do. What do you think?" Alex's face expressed his concern.

"Shit, I don't know," Mac said. "Bringing somebody else in seems pretty risky too. I don't know anybody who has that kind of knowledge and I'm sure you don't."

"Ok," Alex said, "let's take this step by step. First, do we want to settle for ten percent or go for one hundred percent?" He waited for Mac's answer.

"Just like that, huh? Hold on. Let's think about risk-reward," Mac chided. "It might not be ten or one hundred. It might be nothing. How does that sound?"

"Good point," Alex admitted. "Ok. How do we assign a weight to the risk associated with going for one hundred percent? Bluntly, we cut out the Venezuelan government."

"Good question," Mac said, "I don't have a clue. Ask an actuarial?" Alex laughed.

"Our new partner would be an insurance guy?" he joked. "Seriously, how do we figure the risk? If we get caught, can we just say we weren't sure there was anything there and we didn't want to say anything until we were sure?"

"Fuck. This is giving me a headache," the big man said. He rubbed his temples.

"Suppose we had, not an actuarial," Alex grew intense, "but someone powerful enough to protect us if we get caught. Colonel Bautiste, for example?" Mac's eyes narrowed and he spread his palms on the table, fingers spread. He puffed his cheeks and emptied his lungs.

"That," he announced, "would be extremely stupid, and dangerous. In my humble opinion."

"Why? He was a Braga backer, hoping to get something out of the wreck. Now he expects to get nothing. Unless he throws in with us, right?"

"Alex," Mac said, now very serious, "you don't understand these people and you certainly don't understand this man. You're right he is powerful, powerful enough to take away whatever we find and make sure that we are never seen again. Could your daughters stand that?" Mac could see that he had struck a nerve.

"But, could we afford to not cut in Bautiste? And Elise?" Alex asked. "I feel like she is desperate for any financial help. Maybe she could help us persuade him. And, he could be a huge help if we can somehow arrange it that he wouldn't cross us, maybe with her help." Mac shook his head in disbelief.

"Jesus, you're like the world's oldest fucking kid. This world is populated by the desperate and gives no guarantees to anyone. What the fuck? Alex, you don't get it," Mac said shaking his head. "This country is unraveling by the hour. Maduro is weak, but he'll be the next president. In a year, I wouldn't be surprised if there's a full-blown revolution here. Bautiste knows it. He's trying to scoop up everything that he can and, then, he'll probably blow. He's not going to help us. He's going to rob us, if we give him the slightest chance."

"Ok, ok," Alex surrendered, "I get it." He waved his hands. "Let's get back to the recovery problem. That's the unresolved issue. Mac, there's gotta be a way to quietly pull up whatever's there and move it to a place that's safe for us." Alex looked at the big man for answers. The sun was sinking in the west.

"Old man, there's certainly a way to pull up whatever's there without being detected. We can't account for bad luck though. Let's say we're lucky, we recover everything; maybe rebury it, and then what? We're back to the problem of who's going to fence the shit, convert it to cash, and how much we will get on the dollar. Alex, these are real world problems. Maybe I know some people who know some people. Let me make some calls and then we'll talk again. Ok?" Alex was overcome with fatigue. He agreed with Mac. They gave each other a back thump and Alex headed off to Elise's.

As the sun disappeared and before Erin could turn on her apartment lights, there was a knock at the door. Her heart did a weird thump and she went to look out the peephole. She could see the back of Alex's head and, as she undid the chain and the two dead bolts, her heart did the weird thing again.

As soon as the second dead bolt clicked open three men burst into the apartment, shut the door, smothered Erin's screams, and raised the   volume on the television.

187

Erin's eyes were huge with fright as she was roughly thrown into a stiff-backed chair and bound with a lamp's electrical cord.

Alex arrived at Elise's house and was still feeling the buzz of the afternoon beers shared with Mac. Elise was reading a magazine.

"*Hola*, baby," Alex said tripping on the woven mat inside the door. Elise looked at him with amusement. She put aside her magazine.

"*Hola*," she said, "a nice day?"

"Pretty good," he agreed. "Spent the day with Mac at Mac's dinking, drinking," he enunciated more carefully, "beer and playing chess. How was chore, your day?"

"Nice. Went to lunch with Erin at the casino. Oh, and I lost a hundred dollars playing Blackjack. But, that's ok."

"Oh, sorry, babe. Bad luck or bad playing?" Alex asked and immediately regretted the question in spite of his state.

"What? What do you mean? I just had bad luck. It's a casino. You win or you lose. It's not my fault. C'mon *bebe*. You know that." She was squirming around in her chair, agitated.

"No, no," Alex protested, "I didn't mean that. I meant, uh, I guess I don't know what I meant. Anyway, do we have any cookies or something? I've got a sweet craving."

"No cookies," she said, "but I have some chocolate, from the casino. In my purse."

"Can I?" Alex pointed at her purse lying on the kitchen counter.

188

"Go ahead," she said. "Venezuelan chocolate is very good, did you know?"

"I didn't even know there was a chocolate industry here. Belgian, yes. Swiss I've heard of."

"Well, it's not a chocolate industry," she admitted. "It's a cocoa industry. Chocolate made from Venezuelan cocoa is very good."

"Oh, ok. That makes sense," Alex said rummaging through the chaotic contents of her purse. "What am I looking for?"

"Gold covered chocolate," she said.

"Got it," he said. "Mind if I take two?"

"No, go ahead. Can you bring me one? They are free at the casino."

"Here you are." He handed a shiny chocolate disk over. "How about a glass of red wine?"

Erin was paralyzed with fright as she watched the three men go through her things. She asked them what they were looking for and offered to help. Each wore some sort of cloth covering the lower half of their faces. The largest of the three kept looking at her with his dead eyes whenever he passed through the living room. He scared her the most. She found the fact that they never spoke terrifying. She wished that they would say something, ask something. Instead, she could hear them in the kitchen and bedroom opening drawers and closet doors.

Erin realized she had to pee. She asked if she could use the bathroom, but none of the men answered or even gave an indication that they had heard her. They just continued to go through her possessions.

Mac closed the cafe at eight o'clock. Potential Saturday night patrons, Mac knew, would be jamming the casinos and clubs instead of frequenting restaurants or cafes. He went home with his wife to relax. He wanted to tell her about Playa Madrid. They had no secrets and he loved her more than anything. He held back though. He told himself that he felt foolish, pursuing pirate treasure. He would tell her if he and Alex found something. Otherwise, why bring it up except, maybe later, as a humorous story. He did need to make a phone call though. His old buddy, Cor Delaney, another ex-pat, had the equipment that he and Alex needed.

"I'm going to grab a smoke," Mac told his wife. She disapproved of his smoking, but was proud of him, as he had reduced his habit to one or two cigarettes in the evening. She blew him a kiss as she returned to her television program.

Mac stepped out onto their third floor balcony where the ashtray was. The view was hardly breathtaking. Those views cost a lot of money and were out of reach for cafe owners. Someday, Mac thought to himself as he settled into his cushioned chair and lit a cigarette. He pulled out his cell phone and scrolled to Cor's data. He pressed the button that dialed the Irishman's number.

"So how did you meet the black man?" Elise asked sipping wine and nibbling her chocolate. She, like most of the world, believed that racism was rampant in the U.S. and was curious about Alex's basis for any relationship with the *Negro*.

Alex explained how he had been wandering around the waterfront and had randomly chosen a seat at Magrew's cafe.

"So you met him then? And you talked to him? This was an accident, yes?"

"Meeting Mac was random, right, by accident, by chance. Why?"

"White people usually don't like black people," Elise said it as if this were a fact and widely accepted. "Isn't that right?" Alex had to think before responding.

"Probably that's right," he acknowledged, "at least, I think, for my generation." Alex went on to explain that, in his opinion, it was not a matter of "like", but more of "trust". He used a word that had sort of faded from usage: prejudice. He told Elise that this word meant pre-judging, making your mind up before you have the facts. He said that he thought that prejudice was justified.

"What do you mean by that?" Elise asked.

Mac got through to Cor Delaney on the fourth ring.

"Cor? It's Mac. How the hell are you?"

"Mac, you black one-armed bastard. You haven't called in two months. D'ye owe me money? I may have forgotten." Mac knew that Cor could put on a brogue whenever he wanted.

"I've got two arms, you Mick. One's just shorter than the other one." Cor laughed. Mac's wife looked out the sliding glass doors and saw that Mac was on his mobile. Mac noticed her and waved.

"Listen, Cor, I need a favor and I'll pay."

"Go on," Cor said with Irish caution because money was involved.

"I need to borrow your drill rig." Mac was referring to Cor's heavy-duty truck that was fitted with an extendable arm to which a bit could be attached. It could be used to drill deep or to just burrow postholes.

"You mentioned pay?" Cor said.

191

"Yeah, you Mick. Take your choice: a hundred dollars or a half percent." Mac knew that Cor would not ask "percent of what?" That was part of the game.

"Fook your hundred dollars," Cor said. "I'll take the half percent."

"Good choice, you Mick. I'll get back to you."

"Hold on," Cor said, "the truck is on Cubagua," referring to the small island adjacent to Margarita. "I was drilling test wells there. It'll take a couple of days to ferry it here. Ok?" Mac agreed that it was ok. Mac ended the call just as his wife began to slide open the door. He stubbed out his cigarette and rose from his cushioned chair.

"I mean that some people," Alex said, "judge other people based on nothing more than their color. The thing is, it seems that this way of figuring people out is pretty accurate." Alex felt guilty, but he also felt that this was a fresh breath of honesty.

"Accurate how?" Alex felt that he had to choose his words carefully.

"Well, stereotypes exist for a reason. People try to debunk stereotypes by pointing out the exceptions. That's backwards. The stereotypes are there because those groups continue to match the parameters."

Alex went on to use examples of Group A, which had a poor family structure and, thus, performed poorly academically, economically and socially. Another group, Group B, which had a strong family structure performed well academically, economically and socially.

"So stereotypes are established. If you're born into Group A, the odds are against you in school, the job market, and your network. And what happens? Well, sometimes society feels bad and tries to better the odds for you. Society creates affirmative action and equal opportunity, but these don't work, do they?"

Erin was thoroughly humiliated. She could control her bladder no longer. As she relieved herself, the stain on her shorts spread noticeably. Her terrorizers didn't seem to notice or to care. The television continued to blare its program, which added to Erin's inability to marshal her thoughts and make sense of her situation. The three men still hadn't spoken to each other.

Mac's wife asked him about the cell phone call and Mac lied that it was Alex trying to arrange a Sunday chess game or two. He knew that Sonia liked Alex.

"We should go to the beach tomorrow," she said.

"We can do both," Mac answered. "Better yet, why don't we take the boat out? It'll be cooler on the water."

"Good idea," she agreed. "I'll pack us a lunch."

One of the men finally broke his silence and whispered some orders to the other two. Erin could hear water running in the bathroom. The two men reappeared with a towel and a bucket of water. She was beginning to think that they were going to rinse and dry her off. Instead, one of the men submerged the towel in the bucket and pulled it out dripping water on Erin's wood floor. The other man had circled around behind Erin. He immobilized her head with a powerful grip. The towel man placed the heavy cloth over her face and pulled it tight. Erin couldn't breathe and immediately panicked. More water began to pour on the towel. She felt that she was drowning.

Alex was explaining how social programs such as food stamps and subsidized housing removed any chance for the receiving group of people to instill the values of hard work and industry into their culture. Alex and Elise were on their second bottle of wine.

"As long as these things are given to you and you did nothing to earn them, other than belong to the group, how can you value what you have? Anyway, that's what I think. And, something else, for those same reasons, socialist governments, like the one here, will eventually fail. Don't you think?"

"Yes, I agree," Elise said. "I believe in hard work and earning your living. What Chavez did and what Maduro will continue to do only hurts Venezuela. Venezuelans are totally capable of working hard. These politicians just want to appear on a balcony and be cheered by thousands of people who are enjoying cheap gas and cheap food."

"It's the same thing with Obama," Alex said getting excited. "He just wants to be adored. He would extend unemployment benefits indefinitely if he could just so people sitting at home, contributing nothing to the economy, would love him. Politicians are worthless."

Elise drained her glass and held it out for a refill. Alex obliged.

"I always wondered," she said, "and, thank you. I wondered why America elected Obama. Why did you?"

Alex had several opinions. He told her that, initially, Obama had excited young voters and, of course, Black voters. He also had the liberal, Hollywood crowd. That was pretty much enough to carry him. McCain and Palin had little to recommend them, especially after Palin was portrayed as a bubble brain.

"So why was he re-elected after such a poor first four years?" Elise asked. Alex could only offer his opinion.

"By then, the young were disillusioned, as was Hollywood. The Blacks, though, probably egged on by the pastors and preachers of their churches, kept up their support. And, of course, the poor, those who benefitted from Obama's socialism, voted for him. That was enough to carry him over Romney. But he'll be gone soon without that much damage done."

Erin coughed and sputtered and tried to move her head to the side to avoid the water. And then, just as suddenly as it had begun, it ended. The largest of the three men pulled the towel from her face and she breathed freely, gasping.

"Do you know why we are here?" he asked. Erin was still trying to fill her lungs and couldn't yet talk.

"Do you?" he asked again.

"No," she was crying now, "no. I have no idea."

"You tell your boyfriend to make the second trip. Or we'll be back." The large man produced a knife and cut the electric cord. Then they were gone and Erin was alone. The news on the television announced that presidential elections would be held in April.

CHAPTER NINE—A Change of Plans

Alex and Elise were sleeping when the banging came on Elise's front door. It was Alex who opened it.

"Erin. My god," he said, "are you all right? What happened? Elise! Bring a blanket." Elise, to her credit, didn't ask a lot of questions. She just brought a blanket to the front door. She was stunned to see Erin sitting on the floor, soaking wet and obviously in shock. She wrapped the blanket gently around her friend's wet shoulders. Alex had already gone to Elise's bedroom. He returned immediately.

"There's a hot shower running," he told Elise softly. "We should get her in there."

They successfully transferred the nearly catatonic woman still clothed under the warm water. The water soon had its effect. Erin seemed to emerge from her daze as she shivered despite the steamy shower. Alex had gathered four of Elise's bath towels and they now encouraged Erin to remove her t-shirt and shorts and to wrap herself in the towels. After their initial dismay at Erin's condition, they didn't press for information or ask unnecessary questions. Their main concern was to make Erin comfortable. Swaddled in warm towels and with a small glass of Calvados in her hand, Erin began to feel better.

"Thanks, you guys," she said. "God damn it!" She drank down the apple brandy in one gulp.

"What happened?" Alex asked with so much emotion that Elise looked at him.

Erin, with the help of a second Calvados, told them of the three men who terrorized her. She described the complete ordeal and, then, the reason.

"Fucking bastards!" Alex said. "Fuck their drugs. Bautiste, that prick. Elise, you've got a gun, right?" Alex was casting about for a way to hurt Bautiste and violence, maybe surprising, occurred to him first.

"Forget about that, Alex. That would be the worst thing you could do." Elise was the voice of reason and Alex, an eminently rational man, was receptive.

They got Erin settled down and comfortable in Elise's bed. Alex volunteered to stand watch all night. He was too furious to sleep anyway. He spent the entire night thinking, plotting revenge and concocting a plan that would result in a revenge that, in his opinion, would crush Bautiste in every way. As his plan came together he pulled out his laptop. He developed a list of people who would be on the revenge team and assigned roles to each of them. On the team were his daughters, his brother, Magrew, two as yet to be determined firms with very different roles, and a foreign government. Around six o'clock on Sunday morning Alex finally slept.

Alex awoke around ten on Sunday, groggy until he had his first cup of coffee. He was getting used to the bitterness of the Venezuelan brew and appreciated its strength. Erin and Elise had gone to Mass and he had the house to himself. He retrieved his laptop and opened Outlook. He drafted a message to Connie and Jo. He suspected that either of his daughters would know what he was looking for. It took him an hour until he was satisfied that he had it right. He encrypted the email and hit Send. Next he began a note to his brother. As he started, Erin and Elise returned. Alex shut down his computer and turned his full attention to the women.

"How're you doing?" he asked Erin. The depth of his concern was obvious and not lost on Elise who went to brew tea.

"Better. The sleep helped and I realize now they were just trying to scare me so that you would help them." Erin's voice was steady and held no hint of the near-hysteria

197

of the night before. Alex thought she looked beautiful in her church ensemble, a simple blue dress and little makeup.

"I've pretty much made up my mind to help them," Alex announced. "I don't want you or Elise terrorized because of me."

Erin took his hand and squeezed it. "I wasn't terrorized," she smiled, "just scared." Elise brought them tea and served it.

"Ok," Alex smiled, "poor choice of words."

"I doubt that Fernando would try to use me against you," Elise added. "He knows I would spit in his face. I'm not afraid of him." Alex doubted that this was true, but admired her bravado. For his part, he had reached the conclusion that Bautiste was exceedingly dangerous as Mac had said and was becoming more so. The civil unrest since the death of Chavez had, Alex guessed, raised Bautiste's panic level. Alex guessed that Bautiste was probably making arrangements to close down his drug involvement and move on.

"Well, I think you should be afraid of him, both of you." The two women stopped drinking tea and looked at each other. Alex was emphatic. "I think he may be getting desperate. Maybe he doesn't think he can count on Maduro the way he could on Chavez. Maybe he's feeling cut off from Caracas. Anyway, we should be careful. Let me think about it. I'll come up with something." Despite his lack of sleep, he felt the need for physical activity. "I'm too wound up to sit around," he said. "I'm going to take a walk."

"I'll go with you," Erin said. "You?" This was directed at Elise.

"No, thanks. You two go ahead. I'll straighten up here and then I'm going to rest. It's been a busy week for me."

Alex and Erin walked the few blocks to her apartment complex. As they approached her door, Alex noticed that she hadn't locked up. He entered first and saw the shambles of the night before.

"You could have picked up the place, maybe dusted, run the vacuum," he joked.

She laughed and that helped. She wanted to take another shower and change so Alex busied himself putting things away and cleaning. After her description of the three men rummaging, he expected a bigger mess. Apparently, they were just opening and closing drawers and doors and not really looking for anything. Psychological pressure, he thought.

She emerged freshly scrubbed, looked around her place, and hugged and kissed Alex with fervor.

"Thank you," she whispered into his ear. Her closeness and warm breath aroused him, which, under the circumstances, seemed inappropriate so he pulled her tight briefly, squeezed her butt, and broke off the embrace.

"Ready for that walk?" he said taking her hand. She kissed him again.

"Sure. Let's go. Where, though?"

"It doesn't matter. Down by the water?"

They wound up walking an undeveloped stretch of beach within view of the big Porlamar seaside hotels.

"How did it go with Keith Magrew yesterday?" Erin asked.

Alex was going to give her minimal details, but some combination of emotion and logic made him decide to tell her everything. He told how he and Magrew had driven out near Playa Madrid, had identified a location, and how the metal detector had reacted to something. He told her of his Google

199

searches for pirate chests and the trading value of silver and gold. He told her about his calculations. He explained the "treasure trove" laws, as he understood them. He told her how he and Mac had explored the option of concealing whatever there was and making a side deal with a trader.

"If you tried to keep it a secret, how would you convert whatever to legal recognized cash?" Erin asked. Before Alex could answer, she went on. "You would have to deal with people who were in a position to take advantage of your secrecy, people who, like you, would cheat. Why wouldn't they cheat you?"

Alex was impressed with her logic and told her so. He admitted that he and Mac had considered these same points. He told her that, while she slept, he thought he had come up with a plan that solved all the problems.

"Ok, what is it?" she asked frustrated. He had stopped talking.

"Sorry," he said, "just thinking. I haven't even run this plan by Mac yet, so I was deciding whether or not to tell it now." He looked in her eyes. She was squinting in the sunlight and her blonde hair moved in the gentle Caribbean breeze. He put his arm around her small waist and pulled her hip close to his.

"Here's what I came up with," he started. "I wanted to have a plan that accomplished two things." And he explained what the two things were and how he had tried to account for events that would achieve what he thought they needed.

Connie and Jo, who were eating Eggs Benedict and drinking Mimosas, happened to be spending Sunday morning together in Connie's apartment and they, almost simultaneously, received their father's email. Connie, who was wearing a Duke baseball cap backwards, was briefly baffled at the request for a password key then remembered that they had advised their father to use PGP. Jo, who had her dark hair tied back with a white tube sock, read the message in the clear first and waited for her older sister to catch up. This was a small source of chagrin for Connie. The sisters were competitive in almost everything.

"So," Jo said when Connie had decrypted the email, "I wonder what our drug-smuggling Dad is up to now."

"Say hello to my little friend…" Connie said and they both laughed. "What do you think he needs this stuff for?" Connie asked referring to the email content.

"Actually," Jo corrected, "it's just one thing he's asking for. It's a hack that scoops up all documents and emails and copies them to a secure website." Jo adjusted her sweat sock. "As to why he needs it, who the hell knows. Well, I guess Dad knows," she admitted.

"So, you got something that'll work for him?" Connie took a drink of Mimosa.

"I have a couple of things that'll work and a butt load of questions," Jo said. "Doesn't it seem weird that Dad spent his whole life as a super-straight arrow and now he falls face first into the drug trade and stealing emails? What the fuck?" She walked to the glass doors of Connie's balcony, which overlooked a public golf course and idly watched a couple of golfers abuse the rules of the game. "A tradition unlike any other…" she muttered.

"What's that?" Connie asked. She had begun to clear their brunch detritus.

"Nothing. Just thinking. I'll send him what he's asking for and include instructions on how to use it."

"Good. But, I wish I knew what he was up to. Anything I can do?"

"You could if he had asked for iOS help, but…" Jo shrugged.

Alex and Erin had walked miles before they decided to turn around.

"So your daughters, Connie and Joanne?" she asked.

"Connie and Jo. She hates Joanne."

"I like that. So your daughters have a way to help?"

"If anybody can help, they can. Especially Jo, she's the tough one, but it's going to torque Connie an awful lot."

"Torque?" Erin asked for clarification.

"Make angry," Alex said, "piss her off. They're so competitive. She really hates it when her sister has the upper hand."

"I like that, too," Erin said. "Girl power!" She pumped her fist.

Alex and Erin returned to Elise's house after noon. Elise was out and Erin was tired enough to want to take a nap so Alex grabbed his laptop again. He found the response from Jo. It contained an encrypted answer and an attachment. The decryption directed Alex to perform a series of steps, steps that would allow Alex to implement a part of his plan to punish Bautiste. He wasn't certain how this part would work out, and he had a sense that the policeman wasn't operating without his own support team.

Alex decided to follow his daughter's directions later. Right now he wanted to draft another encrypted message, this time to his brother Terry. His message was simple; recruit a Philadelphia law firm, preferably one with international experience. Alex had always held to the maxim that if there was a widely held belief, a truth would be found at the end of the day. The widely held belief in this case was that the craftiness and intelligence of Philadelphia lawyers was unmatched. Alex sent his message to his brother's personal email account and then Googled hotels in Porlamar.

Brother Terrence's Blackberry vibrated as he was enjoying a Sunday afternoon beer and preparing to watch some college basketball in the Common Room. The room was so named because it was a communal gathering place for the Brothers. He considered the NCAA Men's Basketball tournament and the various conference championships leading up to it as the best time of the year. He checked his phone, saw that the email was from Alex, and excused himself from the group of basketball enthusiasts. The Brothers were enthusiastic with good reason. Their team, the LaSalle Explorers, was playing well this year and had a chance of getting to the "Big Dance."

Terry went to his room and logged in to his desktop. He did this because his Blackberry didn't have the software needed to decrypt Alex's email. Terry opened his email client, decrypted the email, and stroked his beard. He, of course, was familiar with several Philadelphia law firms, but he wasn't sure about their international negotiating experience. He would have to ask Brother Roderick who, as the Dean of the Business College, was the most familiar with the specialties of Philadelphia lawyers.

"Rod, got a minute?" Terry said returning to the Common Room. Brother Roderick, realizing that those three words could mean anything, grabbed his beer and a handful of pretzels and nodded toward the door.

"What's up?" he asked when they stepped out in the hall. He munched some pretzels.

"My brother, Alex, needs some help. He's down in Venezuela," Terry began.

"Wow! Ok. What can I do?" Brother Roderick asked.

203

"I'm not sure yet why," Terry explained, "but Alex wants me to line up a Philly law firm which has international experience. You are the only one I know who might know what to do."

"Any idea what country or what part of the world? Is it Venezuela?" Brother Roderick was intrigued.

"Good question," Terry admitted. "I didn't assume Venezuela, but I couldn't tell you why. Let me email him and find out. I'll let you know. Meanwhile, can you help?"

"Sure. I know several lawyers who work for different firms. They all have experience negotiating with foreign countries. Let me know." He stuffed his mouth with pretzels. "Can we get back to watching hoops now?"

"Yeah. Let me buy you a beer," Terry joked. The keg was open to all.

"So generous," Brother Roderick remarked. They went in to watch basketball.

Alex reviewed the plan in his mind. He could think of many reasons why his plan would fail. He couldn't think of alternatives though. He smiled at the thought of how smart his daughters were. Jo had provided software that exceeded his request. He had imagined he would have to sneak a thumb drive into a USB port on Bautiste's computer. Jo's software, he was happy to learn, only required Bautiste's email address. This gave him confidence in at least one part of his plan.

While Erin slept, Alex had spent part of the afternoon finding and reserving adjoining hotel rooms at a medium-priced hotel in Porlamar. He was nervous about the credit card expense, but didn't feel as if he had a choice. While he fretted over his financial future, an email came in from his brother. It wasn't encrypted and Alex was a little nervous about that. The message was a request for more information, to name a specific country so the choice of a law firm would be easier to make. Alex wasn't ready to be specific, but he appreciated Terry's dilemma. He composed a response that specified the nation he had in mind and added that more details would follow.

Terry was enjoying the late afternoon college game so much that he had forgotten Alex's troubles for the moment. The small fraternity shared bonhomie in the way that men do. They all enjoyed the refreshments and the sports and the banter and joking. Terry's group was all over fifty. The younger brothers had their own gathering, he knew, with livelier banter and better joking.

Terry's Blackberry vibrated. It was only the second time that Sunday afternoon and he was glad to see that it was again Alex. He put off decrypting the email until the game was settled, not over, but settled. He went back to his room and read the email *en clair*. He thought he knew the proper law firm, but wanted to check with Brother Roderick first. It could wait, he felt, until Monday morning. He headed down to the refectory for dinner.

Erin awoke around five from her nap. She looked tired when she emerged into Elise's living room and found Alex on his laptop.

"Where's Elise?" she asked with puffy eyes.

"She went to pick up something for dinner," Alex said thinking that, despite puffy eyes, she looked beautiful.

"Great. I'm starving." Erin plopped down beside Alex and, with total lack of artifice, put her arm across his shoulders. "Whatcha doing?" she asked.

"Some emails," he answered, "and making some reservations." He glanced at her to see if she understood.

"For what?"

"Hotel rooms. You're not going back to your apartment except to pack." Erin was impressed with Alex's take-charge demeanor. She squeezed his shoulder.

"Ok, boss," she said. "You're moving too?" Alex nodded. "When do we move in?" She smiled into his face.

"I said 'rooms'," he pointed out smiling back, "but things can be rearranged."

When Elise returned with the ingredients for a chicken and pasta dinner, Alex did not waste time telling her of his plans for new living arrangements. He felt that she was safe enough where she was. Bautiste was not likely to come after her, he felt.

"All right," she said with little emotion. "Let's eat first. Alex, can you open the wine?" Alex thought that she was a fast adjuster.

After they had eaten and Alex had packed up his things, Elise drove them to Erin's apartment where she also packed up a few things. Elise delivered them to the hotel Alex had chosen and, with embraces and kisses, she left them alone to check in.

The hotel honored Alex's reservations, guaranteed by his credit card. The rooms were nice with an adjoining door. Erin was excited at the change and she joined Alex on the balcony in his room.

"Nice view," she said putting her hand on his forearm and stroking the hair.

"It's beautiful," Alex agreed. "It's so nice I can't believe all the shit that's happening. It seems like we're in a different world, temporarily."

"Don't, Alex," she said, "don't ruin it." He put his arm around her waist.

"Sorry, you're right. Look at that!" A shooting star moved from left to right out over the ocean and then another. He kissed her. He felt a small pain in his chest, like a brief muscle cramp. He wanted to say something to her, anything that would explain how he felt and still protect his heart from hurt. He had built a strong defense over the years since his Mary's death. Deep inside he knew he couldn't have it both ways.

He took her face in both of his hands and said, "I cherish you." He kissed her again. She smiled into his face. She understood what he meant and didn't have the words to say. She suspected that she knew why, but would give him time to work it out.

"Thank you," she said, "no one has ever told me that." She held him close. The world seemed far away.

Monday morning Brother Terrence Browning, on the recommendation of Brother Roderick, contacted Jim Davis, Esquire and a LaSalle alumnus.

"How can I help you, Brother Terrence?" The attorney leaned back in his tufted leather chair, pen and paper at the ready.

"Well, it's an unusual request," Terry admitted. "It's coming from my brother actually. Well, actually, there are three things." Terry felt that this wasn't going well and was relieved when Davis took control. Davis was used to clients rushing through their information.

"Why don't I ask some questions and you just answer them," the attorney suggested. "That work for you?" Terry agreed that it would help a lot.

"All right. You mentioned three needs. What's the first one?"

Brother Terrence explained Alex's first need.

"That's not a problem. Any law firm could handle that for you. You could probably even do that online."

"Well, there are certain conditions that complicate things," Terry said.

"Ok. What are they?" The lawyer listened as Terry explained.

"Not unusual and not a problem," Davis said taking notes. "As long as they're both over twenty-one and all U.S. laws are followed." Terry gave his assurances.

"Ok, that's one. What else?"

Terry described Alex's second need. Davis sat up in his chair.

"All right," he said, "that is an area where this firm excels. We can negotiate for you directly or you or your principal can participate. We have close contacts in any event. I'm confident an agreeable contract can be drawn up. Do you have any figures in mind?"

"I don't right now. But I can get back to you. Would that be all right?"

"That would be fine. No problem. What is the third, er, issue?"

"It's similar to the last one. We need you to recruit and contract with a specialized company." Brother Terry explained what Alex had in mind.

"I'll have to ask around to see who has that kind of expertise. It shouldn't be a problem. Anything else?" Davis asked.

"Well," Terry said hesitating, "there is the question of your fee."

"Can you give me a hundred dollar retainer?" Davis asked. He sensed that this was going to be a lucrative endeavor for the law firm.

That same morning Connie Browning was in her office going through correspondence. Samsung was interested in exploring an Android security analysis. Several white hat hackers/programmers had sent in suspected iOS vulnerabilities. These were, in Connie's experience, more imagined than real. She usually tracked them down though. There was another email from Alex and she was surprised that it was sent in the middle of the night. Alex was forwarding the calculations he had done and presented to Magrew. He wanted his daughter to confirm his numbers and also to consider the ramifications of becoming a significant member of the management team if Alex's numbers were correct.

Connie stuck out her lower lip, which was a habit of hers when she was making a major decision. She performed some Google searches and made a bunch of notes. She did the same weight-volume calculations that Alex had a few days ago and came to the same conclusions. Wow, she thought. She wasn't really convinced that Alex's basic premise was correct, that the chests existed, but.... She picked up her phone to call her sister. Instead the cell phone buzzed announcing a call from her uncle.

"Hey, Uncle Terry. How's it going?" she said.

"Great, Connie. Got a minute? Your wayward Dad is keeping me a little busy."

"Uh, oh," she said. "What's going on now? I just got an email from him." She explained about the silver versus gold and large box versus small box calculations. Brother Terry was taken aback by the figures.

"That's quite an amount," he said. "Think there's any possibility? I could use a new rosary," he joked. He trusted his niece's intelligence and instincts. Ever since she was a child, she had an ability to cut through the smoke and mirrors of life and to reduce a problem to its bare bones.

"I don't know, Uncle Terry," she said. "If it were anyone else but Dad I'd say no effing way. But you know how he is. Too logical and level to go chasing Disney dreams." Connie was comfortable being salty with her uncle. She knew he wouldn't be offended.

"Interesting," Terry said. "I agree, but then I thought he was too logical and, what did you call it, 'level-headed' to go down to Venezuela in the first place." Terry remembered his conversation with Alex before Alex left.

"So, what you're saying is that this is all based on a Facebook conversation? You do realize that's totally fucking nuts?" Terry had chided his brother.

"C'mon," Alex had said. "It's like I tried to explain. I just have a feeling that I screwed up the last fifteen years. I haven't been living. I've been existing. I'm old. I want to have one more chance to live."

"So take up big game hunting or Senior MMA, if there is such a thing. This makes no sense."

It was October 2012 in Philadelphia and Indian summer was in effect. The windows were open and a warm breeze was stirring Terry's sheer curtains.

"Well, regardless, I've decided. So, keep an eye on the girls and I'll stay in touch."

"'Level'. I said not 'level-headed', Connie corrected, "as in even-keeled, but, anyway, he is who he is. At the end of the day, we all love him. By the way, as a Dad, he was always kind of nuts. Did   you know?"

210

"No. What do you mean?"

"He was always arranging games. Either sports like bedroom basketball, video games or board games for Jo and me. There was always some sort of competition going on among us three." Terry could hear the fondness in her voice.

"All right," he said. "Shit. I almost forgot why I called. I got an email from your Dad too. He wanted me to get a lawyer to take care of some things." Terry explained what he had conveyed to Davis. "Any idea why?"

"None, but if there's a huge amount of money involved, it'd be smart to have a lawyer, and an accountant, and a tax guy, and a financial guy. Blah, blah, blah."

"Ok, ok. I get it," Terry protested. "And he'd like you to be on the money management team. Did you know?"

"He said that in his email, but I'm not sure what that means. I already have a company. He knows that. Why would I want to spend any time on pirate treasure?" The amusement in her voice was clear.

"I don't know, but let's all just stay loose. By the way, can you pay the hundred dollar retainer fee for the lawyer?" Terry said. "I have a vow of poverty." She laughed.

"You're full of it, Unc," she said. "Email me the contact info and I'll take care of it." They broke off their connection. Terry smiled to himself.

Alex was disoriented when he awoke in the hotel room. Before he even looked, he sensed Erin's presence in the bed. He wriggled toward where she had to be and made contact with her warm, soft body.

"Mmm," she murmured. "Good morning." She put her arm over him.

"Morning," he said. "Should I order coffee?"

"How long will it take to get here?" She snuggled closer.

"Thirty minutes," he answered. He lifted the receiver.

"Room 634," he said. "Yes. Can I get coffee for two and can you bring it in thirty minutes? Great." He hung up and rolled over to her.

Bautiste was in his office early on Monday. The news late Sunday had been of more civil unrest in the capitol. Even though Maduro was the de facto Chavez designee, a challenger had arisen to champion the opposition's cause. His name was Henry Capriles and he was gaining in popularity. Maduro was proving to be a weak and unimaginative leader who was embracing the status quo. The banks had reacted by instituting policies that were sure to lead to increased inflation. Spotty shortages of basic goods were still being reported.

"Is Garcia in yet?"

"No, sir," Sergeant Lopez answered. He knew that the Hammer had spent Sunday in Caracas, but didn't say anything. Garcia usually spent Saturday night visiting the whorehouses and nightclubs of Caracas. He routinely got drunk, got arrested, fought with the local police, spent the night and half the next day in jail, was released, had his record expunged, and returned to Porlamar. Law enforcement, the world over, took care of its own.

"All right. I want to see him as soon as he comes in."

Bautiste had a report in his hand that Alex had left Elise's house. Room 634 the report said. He had also taken Room 635. Technically, this was breaking the law. Alex, as a visitor, was responsible for notifying the authorities of any change of residence. The Colonel knew this was not a big

212

deal and that the law was rarely enforced. He felt that it gave him one more tool to use against Alex to convince the American to return to Miami.

Bautiste's sixth sense was warning him that he should move his assets and cash out of the country and retire. He had had a good run and had used his position to pad his various bank accounts. Now it felt like time to move on. With Chavez, his most powerful ally, gone, he felt that his overall position was weakened. He should probably send the American with one more suitcase and then go.

He walked over to his large office globe. He allowed himself the luxury of imagining where he would go. He spun the orb and stopped it on Thailand. He thought this was a possibility. The Thais were tolerant of all kinds of activities that other countries considered deviant behavior. Bautiste smiled and he salivated, mildly, at the imagined opportunities.

Elise drove to work on Monday morning, in spite of her tough weekend. Once in her office, though, she couldn't concentrate on anything productive. That was unusual. In Alex's absence, the house and her bed had seemed unaccustomedly empty. She was not at all jealous of Erin. That was an emotion as alien to her as it would be to one of the birds flying from branch to branch outside her window. She was disturbed by the thought that an opportunity to gain monetarily had slipped away. Alex and the black man had, she was sure, been up to something, something that they had considered worthy of concealing from others. She should talk to the black man, what was he called? Magrew. That was it. She was sure she could entice him to talk about what he and Alex had been doing. She resolved to have a Monday lunch at his café though she had never been there before.

The Hammer appeared at work around ten o'clock. He had recovered well from his recent debauchery. Sergeant Lopez sent him in.

"Good day," the boss said. "Coffee?"

"Sure. Thanks. What's going on?"

"The American has moved, with Rosen, to," and he named the hotel. "Rooms 634 and 635. It's costing him almost six hundred dollars a night. He's paying with his MasterCard. Doesn't that seem extravagant for someone recently retired?"

"Yes. He doesn't have the resources to pay that much. He's going to have a pretty big debt pretty fast." Sergeant Garcia sipped his coffee and smacked his lips in appreciation. Garcia waited for the Colonel to speak.

"I'm beginning to wonder if there is a resource, real or imagined, that we don't know about. The black man, what do we know about him?"

"Not much," Garcia said. He recited from memory: "Came here in the early Eighties from the US, worked the oil fields, lost his arm at work, used his settlement to buy his restaurant. He lives a quiet life with his wife, a Guaquieri descendant. He naturalized in 1994 or '95, I think. Why? What are you thinking?"

Bautiste wasn't going to tell Garcia what he was thinking. "I'm thinking that we need to know more. Put someone on it. Also, I'm thinking I want you to visit Room 634. I want that American to agree to go to Miami."

"All right. I'll take care of it." The Hammer was not deceived into thinking that his boss considered the fat black man of no consequence. In fact, it was the Colonel's lack of interest in the restaurant owner that convinced Garcia that his boss considered the one-armed man important. "Anything else?"

214

"No. That's it. Just get it moving today." The Colonel returned to his reports.

Alex and Erin went out shopping after breakfast. Erin decided she needed a few things and Alex decided that, after committing to run up the room expenses on his card, what harm could a little shopping do? Besides, at Erin's urging, he had cancelled Room 635 after paying for one night. If his plan worked, he and Erin would have no money worries for a long time. And, if it didn't, he could always come out of retirement. In his mind he wondered at his new cavalier financial attitude.

"What are we after?" he asked after they had arrived at the mall. He wouldn't have been able to explain why, but he thought it was logical that Erin would have at least a mental shopping list.

"Not sure, exactly. I'll know when I see what I need," she said happily, glad that Alex had offered to pay.

"Ok," Alex said not quite as happily. "So, shoes? Makeup? Underwear? What?" Erin laughed.

"Let's just enjoy ourselves," she said brightly. Alex sighed dramatically.

"If you don't have a list," he asked, "how will you know when we're done?" He shrugged his shoulders, palms up.

"We're done when we get hungry for lunch," she announced. She led on, window-shopping as they went.

Three hours and several hundred dollars later Alex was extremely tired of shopping and had an aching back. Erin had teased him good-naturedly and, for his part, he was glad to see her in good spirits, but grumped around to play the part.   To Alex, she seemed to have rebounded marvelously from her ordeal of Saturday night.   He really hadn't been sure how strong or resilient she was, but now he knew she had depths of strength, reserves, which he could only imagine.   She's not like anyone I've ever met, Alex thought and, he hardly needed to remind himself, she's smoking hot.

"So," he said, "are we hungry for lunch yet?"   Erin smiled at him.   Alex had told Erin everything about Mary, in life and in death, so Erin was now very comfortable talking about her.

"Wow, Mary trained you well!   There's so little left for me to do.   Maybe just some smoothing around the edges." Alex feigned surprise.

"Not perfect, huh?   I thought I was," he let the thought trail off.

"Perfect?   No, honey, but soooo close.   Maybe if you were ten or fifteen years younger?"

"Ouch," he said.   "Hey, your time'll come.   Nobody's getting younger."

"Just kidding," she laughed.   "Don't be so touchy.   So what do you feel like for lunch?   Not that I'm trying to change the subject."

"I don't know, as long as the beer is cold.   I need anesthetizing."

"Big word for somebody who wants to be buzzed," she joked.   "How about sandwiches?   Cold food and cold beer?   Sound good?"

Alex agreed that it did and they found a small shop where the sandwiches were huge and delicious and the beer was, indeed, cold.

As he munched, Alex asked, "Did you notice anything weird while we were shopping?" And before Erin could answer, he corrected himself, "I mean while you were shopping and I was suffering."

"Funny," she smirked. "Weird how? I don't think I did. What was it?"

"No tissues to be found anywhere. And no two-ply toilet paper." She laughed so hard she started to cough. She took a drink of beer.

"Really? No, I didn't notice. How did you notice that? The hotel will take care of our paper needs," she teased.

"I don't know." Alex had seen the television news reports. "I notice stuff sometimes. I lost focus on what you were doing sometime during the fourth pair of shoes." She reached over and punched his arm.

After they headed back to their hotel, they were shocked to find an unwelcome visitor in Room 634. Sergeant Garcia flashed his badge, but when he spoke Erin recognized his voice, the leader of her attackers from Saturday night. Although her heart was pounding in near panic, she didn't let on that she knew.

"So the police in Venezuela can enter a residence without a search warrant?" Alex asked, peeved. "Congratulations. Must make your job easier."

The Hammer wasn't sure how to respond and, when he was not sure, he relied on his orders.

"My boss wants you to make another trip to Miami. You should agree and there will be no more trouble either for you or for your friend." He nodded toward Erin.

"Ok," Alex said shrugging. "I'll do it." Garcia hadn't expected this reaction and he had to take a minute to

217

consider his next move. While he was considering, Alex went on, "Give me your boss's email address and I'll make it official."

Garcia pulled a notepad from his pocket and made a notation. He tore the paper from the notebook and passed it to Alex.

"Send it there and he will know that you are willing. You have made a wise decision. The National Police will pay your hotel bill." Bautiste had ordered this bit of gratuity as an additional enticement.

"Great. Thank you very much. I'll email Bautiste tonight. By the way, do you have a business card? I'll copy you on the email just so you know I did it." Garcia got up, handed over a cheap card, shook Alex's hand, was going to do the same to Erin, but her frosty body language discouraged him. He nodded in her direction and left the hotel room.

"Alex, that was one of the guys from Saturday," Erin announced as soon as the Hammer had left.

"That's one big dude," Alex said, "and mean looking. Well, his boss and he are going to be in for one fucking surprise."

"What do you mean?"

"My daughter, Jo, gave me a virus. I'm going to email it to those assholes."

CHAPTER TEN—Big Data

Jo Browning, working out of her apartment that Tuesday morning, was thinking of her Dad. Sipping her third coffee, she was a little worried. She wore sweatpants and a T-shirt that read, "I'm on Welfare. You need 2 Work Harder." She was worried about her father's use of the virus she had emailed. She had every confidence in the exploit itself, but was unsure that he would use it, as she would have. It was a simple program, in fact two programs. They were built on a framework that implemented a hack to take advantage of certain operating system vulnerabilities. The first program gathered information about the target system such as the operating system and it's version. If the operating system was identified as iOS, the program aborted and erased itself. Unfortunately, even with Connie's help attacking iOS, Jo was unable to identify an iOS opening.

If the target operating system was identified as Linux, Android or Windows, Jo's software then determined the operating system's version. Next, it gathered information on the system's installed network services. It passed this data on to the second part of the program, which actually took advantage of another vulnerability by secretly installing a payload, or program, which performed the desired function.

Linux, Android and Windows developers were under constant schedule pressure to add features to their systems. These features often left security holes that hackers could exploit. Third parties performed penetration tests or pentests to find the holes, but it was an upstream swim.

Jo's worry about Alex was specifically based on an event that happened a year ago. A penetration had occurred at a client and when the hack had happened the client had had no idea what had taken place. The intrusion was not detected in a timely fashion and customer usernames and passwords were slurped up. Jo had been mortified at the data loss, but had been able to identify the hacker, a Central European teen who was ambitious beyond his skill level. She notified the authorities, both foreign and domestic, and hoped the jerk would be prosecuted.

Alex had sent the email to Bautiste and Garcia the night before and now had to wait for the program to copy the target data. He was working at a beach cafe with free Wi-Fi, but was using encryption. According to Jo the data flow should begin immediately, if there were no problems. The payload (Jo had called it that) executed as soon as the emails were opened. Alex was staring at his laptop waiting for something to happen. Just then an email arrived. The sender was "348922Hzyfr88" with no Subject. Alex wrinkled his brow. He was using Outlook's preview pane and saw that the body of the message was one word: Incoming.

Colonel Bautiste read Alex's email with satisfaction. The American agreed to go to Miami again. The police officer leaned back in his chair and smiled. He started to calculate how much he would profit from the trip. He could afford to pay the American ten thousand for muling the cocaine. But he wouldn't. The man had shown himself to be weak, so he wouldn't even get the promised five thousand. Bautiste, of course, didn't notice the LED flickering furiously over the Ethernet port on the back of his computer case.

Sergeant Garcia was wary of computers and rarely used his for anything more than official correspondence. He dutifully printed out each email and placed it in a manila folder whose tab was labeled with the classification of the contents. The irony that software icons representing manila folders were available was lost on the Hammer. Garcia opened Alex's email, read it, printed it, and filed it away.

Alex watched with fascination as the directory he had assigned to Jo's software began to fill up. Folders were created and, then, subfolders. Directories filled up the folders. Alex opened and read a couple of files, which were email messages. One was to Chavez, *El Comandante*, himself and seemed to reflect a close relationship. Alex read a couple more and then just watched as the data flowed in.

Jo Browning was having a hard time concentrating. She called her friend, Paul Tanner, just to pass the time. Jo had met Tanner at her gym. He had become her workout/hangout buddy. She thought he was good-looking in a rough sort of way. He was an ex-Navy Seal and had a fanatic devotion to his physical conditioning, which was important for his choice of civilian career, providing physical security for wealthy clients. For his part, he found Jo attractive and admired her professionalism and her computer knowledge. He had no illusions that the future of any security industry would be more and more reliant on technology. He was a full partner in his security firm, Ram Industries, with three of his Seal buddies. They had pooled their funds two years ago and leased office space. Curiously enough, their first three clients were NFL players. Tanner and his friends didn't expect that NFL guys would need protection, but despite the players' intimidating appearances, big muscles and crazy tattoos, they turned out to be not that tough. Ram Industries provided the athletes with bodyguard services and security analyses of each one's domicile. Ram wasn't yet capable of providing the services that home alarm companies could provide, but they expected to be able to expand next year into those activities. For now, the players' word of mouth advertising was working out well.

"Hey, Jaybee," Tanner said answering his phone with his nickname for Jo, "what's up?" Jo smiled at his accessibility. She liked that about him. She knew that he was attracted to her, but he hadn't done anything about it yet.

"Hunk!" she said using her nickname for him. She had told him, half seriously, that even his face had muscles. "Got a minute? Nothing special. Just want to talk."

Tanner was updating computer records. As the only college graduate on the management team, he had volunteered to keep the business side of the business straight. Basically, he didn't trust his partners to do the job correctly yet. They were all enrolled in college and were serious students. They just needed more training, Tanner thought. He was glad for the distraction of Jo's call.

"Sure. I've got all the minutes you need. What's going on? Have you heard from your Dad?" Tanner had met Alex a couple of times and they got along well. He liked Browning's straightforward manner. He also liked the father's relationship with his daughter. Alex and Jo were obviously close.

"Yeah. He launched the payload last night. Assuming the targets open the emails no later than this morning, scooping data should be ongoing right now."

"But you're worried. Massaging your eyebrow?" Tanner had grown to learn Jo's mannerisms. Her nervous tic was rubbing an eyebrow with a fingertip.

"A little," she admitted removing her hand from her face. "Ok. A lot. I think my Dad may be in over his head. You know how you always tell me that the most dangerous situation is the one where you feel like you're in control? My Dad isn't, what, equipped for this Spy vs. Spy bullshit."

Alex, in keeping with his younger daughter's assessment, was feeling anything but in control. The data kept flowing and being stored. There was so much that Alex was overwhelmed. He checked the folder where Sergeant Garcia's data was being stored. It was filling up at half the rate of Bautiste's. Alex read a couple of the files/emails. He knew nothing of what the movies called "tradecraft", the stuff that spies used to conceal information from enemies, but Garcia's messages were pretty open employing no "tradecraft". The one that Alex was currently reading referred to bank deposits and balances. Alex was astonished at the amounts. "Holy shit," he thought to himself. "This clown has over a mil in the bank." Alex's mind now spun up to what his daughter called that "Spy vs. Spy bullshit." He realized he didn't have the skills to do what he wanted to do so the next step was to reconnect with Jo who did have the skills.

Erin was in their hotel room after returning from an afternoon spent poolside at the hotel. She loved living near the ocean, but was not a big fan of swimming there. Pool water suited her better. While she was blowing her long, blonde hair dry, she was thinking about Alex. His age was not a problem to her, but she had a sense that he was concerned about it. There was over a thirty-year difference after all. His body wasn't bad she thought. He could use a little toning and lose a few pounds, but, unless you were twenty-something, who couldn't? She, as a logical person, was tempted to make a pro/con list, but, as an intelligent person, knew this was just a sales gimmick which anyone could rig, consciously or unconsciously. She smiled to herself. She knew that she had already made up her mind. Alex was a "keeper."

Alex was still at the beach cafe, hunched over his laptop, composing another email request for his daughter Jo. He described the software capability he wanted and admitted that he didn't have all the information he needed, yet. To get that information he had to draft another email to his brother. He sent both and closed his laptop. Then he had a thought. He reopened the laptop and navigated to the top folder where Bautiste's email copies resided. He did a quick search and found what he wanted, Bautiste's account correspondences. There were more than twenty references and he would need Jo's help to proceed further here also. He reasoned that if

223

the Sergeant had a million deposited, how much more would a Colonel have?

Brother Terrence read Alex's email. Today he was not annoyed with his brother, but felt a deep affection for him. Although Alex's emails hadn't explicitly stated what his plans were, Terry was able to piece together a broad picture. He picked up the phone and, for the second time, he called Jim Davis.

"Hey, Brother," Davis said with good humor, "you're working me hard."

"Did you get the hundred, Jim?" He had assumed that Connie had taken care of it.

"No idea," Davis admitted. "Can you hold on a second?" Terry could hear him calling out to someone.

"Caroline Browning the one?"

"Yes, Connie. She's my niece."

"Well she transferred the retainer so we're officially and legally a team. I drew it up so that we represent the new corporation. What can I do for you now?"

Terry explained what Alex needed. "Let me see," Davis said. His tone was distracted as Terry assumed he was looking through his computer. "Got it," he announced. "Got a pen?"

"Ready," Terry said after a brief pause. The lawyer read off the information.

"All right," Terry said, "that should do it. Anything else I can forward on?"

"A Florida firm has been identified and contacted. They're not the biggest or best, according to your instructions, but they are legitimate and competent. We're waiting for them to respond to our offer."

"Ok. I'll pass that on to my brother. Thanks, Jim. I'll have my nieces put some money in the corporate account so you can bill the Browning Group for your hours. That work for you?" The lawyer agreed that it would and they ended their conversation.

Jo Browning received her father's second email, decrypted it, and immediately got to work gathering the software that was needed. Alex's requirements were really different from his first request. He needed something that would not only gather up the data, but also transfer it to a new home. She had to admit that her Dad was a lot more interesting since he made his trip to Venezuela.

When she had the software assembled, she decided that she needed to test it. This would need the help of her sister. She called Connie and briefed her on what Alex was trying to do.

"Probably best to use my corporate account. It has the strongest protections. It'd be the best test, if you can guarantee no losses, Sis. It's a corporation, after all."

"Connie, if I could make a guarantee, I wouldn't have to do the test," Jo pointed out. "How about if I promise to cover any losses? That work for you?"

"That'll be fine, but I couldn't let my little Sis pay everything. How about if I pay half?"

"You're the best big sister ever!" Jo said with mock sincerity. "Really though," Jo said, "I'm confident. So half of zero is zero. No worries for you." They laughed together.

"Ok. When do you want to run the test?"

"No rush," Jo said. "Dad doesn't seem like he's ready yet. I'll let you know. Talk to you later?"

"You got it. Keep me posted."

Terry Browning left a voicemail for his nieces to, please, deposit several thousand dollars in the corporate account. He then sent an encrypted email to Alex identifying the Florida firm Jim Davis had found. His email also identified the corporate account the lawyer had set up for the Browning Group. All of the Brownings had deposit and withdrawal access to the account. So did lawyer Davis as minor partner and legal counsel.

Alex didn't find the information he wanted among Bautiste's correspondences, but he did find a key piece. He wrapped up his time at the cafe and headed back to the hotel. Once there he found that Erin professed to be "starving" and was "dying" to go out to eat. They decided to dress and go down to the hotel restaurant. Erin wore a grey dress that had a deep vee-cut front. It would have been a hit on a Hollywood red carpet. Alex couldn't keep his eyes off the half-moons of her exposed breasts. For her part, she was well aware of the effect she was having on him and, apparently, on the rest of the male patrons of the restaurant. They ordered dinner and Erin consumed an impressive quantity of tenderloin tips, mushroom caps and garlic mashed potatoes followed by a New York cheesecake slice.

After dinner they walked around the hotel and pool grounds and enjoyed each other's company. When they returned to their room Alex had one thing on his mind. However, Erin had a voicemail on her phone that turned out to be a mood killer for Alex. It was an invitation from her reporter friends, Ramon and Julia. They had, obviously, learned of Alex's break from Elise and subsequent attachment to Erin. The invitation was to join the reporter's on a trip to a fishing village in the northwest corner of Margarita Island. Erin was excited about the prospect, but was concerned that she was feeling the effects of the champagne they had had with dinner. She was also concerned that Alex might want to just spend time with her alone. She had certainly felt that vibration over dinner.

"Do you want to go?" she asked Alex as casually as she could. Alex was learning that one of the great joys of retirement was the ability to be absolutely spontaneous.

"Sure, if you want to. I haven't seen that part of the island."

"I'll text them 'Yes' and find out what time." Alex was happy because she seemed happy.

The next morning, Ramon and Julia met Alex and Erin in the lobby of the hotel. They greeted each other and then piled in to Ramon's 2003 Toyota RAV4. They headed northwest out of Porlamar.

Margarita Island was really two islands joined by a narrow isthmus. The western, arid side was largely unpopulated and undeveloped except for some fishing villages peopled by descendants of the Guaiqueria Indians who dwelt on Margarita before Columbus visited it. As they drove along a two-lane highway, Ramon and Julia explained that they were working on a story based on rumors that the Caribbean coastal areas of Nueva Esparta had, in the last five years, become a sort of crossroads for the international human smuggling trade.

"Are you talking about illegal immigration or slave trade?" Alex asked.

"Right now," Ramon said, "that's what we're trying to find out."

Alex settled back in his seat and was struck by the fact that the scenery reminded him of drives in the desert outside of Phoenix,

227

Arizona: cactus and rock.

The fishing village had a name that Alex missed. When the quartet arrived, a family of villagers - a man named Luis, his wife and another woman, and four children, three boys and a girl ranging in age from early teens to the six year old girl - were stretching fishing nets to dry after the morning catch. Ramon explained that it was a custom for these fishing villages to accept outside help with the nets in exchange for a few fish. The quartet, following Ramon's lead, pitched in with the stretching. They were, however, reluctant to accept any fish.

The family insisted, however, so the fish, wrapped in newspaper, were accepted. Alex and Erin had had a large thermos of coffee prepared by the hotel and they offered it around to the fisherman and his family. The fisherman's wife produced cups. She had some bread to offer. A fire was lit and, after a pan was oiled and fish were fried, they enjoyed a wonderful breakfast on the beach while the fisherman, Luis, who wore only board shorts and sported a ponytail, described the various boats and their functions to Ramon and Julia. Ramon translated the patois for Alex.

There were fishing boats from which the nets were spread. There were large refrigerated company boats, which purchased the fish from the fishermen and then sold the catch to the restaurants and hotels. Representing the oil industry, there were barge-type slurry boats both single hull and catamarans. These collected slurry or drilling mud from the slurry pits around oil wells and dumped the slurry out in the ocean. This was the kind of boat, Alex knew, that Mac occasionally captained. The slurry, when dumped, settled harmlessly on the ocean bottom to mix with the existing sand and silt. There were many kinds of pleasure boats shiny and white, cruise liners further out, the ones that never came to Margarita, and fast cigarette-type boats typically used by smugglers of different things including drugs.

Ramon asked Luis if any of the boats were used for human trafficking. Luis shrugged almost imperceptibly. He

228

tipped his chin toward a large pleasure boat traveling slowly parallel to the beach.

"Like that one?" Ramon asked indicating the yacht. Luis nodded once, clearly knowledgeable, but also uncomfortable with the subject matter. Alex suspected that Luis might have supplemented his fishing income now and then.

"Do you know about the *Little Ranger*?" Erin asked changing the subject.

"Why not? Of course," Luis answered.

Erin asked if the fisherman believed there was treasure on the ship. Luis appeared to consider carefully. Then he answered that, in his experience, money, illegal and legal, had always found its way to Margarita Island. The quartet took leave after breakfast and headed back toward the east and Juangriego.

Wednesday morning for Connie Browning was normal. She worked out on her exercise bike, did three sets of push-ups and sit-ups, and ran on her treadmill for thirty minutes. She showered and then, toweling off, admired her body. She was holding on to her figure fairly easily and was glad for her good fortune.

Later, when she went through her emails, she found the one from her uncle asking that his nieces deposit no less than seven thousand dollars in the account for the newly formed corporation. Connie, whose business was flourishing, sent an email to her sister that she would cover the deposit and pay any future attorney's fees.

After sightseeing around Juangriego and viewing the French activity around the *Little Ranger*, Alex and the group found an upscale grocer. They had decided to buy some

229

beef filets, a treat on any Caribbean island and outrageously expensive, and take them back to Luis and his family. In this way they would repay the villagers for their kindness. The grocer sealed the meat in butcher's paper and wrapped this with taped plastic bags packed in ice. The group headed back to the village. Luis and his two oldest sons were tending to their boat. Nearby on the beach were discarded fragments of old fishing nets. Alex put the sealed meat in a fragment of net and had Ramon, with a straight face, call for help in hauling the net up the beach. Luis good-humoredly played along with the gag while his sons looked on in confusion. Ramon explained that they insisted that the fisherman and his family share in the bounty. When the meat was unwrapped, there was a lot of oohing and aahing at the sight. Again the pan was oiled and the fire fed. Bread was produced as well as a salad of local vegetation that turned out to be peppery and sweet. After enjoying a second delicious meal prepared and eaten on the beach, they headed back to Porlamar, again crossing the isthmus and then swinging south to take the leisurely coast road. Ramon and Julia were curious about Alex's background. He attributed this to the inquisitiveness of people in their profession, but answered all their questions.

Bautiste was distracted that afternoon. The reports of unrest appeared to be limited to the capitol. However, the incidents were becoming more frequent and more violent. If he hadn't been distracted, he may have attached more significance to his tech support Sergeant.

"*Mi Colonel*," Sergeant Lopez had asked, "have you been backing up your email?" The Sergeant had noticed a large transfer of data captured by the server logs.

"Maybe," Bautiste had answered. He was studying reports. "It's automatic, isn't it?" Bautiste had asked.

"Yes." the Sergeant agreed. "I have set it up that way. But everyone can create an archive at any time."

Bautiste had already checked out of the conversation.

"All right," he said dismissing the Sergeant to go about his duties that apparently, to the Sergeant, included consuming large amounts of soda and candy.

Alex was asked how he and Elise had met. He explained how he had an advanced degree in teaching English and how Elise was a student. He said that he was married at the time, but was definitely attracted to the young Venezuelan. He supposed that she was attracted too. He told how nothing happened, but that, for him, the memory was always an interesting part of his past. He described how he had moved on, had a couple of daughters, and got out of the English teaching business. He told them how he had earned a third degree, a Bachelor of Science in Computer Science. He guessed that he saw the future and the future was computers and the software that ran them. He said that software made sense to him from his very first exposure. I = i + 1, while, if not lunacy, certainly heresy to mathematicians, made eminent sense and was clearly the power of computing: being able to change values in midstream. A move to the U.S. defense industry completed the career transformation. The death of his wife, the graduation of his daughters, also in Computer Science, and acquiring good paying jobs, retirement, and that brought them all up to date.

They asked how he was adjusting to Venezuela and life in a foreign country. He opined that measuring the character of a nation by those you met in your own country was skewed. People who travel were not representative of those remaining at home. People who travel had open minds and were more likely to be open culturally. They changed the subject.

"Mr. Jim Davis, please." Connie was intent on executing her part of Alex's plan, which meant getting money into the account so that their legal counsel could be paid. As a business owner, she was familiar with lawyers and their value. They were similar to mountain guides. You hired them to show you the safest way to your goal. They might even cook your dinner on the way to the top.

"This is Jim Davis."

"Mr. Davis, this is Caroline Browning," Connie said using her full name. "You've been speaking to my uncle, Brother Terrence Browning, about our company, the Browning Group."

"Yes, Ms. Browning. Actually, I filed the papers for the corporation. What can I do for you?"

"Well, it's something that I can do for you. I have a check that I'd like to leave with you, kind of an escrow against your services. Obviously, my uncle doesn't have the resources to retain your firm, so I'll put up the funds."

"Do you want to drop off the check personally? We probably should meet anyway."

"That's what I had in mind. When's a good time for you? My schedule's kind of flexible."

"Can you come over this afternoon? I have a ton of paperwork I'm trying to clear so I'm going to be here for quite a while. Say around five o' clock?"

"See you then."

The conversation during the rest of the trip back to Porlamar centered on Bautiste. Alex was fascinated to learn that Julia had been investigating the reign of the top law enforcement officer. Rumors had been flying linking Colonel Bautiste to several illegal activities.

"His connection to a bunch of shady characters, including Magrew," Julia pointed out, "makes him even more suspicious."

"What's the matter with Magrew?" Alex asked, guessing that he already knew the answer.

"He's a wanted felon back in the U.S." Julia answered. "I never looked into what he did, but I bet it wouldn't be hard to find out."

"What about Bautiste? How hard has that been?"

Julia explained her frustrations. She hadn't been able to find anything solid just the afore-mentioned rumors and innuendoes.

"So I was assigned to help the young reporter," Ramon interjected with a smile. "And how did that go?" he asked rhetorically. "Not good. I found what Julia found." He went on to say that Bautiste was living well. Alex had seen that for himself the night of the welcoming party. Julia added, as Ramon drove, that Bautiste was living more than well, he was living way beyond his means. He had expensive cars and a boat that would have put a sizable dent in a multi-millionaire's fortune. The cars and boat, as well as the reporters could determine, were paid for, but the Colonel was apparently learning that there were massive expenses associated with maintaining a certain lifestyle. Bautiste had put out the story that he benefitted from investments and an inheritance, but Julia said, she and Ramon hadn't been able to substantiate any of that.

Julia went on to say that the oddest thing the two reporters had observed about Bautiste was the lawman's early obsession with the *Little Ranger* and the ship's alleged treasure. Ever since the wreck was exposed six years ago and linked to the journal, Bautiste's fingerprints were on every activity associated with it. Either he or one of his men supervised everything from approving who could approach the wreck site to managing the release of information to the

233

press. Julia reiterated what everyone knew: Bautiste was responsible for hiring Dr. Vitorino Braga and bringing him to the island. It was only after Braga and his team definitively determined that there was no treasure around the *Little Ranger* that Bautiste appeared to lose interest in the wreck and recommended turning it over to the French.

Connie arrived at the law firm a few minutes early. She was wearing a skirt and blouse that showed off her figure. She wore low heels.

The building was a nice downtown Philadelphia address. Connie had been at this high rise before and had no trouble locating the law offices. She announced herself to the receptionist and was asked to have a seat.

The receptionist, Sarah, alerted Jim Davis that his five o'clock had arrived and was discreetly described as a "ten". Sarah and Davis had a longtime friendship filled with joking and bantering and teasing about each other's imagined love lives. So when Jim came out to meet Connie, he wasn't sure what to expect: a beauty or a troll?

Davis was caught off guard when he first spotted Connie sitting in the reception area. A nice display of leg and draping blond hair as the young woman studied her cell phone.

"Ms. Browning?" he said as he arrived and stood in front of her. She looked up and he lost the thought he was about to express. Connie's slanted blue eyes were unfocussed when she looked into his. She looked back down at her phone, pushed a button, and started to rise extending her hand. At full height, Davis found her even with him and completely captivating. He took her hand and, instead of shaking it, which he had planned to do, lightly squeezed it in an awkwardly intimate gesture. Connie, well aware of the effect she was having, was amused.

"How are you?" she said. She had a deep, throaty voice Davis noticed.

"Well. I'm well," he answered and thought to himself 'Christ. Get a grip.'

Sarah, the receptionist, came to his rescue, although inside she was howling with laughter.

"Will you need the conference room, Mr. Davis?" she said. That brought the lawyer back to business.

"No, no. Thanks. My office will be fine. Ok with you, Ms. Browning?" He had dropped her hand after an awkward beat.

"Sounds fine," Connie said. "I shouldn't need much of your time."

Davis avoided looking into her face and found that this made it easier for him to achieve full lawyer mode.

"It's this way," he indicated that she should precede him, "just to the right." Connie entered a hall of glass walls.

"Third door on the left," Davis directed. His view of Connie's back did not disappoint. She entered the door he had indicated. It was an office that could have belonged to any midlevel member of any profession. Windows looked out on Broad Street and regulated air circulated with a low hum.

"Have a seat," he said gesturing toward a chair that was one of a pair facing his desk. "Can I offer you something?"

"No, thanks. I'm fine." The offer, though, made Connie realize that she had skipped lunch again. To her embarrassment, her stomach growled so loudly that she was sure that Davis must have heard it. He gave no indication that he had.

"Ok," he said leaning back casually, but studying the papers on his desk. He was still avoiding looking at her. "So you want to set up a kind of escrow account against our service billing, right?"

"That's right. My thinking is that, with my father out of the country and my uncle limited in his ability to pay, I should make it convenient for your firm to get paid in a timely manner." She tried to make eye contact, but every time he allowed his eyes to meet hers, he glanced away. She thought he might be shy. She had noticed that he wasn't wearing a wedding ring.

"That's really considerate. I must say that there aren't a lot of clients who're concerned that their attorneys get paid. In my experience," he added. "That's nice of you." This time he looked her in the eyes wanting to show that he was being totally sincere. There were those blue eyes gazing coolly back at him.

"You're welcome," Connie said. "As a business owner, I appreciate being paid promptly."

"Oh. What kind of business do you own?"

"Software security," she said. "Give me your cell number and I'll text you my web address." He gave her the number and she typed the address.

"Say," she said, "I'm starving and I haven't eaten downtown in ages. Can you recommend a place nearby?"

"I can do better than that," he said confident now. "I'll guide you to it if you don't mind."

"That would be great, but are you sure? It's not too much trouble? I thought you had a lot to do." She was annoyed at herself for trying to talk a nice-looking, eligible man out of having dinner with her. He just laughed.

"Well, I can't be gone for hours or get shit-faced drunk, but I can slip out for an hour or so." She laughed from her belly at his frankness. He liked her laugh and smiled his most genuine smile.

"Let's do it," she said enthusiastically rising from the chair. He signed out at the receptionist's desk even though Sarah had already left for the day.

"So call me 'Jim'," he said as he led her to the elevator.

"Connie," she said laying her hand on his shoulder. Muscles, she thought to herself as they rode to the street level.

"What kind of food are you in the mood for, Connie? We've kind of got a large choice within a two block radius," he said as they arrived on the sidewalk. "Or I can drive us somewhere." They were both aware of the man-woman tension between them.

"Nothing bland," she answered. "I want something with a little kick tonight." She gazed at him levelly. He liked that.

"How about Szechuan then? A little spicy and filling if you order right."

"Lead on," Connie said gesturing openly to the world around them. Connie pulled out her phone and followed Davis' lead.

Jo Browning and Paul Tanner had arranged to get together for a drink after work. Since they both owned their businesses, "after work" was indeterminate. By unspoken agreement, they met at 5:30 even though each thought of this as only a break. Their favorite spot was on Broad Street downtown, a little place called Lippy's. Lippy's served alcoholic and non-alcoholic drinks and so was popular with the young, health conscious clientele that was rapidly becoming a majority to downtown Philadelphia businesses.

Sam Lipynski owned Lippy's. He was the Jewish American son of an Auschwitz survivor. He was a tolerant

237

man and a loyal friend to Jo and Connie. He treated them as if they were his own daughters and he was paternalistically suspicious of Paul Tanner. For his part, Tanner was amused at Lipynski's protective attitude toward Jo and her sister. He liked the old man.

"Jo-Jo," Lipynski called out when he spotted the couple. It was his pet nickname for her. "Come let me look at you. You don't eat enough. Let me fix you something."

"I'm fine, Sam," Jo said. "How about a quiet table and some white tea? Can we have that? Slow in here tonight, huh?" The bar and grill was located on the first floor of a brick and mortar six story building. It was narrow, but deep and the tables were spaced nicely around the open area. The bar itself lined the left side of the room. The simple kitchen was in the back. The proprietor signaled for a member of the wait staff to approach and mumbled several words. He then departed.

The young waitress, a girl named Jenny, took their tea orders, recommended the scones, took scone orders, and walked away. Jo felt her phone vibrate. She pulled it out. Jo and Paul had a rule: no business when they were in "down time" together. Paul cleared his throat and, when Jo looked at him, he raised his eyebrows.

"It's Connie," Jo said by way of explanation holding up her phone. "She's going out to eat with someone. Wow! Can you believe it?" Jo texted Connie that she was having tea with the "Hunk", their nickname for Paul Tanner.

Shortly, Connie texted back.

"Connie wants us to join her and her new friend at Szechuan's. What do you think? We can still have tea. And fortune cookies." Tanner was happy to be anywhere with Jo, but he wouldn't let her know that.

"Sounds like she needs us to check out this new guy. What do you think?" He smiled and rolled his bulging shoulders.

"I think we should get some fortune cookies," Jo said. "Sam will understand." She got up and went looking for Jenny to cancel their order and tip their server ten dollars for her trouble. Jo had learned from her Dad that a show of appreciation for those who worked hard to bring a little extra service to their customers was, in turn, genuinely appreciated. She returned to Paul.

"Ok. Let's go." Paul got up and trailed her out of the little restaurant. The March evening was cool.

"Warm enough?" he asked Jo. He had a leather jacket, but all she had was a knitted, belted cardigan.

"I'm good," she said as she wrapped her arm under his and leaned in close. "Let's go see what Connie's up to."

Jim Davis led Connie to Szechuan's and they entered to a delicious smell of food being prepared.

"A table for two," Jim said to the Asian maître D. The man reached for menus when Connie interrupted.

"Can you make that for four?" she said. Jim looked at her.

"What's up?"

"My sister texted earlier and she wants to join us. She's with a friend. Is that ok?" Connie turned up the wattage of her blue eyes.

"Sure," Davis said overwhelmed by the wattage. "No problem."

The distance from Lippy's to Szechuan's was only three blocks. Jo and Paul didn't talk much as they covered the distance. Jo was thinking of how safe Paul made her feel even though they were walking the rough streets of a major

239

American city. It was just then that she felt the tug on her purse strap and, instinctively, let go of Paul's arm to secure the bag. It all happened so fast that Jo now understood how eyewitnesses got confused. She had the impression of a young black male slicing the bag strap from her shoulder and was impressed by the finesse and the sneakers. Her next impression was of a brown leather flash as Paul reacted. Jo just remembered thinking that he was incredibly quick. He caught the robber before the thief had gone three steps. Jo could picture later that Paul's left hand had gripped the youth around the neck area and his right hand had grabbed a fistful of jean material. Then Paul had upended the young man and slammed him to the sidewalk where he lay still. Before retrieving Jo's purse and their assailant's knife, Paul had slowly eyed the area around them for more threats. A younger accomplice watching from a distance merely turned and ran. Paul picked up the purse and returned it to Jo. He also picked up the knife.

"Jesus, thanks," Jo said. "Is he ok?" Paul was knotting the purse strap ends for her.

"Who cares?" he answered. "Are you ok?" She nodded. "Then let's go get some Chinese food. Now I'm hungry." He closed and pocketed the knife.

CHAPTER ELEVEN—Making Plans

Szechuan's was not that busy on a Wednesday evening. Connie and Jim Davis were enjoying green tea as they waited for the other couple to arrive. Connie spotted Jo and the Hunk and waved.

"Holy crap!" Jo said as they were seated and given menus by the not-very-busy staff. "You won't believe what happened walking over here. We were at Lippy's and decided to walk." She recounted how, as they were just minding their own business, the mugger had come out of nowhere and tried to take her purse.

"Tried?" Paul laughed. "He had it in his hands."

"Oh, sorry," Jo said. "Paul's right and, Paul, you know Connie and this is her friend. Who are you, friend?" Jo asked.

Jim Davis laughed, introduced himself, and shook hands all around. "How did you get your bag back?" he asked. He noticed the knotted strap. "Looks a little worse for wear or is that the new style?"

"Maybe it will be," Jo joked. "Paul got it back for me." She looked at her companion with appreciation. "This guy moves faster than anyone I'd ever seen." She took a sip of Davis' tea and described how Tanner had snagged the thief and threw him to the ground. Connie and Davis were obviously impressed.

"So what happened to the strap?" Davis asked.

"The guy sliced it," Jo said. Connie's eyebrows shot up.

"He had a knife?" Paul produced the object. The Asian server was serving tea throughout this whole exchange. She decided   to get involved.

"You call police?" she asked. Jo said no, it was all over so fast it didn't seem like there was any need. The server left.

"He's a retired SEAL," Connie told Davis indicating Tanner. Paul looked uncomfortable.

"I thought it was something like that," Davis said. "Either that or a pro athlete; muscles on muscles," the lawyer said. "Ballsy, though, going up against a guy with a knife."

"I'm just a business man now, Jim" Tanner said casually. "This is actually the first time something like this has happened to me since I left the Navy."

"What business are you in, Paul?" Davis asked as the server arrived with their soup orders. Hot and Sour was the group consensus.

"Security," Paul answered sipping the spicy concoction. "My partners and I provide physical and electronic security to our clients and their families. It lets us take advantage of all the training the military gave us."

"So all of you are ex-military?"

"We are, although lately we're exploring adding on some jocks, ex-NFL or NHL types. They tend to have the same type A personality we look for. And they have some pretty good contacts with money." Tanner smiled sipping more soup.

They had just given their entree orders, when two Philadelphia police officers in uniform approached their table.

"Had a little trouble tonight folks?" the first officer asked of no one in particular. Davis, as an officer of the court, felt he should speak up.

"I am an attorney, Officer. What kind of trouble are you referring to?" The policeman was nonplussed.

"The kind that gets the police involved," he said. "Just trying to gather some facts. The restaurant manager called us and we already had a report of an incident a few blocks from here. Was that you?" He looked at Tanner and sized him up. "Maybe you?"

"I was there," Tanner admitted. "Was there a complaint?"

"Ha," the officer laughed, "that punk was in no shape to complain. He's what we call a habitual offender, but he won't be offending for a while. So, that was you?"

"Ah, Officer, is my client in trouble? If so, I advise him not to answer any more questions," Davis started to rise.

"Settle down, Counselor," the officer said, "no one's in trouble as far as I know. Except for that piece of shit, excuse my French, ladies, your client left on the sidewalk." The policeman turned his attention back to Tanner. "You look like you can handle yourself. Where'd you learn that?"

"SEALs," Tanner answered. "Got to use some of that in eastern Afghanistan, too." The officer nodded his head.

"I was there," the officer said. They exchanged dates, locations, and duties.

"My dog, Bertie, I've still got her," the officer said. The group was fascinated at all of this. "I wanted K-9 when I joined Philly's finest, but there are a really limited number of spots. So, I'm regular patrol." He shrugged. Davis could sense a steep drop in tensions and was embarrassed that he had aggressed. He drew back mentally.

"Well, dude," Paul said, "Glad to hear about your, Bertie was it? You guys did real work over there and I appreciate it." He stuck out his hand and the cop took it.

"No problem," he said. He looked at his partner, who had remained silent throughout the entire encounter. "Let's go, pard. Nothing here."

243

The policemen left as suddenly as they had arrived.

"Wow," Davis said. "That was interesting. Band of brothers type shit, huh?" He looked at Tanner with respect.

"Something like that, but really a common misery. Sad to say, but more like that than some glory shit." He sampled his soup, which was now cold. He signaled the waitress who approached. He asked for a refill and the server took his bowl and went to the kitchen.

"I think that's cool how you guys can immediately empathize with each other once you identify the common ground," Connie said. "Is that a guy thing?" she asked Davis.

"I think it's just a people thing." Tanner nodded as he was served his steaming bowl. "It's kind of like the same for women, just a different sphere of experience. For example, I remember when friends of mine had their first child, a little girl. Don't ask me why, but they invited me to join their Lamaze class reunion."

"Dubya Tee Eff?" Jo reacted enjoying her soup. "And you went?"

"Like I said, don't ask me why. Yeah, I went. Anyway, the point is that all of the moms shared a similar story: women at church, at the grocery store, at school all came up to see the newborns and to empathize, a people thing. Sharing that common experience." Connie looked at him considering.

"Still can't believe you went to a Lamaze class reunion and — no baby," Jo said laughing. Tanner shrugged a little embarrassed.

"Had to be there I guess," he said just as their entrees arrived.

Ramon and Julia dropped off Alex and Erin at their hotel. They were tired, but happy after their day in the sun and sea air. All the walking had contributed to their shared sense of fatigue and well-being, too. There were two messages on the hotel's answering machine: one from Terry Browning and one from a garage that was trying to give Erin a quote to repair a rust spot on her car's radiator. The couple was too exhausted to respond to the messages and, so, they stripped down, washed up, put on robes, and ordered room service. Their late dinner meant that they agreed to split an appetizer sampler platter and a pitcher of beer. Erin tuned the television to the local news. It wasn't good.

"Geez," she said. "Maduro's got no control. Who's running things? It's like these jerks on motorcycles are acting on their own." She was commenting on the news reports that more militias in Caracas had popped up and were "enforcing" the peace on the streets of the capitol.

Alex stretched out on the bed and found the posture luxurious. He reached toward the television screen with the tips of his toes. The extension of musculature felt great to his tired body.

"I didn't realize that Hugo had such an iron control during his Presidency," he commented, pronouncing the deceased President's name as "hyou-go".

"He was beloved by the people, except for the people who had something to lose," Erin said. "He called them 'fascists', the ones who opposed what he called reform. The funny thing was that he didn't, usually, need to intimidate or bully. He controlled by, what, charm?" She was sitting at the foot of the bed looking over her right shoulder at Alex propped on a bunch of pillows.

"Interesting how these guys, I guess they're usually guys, are so charming and charismatic. How is that possible? They're all the same. Where does that come from? And, guess what? I'm including Bill Clinton into the mix." Erin laughed.

245

"Ok. I guess that's fair. But, let me try to answer your question. I think it's in the nature of the beast. And, maybe 'beast' is the right term. These guys, and I think you're right, they're mostly guys, pursue power as a means to another end. Maybe it's sexual, maybe it's egotistical, and maybe it's maniacal. But, whatever it is, they use power to get what they really want. Anyway, that's what I think. What do you think?"

Erin looked deeply into Alex's eyes. He returned her look and a lump formed in his throat. He forgot her question.

"Who gives a shit?" he said sitting up and sliding down the comforter. He reached for her and she scooted up the comforter to meet him. A knock came at the door.

"Oh, shit," Erin exclaimed. "Our room service."

The woman who rolled the service cart into the room was puzzled. She usually was greeted with enthusiasm and good humor. This couple seemed put off. She laid out the food and drink and proffered the slip for a signature. Alex accommodated with a healthy tip.

The woman left with effusive thanks and apologies if she had disturbed them. For their turn, after tuning the TV to a game show, they dug into the food. Alex poured frosty glasses of beer.

Later, sated, they lay next to each other while a Latin version of Wheel of Fortune played out. Alex had his left arm over Erin's shoulders, his left hand resting on her left arm. He squeezed her close.

"I'm a little afraid of how I feel about you," he admitted. She snuggled closer without saying anything. "It's hard to explain," he went on. "I'm guessing it's a relationship thing."

"Meaning?" She studied his face.

"Meaning, I think, for me, relationships some time ago became high risk. Sorry. That sounds stupid. I mean, I think, a relationship, at this time in my life, is a hard thing. I feel like relationships, at this phase, should come with warnings, like the ones that come on med bottles. 'May cause drowsiness. May cause dizziness. May cause nausea. May cause diarrhea.' I don't know. It's surprisingly hard for me, sweetie." He leaned down and kissed Erin hard on the mouth. "I'm sure you're wondering about Elise and me. What can I say? It was an experiment, something that I was trying to resolve. The resolution was a bit of a surprise, though. I thought, what, Jesus, Alex, so much time has gone by. You can't commit?" Alex pulled Erin closer. She could see the pain in his eyes and that pain brought the beginning of tears to her own eyes.

"So, Alex," she said and he could feel her emotion, "can you commit?" She put her head on his shoulder a little afraid of the answer. Several heartbeats intervened before Alex spoke.

"Yes, Erin," he said, "I can. With you, I can. You're an amazing woman. The surprising part, for me, is that I can imagine introducing you to my daughters and I can see them just embracing you." He kissed her offered lips long and tenderly. "Would you like to meet my daughters?"

"I'd be honored and intimidated by meeting your daughters. From what you've told me, they're a couple of amazing women themselves." Alex laughed.

"No need to be intimidated. These are the little ones whose bottoms I cleaned not so long ago. But, I agree, they are amazing. And they'll be amazed when they meet you."

Alex released her and slid off the bed. "Now, let's eat some more."

They sat at the table just inside the glass doors leading to the patio. The leftovers were a little cold, but still good. The beer was a little less cold, but still good. Alex looked at Erin who was chewing and was astonished at his luck. It was still good.

The next morning, Thursday, Alex had a call from Mac as breakfast was being served in the hotel's dining room.

"Got a minute?"

"Sure. Just sitting down to breakfast. What's up?"

"Remember my buddy Cor? Well, he moved the equipment we need from Cubagua. It's here on Margarita ready to be moved where we want it. Can we hook up later today and get this going?"

"Sure," Alex said, "call me later with when and where and I'll be there. Ok?"

"Good. Talk to you later."

"Mac," Alex told Erin. "We've got some equipment to set up to do a, what, a test dig? I don't know what you would call it."

"The boxes?" The way she said it sounded to Alex like she thought he might be wasting his time.

"Right. You don't think it's worth checking?"

They ended up talking about the issues of money, religion, work ethic, and politics. Where money was concerned, they both realized that neither was very fascinated with the idea of wealth. They were both comfortable, within reason, with their respective stations in life. Alex admitted that he had a core belief that people should work for what they had. Things like inheritances, winning the lottery, or getting lucky in the stock market didn't seem to Alex to prove anything about the person who gained. It didn't prove that they were smart or industrious or deserving. Erin agreed. She brought up the issues of taxes

248

and other legal claims. She made it sound like being rich was hell.

"People would be coming out of the woodwork to get a piece of the action," she pointed out. Erin compared some people's commitment to money to their commitment to religion.

"I would even say that some people's religion is money," she said. He laughed at the easy platitude, but then considered it seriously. He had obviously given religion some thought in the past.

"You know, I've come to the conclusion over the years that the very idea of religion is somehow a fundamental need in human nature." Erin started to respond, but Alex went on. "And I think it's totally irrational."

"I agree," Erin said enjoying herself. "I was going to say that the fundamental need is a need to believe that there is life after death. We just don't want to accept that this is all there is." She gestured to include the restaurant and its patrons. "Some people seem to have a need to believe that there is some ultimate force steering their lives. Think about that. It's not chance. It's not my lack of effort. If I follow the rules, pray, and avoid trouble, I'll be ok. What do you think about that?"

Alex sipped his coffee thoughtfully. "I don't begrudge anyone what they believe. Remind me to tell you about my brother. It's ok with me if that's how you want to live your life. I guess what bugs me is when you feel compelled to convince me that your beliefs are right and that I should join you. That really pisses me off.

"I'm convinced that if we work hard, get a good education, and keep most of our opinions to ourselves, we'll prosper."

"And live long?" Erin joked. "But, seriously, keep our opinions to ourselves? What's that about?"

"Ok. I should have qualified it to unless we're asked. Better?"

"Better," she affirmed.

"Oh, and by the way, that includes political opinions. You wouldn't believe the current political atmosphere back home in the U.S. It's like the current religious atmosphere."

"What do you mean?"

"I mean that people these days, and I'm including members of Congress in this, are holding on to their ideologies with such unbending conviction that there's no room for debate or compromise or even tolerance. It's crazy. I don't know if you've been following the news, but the U.S. government is getting nothing done under this administration. And it's not just the President's fault. Our politicians have become professionals."

"What's wrong with that?" Erin asked looking for a wait staff member to bring the check.

"It was never meant to be that way. The drafters of the Constitution, I bet, never envisioned that. I learned in school that the people sent to Congress were supposed to be chosen by their communities to represent the community's needs. They could be teachers or dentists or shop owners, whatever. Not professional politicians. That is probably the worst makeup for a system of checks and balances. If politicians were mostly concerned with keeping themselves in office, little would get done that benefitted the governed." He realized that he was ranting and stopped, embarrassed.

"Go on," Erin encouraged him. "It's interesting."

"Well, the end result is gridlock, which is what we have today. The funny thing is that voters have such short memories. They keep electing the same fools term after term. It's amazing." He shook his head.

250

"Things in Venezuela are pretty much the same," Erin said softly so as to not be overheard. "Power is centralized and there is little chance that those at the core of power would ever willingly give it up. Anyway, let's pay the bill. I want to go for a walk."

As they walked along the seaside promenade, Alex thought that life couldn't be much better. Except for fucking Bautiste and his crap. He considered that after the next run, his involvement with that dick would be over. Besides, if his plan worked, Bautiste wouldn't be in any position to entice Alex.

"What are you thinking about?" Erin asked. "You look worried."

"Not worried, really," Alex answered. "Just thinking."

"About?"

"About us. Where do you see us going?" He gestured to a free bench on the promenade. They sat in the sun with the ocean sounds and smells around them.

"Not back to the U.S.," she said. "Too many bad memories for me. And, I guess I don't really fit in there. I'm not that kind of competitive person that the U.S. admires. I don't have that fire that it takes to succeed there." She shrugged. "How about Europe or some place like Belize or Costa Rica? Would you go there?"

Alex seriously considered these possibilities, but his thoughts kept returning to the same thing. "I could live in any of those places with you. I'm pretty sure we could afford it. The only thing is," he trailed off.

"Is your family," Erin finished for him. "I understand."

"Yeah, even though we didn't live close to each other, I still felt like they were a couple of hours away by plane.

And, the convenience of a cell phone call, I'm not sure that would be there from Europe or Central America. I know I sound like a puss. I'm sorry. It's just that, I guess, I feel like at this time in my life, I want to have them close. That's stupid I guess, considering I came all the way down here. I don't know what my expectations were. Am I making any sense?" He looked into her face searching for help.

"Not at all," she said with a smile. "But, let's leave it at that. Maybe I need to meet your daughters and brother before we make any solid plans. How does that sound?"

"That does make sense. Let me call and set up the meeting with Mac and his buddy and I'll catch up with you later. Start thinking about what I can bring back from Miami for you. I'm going to go pretty soon I've decided."

Mac got Alex's call as the midweek lunchtime crowd dwindled to just a few diehards who had apparently decided to have a few drinks and not return to work. They arranged to meet in an hour near the spot they had identified a couple of days ago.

When Mac and Alex arrived, Delaney was already there. Cor Delaney was Alex's stereotypical image of an expatriate Irishman. He was no more than five and half feet tall, but was thick everywhere. His neck, his chest, his forearms and his calves were thick. His reddish, grayish beard was thick. His ponytail was thick. His eyebrows were thick. And when he spoke, his accent was thick.

"Please ta meet ye," he told Alex when Mac introduced him. He was smoking a cigarette, a brand that Alex recognized as British, and offered one to Alex. Alex hadn't smoked since Jo was born, but he surprised himself and accepted the offer. The nicotine initially made his head spin and he felt the need to sit. He recovered quickly, though, and watched with interest as Mac and Cor backed Cor's specialized truck into position and made some adjustments. The business part of the rig reminded Alex of a scorpion's stinger. Instead of a sharp stinger though, the terminus was a spiral of steel. The diameter of the spiral was smaller than Alex had imagined, maybe no more than six inches. It was about eight feet long and then was connected to a sort of hinge.

"Is that long enough?" Alex asked and then felt stupid for questioning their professionalism. They were quick to respond though.

"That's what she said," Mac brought out the well-worn line and Delaney laughed.

"Long enou' fer where we gonna stick it," Delaney said and Mac laughed. They continued with the set up and Alex was content to be quiet and smoke. When they were done, Cor flipped some switches and air was filled with a deafening din. Alex dropped his cigarette butt and stomped it out. He stepped back as the drill bit was extended.

"We're just going to see how the soil is here," Mac shouted above the engine noise. He put on a pair of heavy work gloves and a pair of clear plastic safety glasses.

Jo Browning's phone rang for the first time that Thursday. The caller ID announced that it was Connie. Jo had been controlling herself all day, wanting to call her sister and discuss Jim Davis. The dinner of the night before had devolved into a sort of double date, Jo felt, and she wanted to know if her sister felt the same thing. She had watched the lawyer watching her sister and was amused at his undisguised interest.

"What's up, Sis?" she asked with a lot of energy.

"What's up with you— and the Hunk?" Connie said brightly matching her sister's energy.

"What? What are you talking about?" Jo was caught off guard.

"You guys were obviously vibing off each other. Was it the near mugging? That's what I thought it was." Jo was baffled now.

"What the hell are you talking about? One: the Hunk and I are and have always been platonic. No vibing going on. C'mon. And two: you and your lawyer buddy were the ones vibing. Jeez, Hunk and I could feel it all the way across the table. What's up with that? He's cute, by the way, for a lawyer." Connie laughed.

"Nothing's up with that." She realized she didn't sound convincing. "Well, maybe a little some something is up. He took me out for a drink after dinner. I had a blast."

"I knew it!" Jo squealed. "Tell me everything." And then she realized that it was the middle of a workday. "If you have time," she added. She waited as her sister's silence filled the space between them.

Cell phones and, maybe, all phones employed a digital signal. This meant that there was either a transmission or there was not. This made it difficult for either party to tell the difference between a silent connection and a broken connection.

"Connie? You there?"

"Yeah. Just thinking for a sec." Connie had gathered her thoughts. "So, we went to the Saucer," she said naming a downtown bar, The Flying Saucer, that was popular with young professionals. "We talked about you guys and your relationship." Connie could hear Jo start to protest, so she powered through. "Jim really liked you and the Hunk. He admires what the Hunk is doing. We talked about each other's careers and how committed we were to our jobs. We realized that we're both pretty fucking committed." Jo laughed.

254

"What else?" Jo giggled. "I feel like we're in high school."

"Well, he held my hand and told me he wanted to go steady and he asked if I would wear his ring and his letterman jacket."

"Get the fuck out!" Jo said in astonishment and then, as she heard her sister's laughter, realized Connie's joke. "Asshole! Really. What else happened?"

"Not much," Connie said, serious now. "Honestly, I like him. We talked about ourselves and, you know how you can tell when a guy is full of shit? Well, he isn't. He's a really nice guy. Loves to cook, believe that? Has a little terrier named Casper or Captain or something. Likes travel. Blah, blah, blah. Anyway, we Uber-ed home and when I thought he was going to make his move, he gave me a hug and said good night and just left. I'm still tingly thinking about it." Connie stopped talking and waited for Jo's reaction. When the silence went on, she said, "What do you think?"

"I'm thinking about what I think," Jo said. "I think he's a good-looking guy and that he probably knows that." Jo could sense her sister was about to make an objection. She kept going. "Not that there's any surprise there. Let me ask you this, though. This just occurred to me. Isn't there some kind of ethical thing for lawyers dating clients?"

"I don't know. That sounds familiar. Probably. I'm not going to push the dating thing, though. I guess I should ask him about it. Shit. I don't want to get him in any trouble. Do you think that's a big deal?" Jo thought that Connie sounded worried.

"I don't know," Jo admitted. "My guess is that there's probably a loophole, I mean being a lawyer and all. Anyway, the heart wants what it wants, right? Isn't that what they say? So, talk to him about it. He'll know what he can and can't do." Jo stopped talking to give her sister a chance to express herself.

"Right. I'll talk to him about it. We're having lunch tomorrow. I guess if things get serious, I can always resign from the board or whatever. Hah, I'm on a board."

Mac and Cor drilled several test holes. Alex could tell that they were enthused with the results. He had no idea why. Mac explained.

"Two things you hope for when you're drilling," Mac said. "Well, actually, you hope that two things won't happen. First, you don't want the soil to be too soft. Sandy. That's bad. The hole will collapse on itself and you have to line it with pipe. Second, you don't want the soil to be too hard. Hitting rock will not only slow the drilling process, but it will wear out the equipment." Mac paused.

"So?" Alex asked. "Which is it?"

"Naytha," Delaney answered for Mac. "It's goot daht. We got goot daht." Alex was pretty sure he understood but looked to Mac for confirmation.

"Good dirt," Mac translated. "Should be an easy dig. We're going to switch out the drilling bore to the big one and then we'll call it a day for now. We'll do the real dig tomorrow morning. What time, Cor?"

"Way white? Sen, ok? Mebbe, ite? Whadya thank?" Alex looked to Mac.

"Seven or eight?" Mac asked Alex, helping to interpret once again.

"Eight. Ok? Not too late?" Alex asked the both of them. Eight was acceptable and that was it. They departed in their various vehicles. Alex drove back to the hotel.

Alex and Erin went to the beach for the afternoon. It was another perfect Margarita day with warm sun and a cool ocean breeze. They had the hotel pack towels and refreshments. Since it was a Thursday, the beach was fairly empty. They spread their towels down by the water where small waves lapped the sand. Alex couldn't relax. He had so many thoughts running through his mind. He remembered what Erin had said that morning about wanting to meet Connie and Jo. He had tried to process how he felt about that while he drove to and from his meeting with Mac and Cor Delaney. In the end, he decided that he was excited at the prospect.

"Hey, babe," Alex said. "Remember what you said this morning about wanting to meet my daughters, Connie and Jo?" Erin rolled over on her towel and squinted at Alex. She nodded her affirmation. "I think my daughters and I would be psyched for you to meet them and for everyone to get to know one another, even my brother. I know that they would feel the way I feel about you. I love you." Alex flushed at his admission. The relationship between Erin and him up to this point had been defined by sexual attraction and general good humor. Now, with his declaration, the game had changed. He had made a promise.

"What?" Erin stammered, not certain of what she had heard. "What was that?" She knew she was buying time until she could recover from what she thought she had heard. She tried to penetrate Alex's expression cloaked by his Maui Jim sunglasses. She squinted at him waiting.

"You heard me. Stop messing around. Do you?" Alex's heart was pounding. He wanted to treat Erin the way she had never been treated. But, even at sixty-seven, he felt the doubts that a seventeen year old felt: does she feel like I feel? What if she doesn't? Shit!

Erin, for her part, was touched beyond words. She knew exactly how she felt. She gathered her thoughts and focused on what she wanted Alex to understand.

"I could draw this out by asking do I what," she began. "But, neither of us are kids. I love you, too. Let's figure this out together. All of this craziness, Bautiste and pirates, we should forget about all of that and get on the first plane out of here." She grabbed his forearm and held it tightly.

"I don't know if Bautiste would let me walk away at this point," Alex said sadly. "I think he's desperate for me to take another suitcase to Miami. And frankly, that big guy who he hangs around with scares the shit out of me. After Bautiste is satisfied, then we could get on a plane." Alex didn't mention the progress he and Mac had made. "It's going to feel good leaving this mess behind. With you." Alex put his hand over hers and leaned over and kissed her.

"Can Bautiste stop us, do you think?" She sat up and propped her head on one elbow. Boats cruised by on the bay's water and the sound of their motors drifted to the beach.

"I'd like to think no, but, honestly, I think he can do whatever he wants. I guess we could go to the American Embassy in Caracas, but I'm not sure that our government wants to tangle with Maduro right now. Maduro's government is on the ropes. They're blaming the U.S. for supporting unrest. Would the embassy want to add our little troubles to the stew they've already got cooking? I don't think they would." He blew out his breath. "Once Bautiste gets his money from my trip, then, I think, we'll be able to leave.

"Also," he continued, "I want to see this thing with Mac through to some resolution. Who knows, maybe we'll come away with a little cash."

"With my trust and your pension, we'll have enough to be comfortable, maybe not in the big cities of the world, but somewhere nice. How expensive is it to live in Philadelphia? Could we afford to live there?" She had obviously reconsidered her aversion to living in the U.S. "I could get work, I guess." Alex laughed at the prospect of living in the City of Brotherly Love.

"I'm sure Connie and Jo would be thrilled to have me living in their city." He sarcastically emphasized the word "thrilled".

"Why? What's the problem?" Erin was genuinely mystified Alex could tell.

"Would you have wanted one or both of your parents living nearby when you were out of college and on your own?" She pouted.

"Yes, if they were alive, even my adoptive parents. They were always close to me. It's the old world way, I guess. Isn't your family close that way?"

"Not in, what did you call it? 'The old-world way'? It's interesting that there's a difference defined that way. I guess I'd have to say that we're close in the New World way. We stay in touch regularly, but give each other their space. We get together for the big occasions when we can. We support each other's efforts as we can." Alex chuckled. "Have you ever heard the term 'helicopter parents'?" he asked.

Erin admitted that she had not. She asked what it meant.

"It means those parents who hover over their kids like helicopters, not giving them any room to grow or develop." Erin nodded that she understood. "It's usually used to describe parents of young children, but I guess it could apply at any age. Once you become a parent, you've signed up for a lifetime gig." Alex lay back on his towel.

"I bet you're a great Dad," Erin said stretching out on her own towel. Alex hoped that she was right.

Cor Delaney loved his work and he loved his beer. After leaving Mac, he drove to one of his favorite pubs in Porlamar, Uncle Julio's. It was a workingman's establishment. The beer was cold and the tables, chairs and windows were filthy. An evaporative cooler hummed uselessly unable to cope with the Caribbean humidity. Ceiling fans stirred the air, which smelled of stale beer, stale smoke, and stale body odor. It was a pub because almost all of its customers were UK expats, workers from England, Wales, Scotland, and Ireland and because it had a dartboard. The custom was for the workers and their friends to gather in the early evening. Delaney was earlier than the custom dictated. Besides the owner, who was named Alfonso and who was also the bartender, there were only two customers in the place. Delaney recognized one of the men as a friend of Mac's, a fellow slurry boat captain named Manny Velez. Velez was Venezuelan, but he preferred the rough company of the expatriate community.

"Hola, Manny," Delaney said after receiving a pint of Guinness from Alfonso. He lifted his glass in salute. Manny looked confused at first and then smiled in recognition.

"Hola, drilling man. How does it go?"

"Well. Very well. May I join you?" Delaney indicated one of the empty chairs at Velez's table.

"Yes, of course," Manny said pulling out the empty chair. He introduced his companion as Leo Graham. Graham was a Brit who had worked the North Sea oil fields and had decided two years ago that he had had enough of the cold weather. He had drifted south for three months until he finally settled on Venezuela. Delaney recognized Graham as an Uncle Julio's regular, but they had never been introduced.

"Was working with a buddy of yours earlier," Delaney said to Velez. He drained his glass and ordered another round for the table.

"Who's that?" Velez asked as the drinks arrived. Service at Uncle Julio's was excellent since Alfonso attended to his customers instead of concerning himself with other niceties such as cleanliness.

"Magrew," Delaney said naming the black man. Mac and Alex had tried to impress on the Irishman that their drilling activity that day should be treated discreetly. They didn't come right out and swear him to secrecy, but they thought they had convinced him of the need for circumspection.

"So what's going on with Mac?" Velez asked. He signaled Alfonso for another round, which was also the signal for everyone to finish their drinks.

"Little drilling project," Delaney said upending his glass. He was oblivious to the fact that he sounded mysterious. This piqued the interest of Velez and Graham.

"Drillin'?" Graham asked.

"Where you drilling?" Velez asked. "I thought you was working Cubagua."

"I was and then Mac made me an offer." Again, the Irishman had no idea he was seemingly evasive.

"An offer to do what?" Graham asked and then Velez said, with some exasperation, "Why don't you just tell it, Delaney?" So, Delaney told them about the deal to bring his rig to Margarita and how he had moved it, at Mac's direction, to a spot near the north shore. He told them how he and Mac and the American had drilled a soil sample and had determined it to be good. Finally, he told them that the big bit was going in tomorrow.

"So what's the Negro after?" It was Graham who asked with seeming nonchalance. The Brit could hold his alcohol better than any of Uncle Julio's customers, which was quite a distinction. He sensed an opportunity for financial gain.

"Don't know," Delaney admitted. "But I know this. It's your turn for a round and, whatever Mac's after, it was worth dollars to him to go get it."

Bautiste was in his office reading reports. The national reports were not good. Thursday had brought no stop to the rioting and protests on the mainland despite a heavy police crackdown and many arrests. More shortages of consumer goods had appeared and these fomented more unrest. Social media was contributing by fueling rumor after rumor. The Colonel shook his head thinking that this would have never had happened if Chavez were alive. He moved on to the local reports. The news here made him feel better. There were no protests on Margarita and he was proud of that counting it as a personal achievement. Finally, he opened a sealed envelope, which held the last report he had to read. He was very interested in its contents.

He flipped through the pages, which described the American's activities for that day, a walk on the beach, a drive to the north to meet with the black American, an afternoon taking the sun with the Jewish woman. Then Bautiste returned to the paragraph, which described Alex and Mac's meeting. A third man was present and he had been driving a most unusual vehicle. The report didn't say how the vehicle was unusual and this irritated the Colonel.

"Lopez," he called loudly and the young, fat Sergeant cringed at the tone. He got up from his computer as fast as his bulk would allow.

"*Mi Colonel*?" Lopez said sweating as he stopped in Bautiste's office doorway.

"Who submitted this piece of shit?" Bautiste asked waving the papers he was holding.

"Which piece of shit is that?" the young Sergeant asked indicating the papers. Bautiste was inwardly amused at the question thinking 'Exactly'.

"The sealed report. Who submitted it?"

"Let me check the log," the Sergeant said backing toward his desk. He was sure it was a Detective named Rodriguez, but he wanted to be certain that Rodriguez's name was entered in the official record. It was.

"Detective Rodriguez," the Sergeant announced. Bautiste was a little surprised. The detective was usually more thorough than this. He made a decision anyway.

"Get me Rodriguez and then get me Garcia," he commanded. The Hammer was going to have to look after the American personally.

When Rodriguez called in, Bautiste demanded to know more about the vehicle in the report. Upon further description, the Colonel was able to determine that it was a light-duty drilling vehicle.

"Interesting," the Colonel thought as he dismissed the detective. Sergeant Garcia's call was announced.

"Garcia," the Colonel said, "I want you to be responsible for the American. Rodriguez is getting sloppy. I need to be sure that the American is available to go to Miami on Saturday."

"And after that?" Lopez growled in his deep voice. Bautiste considered his answer briefly.

"After that we don't need him. You can take care of that   too."

CHAPTER TWELVE—Some Surprises

Alex had ordered a wakeup call for seven o'clock that Friday morning and he answered it and got ready to meet Mac and Cor as Erin slept. He drove his rental to the place they had met yesterday, a place sheltered by scrubby and stunted pines and tall sea grass. He was the first to arrive and wished he had bought a pack of cigarettes at the hotel gift shop. As he waited, he wondered if he was getting sucked back in to the nicotine habit.

Mac arrived next. He greeted Alex and smelled of coffee. He was also bearing a thermos. He offered coffee and Alex accepted. Mac poured two portions into the cups that were part of the thermos and they sat on the tailgate of Mac's pickup truck watching the day lighten the Eastern sky. Alex was content in the moment. Mac was a little nervous in anticipation of the activity to come.

"Got a cigarette?" Alex asked completely embarrassed at the question.

"I didn't know you smoked," was Mac's response. Alex hesitated.

"I quit when Joanne was born." Mac considered this.

"I thought she was like twenty-five years old," Mac said.

"Right," Alex answered. "Got a cigarette?" Mac shook his head emphatically.

"Fuck no. Expensive habit," he observed not admitting his own one to two sticks a day habit. Alex, obviously disappointed, sipped his coffee and admired the brightening day from the leg-swinging height of the tailgate.

His attention was diverted to a revving motor sound as Delaney's drilling rig arrived.

The short Irishman was, clearly, in bad humor that morning as he exited his vehicle slamming the door. He glared in challenge at Mac and Alex who looked away and who would have whistled in exaggerated casualness if that had not been too obvious. Delaney dug into his shirt pocket and pulled out a pack of Marlboro's. Alex hopped from the tailgate and approached the diminutive man.

"Got an extra one of those?" he asked as the Irishman struck a match, shielded the flame from the negligible breeze, and lit his cigarette.

"Nape," Delaney answered. "Ony got twenny in the pack." It was an old smoker's joke and Alex wasn't amused. He fished a fistful of Bolivars from his jeans' pockets and thrust them toward Delaney.

"Gimme a cig," he said, not exactly threatening, but not in friendly demand. The short man reached into his shirt pocket to retrieve the cigarette pack. He tapped one out and offered it to Alex.

"No chahge," the little man said pushing Alex's hand away. Alex took the Marlboro with his left hand as he stuffed the money back into his pocket with his right. Delaney was ready with a match as Alex put the cigarette to his lips.

"Thanks," Alex said. He retreated to the tailgate and resumed his previous position. He wiggled his half full coffee cup at Mac who opened the thermos once more and topped Alex off with more of the steaming brew. Now Alex was really content. At the moment, the combination of caffeine and nicotine, coupled with the fresh, beach air and the quiet of the location, was heaven. The quiet didn't last long.

"Hey, Mac?" Delaney said. Mac looked up from his seat on the tailgate as he secured the stopper on the thermos.

"Yeah?" he said sensing trouble but not knowing why.

"Ize watchin the telly ta otha nayt an theyz talkin bout a spidah. This spidah, she put all her babies on her back an crawls to the highest pint aroun. Dere she shakes all dem babies loose an dey fly off on a strang of web tooken bay the wind."

"What's your fuckin' point, you limey bastard?" Mac asked, figuring Delaney was working up to some personal attack and knowing that 'limey' was the most powerful insult he could give to the Irishman.

"Um Irish," Delaney said, "and me pint is that the spidah is givin her young a random chance fer survival. Unnerstan? Now yer people's doing the same thang with yer ghettoes and such. I thank the spidah's got a better chance than yer people. What ya thank?" The Irishman smoked his cigarette to the filter and then stubbed it out on a pine trunk.

"Interesting," Mac said. "Didn't know you was such a deep thinker, Cor." He hopped off the tailgate. "Had a tough night, didn't ya?" he asked.

"Lil bit," the Irishman admitted. "Wen ta Uncle's. Had a wee bit."

"Well, get your shit together, limey. We got work to do," Mac admonished. Delaney bowed and shook his large head from side to side. He gathered himself.

"Um ok," he reassured Mac. "Ah ken do mah job." Mac clapped the Irishman on his shoulder and the little man seemed to take heart.

"Let's do it," Mac encouraged.

Alex watched Mac put on the heavy gloves and plastic glasses he had worn the previous afternoon. Alex had brought, thanks to hotel staff, heavy gloves of his own and put them on. He walked up to Delaney as the Irishman readied the drill bit.

266

"How deep do you think we have to drill?" Alex asked. The little man looked at him like he was from Uranus. He just shrugged as Mac entered their sphere.

"We'll dig as deep as we have to," he answered Alex. Delaney nodded in agreement. He moved the wide bit into position and, as he had done on the previous afternoon, he shattered the morning quiet. The diesel motor's din announced that it was ready for business. Cor Delaney maneuvered the tip into position.

The drill dug in immediately and Alex was struck by the smell of freshly turned earth. It was the odor of planting new trees and bushes in the spring, but also the odor of a freshly dug grave. The bit slowly brought the dark earth to the surface as the three men watched. After the first half hour, nothing happened. More dark moist dirt was brought to the surface and an extension was affixed to the drill bit. The drilling continued slowly under Delaney's supervision. Around mid-morning Delaney's beard and ponytail were limp with sweat. Alex and Mac were also soaked. The up and down drone of the engine had lulled the men into a state of non-expectation. So, it was with great surprise that Alex was the first to notice a shiny revelation partially covered by dark, moist earth and tiny roots. He yelled at first and, then, realizing that the diesel noise was drowning out his shouts, he waved his arms to get the drillers' attention. Cor saw him first and switched the engine off. The silence was immediate and so incongruous that Alex doubted his ability to hear for a brief second.

"Got something," he bellowed to the others, maybe more loudly than necessary.

Alex recovered quickly and went to find the bright object amid the grime and grit. He dug around for a little bit and then found what he was looking for. It was round, yellow, shiny and heavier than he expected. He wiped it on his shirttail and held it up between his thumb and forefinger for the others to see.

267

"Wha the fook?" Cor said squinting at Alex's hand as he approached the American. He took the gold coin and turned it in the mottled morning sunlight.

"Fook," he exclaimed, bereft of other words. He motioned for Mac to come over and have a look.

Mac took the coin, spit on it, wiped it and placed it in his palm. He gazed at it with his dark brown eyes. He turned it over and studied the other side. Unlike Cor, he had spent some time online researching the value of gold and silver coins of the eighteenth century. So, although, his knowledge was minimal, he conservatively estimated the worth of the coin at fifteen hundred American dollars. He kept his estimate to himself.

"Nice," he remarked and returned the piece to Alex. Alex pocketed the coin and shrugged at the others.

"Shouldn't we keep going?" he asked. He looked at the two men. After a moment of inaction by both, it was Delaney who snapped out of his mesmerized state.

"Right ya are," he said as he took the couple of steps to the engine's control panel filled with toggle switches and gauges and indicator lights. Delaney repositioned the drilling bit. He flipped a toggle switch. The engine coughed, sputtered, and caught. Delaney expertly guided the steel spiral back into the hole. It drilled nothing but air for a few seconds and then the dirt once again flowed to the surface and piled up there. Six eyes studied that pile of dirt. And minute after minute as the time added up, nothing appeared but more dirt. Then, maybe after ten minutes, something was propelled to the surface that was so obviously not a gold coin that the trio stared in unison — and in shock. None of the three had ever been exposed to violence.

"Is tha a fookin head?" It was Cor Delaney who had recovered first. Alex's first thought was to correct the Irishman. This was not a head, he thought. This is a skull, a human skull. Delaney had flipped the engine switch again invoking silence.

The thoughts that had simultaneously occurred to each man were as diverse as were their owners. Delaney thought that this was bad luck, an omen, a curse on their endeavors. Alex thought that this was confirmation that his plan was going to work. Mac thought that this was an unneeded complication, possibly a legal hurdle that fucked things up.

"We should keep working," Alex said, interrupting the thought processes of the other two. Delaney looked at Magrew for guidance. Magrew shrugged and then nodded affirmation. Delaney went to the control panel, Mac went to the dirt pile to retrieve the skull, and Alex went to the tailgate of Mac's truck. Alex craved a cigarette.

Despite the shock of encountering a human skull, the trio resumed work. To Alex, the drill bit seemed to be progressing even more slowly. No human (or other) artifacts surfaced over the next fifteen minutes. The air was growing heavier as the sun moved along and no breeze stirred the sparse vegetation. Then, the next twenty minutes produced a continuous flow of material consistent with an ossuary. The bones piled up as if after a giant, gruesome chicken dinner, some totally intact and some destroyed by the large drill. Alex grew more and more concerned that someone might discover them with their disturbing find and that same someone might have the authority to arrest them. As the flow of human remains began to taper off, Delaney slowed the rotation of the bit and the decibel level reflected the change. Mac was a little irritated at the reduction in production. The drill went inexorably downward. After another ten minutes a few more shiny coins appeared. Delaney cut the power to the engine.

"Thas it," he announced raising the bit out of the earth and folding it into place.

"What the hell, Cor?" Mac protested. He voice was abnormally loud in the new silence. Delaney summoned the two Americans close and, in hushed tones, explained that it was a seriously criminal act in Venezuela, as it was in most nations, to disturb the graves of the dead.

Alex, imitating Cor's low tone, argued.

"I don't think this is a grave, guys. This is like a jumble of piled up bodies. Look at some of this stuff. There're pieces of metal, rotten leather, other crap. These poor suckers weren't lovingly laid to rest. They were dumped in a hole."

Delaney wasn't convinced, and besides, he said, just because there wasn't a marker, that didn't make it any less a gravesite. Mac pondered this.

"He may be right," Mac addressed Alex. "What should we do?" Alex reached in his pocket and pulled out the gold coin.

"This is what we're after," he said holding the coin up between his thumb and forefinger. "I think we should dig a few feet more and see if we turn up more of this." He raised his hand. "Then, regardless, we should shut down, cover up and consider our options. Agreed?" He looked at his two partners. Cor Delaney was obviously uneasy. As the one with the least to gain if they found more gold, he was nervous about proceeding. His agreement to accept a thousand dollars didn't look like a smart move right now. Mac sensed his hesitation and guessed the reason why.

"Rethinking our arrangement?" he asked the Irishman. Alex could read regret on his face. "How about a half percent share?" Mac offered.

"Instead of the thousand," Alex added and then realized how stupid it sounded. "Sorry," he said. Delaney was chewing his lip. He looked again at the gold in Alex's palm. The little man was good at math. He calculated that to make up the thousand at a half percent they would have to recover around a hundred and thirty coins.

"Doon," he said extending his hand. "Les dig a lil more. Den we should pudda bones back and clean oop." There were smiles all around. Delaney went over and restarted the engine.

Alex felt elated and a little vindicated when, after less than a quarter hour of additional drilling and a "few feet more", two more gold coins were brought up. Mac saw them first and moved his bulk quickly to Delaney's side and motioned for Cor to shut down the drill. Delaney complied and looked where Mac was pointing. Alex and Mac held back to allow the little man to have the chance to be the first to pick up and hold the two gold coins.

Delaney, who was somewhat superstitious, clearly circumvented any of the bones and other debris as he delicately brushed dirt. Alex and Mac watched the thick Irish fingers pluck the first gold piece and lift it to Delaney's lips so he could blow the dirt away. The little man spit on the coin and rubbed it clean with his shirt. He held it up for the other two to appreciate the glint. He tossed it to Alex who initially panicked and then recovered sufficiently to make a clean athletic catch. Delaney went after the second coin and repeated the previous process.

With the gold secured, Mac urged them all to hurry and hide the evidence of their digging. Cor had shovels and rakes in his rig so they split up the tools and went to work. The bones were pushed back down the shaft Delaney had drilled. There wasn't any concern for reverence. Alex felt like the dead were dead. These were just bones. The only problem was that the bones would not compact neatly and they quickly refilled the hole. The trio couldn't bring themselves to break any of the bones so they just threw the dirt on top and raked it around a bit. There was a small mound at the finish, but they felt that this was acceptable.

Alex beckoned the other two close after they had stowed the tools.

"Here's the next step:" he said, "I'm going to Miami tomorrow. When I get back to the hotel in Porlamar, I'll take some pictures of the coins and send them to my daughters. They'll get them to my lawyer and he can use them to convince our 'sponsors' that this is the real deal. That's the plan. Any problems?" It was Mac who spoke up.

"Not a problem," he said. "More like a suggestion." He hesitated and then went on. "How about you take the gold we have to Miami, kind of like samples, and use them to what did you call it? Convince our sponsors that this is the real deal? Nothing works for the real deal like the real deal, yes?"

"Ok," Alex said. "Good idea."

Alex went right back to the hotel. He hugged Erin tightly when he entered their room. He was afraid he might be pulling her into a danger from which he could not protect her. He held her for a while and she grew increasingly uncomfortable as he pressed her to him. She wriggled free to gaze into his eyes.

"What's up?" she asked. She looked from one blue eye to the other.

"We found this," Alex said dramatically. He threw the three gold pieces on the bed. Erin's reaction was a testament to the power of the yellow metal.

"Holy shit! Is that real?" Erin walked over to the bed, but stopped well out of touching distance. It was as if for her, the gold was evil, something that could taint her.

"Damn right it's real!" Alex said misinterpreting her reluctance for doubt.

272

"I can see that, asshole," Erin said smiling. "What the hell? Where did this come from?" Alex couldn't know, but Erin was suddenly afraid for both of them.

"Maybe it's better if you don't know that," Alex said. He looked into her gray-green eyes and immediately regretted his statement. "Sorry," he said honestly. "We dug them up." He awaited her reaction. It wasn't what he expected.

"Ok. Was that hard? Now, what can I do to help?" She kept her gaze level and penetrating. He felt her toughness and squirmed inwardly.

"I don't know," he admitted accepting that the truth was what Erin deserved and nothing else. "I have an idea though," he told her. He explained his idea.

They spent the early and late afternoon shopping. Alex wanted Erin to enjoy the rest of their day together before he left in the morning for Miami. He knew he was racking up quite a credit card bill, but he hoped that Connie was keeping up with him. He knew he would repay her even it meant selling his California house.

When they returned to the hotel Alex was exhausted and Erin was elated. He headed for the shower in search of revival. He found it and inspiration. He toweled off and joined Erin.

"Let's go to a casino tonight," he said. She was watching the local news. She muted the television.

"Ok. Didn't know you were a high roller," she said. She waited for his response.

"I'm not," he said. "There's something else I want at the casino. Want to go?" He smiled and she tossed her hair and walked into the bathroom.

273

The casino was opulent by any standard. It was built to entice the tourists of Europe and Asia who had money to risk. The Venezuelan government guaranteed the honesty of the games. So, although the tourism traffic had fallen off, the games were still deemed to be fair.

Alex dressed in a dinner jacket and formal shirt. Erin wore a pale green dress that was neither too formal nor too casual and which revealed an enticing amount of skin. She walked on matching heels. Alex was enthralled.

"Fuck, you look good," he murmured as they headed out of the hotel lobby. The walk to the casino was brief, at least for Alex. Erin's heels leant a whole new dimension to the distance. When they walked up the steps to the casino lobby Alex's thoughts were that this was nothing new. He had been to Vegas, to casinos in Nice back when the Riviera was something. The lobby was as he remembered, a piratical theme. There was the usual treasure chest of foil-wrapped chocolate. Alex reached into the chest and pocketed a handful.

They made their way to the Blackjack tables. Alex had read about counting strategies many years ago. He had forgotten most of what he had read, but he knew the basics. He pulled out a chair for Erin and then sat beside her at the green felt table.

Despite their lack of knowledge, Erin and Alex did quite well. In fact, they cleared over five thousand dollars in winnings. The cards simply fell in a pattern that was extremely lucky. Every time Alex had a face card, an ace would follow. Erin's play was pretty much the same. When either Alex or Erin had matching cards, they 'doubled down' and won. Alex, after the time with Mac and Cor, was feeling like this was surely a day of good fortune. Alex and Erin took their winning chips and moved to the roulette wheel.

Roulette odds were set strongly against the players. Early on, the numbers were one to thirty-six and black and red. However, the gambling houses realized that these odds

274

were not favorable enough. The numbers were increased to include double zero and the colors were increased to include green. If any other game cheated like this, for example, chess had added a black queen but not an additional white queen, uproar would have ensued. No uproar ensued, however. The casinos were the masters of their own domains. Worldwide the odds were adopted and the players either accepted them or walked away. Occasionally, however, the players got lucky.

"No more bets," the croupier chanted in a voice deader than a monk chanting the litany of the saints. The wheel spun, the ball entered the wheel, and the click, click as the ball sought a resting slot enticing the gamblers with promises of hope and despair. A roar of approval/disapproval went up as the ball settled.

"We won," Erin exclaimed. "Holy shit." She hopped slightly in joy. Alex calculated their winnings as chips were piled in front of them, thirty-seven thousand dollars and change.

"Yeah, we did," Alex said calmly. "Should we quit?"

When they returned to the hotel, Alex dumped their cash winnings on the bed. They laughed as they counted the bolivars. It converted to around thirty-eight thousand dollars. They had actually been ahead about fifty thousand when they both decided to cash in. The casino, acting on behalf of the Venezuelan government, in the tradition of governments everywhere, withheld twenty-five percent as a potential tax. Alex was tired, but had a couple of things to do before he could relax.

The first thing he did was to arrange the three coins on the back of his discarded jacket and take a series of phone camera pictures. He photographed the fronts and backs of the coins. Then, he emailed the photos to his daughters. He wrote that Connie should feel free to share

275

them with their lawyer and no one else. The lawyer, Alex wrote, could share them with any of their potential partners he felt would be useful to help cement negotiations. Next, Alex called the number Bautiste had provided. The call was answered by an unexpected voice.

"Is the Colonel there?"

"You talk to me," the voice growled and Alex knew it was the big Sergeant who was always hovering around Bautiste. He couldn't remember the Sergeant's name.

"Ok. Sergeant, this is Alex Browning. I assume you know about my trip to Miami. I'm supposed to go tomorrow, but I don't have any information." Alex waited for the Sergeant's response. The Hammer took some time before he said, "I send email." Then he hung up.

"Have a nice night," Alex said into the dead connection. He checked for the Sergeant's email, read it, and deleted it. Basically, it said he would be picked up at nine in the morning and driven to Porlamar's airport. Everything this time was to be as before. No changes. He packed a small carryon with his toiletries and joined Erin in the large bed.

Saturday morning Jim Davis was pleased that his first call of the weekend was from Connie. They hadn't had a chance to get together the last couple of days and Davis was looking forward to spending some of the weekend with her.

"Hey, Connie," he began, "this is a nice surprise. Business or pleasure?" She was happy to hear the delight in his voice.

"Business, pretty much, Jim," she said with some regret. "I got an interesting email from my Dad last night." She went on to explain the pictures, a hyperlink that Alex had included to a website on Spanish gold, and Alex's directions to provide the lawyer with that information in case it was needed to bolster his   dealings on their behalf.

276

"Ok," Davis said, "send them to my private email." He gave her the address. "You know," he added, "it would be better if I had the actual objects. Can you make that happen?"

"I don't know," she admitted. "Let me see what I can do." Their conversation moved on to personal matters and they arranged to have dinner that night.

As Alex prepared for his trip that morning, his phone vibrated briefly. It was an email response from Connie. It was to the point: any way he could send her the coins? He revealed that he was going to be in Miami that night for only the one night. Could she meet him in Miami? She agreed and got his hotel information. The hotel phone rang and Alex had to go. His ride was there.

Connie called Davis for the second time that morning. She explained about Alex's trip to Miami and the coins. She apologized about dinner. Then Davis had an interesting thought.

"Why don't we fly to Miami together? I could meet your Dad and we could have dinner there. We could fly back tomorrow. What do you think?" Connie could tell that he was clearly spitballing, but she was excited at the proposition. She wanted to make one thing clear, however.

"Separate rooms," she said. He laughed.

"I was going to insist on that anyway," he said.

"Riiiight," she said drawing out the word. He laughed again. "My schedule's pretty flexible so you make the arrangements," she said. "Get us into this hotel if you can," she named the hotel where Alex was staying.

"Ok, talk to you later," he said. He put the phone to his lips and then set it on his desk. He started to compose a couple of emails, humming as he typed.

Alex met the Hammer in the lobby of the hotel. He still hadn't recalled the Sergeant's name. He put out his hand and the Hammer ignored it.

"We go," he said and turned on his heel. Alex, carrying his small bag, followed.

"I don't remember your name," Alex said to the broad back. The Hammer paid no attention. He led Alex to a black Toyota Forerunner. He got in the driver's seat and hit the button to unlock the passenger door. Alex took the passenger seat and held his bag on his lap. He glanced in the back seat and saw the large suitcase, just as before. The Hammer started up and took off for the small airport.

Garcia dropped Alex off with no niceties. He had made it clear during the drive that Bautiste would no longer have any direct contact with Alex. This revelation made Alex uneasy, but he couldn't figure out why he felt that way. The check-in was trivial and his large suitcase was checked through to Miami, USA. He enjoyed a cup of coffee during the short connector flight, although the ten thousand dollars in bolivars strapped around his waist made him a little nervous.

He made the connection in Caracas without incident. He was surprised that he was more concerned about carrying the cash than he was about the cocaine. He ordered a Bloody Mary and tried to relax.

Hours later Alex emerged from the air-conditioned comfort of Miami airport into the humidity and heat of the city. He had had some interesting moments since his plane landed in Florida. ICE or Immigration and Customs Enforcement had given his two bags more scrutiny than they had done during his first trip. He wondered if Pete Simmons was responsible. Fortunately, the officers had focused their entire attention on the bags and had not checked Alex personally. In any event, Alex had apparently passed muster with the agents and was allowed to leave. He had immediately headed for the men's room and had removed several wads of bolivars from around his waist. He went to the exchange window at the airport and, getting a truly lousy conversion rate, walked away with a pocketful of dollars.

Outside, Alex set the large suitcase on the sidewalk and waited for Bautiste's man to appear. He didn't have to wait long. The same man as before approached with a matching bag and set it beside Alex's. As before, he didn't look at Alex or acknowledge him. He took out a cigarette, lit it, and looked around. Then he picked up the cocaine bag and left. Alex watched him leave. He felt nothing. Not fear, not guilt, not anger.

Alex, of course, had no idea but the surveillance was also there as before.

Jim Davis received the coin photos from Connie. He studied them and wished that Alex had put something in the picture, like a dime or nickel, for perspective. He forwarded the photos to the firm in Florida that he had previously contacted. Even though they were still negotiating, he wanted them to know that his client was serious. He doubted that photos of three coins would be enough to convince them to commit to an operation in Venezuela, but he did feel that it probably couldn't hurt.

Davis sent an email to the other party with whom he was negotiating. He attached the photos to this email, too. He reasoned, again, that the photos couldn't do any harm at this stage. Probably, Davis thought, they won't make any difference at all. He wondered if he was right. He'd have to check with Chuck Murtaugh. Chuck was the in-house expert on those guys.

Davis made online reservations for a flight to Miami that would get Connie and him there about five. The round trip would get them back to Philadelphia on Sunday afternoon. He then used the hotel's website to reserve and pay for two rooms for the night. He found that he was excited about the trip and meeting Connie's father. He forwarded the flight and hotel information to Connie's email and got back to work.

Early in the afternoon, Davis got an email on his work account. It was a response from the Florida firm, thanking him for the photos, and did he have any guarantee as to their authenticity? Also the firm wanted to know if Davis had any estimate of the volume involved. Davis guessed that they were a little interested and were trying to figure out what size vessel they would have to move into position. Davis put off answering them. As the time neared for him to pick up Connie and leave for the airport, he was finding it more difficult to focus on work. Finally, he just gave up, notified his boss that he was leaving for the day and might be in late tomorrow, and left to pick up Connie.

Alex checked into his hotel and let the bellhop take his bags up to the room. He tipped the young Hispanic healthily and called down to room service for a bottle of Woodford Reserve and a suitable glass. Deja vu, he thought to himself. Next he pulled out his cell phone and looked up Pete Simmons' number. He called the FBI agent.

"Simmons," the agent said in a flat tone.

"Hey, it's your favorite cocaine smuggler."

"Alex! How come you're not in jail?"

"There's still plenty of time for that. How's it going?" Alex wanted to know if he was in any trouble and how serious the trouble was. He tried to sound more relaxed than he felt. He paced his hotel room and watched his reflection in the mirror.

"Not bad, and if you were worried about the DEA, don't. They understand what happened. I've been talking to a guy named Reynolds, John Reynolds. He appreciated the information you gave us."

"Well, good because I've got more information." Alex explained that he was again in Miami and, again, had delivered a suitcase of contraband to George Volek.

"Same as before?" Simmons asked.

"Exactly the same," Alex affirmed. "I've got the switched bag with me in my hotel room. What can I do to help?"

"Nothing for now. I shouldn't tell you this, but you and Volek were under surveillance the first trip you made. Sooo, I'm guessing you two were being watched this time, too. I'll get a hold of Reynolds and confirm that. You headed back to your island tomorrow?"

"Right, but first my daughter and our lawyer are joining me here tonight." Alex hurried on before Simmons could react to the word "lawyer." "It's something separate from this drug thing. It's a separate issue." When he spoke, Simmons didn't sound convinced.

"Yeah. What's it about then?"

"Nothing that you need to worry about, honestly. We're just exploring some other stuff and there're legal issues that need to be addressed. Nothing, really, Pete." Simmons' radar was up as he sensed Alex being evasive and too reassuring.

"Ok. Expect to smuggle any more powder in the near future? I'd like to get a heads up so I can pass it on to Reynolds. Makes me and, more importantly, you look good."

"I'm pretty sure this is it for me. The guy, who you'll remember is law enforcement, seems to be less than enthralled with me. I don't think he's going to use me again."

"That's disconcerting, then, bud," Simmons said without mirth. "I don't want to worry you unnecessarily, but when druggies do that, they usually follow up with something permanent. You need to watch your back." Alex didn't like this turn of conversation.

"Meaning?"

"Really Alex. One hundred percent of the time when someone's cut loose, it's permanently. Can somebody protect you?" Alex thought this over.

"I've got some friends on the island, as you put it. They're pretty tough guys in their own ways."

"Alex, what the fuck? They have to be more than 'pretty tough'. What's going on?" Simmons' voice conveyed a modicum of panic.

"Nothing's going on. Are you ok?"

"I'm fine. I just want to know that the people on your island are stiff, you know? Tough fuckers."

"I think they are," Alex said without conviction. "I mean I hope they are. They act all tough, drillers and stuff. I don't know," Alex admitted.

"Ok, Alex, relax," Simmons said. "We can't really infiltrate anyone, but we can keep an eye on things from afar. Ok?"

"I don't even know what that means, but ok if it keeps everyone safe." Alex thought of Mac, the diminutive Irishman, and their families. He gave Simmons his best wishes and broke off.

Room service knocked discreetly. Alex tipped the young staff member more than he could ever have hoped for. Alex poured three fingers of the brown liquid into the Waterford Lismore crystal glass that room service had provided. He enjoyed the burning sensation as he downed the bourbon. He went out on the balcony and enjoyed the ocean view with his drink.

Alex had a good buzz on when his cell phone rang. It was Connie.

"Hey, baby girl," he said careful not to slur. That was the signal to Connie that he had been drinking.

"Hey, Dad," she said. "Guess what. We're here. We got rooms at your hotel. Ready to get together?" Alex looked at his watch and was confused to see that it was already seven o'clock.

"Holy crap," he said. "I lost track of time. Absolutely, let's meet up in the hotel dining room in thirty minutes." He headed to his room's fabulous shower arrangement. The hot water helped clear his head. It was a multi-head, multi-jet tile and glass marvel. It even had a bench seat which Alex took advantage of letting the hot streams massage his aching leg joints.

After dressing, Alex found that he still had five minutes before joining his daughter and her friend. He also found that he was famished. He realized, that with his travels, he hadn't really eaten a decent meal all day. He decided to head on down to the dining room.

The dining room decor was in keeping with the promised luxury of the rest of the hotel. Discreet lighting and exquisite quiet were the main features. Alex announced himself to the maître d and was expertly guided to a table set for three. Alex liked the location of the table near a joining of two walls, not exactly a corner because of the angle. Alex asked for a wine list and a Woodford Reserve. The waiter disappeared.

"Dad, holy shit, look at you!" Connie delivered in a delighted tone catching Alex by surprise. Her companion, who was a tall, fit looking thirty-something man, laughed.

"Nice daughter talk," Davis commented. Alex liked him immediately.

"She's always like that," Alex said rising and extending his hand.

"Dad, you look amazing! Tan, and you must have lost ten pounds. Holy crap!" Connie was not to be distracted by the men's banter. Alex laughed and shook Davis' hand.

"Alex Browning," he said, "proud dad of this one and her little sister. You must be our lawyer." Davis laughed and relaxed.

"For tonight, let's just make it friends. Jim Davis," Davis said. "No billable hours. Pleased to meet you, finally. We can talk some business, if you want," he offered. "No billable, but I have a lot of questions."

"Hey, that reminds me," Connie interjected, "if we're dating is there some kind of lawyer/client breach of ethics? I want a drink, too," she said pointing at Alex's bourbon as it was delivered. It took Davis a second to regain his equilibrium and Alex smiled as he sipped his bourbon. "That's my girl," he said smacking his lips.

"I, well, I don't," Davis searched for the right words. "We're dating?" Connie looked at Alex and shook her head. Alex raised his glass in a toast and said, "He's a keeper." The waiter who had brought Alex his drink looked confused as he hovered to see if there were going to be more pre-prandial orders.

"Yes, we're dating and if that's against some kind of lawyer ethics then I resign my spot on the board. Now," she turned to the waiter, "can I get a Tanqueray and tonic, plenty of lime and ice?" The waiter made a note and looked at Jim Davis inquiringly.

"The same," Davis said still processing Connie's last proclamation. He looked at Connie and realized that with all the drama, they hadn't taken their seats yet. He pulled out her chair.

"So," Alex said to Davis as the lawyer took is seat, "I think you said you have some questions?" Connie smiled knowing her father's machinations. Davis was clearly gathering himself and attempting to regain his self-control.

"Yes, sir. As counselor for the corporation, your communications are protected by client/attorney privilege. That includes anything you tell me tonight. But," Davis paused and smiled, "first, I want to know." He looked at Connie. "We're dating?"

Connie and, then, Alex laughed. The gin and tonics arrived. Connie and Jim sampled them and, obviously, approved.

"Yes, dumb ass," Connie clarified. "Dad, what do you think of this moron?"

"Well," Alex began judiciously, "dating is possible. But, you guys, after that exchange, could also be married. Con, he seems like a moron with a good heart." Alex took a sip of his drink. "Could be the bourbon talking, though." He beamed at his daughter. She laughed as she sipped her gin and tonic and stroked Jim's hair.

"He does have a good heart, Dad," she said. "I had a Private Investigator get a copy of his EKG and, yeah, it's good." She mussed Jim's hair. Davis took a long draw on his gin and tonic.

"I see that this family is going to be a problem," he said. "Shall we order dinner before someone," he looked knowingly at Connie, "says something embarrassing?"

"Great idea," Alex said. "I mean about ordering," he said. "Connie can take care of herself." He smiled at his daughter. The three of them perused their menus. Alex saw

285

a selection he liked. The waiter, professionally, took each order: shrimp and crab legs and salad for Alex, tournedos and salad for Connie, beef Wellington and salad for Davis. Connie looked at Davis.

"Are you sure you want all those calories, and, the EKG wasn't that good?" she asked. Alex laughed in delight at his daughter.

"He's fit and trim, baby girl," he told his daughter. "Let it go." It was Davis turn to laugh now. He raised his glass in toast to Alex.

"Salud," he said, "to you and this lovely girl, your daughter. I drink to the both of you." He drained his gin and tonic soundly rapping his empty glass on the table. It was an overly dramatic toast, but he was having a good time with the Brownings.

CHAPTER THIRTEEN—Some Exchanges

The dinner turned out to be a tremendous success both gastronomically and socially. The hotel's restaurant did not disappoint in any aspect.

Alex leaned back and would have loosened his belt if he were in a more private setting. He was content. The banter between his daughter and her lawyer friend had amused him throughout the meal.

"Jim," he said, "you said before that you had some questions, a lot of questions. I assume you meant about the corporation and what I'm up to." They were having coffee and iced Bailey's.

"The questions aren't just mine," Davis admitted. "Our friends here in Florida and in Europe are also asking for more information. Europe," Davis went on and, here, Alex appreciated and admired the lawyer's circumspection by not naming the country. They seemed to be free of eavesdroppers, but why take a chance? "especially, would like some more specifics before they agree to the numbers. They're nervous because their own experts can't imagine that they have a ship out there that they don't know about."

"Crap, I forgot all about these," Alex said reaching into his pants pocket. He produced the three gold coins wrapped in tissue and discreetly covered them with his napkin. He pushed the napkin over to Davis. "Are those specific enough for Europe?" he asked. Davis unwrapped and palmed one of the coins and looked at it below the table level.

"These are the ones in the picture?" Alex nodded that they were. "Bigger than I guessed. These could help a lot in convincing our partners." He replaced the coin under the napkin and slid it over to Connie. "Are there a lot more of those?" Davis asked.

"We think so. We didn't get to finish our drilling. We hit a, um, snag." Davis could see Alex's discomfort and was, in turn, discomfited.

"What kind of snag?" Connie pushed the napkin back to her Dad who bundled the coins in the cloth and placed it in his lap.

"What happened, Dad?" she asked.

"There were bodies buried where we estimated the boxes were," Alex answered softly. "Well," he went on as they listened intently, "not exactly bodies. There were bones. Lots of bones."

"That's horrible!" Connie said.

"You hit a grave site?" the lawyer probed. He was sensing unseen legal issues.

"That's what we wondered," Alex admitted. "We don't know what we hit. We're pretty sure no one knows what we found, so we covered the bones back up and decided to think over what our next move should be."

"Any chance the bones could be the remains of the legal owner of those?" Davis said indicating the cloth bundle on Alex's lap. "That would be a complication. I'm thinking of descendants."

"What if the remains belong to the *illegal* owners of those?" Connie asked. "I mean we are dealing with pirates, right? What if the gold was stolen from some unknown third party? Then what?" Davis mulled this.

"Then, if I remember correctly, the gold will belong to whomever finds it."

"Well, we're done here, right?" Alex asked. He was not comfortable discussing all of this in a public place. "Let's go up to my room and I'll tell you what I'm planning." He pocketed the gold pieces and called for the check.

They sat around Alex's room as he explained about the *Little Ranger*, the boxes, the journal, and Mac and Cor.

"So, my idea is to get the French to agree to take 90% of whatever we find up to $100 million, and then to flip the numbers after that. We get 90% of anything over $100 million." Alex looked at them as they thought this over. The lawyer spoke first.

"It's a good deal for the French," he commented. "Not so much for you. I can't imagine that they wouldn't agree. Especially, since you're guaranteeing that they have a clean, incontestable claim to whatever you turn up."

"Here," Alex said handing the three gold pieces over to Davis, "you take these and share them with whomever you judge as necessary. Let's get this done, ok?" Davis took the coins and rubbed each one between thumb and forefinger. The weight of each felt the same to him. The lure of gold, he thought. There was certainly something to it.

"May I?" Connie said putting out her palm. Davis clinked the coins into her hand. "Heavy," she said hefting the three pieces. She rubbed each one as Davis had done.

Alex watched her smiling. He appreciated what his daughter was experiencing. "They're something, aren't they?"

"They are something," Connie said. "I was just thinking that they're like little baby coins. They've hardly been anywhere. Just sitting in the ground for almost four hundred years." The trio grew solemn then.

"Interesting way to put it," Davis said. "I guess the bones have been there for four hundred years too," he opined.

"I wonder what happened to those people," Alex said.

"if they were pirates," Connie said, "I'm guessing they died violently. Do you think they were murdered, killed in battle, died from disease, or what?" she asked. She bounced the gold pieces in her palm.

"We'll probably never know," Alex answered, "but seeing those bones and putting them back in the earth. That wasn't something I was ready for. It kind of made it too real. That people were on that spot four hundred years ago. They probably had relatives who wondered whatever became of them, unless there were survivors who took the tale home, eventually. Really interesting," he observed.

Jim Davis nodded in agreement. As an attorney, he considered the idea of relatives and heirs. "I'd guess that if there were relatives who knew what happened to those deceased, they'd have gone searching for the remains long ago. I don't think there will be any claimant issues." He pointed at Alex's bottle of bourbon. "Could I have a small one?" he asked holding his right thumb and forefinger about a half-inch apart.

"Absolutely," Alex said. "Sorry. I should have offered. Help yourself. The glasses are clean. Connie? Want anything? Room service?" Connie said that she was ok.

"Jim," she said, "I've been thinking. I mean I don't, obviously, know how these things work, but since we're already here in Florida, would it make sense to take a side trip tomorrow and talk to the people at the marine company? We could show them these." She held up the coins.

"Not only does it make sense, but I'm embarrassed that I didn't think of it. Let me go to my room and change our plane tickets and I'll catch up to you guys later. Ok?" They all agreed and Davis left the father and daughter alone.

"He's nice," Alex said getting a bourbon for himself. "Serious?"

"TBD," Connie answered. "We get along great so far and I like that he's not intimidated by me. He treats me like an equal." Alex laughed.

"I bet you're more than an equal and he knows it. By the way, I've met someone too." He took the next half hour explaining how it hadn't worked out with Elise. He told how Erin had attracted him immediately and how they had grown close to each other in such a short time. He described her intelligence and wit and her ability to keep him centered and focused on whatever the issue was at hand.

"She sounds cool," Connie said. "You haven't said anything about what she looks like though. Have any pictures?" The ubiquity of cell phones and their concomitant cameras made this a natural question for Connie. However, as a member of a different generation, Alex had never gotten used to the idea of unlimited photography.

"No," Alex admitted. "I guess I didn't think of it. Anyway, she's blonde, tall, tan, and has gray eyes. She kind of looks like that actress, the one with the big smile, all lips and teeth. *Pretty Woman*," he said. "That one. I can't think of her name." Connie thought for a second.

"Yeah, I can picture her. She was in that lawyer movie, with the boobs, too. I know whom you mean. Julia Roberts!" she exclaimed.

"Right," Alex said relieved. "A young Julia Roberts. That's whom Erin looks like, a little, anyway. What was the name of the lawyer she played?" Connie remembered immediately.

"Erin Brockovich. But she wasn't a lawyer," Connie corrected. "She was a legal clerk or assistant or something. Remember?"

"You're right. Jeez, I can't remember anything anymore. Good thing for Google, huh?"

"Good thing for old people like you," Connie teased. She pantomimed a kiss toward Alex.

"Thanks," he said with unveiled sarcasm. "Anyway, Julia Roberts. Somewhat. More importantly, Erin, the real Erin. I feel close to her, really close. That hasn't happened for a long time."

"Oh, Dad, I'm happy for you." She went over and gave him a hug. "By the way, Jo and the Hunk were almost mugged Wednesday night."

"What?" Alex said, "What happened?" Connie described how Jo and Paul Tanner were approached and how Tanner had handled the would-be mugger. She explained that her sister and Tanner had joined her and Davis for dinner that same evening.

"I guess that punk got the surprise of his life messing with an ex-Seal. It's surprising to me that the D-B didn't see that Tanner was in great shape.

"I know. It's stupid. But, also, I didn't get to tell you another thing. It looks like Jo and the Hunk are becoming an item. Jim and I both noticed it. Jo pretty much denies it though. As you'd expect." Connie shook her head. "Sisters know these things. Anyway, so maybe the Brownings are all getting lucky." She took a Coke from Alex's mini-fridge. "Ok?" she asked holding up the can. Alex nodded.

"Of course," he said.

"Or maybe it's just that it's spring," Connie observed, opening and sipping her drink. Alex smiled wryly. He was thinking that this young lady was someone he didn't have to worry about. She understood the world and handled it well. Just then there was a tapping at Alex's hotel room door. Alex opened the door for Jim Davis.

"All taken care of," he said. "I even called the salvage company owner to make sure he would be in the office tomorrow. He sounded interested to meet with us, but I got the feeling that he has a healthy amount of skepticism."

"That's probably a good sign," Alex said. "I wouldn't be too confident in someone who was ready to jump in with both feet based on the little information we've given them so far." He noticed that Davis emptied his bourbon. He offered his own glass. "Want to finish this? I'm switching to water for the rest of the evening." Davis poured Alex's drink into his own glass.

"Thanks," he said. "You're right, I think. Their reactions have been exactly those of a responsible company trying to expand its business. Well, we'll find out tomorrow."

Sunday morning found the three saying good-bye in the hotel lobby. Alex had asked Connie to keep his credit card paid down and Connie agreed. Connie had insisted on paying Alex's hotel bill and he knew better than to argue with her when she was insistent.

"Oh and, Dad," she said as she hugged him, "don't know if you remembered, but today is Selection Sunday. Gonna watch?" She was referring to the yearly college basketball tournament. The teams were announced on a Sunday.

"I forgot all about it, so much going on. Thanks for reminding me. Next weekend is my favorite weekend of the year." He kissed her on the cheek. "Tell Jo I love her and miss her. Take care and I'll email you tomorrow. You too," he directed this last to Jim Davis. "I'll be interested in how it goes with the marine company." Davis shook his hand.

"You take care, too, sir," he said to the older man. "Be careful," he added for wont of nothing else to say. Alex's shuttle van to the airport was the first to leave so he got in, waved to the two, and was driven off.

"Your Dad's a good guy," Davis told Connie, "but you already know that."

"Yeah, I do," Connie said taking Davis' hand and squeezing it. "How do you want to handle the marine company guy today?" she asked straightening her back. "Good lawyer, bad lawyer?" Davis laughed so loudly that the hotel staff and guests in the lobby stared at him.

Their flight to Fort Lauderdale was so short that they hardly got settled in their seats before the propeller plane began its descent. Connie noticed that the cabin hadn't even begun to cool from the air-conditioning.

They disembarked into a gentle warm breeze that the Fort Lauderdale Chamber of Commerce would have been proud of. They rented an SUV just for the extra visibility, set the navigation destination to the address of the marine company, and drove off.

The company was in a part of town near the water, but was lacking any oceanside charm. There were docks; shops dedicated to various boating endeavors, and maintenance businesses for boats both small and large. Their destination had a parking lot with only four spaces. Three were empty. A large door stood open leading into an equally large workspace. Connie followed Jim into the workspace and was blind because of the transition from sunlight to poorly lit interior.

"Hullo?" Jim called into the darkness. There was a machine motor running back in the dimness. "Hullo?" he called again.

"Hullo," a voice called. "Mr. Davis?" The voice turned out to belong to a man that Connie imagined would be on the poster for a guided fishing business. His face was deeply tanned and creased. He had short gray hair and muscled arms and legs. He wore tattered cargo shorts and a faded blue denim shirt with the sleeves cut off. He was barefoot which, to Connie, seemed insane given the man's work environment. Davis stuck out his hand.

"Mr. McDonald?" Davis asked. The two men introduced themselves and Davis introduced Connie using her first name only. Davis was purposely vague about Connie's role in the meeting. Connie knew that McDonald was the owner of the business. McDonald ushered them into his small, attached office where an air-conditioner whirred. He took his place in a chair behind a desk that was more of a table. Connie and Davis sat on stools facing the owner.

"So, your office," McDonald was obviously including Connie, "said you have a salvage job you want me to bid on?" Davis answered.

"There won't be any bidding. The job is yours if you want it." McDonald ran his palm over his short gray hair.

"Why's that?" he asked with undisguised suspicion. His thought was that something illegal was being proposed. He looked at the couple casually.

"Your company has the exact reputation our firm is looking for," Davis answered. "You go in, get the job done, minimize the drama, and move on." McDonald was unconvinced.

"And why is that important to you?" He directed this last at Connie, challenging her to speak up.

"It's important because," Davis started to say. Connie interrupted.

"Because several governments are involved," she said smoothly, "agreements are signed and in place, and we need someone who won't fuck it up." She smiled sweetly. McDonald looked at her to see if she was mocking him and then he laughed.

295

"Ok. Ma'am, you may be the first lawyer in my entire life that spoke honestly to me. So, what's next for us?" He directed this at both of them. Davis sensed the tension was broken and some friendly line had been crossed.

"Well, we need to get your commitment to the project. And to decide on your compensation." Davis watched as McDonald thought this over.

"First of all, call me Travis or Trav since I'm going to do your project. Second, my compensation will be one million dollars. Guaranteed." Davis held his expression, but he was thinking that the friendly line hadn't been crossed by much.

"Mr. McDonald, er, Travis, er, Trav. Wouldn't you consider a percentage of whatever is recovered? That could mean much more that a million dollars to you. And, why a million dollars? I've got to ask so I can report to my client."

"Well, son, no I wouldn't consider a percentage," the Florida man began, "first, because this is my business, not yours. The chances of recovering something of significant value from a wreck are running, right now in 2013, at less than 15%. You're a smart lawyer, so I don't have to tell you that that means an 85% chance of coming up empty.

"So, the million is for two reasons: to pay me for my trouble and effort and to test your commitment to the project." McDonald sat back and folded his arms across his chest. Connie had a thought.

"Travis, would you take a look at something before you make your final decision?" she asked. Without waiting for his answer, Connie urged Jim to produce the gold coins.

"What do you think?" she asked when the coins were placed on the table surface. McDonald leaned forward, reached for his glasses, and peered at the gold with a scientific intensity.

"Where'd you get these?" McDonald asked. "May I?" He indicated the three pieces on the table. He knew to ask before touching.

"Sure," Davis said, "go ahead." The gray-haired man picked up all three in his tanned and mottled hands. He turned them over and studied them. He pulled a drawer out on his side of the table and produced a large magnifying glass. He put the glass to work as no one spoke. Connie tried to read McDonald's expressionless face, but he could have been an experienced poker player without the sunglasses and hat. He seemed to have reached a conclusion as he returned the coins to the table.

"These are something," he said. "How long are you going to be in town?"

"We're leaving this afternoon," Connie said. McDonald seemed disappointed.

"Well, here's the deal," he said. "I'd like to research these if I can. There are a few sources I'd like to check. Would you trust me with them?" He looked at the young couple for an answer. It was Davis who, being a lawyer, sensed a chance for leverage.

"Would photos be good enough for your research?" Davis asked, already knowing the answer.

"No, you already sent me photos," McDonald answered, "and photos can be tampered with. Besides, I want to do metallurgical tests as well as some provenance checking. Understand?" He looked to the lawyer for comprehension.

"Oh, I understand," Davis asserted. "How long would you need the coins for?"

"Let's see," McDonald stared at the ceiling of the room, "today's Sunday. How about Wednesday? That suit you?" It was Davis' turn to look disappointed.

"No, sorry. That's too long. Look, I'll be honest with you. One of the governments involved needs to be convinced as to our sincerity and capability. Would you be willing to vouch for these," Davis indicated the coins, "as soon as you're satisfied? Give your approval to the government we're working with?" McDonald was used to this kind of negotiating and he stretched out his hand.

"Deal," he said. "As long as these prove out. I've dealt with most of the governments in the world and they know me. If these are the real deal, I'll let them know and, trust me, that'll go a long way toward establishing your bona fides." Davis thought this over.

"I believe you. Ok. Hold on to these. Satisfy yourself and I'll be in touch on Monday to check your progress. Ok?"

"Sure. Just remember: a million dollars guaranteed." Davis smiled grimly.

"We'll see. I'll do what I can. My client is not a wealthy man." They took their leave, returned the rental to the airport, and caught their flight, through Atlanta, back to Philadelphia.

By the time Connie and Jim had left Atlanta for Philadelphia, Alex was landing in Caracas. He had grown accustomed to the routine having gone through it three times in less than three weeks. He caught his connector flight to Porlamar and relaxed and watched the blue water pass below him. He smiled as he fondly remembered the previous night with his daughter and Davis. The smile vanished as he looked ahead to his coming meeting with Bautiste. Alex was surprised at how quickly and how strongly his feelings had turned against Fernando. He knew he had been shamelessly manipulated by the law officer and was embarrassed by that fact.

"Would you like anything else, sir?" the flight attendant asked. She was attractive and had been flirting with Alex since he had boarded. Alex thought, jeez, it's like I'm on a roll.

"No, thank you. I'm fine," he answered reclining his seat and closing his eyes. He realized he was bone-tired after the last three days. He couldn't wait to get back to the hotel and Erin.

That Sunday evening, Alex felt sufficiently recuperated after a light supper. He and Erin had brought each other up-to-date. Alex found an email from Davis among the usual notices of offers to save money by buying stuff. Alex whistled and Erin asked why.

"The marine company wants a million dollars," he answered. "In advance of any activity on their part." Erin looked over his shoulder to read the email for herself.

"How can you pay that? Do you know anyone who has a million dollars?" she asked rubbing his shoulders.

"No," he admitted, "and even if I did, I wouldn't ask them to risk their money in this situation. That wouldn't be fair, would it?"

"I know," she said, "but what are you going to do?"

"I don't know," he said taking her hands. "I'll think of something."

That same day, back in Philadelphia, Jim Davis had gone in to his office. He was dressed casually even though it was Sunday. As he was composing the email to Alex, detailing McDonald's demands, Chuck Murtaugh entered Davis' office, and walked up to look over his shoulder.

"A million dollars?" Murtaugh read. "What's that for?" Davis was irritated at the interruption and at the snooping. But, he needed Murtaugh's help since Chuck was the firm's expert on dealing with the French government. Besides, Murtaugh was notoriously socially handicapped. Murtaugh was also dressed casually.

"For services a Florida firm is going to provide our client," Davis answered. "How are you, Chuck? What are you working on?"

"The French are requesting clarification on that Expressway thing." Their law firm was acting as the mediator between a Paris-based construction company and the State of Pennsylvania. PennDOT, the state's Department of Transportation, had put out an open bid for infrastructure repairs to the part of Interstate 76 that ran through Philadelphia and was known as the Schuylkill Expressway. The job was worth, with incentives, up to a billion dollars to the winning company.

"What's not clear?" Davis asked. He was naturally curious as a lawyer when communication was unclear, and was partially leading Chuck away from questions about the part of Alex's business taking place in Florida.

Murtaugh took a deep breath and, picking his nose, explained that the French wanted to know more about how Pennsylvania's incentive program worked. A construction firm could be rewarded with millions of dollars above and beyond its negotiated fees if it performed well, beating schedule and budget milestones.

"So I have to hold their hand and walk them through it," Chuck said. "Oh, by the way, on your thing: they are clearly interested in making a deal. They're reviewing the numbers to see if they're ok. I expect I'll have an answer for you tomorrow. Work for you?"

"That'll work," Jim answered. "Appreciate it. Now, I've got to get this done." He indicated the computer and hoped that this was enough of a signal to Chuck that they were done conversing. Murtaugh exited Jim's office without further comment.

Davis continued to draft his email to Alex. He was realistic enough to know that Alex wouldn't try to borrow that much money against the possibility that there was an enormous treasure in his future. Davis considered approaching a competitor of McDonald whose demands might be significantly less than the Florida man's. Davis, however, had no authority to open further negotiations. He felt as trapped as Alex would feel when he read the email.

Davis focused his attention on what Murtaugh had said. The other partner was interested. That was great news. He included the information in the email. Maybe Alex would feel better about that.

Davis clicked on Send when he finished composing Alex's email. He wondered how the old man, which was how he thought of Alex despite his fondness for him, would take the news.

Joanne Browning was working that Sunday also, although she was at home in her apartment. She was browsing the Internet for anything connected to her job. The hacker forums were buzzing with conversation concerning a virus. BlackShades was a RAT, a remote access tool, a software program that, once installed, allowed a hacker to control a computer remotely. Control, in this case, meant recording keystrokes, accessing a hard drive, and even turning on a webcam. Jo knew all about BlackShades and had known for a year. But she was worried that the idiots on the Web were now talking about it openly. It had been written by a Swedish programmer and was for sale to anyone who could come up with the price. She had bought a copy and had reverse engineered the program improving it. She had only made it available to one other person.

301

BlackShades was undetectable to the victim. In its original form, it installed itself on the target system when the victim clicked on an enticing link. Joanne had modified the program so that it installed itself even when the victim only viewed an email. Of course, a wary email user could hit Delete when something came in from an unfamiliar sender. In that case, no install would occur.

Joanne's variation of BlackShades, which she called BlackShadesMe, was the program she had sent to her Dad. She was surprised that he hadn't contacted her by now. She knew he had travelled to Miami and met with Connie and Jim. She smiled at the thought of Connie and Jim. They were perfect, in her estimation, for each other. She wondered, though, if her Dad had had a problem with her program. She had sent him an email earlier in the day, but hadn't received a response yet.

Alex and Erin were having a relaxing Sunday evening. After checking his email inbox, Alex had decided to take it easy for the rest of the night. After all, as Connie had reminded him, today was Selection Sunday. Erin had admitted that she was a closet college basketball tournament junkie, although, she had said, she favored teams from the East. She told Alex, to his delight, that East coast basketball was more complete. When asked what she meant, she explained that teams from the East emphasized defense as well as scoring. Game totals might be lower than those played in the West, but they were more exciting because of the defensive tension.

Alex was delighted with her analysis. They spent the part of the evening lounging at the hotel pool. Erin was a people watcher and kept up a running commentary on their fellow bathers. Some northern Europeans were taking early vacations, but most of the holidaymakers were Venezuelans from the interior provinces.

Later they went up to their room to clean up. Then they sought out one of the hotel bars that had a sports theme. The Selection show was being rebroadcast. The so-called experts presented their opinions as to which teams should be selected for inclusion in the tournament and why. After the official Selection Committee revealed their choices and the tournament seedings, the so-called experts gave their analyses as to why the Committee had erred and the experts were right. To Alex, this was always a funny CYA moment. Funnier still to Alex was the moment when the experts revealed their brackets, the predicted winner of each game round by round including the eventual champion. The next two weeks were so much fun.

"And in spite of all that, you know why I really love the tournament?" Alex asked Erin as they were served beer and peanuts.

"No, why?" she smiled.

"I'll give you a hint. It's the same reason I love the Little League World Series and the Women's FIFA World Cup." Erin thought this over looking for a common thread. She took a sip of her icy cold beer.

"Is it the win or go home mentality?" she asked.

"No, lots of sports events have that. Although," Alex reconsidered, "that is a part of it: win or go home."

"Ok, I give up," she said. "What do those three have in common that you love?"

"You're going to think I'm twisted, but hear me out," Alex warned with mock solemnity. "The thing that I really like about these competitions is that the losers cry." Erin laughed and then rolled her eyes.

"Yes, you're twisted," she started, but Alex interrupted.

"No, really, think about it," he said, "I wish that all competitors cared so much that they cried when they lost. Think how great that would be," he exhorted. "The World Series Little Leaguers are the best. Raw emotion."

"What about the winners? Don't they show the same amount of emotion, only joy?" Erin argued.

"Sure," Alex answered, "but all winners show that joy. To me, it's the losers who show how much the players care, how much the game meant. It's cool, don't you think?"

"I don't know," Erin admitted. "Maybe I'm just not as twisted as you," she conceded. They watched the replay of the selection program.

Watching a live broadcast of the selection program were Jo and Tanner. Jo had called the Hunk after she finished her work. They were watching at a sports bar near Villanova University's main campus. The bar was packed with Villanova faithful, hoping and expecting that their team would be not only picked, but also highly seeded. It didn't take long for the Selection show to reveal that Villanova was selected, placed in the South region, and as a middle-of-the-pack 9th seed, would play North Carolina in the first round. The bar was filled with groans when this news was announced. Villanova fans expected a seeding no lower than fourth.

The Hunk, as a Villanova night school attendee, was a Wildcat fan. Jo didn't really care that much. She hoped for a good showing from Philadelphia's teams and, especially, hoped that La Salle, for her Uncle Terry's sake, would be picked. Her T-shirt this day read: "I fought the lawn and the lawn won" with a picture of several dandelions. To her delight and dismay, La Salle was selected as a provisional 13th seed. What this meant was that La Salle was part of the recently introduced "First Four", four teams who would play to determine who would gain access to the field of sixty-four. La

304

Salle would play Boise State University who was also a provisional 13th seed. The winner would go into the South region and play Kansas State University in the first round.

"That sucks," Jo commented. "If they're good enough to be a 13th seed, they shouldn't have to play themselves in. That's going to make it tough." Jo was referring, Tanner knew, to the fact that the First Four winners had to play twice in the first round while other teams played only once, a distinct disadvantage.

"Agreed. I never have understood why they had to game it up. All about the money I guess." After this observation, the rest of the selections were not of much interest so Jo changed the subject.

"I heard from Connie that Dad installed my BlackShadesMe program." Tanner knew what she was talking about. They had often discussed the possibility of future warfare being fought through technology. As someone who had faced, and smelled, his enemy, Tanner was comfortable with the idea of gaining any edge through technology. He applauded the use of drones. He would have like to have seen the military use robots more. He knew that software was key to gathering intelligence and would be even more so going forward.

"So what's he doing with the intel?" Paul asked. He knew that the data flow could be overwhelming, to say the least.

"I haven't heard from him yet, but I think he's just going to store it," she answered with a tone of regret. "I'm going to ask him tonight to upload it to the cloud so I can analyze it."

"Where's he storing it now?" Tanner asked. He was aware that the vastness of the cloud made for safer storage than someone's local drive.

"Local drive I guess," Jo said. "Dad knows a lot, but he hasn't had to worry much about system security, other than passwords, during his career. His company had departments to take care of that." Tanner had a thought.

"Isn't he going to run out of disk space eventually?"

"I know. I'm worried about that too. Half a terabyte should be enough, though," she answered. Tanner could tell that she was now distracted. The television experts were going on and on advising America how to fill out the winning office bracket.

"I've seen enough of this. You?" Tanner asked. Jo agreed and they settled their bill and left. Sunday nights for young singles could be a lonely time in Philly. Tanner said, "Want to come over? I've got Game of Thrones Season 2 on DVD." Jo thought for a minute.

"Sounds good. Got beer?" she asked mocking a familiar ad.

"Yes I do."

"And, can I use your computer? I want to send an email to my Dad."

"Absolutely. I have popcorn, too," Tanner said.

"Microwave or kernels?" Jo asked. Tanner scoffed at the audacity of the suggestion.

"Kernels, of course," he said with affected wounded pride.

A roar went up in the Common Room as the announcement was made that the La Salle Explorers would represent the University in the Tournament. In contrast to his niece's disappointment at the Explorers' play-in status, Brother Terry and his fellows were extremely pleased at the team's inclusion. They all knew that the exposure for the University was a priceless bit of advertising. Most universities experienced a jump in enrollment of from fifteen to twenty

306

percent the following year. Student enrollment was the fuel that kept the University's engine running.

"How good is Boise?" asked Brother Roderick of no one in particular.

"They're good, but slow," Brother Edward shouted. Brother Edward was passionate about college basketball, men and women's, and had an encyclopedic knowledge of the sport. He had, for forty years, been the go-to guy when anyone in the community needed a fact or an informed opinion where college basketball was concerned. The Internet, however, had leveled the playing field and nowadays anyone with a laptop, tablet, or smart phone had access to the same knowledge, unless Edward was nearby and the question was about sports trivia from the '70s or '80s.

"Thanks," Roderick gave Edward a thumbs up. "Can't wait for Wednesday." That was the day La Salle was scheduled to face Boise State University in Dayton, Ohio.

Brother Terry hummed as he headed for the Refectory. He was delighted that the Selection Committee had included the University. He knew that his brother and nieces would also be delighted. He wondered how Connie had made out with the lawyer. What was his name? Jeff? John? Jack? Jim? That was it. Jim.

He also wondered how Alex was doing. Was his brother safe? Was his crazy plan progressing? Was there anything that Terry could do to help? He decided to call his niece, Connie, after dinner.

Dinner was typical Sunday fare. Sliders, shrimp boil, and crab legs served buffet style. Terry piled a plate high and searched for a table populated with those Brothers he enjoyed. He spotted Roderick and Edward seated with a couple of the younger Brothers. As a member of the Administration, the younger members of the community held Terry in awe. He sat down, greeted everyone, bowed his head in grace. and then asked, "Well. What about it? We're in the Dance!"

Brother Lawrence, who would be the least likely of those at the table to have a sports opinion, said, "We're not exactly in the Dance, Terry. We're in the playoff to the playoff, the play 'IN' game. It's not the same." Terry took a large bite of slider garnished with cheese and onion.

"We're a thirteen seed," he pointed out loftily while chewing. "That is 'IN'. Don't worry. We'll handle Boise. Right, Ed?" he asked of the acknowledged expert.

"In my heart, I hope so," Edward said fervently. "But," he cautioned, "it's the Tournament. You never know. Remember North Carolina State? Remember Villanova? That's why it's so compelling."

"It's not the tournament," Lawrence protested, "it's a fucking play in game. Christ forgive me," he murmured bowing his head.

"He forgives your potty mouth," Terry assured, gobbling a shrimp, "but not your stupidity." He burped softly. "Excuse me."

"Why is it stupid?" Lawrence protested. "It's just a play in game. We're not in the field of sixty-four. Yet," he amended.

Roderick, ever the peace maker, asked, "Will we get in, Ed? Will we beat Boise?"

"I think so, Rod," he said. "We're more athletic, quicker, better offensively. Let's just say we should beat Boise."

"And there you have it, sports fans," Terry said talking into a crab leg as if it were a microphone, "the Prediction. You heard it first here, La Salle over Boise, a guarantee from Brother Ed. Let's hear from a young fan." He stuck the crab leg in Brother Lawrence's face. "What's your reaction, young man?" The whole table was laughing now, as well as the occupants of the adjoining tables, typical Refectory levity.

"As an avid Explorer's fan and a realist, I predict," Lawrence paused for dramatic effect, "La Salle will win easily by ten." The whole Refectory roared in approval. Terry hoped he was right.

CHAPTER FOURTEEN—Arrangements

Monday morning was sunny in Porlamar. Alex had gotten acclimated to the constant sun and humidity. He stood on the hotel room balcony and watched as the hotel pool crew did their work. A couple of them were working with brushes on long poles while two others were on their knees using hand brushes to scrub the decorative tile. He sipped his coffee as he watched them and considered Joanne's email. The owner of the salvage company needed a million dollars to accept the job. He wouldn't take a percentage, which would have been Alex's preference. He hated to do it, but he would have to involve Joanne. He had thought about it last night. Jo's software was reaping a mountain of data and Alex had no idea what to do with it. He thought, though, that Bautiste's data might hold the key to the salvage company's fee.

"What're you thinking about?" Erin asked. She held a cup of coffee and wore a hotel robe.

"The Florida company. I've got to find a way to pay them. They're essential to the plan." He raised his cup and realized it had gone cold. "And I think I'm going to have to take Jo up on her offer." He entered the room and poured more from the thermal carafe.

"You're afraid she'll be in danger, aren't you?" Erin rubbed his arms and rested her chin on his shoulder.

"Well, yes. We both know what that prick Bautiste is capable of. I'm not going to let her do anything that would even remotely endanger her." Alex turned to Erin, clearly struggling with his dilemma. "But I need her help." He shrugged. "I'm going to send some emails, ok?"

"Of course," Erin hugged him. "Do what you need to do. I'll stay out of your way."

"You're not in my way, sweetie. I feel better when you're near by. It's easier to focus. Sit near me." He grabbed his laptop and sat at the room's small table.

Alex first sent an answer to Jo. She had encouraged him to move Bautiste's data from his laptop's external drive to the "cloud", meaning any available server space on the Internet. She explained that she wanted to process the data, in other words, sort it and organize it. With so much data, she wasn't going to do this manually. She had more software that would do the processing for her.

She suggested that Alex rent space on some company's servers and upload his cache of data there. He could send her the access info.

Alex uploaded Bautiste's data, all four gigabytes of it, to the website that sold everything. The company made it amazingly easy. In his answer to his daughter, he included the access information and hoped that would be enough for her. He then turned his attention to his brother's email. Terry had warned Alex to be ready for word from France. Brother Roderick had used his back door contacts to feel out how Jim Davis' negotiations were going at the French end. The answer was encouraging. The French, as Alex had guessed, saw no risk in the offer and a fairly large reward. Terry had said to stand by. Alex judged that no reply was warranted.

Alex then had to consider an email from Mr. Travis McDonald, the owner of the Florida firm. Jim Davis had forwarded the email with a two word comment: "Please advise." Alex had to decide with whom to share McDonald's information. Alex's was used to "need to know" situations. He had been involved with them his whole career. This was plainly good news, but, in McDonald's words "sensitive."

McDonald had spent his Sunday running around Fort Lauderdale, visiting a variety of experts. First he visited a local historian, John Colletta. Colletta was an old man whose eyes had failed him long ago. He wore thick glasses and his office was equipped with a number of other optical aids. McDonald and he were uneasy allies, never friends, but often cooperative antagonists. Their antagonism went back to the '60's when both men were in their early 20's and motivated by greed and a competitive urge that could have easily been characterized as unreasonable. Back then both men chased every rumor of sunken treasure as if their very lives depended on it. As it turned out, Colletta's life almost did. In 1972, McDonald located a World War II wreck off North Carolina. McDonald quickly identified it as the *U.S.S. Harding*. The *Harding* had sailed out of Galveston, Texas with a load of Lend-Lease gold destined for the British government. Colletta, a smooth talking Italian-American with a friendly demeanor, had earlier convinced, *c'est a dire* "bribed", a clerk at a certain Federal Registry to alert him if ever an interesting claim was made. An interesting claim was made, Colletta was alerted, and a war of claims and counter-claims ensued. Unfortunately, for Colletta, McDonald had obfuscated the exact location of the *Harding* so that, when pressed for details of his claim, Colletta, stammering and stalling, was less than convincing and the claim was awarded to McDonald. The recovery was sufficient to launch McDonald's company. Bad blood had existed between the men since then. Neither man had seen the other since that time. Colletta had given up treasure hunting and had established himself as an expert in wreck provenance over the intervening years.

McDonald offered his hand to Colletta.

"John, it's good to see you." The historian hesitated ever so slightly before taking the proffered hand.

"Travis, it's been a long time," Colletta said noncommittally. "What have you been up to?" His voice left no doubt that he no longer cared.

"This and that," McDonald answered equally noncommittally. "Mostly this," he said as he produced the three gold coins and deposited them on the expert's desktop.

They lay there glinting in yellow challenge. Colletta stared at them for a prolonged minute and then reached and picked one up. He examined it. Then he fetched a magnifying glass from a nearby surface and peered more closely. In spite of himself he whistled softly. McDonald noticed and had a visceral response. He wanted to ask questions, but controlled himself and remained quiet.

"These are some shit," Colletta admitted. "Where'd you get these?" He picked up another gold piece and studied it. "Shit," he said. McDonald had anticipated the question and had formulated his answer.

"You don't need to know, John," he answered. "So they're the real deal? What century, do you think?" He looked hard at the historian's face trying to detect any effort at deception.

"Early eighteenth, I think. The quality is unbelievable. Where are these from?"

McDonald ignored his question. He retrieved his gold and moved on to his next stop.

Lauren Chastain was a weasel. But she was also the foremost numismatist in Fort Lauderdale. And she loved making deals.

"Travis, I want to help you, but you have to show me what you have." Her voice was nasally and full of phlegm. McDonald had attempted to gain the coin woman's cooperation by describing the gold pieces and adding Colletta's evaluation. He was unsuccessful.

"Ok. Here," he said and handed them over to Chastain. She took them in her small hand and reached for the switch on a magnifying contraption usually used for circuit board manufacturing. The switch turned on a fluorescent bulb. The gold was illuminated and magnified.

"These are amazing," she said softly as much to herself as to McDonald. "Where are these from?"

McDonald's next visit was to Dan Carney. Carney was a gold trader by name. In fact, he was a failed trader who started in the '70's pushing gold as a safe haven, a hedge, from the rampant inflation of that time. He sold futures, mining stock, and the hard commodity. The panic of the 1970's never happened and the investors grew impatient and drifted away. Now, Carney worked cold calls trying to convince widows and retirees that gold was the smart haven for their cash in this time of terrorism.

"Travis, my friend, welcome, welcome," Carney oiled forth. "What can I do for you?" He grabbed McDonald's shoulder in an unwelcome gesture. McDonald flinched involuntarily.

"Dan, how've you been?" Uninvited, he took a chair in Carney's small office. It was cheaply paneled and carpeted and reeked of failed business.

"Great. Never better," Carney replied. "Kind of busy so how I can I help you?" he reiterated. McDonald decided not to waste of any of his own time.

"These," he said producing the coins, "you can help me with these. Give me a valuation on these. What are these worth?" Carney leaned in to get a better look at the gold.

"May I?" he asked reaching for the coins. McDonald handed them over. Carney looked at them carefully.

"Mind if I check my materials?" he asked. McDonald merely shrugged. Carney took down several large references from the shelves in his office. He picked out a coffee table-sized book that had seen better days. He thumbed through the TOC and apparently found what he was looking for.

"Your guys are Spanish," he told McDonald. "They look like 1719 mint, but the weird thing is they don't show much wear. Like they were never circulated. See what I mean?" He held up a coin. McDonald only saw that the coin was gold.

314

"No," he answered. "How do you figure 1719? I don't see that."

"The Spanish minted their gold in many places at that time. These were minted in Mexico City. See these dots. Mexico City was the first to get them so precisely. Dates weren't always stamped, but Phillip V was King at the time." He paused. "I'm just guessing 1719, say plus or minus a year. What's the wreck? I could nail it down closer for you." And figure out where the gold is, McDonald thought.

"Don't know," he answered honestly. "Client is playing it close."

"Too bad. Want the valuation?"

"Of course."

"Two hundred dollars." McDonald stood up.

"You fucking thief," he started.

"As my fee," Carney said quite calmly. McDonald sat back down.

"Ok," he said fishing out his wallet. Carney produced a digital scale and weighed one of the coins.

"Fifteen hundred, give or take a hundred," he said. "Of course, the historical value would only add to the valuation. Say, double to a collector. Happy?" He handed the coin over to McDonald.

"Happy," McDonald confirmed.

McDonald's final stop was at a lawyer friend of his, Tony Stockton, Esq. Stockton gave advice and charged for it. His fees were calculated according to the complexity of the question. McDonald's question was simple.

"How do I know if there's some legal bullshit around the corner?"

"Not your worry," was the lawyer's answer. "The client assumes the legal risk. You're just the vacuum cleaner." He placed his palms up for emphasis. "Where'd you get these?" he asked admiring the coins.

McDonald returned to his office and thought about the information he had gathered. McDonald was not disappointed. He emailed the facts to Jim Davis and asked if the lawyer would reconsider the million-dollar fee in exchange for a percentage of the salvage. Davis forwarded McDonald's idea to Alex with just a two word comment: "Please advise."

Alex considered McDonald's proposal. The coins had been certified by a myriad of experts. This did bode well for Alex and everyone. Alex could see no reason to give the man in Fort Lauderdale a percentage. Obviously, McDonald considered a percentage more valuable than the million dollars already agreed to. The problem was that Alex still had no idea from where the million dollars would come. He decided two things.

The first part of Alex's response to Jim Davis was to tell the lawyer to stall McDonald. Alex had no doubt the lawyer would come up with some credible excuse. The second part of the email was to give Davis permission to share McDonald's findings with the French. Alex hoped that this would push them to make a decision. Alex pushed Send and turned his attention to Erin.

Jo spent Monday morning visiting a client whose website had been hacked and whose customer information was believed to have been compromised. It still surprised Jo how careless a company could be with their customer's data even when the company was small. Fortunately, she had advised this company to store customer's personal data such as phone numbers, email addresses, and names in one database and customer's financial information and password information in a separate database. Only the personal information had been hacked. The client would have to alert their customers, but the damage had been mitigated. Jo always felt good when she saw the relief on her clients' faces. She enjoyed delivering good news.

When she checked her smart phone as she drove back to the office, she saw that she had a response from her Dad. Joanne had made it a practice long ago to make sure that her phone was turned off when she was with a client. Not set to Vibrate or Do Not Disturb, but Off. She was aware that many of her clients did not bother to return the courtesy, but, Joanne reasoned, they were the clients. She was tempted to sneak a peek at the email, but Pennsylvania and Philadelphia had very strict "Texting While Driving" laws and enforced them seriously. Besides, Joanne recognized the validity of the concern behind the laws. Every day she saw other drivers poorly controlling their vehicles while they gave their attention to some digital nonsense.

Back at her office, Jo logged in to her laptop and opened her email client. She browsed nineteen new items in her Inbox and opened the one from Alex. She smiled as she saw that he had taken her advice and copied all his stolen data to the Cloud. She got up and went to her mini-fridge, removed a bottle of Starbucks' Frappuccino, opened it, and returned to her laptop. She wasted no time using the access information Alex had sent.

As she had suspected and discussed with Paul, there was a lot of data. It was poorly organized, which was to say, totally disorganized. Joanne made a note and attached it to Alex's email to remind her that she should rewrite BlackShadesMe so that when it reaped its haul, it would sort the bits and bytes according to at least some broad classifications. She did a quick browse of the jumble. She saw emails, draft documents, spreadsheet contents, chart pitches, photos, and some video content.

Jo realized that looking through all of this would be a "time suck", as she mentally phrased it, so she opened a

TextPad session and loaded a Perl script she had been working on. She had conceived the script as a tool to attack what was known as "big data", the massive amount of content being scooped up every second of every hour of every day by companies like Google. There was so much data that no one yet had solved the problem of how to use it, let alone how to organize and make sense of it. Jo had a feeling that there were underlying commonalities among different parts of data that would identify them as belonging to a set. She reasoned that these sets could then be further divided into subsets and so on. Her hope was that software could penetrate the jumble of apparently unrelated items and begin to pull out pieces and place them according to some sense. She got to work modifying the script.

Magrew had had a lazy Sunday. The cafe was closed on Sunday so that he and Sonia could take the family to the beach or rent a boat and cruise around and do some fishing. They had, indeed, rented a boat and Mac had puttered it around intending to circle the Island heading East out of Porlamar, turning North, cruising West, then South and finally returning East to Porlamar. Mac paid special attention as Playa Madrid and the wreck site with its moderate Sunday activity drifted by. The trip took all day and they had made stops for food and fuel. Sonia and Mac had always enjoyed the water, but had been too frugal to buy their own boat. Sonia had felt that the fortunes of their small restaurant were too undependable to commit to a payment plan. She insisted that they pay cash for everything.

Monday morning found them back at work, preparing the lunch menu and putting out the chairs and tables. Mac made time to do some scraping and painting and general sprucing up. He hadn't talked to Sonia about it, but he was anxious to get together with Cor and Alex and finish the digging. He felt that he HAD to know, one way or the other. As he painted, he wondered if Alex felt the same. The old man had seemed confident that there was something to recover. Mac toyed with the idea of telling Alex his whole

318

story and then dismissed the idea. He finished up his chores, checked that Sonia, naturally, had everything in the kitchen under control, grabbed the newspaper and a Tulia, and sat outside where Sonia could not easily see him. He opened the paper and turned to the Sports Section. Because of their boat trip yesterday, he hadn't had a chance to catch up on the Selection Sunday news. He faithfully filled out a tournament bracket every year, although he hadn't competed against anybody else's bracket since he left the oil fields. He studied the selections and their seeds enjoying his Monday.

Jim Davis got Alex's response and was pleased with his acuity. In the lawyer's experience, not many clients were smart enough to strategize *and* follow their lawyer's advice. He had a couple of emails to compose and set to work.

The first was to the French, forwarding a summary of what McDonald had been told and adding a few phrases of explanation. He knew that the French government was on the fence, not for any good reason. They just were wary of a deal that seemed too good to be true. He hoped and expected that McDonald's information would set their minds at ease.

His second message was to McDonald. He understood the salvage man's ploy to try and increase his share of any salvage, and he didn't like it. As an attorney, he felt that a deal had been negotiated and agreed to. Now McDonald was trying to change it. He advised McDonald that his new offer was interesting and that, unfortunately, he was unable to reach his client for a decision, so he would have to get back to him later. Davis expected that would hold the Florida man for now.

Roderick had no Monday morning classes and was in his office grading papers when his Blackberry buzzed. As the red light alerted him to what he already knew, he punched some buttons on the keypad and brought up the new email. It was from his friend in the French government. Roderick, from the message, understood that the French were going to agree to Jim Davis' terms. Roderick, however, didn't comprehend the second part of the email, which alluded to "certification" and "authentication". He had no idea what this meant, but dutifully forwarded the message to Terry.

Terry noticed the message just as he was about to go to an early lunch. He smiled and considered alerting Alex that the French were fully onboard. Then he reconsidered, thinking that Roderick's information, while usually reliable, was not official. He decided, instead, to send Alex further encouragement that, according to his sources, the French would soon agree to all of Alex's terms. It looked like the Florida data did the trick. He passed this information on to Alex, also. Then he headed for lunch.

Jim Davis was getting ready to go to lunch when Chuck Murtaugh entered his office.

"Dude, the partners are confused and that's never good," he said sitting down and flicking imaginary specks from his shoulder.

"Confused about what, *dude*?" Davis resumed his seat behind his desk.

"Billing," Murtaugh said. He flicked again.

"What about billing?" Davis was getting nervous. He hadn't billed his hours for The Browning Group despite the balance in their account. He had held off because he knew the fledgling company, mainly Connie, might not have the finances currently to continue to meet obligations. He also knew that McDonald was demanding a cool million before he moved a ship toward Margarita Island. He was trapped.

"This Browning Group thing. The partners haven't seen a dime or a suggestion of a dime from your activity. What's going on?" Murtaugh flicked.

"Well, the truth is I've been busy. Out of town. And I didn't judge that it was something the partners would get in a twist about. I'll get on it if that's what they want." Davis opened his laptop so that it was a barrier between Murtaugh and him. Murtaugh stood up.

"I think that's the plan," he said and left the office.

Davis mentally kissed his lunch good-bye and opened his spreadsheet application. He calculated the hours times the rate and emailed the results to Connie, Alex, Jo and Terry in the form of a bill, a bill that practically depleted the Browning account. He copied the partners on the email and left Murtaugh off the distribution.

Jo finished her Perl script and, though it was time for lunch, logged into Alex's cloud account. She took some time to familiarize herself with the interface and how the data was stored. It was a bulk data storage schema. Good, she thought. A database, although well within the storage company's capabilities, would have made her script useless and forced her to code up an SQL query.

She downloaded the entire contents to a four terabyte external drive and launched her Perl script. She sipped a Red Bull as she watched the script churn its way through the huge amount of data. She went to a cabinet that was usually stocked with snacks, both salty and sugary. She grabbed a package of Twizzlers and returned to her desk. She ripped open the strawberry-flavored stretchy stuff, picked one out, and bit off a mouthful. She chewed thoughtfully as she watched her script drop bits and chunks of data into separate folders.

It took an hour for all of the sorting to finish. Folders had been created for emails, documents, spreadsheets, financials, charts, and images. Now the hard part began. Each folder had to be submitted to further filtering by Jo's script. The software parsed the data at a speed in keeping with the hardware's capability. Jo was looking for anything that could help her father. At 1:06 P.M. she found it.

Her script had sub-sorted email and one of the subfolders was <u>Business</u>. As she scanned the dozens of emails, she found two that excited her. Holy shit, she thought to herself. The first email was a correspondence between Fernando Bautiste and a bank in the Caymans. It contained account balances and, more importantly, the account numbers. There were three accounts and they totaled more than ten million dollars.

The other email was similar except that instead of Bautiste it belonged to someone named David Garcia. The account balance, for a numbered account at a bank also in the Caymans, was almost a million dollars.

Previously, Jo had browsed a folder of documents. There were a lot of documents, but one file named "Shh" had caught her attention. When she had tried to open it, she found that it was password protected so she had moved on. Now, she came back to it. She ran a password-cracking tool on it and had it open in less than ten minutes. The file contained Bautiste's list of login usernames and passwords. Apparently, the Venezuelan policeman had trouble remembering his access codes. The bank passwords for all of his accounts were there. The Garcia account … Jo got to work knowing what she would do.

Jo worked slowly and methodically. Her first task was to open an account at another Caymans bank. Her previous research had told her to open the offshore account. Since she had no intention of avoiding U.S. taxes and only intended to use the account as a parking spot, she had no need for most of the rigamarole associated with a Caymans account.

Her next task was to access the millions already on deposit in the various accounts belonging to the two cops and transfer their money in a series of transactions. She had reasoned that smaller transactions performed sequentially would attract less attention than one large move. Also, she hoped that electronic transfers between Cayman banks would allay any suspicions that the financial institutions might have. She logged in to the first account and entered the password. The screen flickered and settled into a display of account balances and available options. Jo selected Transfers to External Accounts. At first there was a delay as if the computer were considering the transaction. Then the display offered several fields: account to transfer from (there was only one choice), receiving account, transfer amount. She had started the first robbery of her life.

To her surprise, the transfers were unbelievably easy. In less than twenty minutes she had moved over ten million dollars. The ease gave her confidence and she transferred all of the money from the smaller account.

Now she had to move the money (or most of it) out of the Caymans account and into the Browning Group corporate account. Her heart was thudding as she typed the commands that moved a fortune from the Caribbean to Philadelphia. She sipped a Red Bull as the early afternoon moved along. She watched as the local account bulged with transferred wealth. Fuck, she thought, I did it. She wished she had a celebratory cigarette. Like Dad, she was a former smoker. The Browning Group corporate account was flush with over eleven million dollars.

Jim Davis felt guilty as hell. It was late afternoon. He had billed Connie and her family an amount that he knew was fair but felt was obscene. Guilty? He felt like shit. He pulled out his cell phone and started to look for Connie's number. She was under his Recent Calls list. He pushed the button to make the call when Chuck Murtaugh interrupted him.

"Good job, dude," Murtaugh said.

"Ok," Davis said hesitantly. "For what?"

"C'mon," Murtaugh said flicking at his shoulder and taking a seat, "ten million? That's chill." Davis was confused, but Murtaugh had no clue. "The partners got the word fifteen minutes ago and, may I say, they are pleased." Davis had no idea what was going on.

"Ten million? For what?" Davis asked seeking clarity. He had a sense of what was to come.

"Well, that's TBD, isn't it?" Murtaugh answered. "Your client, Browning Group, filled up the billing account, and how. Actually, a little more than ten." He pumped his fist.

"What the hell?" Davis said. "The hours were like sixty-five hundred. Maybe a bit more." He held his palms up. Murtaugh smiled.

"Your client must have wanted to build up a little credit," he observed.

Davis was concerned for Connie and wanted to contact her. He dismissed Murtaugh.

Davis logged in and immediately checked the Browning Group account.

Holy shit, he thought, ten million plus. Where did that come from?

Davis called Connie and was glad to hear her voice.

"Jim, great to hear from you. I'm just wrapping up a couple of things. Want to do lunch?"

"I can't, Connie," he said with obvious regret. "Too much shit going on, but I have a question."

"Shoot," she said. She had come to really enjoy talking with Davis, although she enjoyed spending time with him much more.

"Ok. Did you know that ten million dollars was deposited in the Browning Group's account this morning?" Davis could tell by her silence that she did not.

"What? Ten. Million?" Her incredulity was clear. He felt some guilt at surprising her like that.

"Sorry, Connie. I couldn't think of another way to ask you. Yeah, more than ten million showed up in the account this morning. Could it have been your Dad and the treasure thing?" It occurred to Davis that he hadn't yet questioned the source of the funds, only the amount.

"Let me check," Connie answered accepting the premise that it could have been Alex, especially with all the weird stuff going on.

"All right. Get back to me. Get with you soon," Davis said breaking off.

Connie contacted Jo as soon as she broke the connection with Davis. She had a warm feeling still after speaking with the attorney. Jo answered immediately.

"Big Sis!" she said delighted. "What's up?"

"Lil Sis!" Connie completed the greeting. "Some money stuff is up. Ten million. Know anything about it?" She doubted that her sister did know anything, but this connection was easier than one with her Dad.

"As a matter of fact." This wasn't the answer Connie expected. She waited for more. "I put that money there," Jo said. Connie was incredulous and had to ask.

"From where?" Jo explained about the software and her additional parsing software. Connie, of course, grasped both concepts.

"Wow. Stealing, Jo? What if somebody finds out?"

"When those two cops notice it's gone," Jo explained, "they'll have no idea where it went." She explained how she had double-blinded the transfer through an untraceable Caymans account to Philadelphia. Connie was impressed, but skeptical.

"Sounds like you did a nice job covering your tracks, Sis, but what're the chances you're wrong? It could be Dad's ass, not yours."

"Didn't think of that," Jo admitted. "But I'm pretty sure I'm right." As it turned out, it was neither Alex's nor Jo's ass that was on the line.

An hour and a skipped lunch later, Davis got even better news. It was a phone call.

"Eh, Mister Davis?" the accented voice inquired.

"This is Jim Davis," the attorney confirmed. His heart beat faster knowing it was the French government. "What can I do for you?"

"I want to discuss your proposed agreement. Oh, by the way, I am Monsieur Gerard. The Bureau of Antiquities employs me. I am also the friend of Chuck, (pronounced as 'Chook'), Murtaugh. I have good news, I think, for you." There was a pause and Davis waited until it was clear it was his turn to respond.

"Well, thank you," Davis said. "What's the good news, if I may ask?" He rubbed his thumb on the smooth surface of the phone.

"It is this," Gerard said. "Speaking for the French government, I am authorized to tell you that we have accepted the terms of the, what did you call it, recovery?" There was a pause and then Gerard went on. "To reiterate, 90% for us up to one hundred million dollars US, and 90% for the recovery team for anything above one hundred million. The French government retains ownership of the shipwreck. We will be in charge of evaluating anything recovered and will pay in US dollars. We will also take possession of whatever is recovered. We are responsible for the disposition of everything after the recovery. The operation is to be treated with the utmost discretion. Is that it?" Davis was impressed.

"I'll tell Chuck that you were extremely cooperative. That's it. So, we're agreed?" Davis could still not quite accept it.

"*C'est tout,*" Gerard said and hung up. The Frenchman smiled, thinking that he had just helped his government acquire a large quantity of US dollars, dollars that it desperately needed.

Davis' phone rang almost as soon as Gerard broke his connection. It was Connie. She was in a hurry and explained quickly what Jo had done.

Davis' next action was to move one million US dollars from the Browning Group account to an escrow account. He then phoned Travis McDonald in Fort Lauderdale.

"Mr. Davis," McDonald said. He was laying on his Florida twang. "What kin Ah do ya fo?" Davis was a little irritated with this bumpkin, but did not let it show.

"Mr. McDonald, there is a considerable sum of US cash sitting in an escrow account just waiting for you. Have you got a pen?" There was a delay as McDonald clearly scrambled for a writing instrument.

"Got it," McDonald said. "What is it?"

"Here's the account number," Davis said and he recited a ten character alphanumeric string. "Got that?" he asked.

"Lemme read it back," McDonald said and he read back the string.

"That's it. Now here's the password," Davis said. He rattled off another ten-character alpha-numeric-special character string that included upper case. "Read it back to me." McDonald complied faultlessly.

"Again, that's it. Did you write it down?"

"Got it," McDonald answered.

"Ok. Well, you can't do anything with them right now except verify the account balance. Understand?"

"Yeah. I can't get no money until I get your shit. Right?" Davis smiled at his office wall. Not as fucking dumb as he acts, he thought.

"Pretty much. When the time comes to get the money, we'll login with our password here and you do the same and *voila*. You're a millionaire!"

"La, whatever. I'm rich already. Ok, I'll move a boat into early position as soon as I see the balance. Then you'll have to tell me where the boat should go."

"Agreed. You'll need to have that boat pre-positioned by tomorrow. I'll email you the lat and long so there are no mistakes."

"Anywhere in the whole wide world. I kin get a contract out and a boat in place. Don't doubt it." Davis could imagine McDonald pointing a forefinger at an imaginary camera as if he were making a car commercial.

By Monday afternoon, Mac's quiet time had vanished in a literal storm. As he had worked his picks into the Elite Eight round and nursed a Tulia, the skies had darkened and opened up and doused the patio in a drumfire of huge raindrops. Mac had retreated to the restaurant's interior and continued to work on his bracket. Around two o'clock as he looked out the windows and marveled at the waste of such a storm pouring into the sea, he thought of the boon this would be to the slurry barges. The slurry ponds would be overflowing and the barges would be needed to pump them out and move the slurry out to sea. Extra income, he thought. This storm's intensity reminded him of the Houston, Texas storms he had experienced as a young man. He was interrupted in his reverie by the welcome and somewhat funny sight of a dripping Alex entering the restaurant.

"What's up?" Alex asked shaking his bare arms.

"Hold on," Mac said, "let me get you a towel." He retrieved one from the kitchen.

As he dried off, Alex glanced down at Mac's bracket.

"Louisville? Really?" he chided. "That's what you think?"

"Actually," Mac said folding the bracket and putting it out of sight, "when you arrived I was thinking of my youth. Sit down. Let me get you a beer and tell you all about me." He had made his mind up to tell Alex all. He went behind the bar and got a Tulia for Alex. He settled his bulk opposite the old man and started his story.

"I was a high school dropout and that wasn't my first mistake, but it was probably my second biggest," he began.

He recounted that he had felt invulnerable back in those days like all young people and that he had done a stupid thing that would change his life forever. He had had a good job in a refinery back then, but he wanted to be his own boss. He had gotten a line on a bar for sale - the seller had wanted $50,000, cash only, to close the deal. So he had

329

done what a rudderless young black man did. He got a gun, donned a floppy brimmed hat and a kerchief, and robbed a Houston Savings and Loan.

"Remember Savings and Loans banks?" he asked of Alex.

He had had the $50,000 and the gun in a brown bag on the seat next to him when he had sailed the wide-brimmed hat out the car window as he sped down the Interstate. He had disposed of the kerchief similarly just as he had noticed a patrol car noticing him. He exited the freeway and entered an area of small businesses that, maybe, had once been residences. Mac had made two quick right turns and had stopped the car. He had quickly hidden the brown paper bag behind some landscaped bushes, noted the location, and hopped back in the car. Three minutes later he was in handcuffs.

"So they had me. I was what? Twenty? My lawyer wanted to plead, but I was pissed off and said no."

The trial was short. The evidence was the car and the surveillance photos from the S and L despite the disguise. It was adequate for a conviction, but the prosecutor was willing to minimize the sentence if Magrew returned the money. Magrew, against the advice of his public defender, protested his innocence. The prosecutor asked for the maximum sentence of twenty to twenty-five years and got it.

Magrew went to prison, but not before he told his father about the hidden bag and the deal for the bar. He made his father promise that he would take him on as a partner in the ownership when he was released. His father agreed, bought the bar, and turned it into a thriving business. Magrew was released on probation in six years for good behavior and, as his lawyer loudly argued, because of the less than compelling nature of the evidence.

"So when I looked up Papa Magrew, guess what? Papa acted like he didn't even know me. He wouldn't sign

330

the papers making me a partner. Now, I think I couldn't have owned a bar anyway, since I was a convicted felon, but I was pissed then."

Mac, without any further prospects, bitter and ignoring the conditions of his parole, had hopped a freighter heading south and turned his back on his past life.

"Now, here I am with half a left arm gone and thirty-five years older." He smiled. "Don't know if I'm any smarter. But I am more philosophical. I work the jobs I can get. That, in addition to what Sonia and I make with this place, lets me live anonymously and a little comfortably." He took a swig of beer. "And that's why I'm nervous over this treasure thing. I feel like it's gonna wreck our life." Alex thought it over.

"Well, there's probably nothing there anyway, so nothing to worry about." He lifted his beer bottle in a toast. "How did you and Sonia hook up?" he asked partly out of curiosity and partly to change the subject.

"That's more her story than mine," he said. "But I will say that we married back in the day, her and her three kids. We saved our money and, with the insurance settlement for my arm, we bought this place out right. Over the years, she kept me out of trouble. Then, one day, Bautiste showed up. All smiles and confidence, he offered me a chance to make some good side money moving 'cargo.' I knew it was drugs, but we needed the extra money. After this place got going good, I refused to haul any more drugs. Bautiste just smiled. He knew about Houston and the Savings and Loan. He tried to blackmail me. I had no idea whether I could be extradited or not, but I called his bluff. He sent that big Sergeant around trying to scare me. I put a shotgun in his face and told him if I ever saw him again I'd take his head off. He got pissed, but he left us and didn't come back." Mac fell into a silence that worried Alex. The big man had unloaded a lot. Alex was about to say something.

"Fuck it!" Mac said. "Let's do it. Let's dig." Alex was elated.

"Ok. When?"

"Tomorrow."

Fernando Bautiste was in a celebratory mood. He went to his file cabinet and retrieved a bottle of Ron Anejo Pampero Aniversario Reserva Exclusiva Venezuelan rum. The bottle was wrapped in a supple leather bag. The Colonel removed the bag, got out two glasses, and summoned the Hammer.

"Eh?" he said holding up the bottle so the label could be seen. The Hammer grinned.

"*Bueno,*" he said reaching for a glass. Bautiste filled the two glasses halfway.

"Soon, my friend," he said raising his glass, "we will leave this all behind and retire where ever we want." They touched glasses.

CHAPTER FIFTEEN—Rewards

Once they made the decision to drill on Tuesday, Mac and Alex tapered their Monday beer drinking. Alex had left after the storm subsided and Mac had contacted Cor Delaney. The arrangements were made to get together and all three passed separately restless nights.

Alex finally arose before dawn on Tuesday. He had slept little thinking of the implications if there were a million dollars in treasure to be recovered. He dressed in the dark trying to avoid waking Erin. He went down to the lobby where there was an all night stand that sold sundries, snacks, and coffee. The attendant was half-asleep as Alex ordered a coffee and a pack of cigarettes. As he sipped through the slit in the plastic lid, he appreciated the caffeine even though the coffee had been warming for hours. He took his coffee and headed to the parking garage and the rental car. He had stopped concerning himself with the legalities of driving in a foreign country. He drove north to the digging site.

Cor Delaney woke a half hour later than Alex. He was hung over, but since this was normal for him, he felt ok. He wet his hair with cold water and finger combed it straight back. He locked the door to his shack and hopped up into the cab of his drilling truck. He started the big engine and headed to an early morning place that sold coffee and bread. The radio in the truck was broken so he hummed an Irish folk tune the lyrics to which he couldn't remember as headed to the coffee place.

He ordered a black coffee, a small bread, and a wedge of cheese. He drove west as he sipped and chewed. His mind now was imagining the coming task, the problems that would be encountered, and how to solve the problems. He resumed humming as he thought.

When Mac arose, Alex was already at the digging site smoking a cigarette and Delaney was approaching location. Mac made and packed some fish sandwiches for everyone and filled two thermoses with hot coffee. He filled a third thermos with dark Jamaican rum. He poured a paper cup full of hot coffee, snapped on a lid, and carried the lot out the front door. Then he locked up the restaurant, started his truck, and headed north along the route Alex had taken. He, too, sipped coffee and hummed, a Tears for Fears song from 1985, <u>Everybody Wants To Rule The World.</u>

Delaney first and then Mac joined Alex at the site. The sun was just rising. Alex was glad to have company. He found the site creepy alone in the dark knowing that there was, in essence, a mass grave a few yards away. As Delaney set up the big drill bit, Alex offered cigarettes. Mac declined, Delaney took one, but held it unlit between his lips as he worked. He placed the bit just over their previous hole and lowered it until the sharp tip just touched the soft ground. He walked around the truck's side and flipped some toggle switches. He checked some gauges and then pushed the starter. The drill's motor coughed briefly and then roared to life. As before, the noise was deafening. Delaney lit his cigarette with a lighter from his pants pocket. He walked up to the control levers, puffed his cigarette without handling it, and started the drill revolving. Six eyes watched as the drill, at first, pulled up an amount of fragrant earth and then pulled up some of the reburied bones. Cigarettes were puffed and cigarette filters were bitten down on as the big bit made slow, but inexorable, progress. More dirt surfaced as a bone here and there was noted in the debris. Delaney slowed the drill's progress, so that it was easier for his partners to spot foreign material between the growing amounts of dirt and rock.

Ten minutes in to the drilling, more bones, many more bones, surfaced. Delaney halted the drilling, unsure of the protocol. He looked to Mac for guidance. Mac shrugged as the drill motor idled.

"What da ya thank?" Cor asked. He was clearly a little rattled.

"Don't know," Mac admitted. "Creepy. Alex?" He looked over at the American who was casually smoking another cigarette.

"No balls, no babies," Alex said famously quoting. "Let's keep going. We can get a priest to bless the bones later." Mac and Cor looked at each other. Mac stuck out his lower lip and shrugged. Cor nodded affirmation.

"Ok," Mac said, "let's keep going. These poor fucks are in no condition to complain."

Delaney put the motor back in gear. The drilling resumed. More bones and fragments of garments, including an unmistakable leather boot fully intact, revealed themselves. Alex waved his arms over his head in a signal to Delaney. Delaney noticed and the motor went back into idle.

Alex stepped forward, picked up the boot, backed away, and signaled a circular motion with his extended forefinger. Delaney nodded and the motor went back into gear.

More bones, dirt, pieces of clothing and unidentifiable detritus were brought up. More pauses were signaled and the bits evaluated. Nothing significant was found and time stretched on. Alex noticed that his mouth was dry and tasted awful from the many cigarettes he had smoked. He thought of how disappointed his daughters would be that he was smoking. He reasoned that he was not really back to smoking, just having the occasional Marlboro, not habitually. Alex filled a plastic cup with the contents of one of Mac's thermoses. The coffee was still hot and Alex swished it around in his mouth. It really didn't help with the bad taste, but it didn't hurt either. He continued to observe the progress of the drilling. It was thirty minutes into the drilling process when the first rewards were produced. Alex was the first to notice.

"Hold it, hold it," he shouted over the din waving his arms as before. Delaney recognized the signal and slipped the motor into idle. He shrugged his shoulders.

Alex rushed up to the hole, careful to avoid the proximity of the motionless bit. Mimicking a power shovel, he scooped a double handful of freshly dug earth. There was more than one shiny object. Alex brushed away intervening dirt and exposed a gold piece. He recognized it as similar to those the trio had found before. He flipped it to Delaney. Then Alex bent to pick up a glinting, thumb-sized lump. He spat on it and rubbed it on his shirttail. It winked in the morning sunlight. He rolled it between his thumb and forefinger and held it up toward the rising sun. The resulting refraction painted a spectrum of color on his face that only Cor and Mac could appreciate.

"What the hell is that?" Cor asked.

"Prism," Mac said with conviction.

"Almost looks like a diamond," Alex added. "Couldn't be, though. Too big." He tilted it to and fro in the morning light. He tossed it to Mac and returned to the dirt pile and resumed his power shovel imitation. There were many more, both large and small, pieces of dulled crystals. They existed in varying colors. Besides white, red was next dominant. Alex was confused, but focused.

"Some gems," he announced. "Keep on digging?" he questioned. Both partners agreed.

"Let's do it," Mac said aggressively. Delaney again shifted the motor's gears and engaged the gears. The bit dug deeper.

Dr. Braga, now essentially an employee of the French government, was confused by the latest messages from the French Antiquities Administration. The messages were not addressed to him, but to JJ Wilson. Wilson had shared them. In essence, they said that the French government had now agreed to use the services of an American company that would subcontract the services of a Florida firm to recover and turn over anything that would be recovered on an as yet to be identified shipwreck. Details to follow. Braga wished them better luck than he had had.

The three men watched as the machine did its work. At first there wasn't much more reward. Then glitter began to flow in a steady stream. Alex grabbed a rake from Delaney's assortment of tools and began to move the dirt back and forth, sifting the larger, more solid objects in to a small pile. The objects were multi-hued: red, green, blue, white, and, most of all, gold. Alex bent down and picked up a glinting red lump. He assumed that it was a ruby, but why was it so large? In his experience, rubies were the size of peas and were multi-faceted. This stone was the size of a walnut, dirty and, yet, filled with reflected light. Alex reached for a green stone. It was also the size of a walnut and full of the morning light. He called over Mac and Cor.

"Look at this," he said, "what do you think about that?" He pushed a red stone into Mac's hand and a green one into Delaney's. Both men licked their fingers and wiped their respective stones clean. Mac held his toward the East.

"This the real thing?" he asked. "Should be worth ten thousand, at least." He was mesmerized. Delaney rotated his stone in the same sunlight.

"It's un emarald, ain't un?" He didn't wait for an answer. "She's a beaut." He twirled the stone between his thumb and forefinger.

337

"I think so," Alex said. "And that's a ruby." He pointed at Mac's stone.

"We need to set up some kind of sifting deal. Something to separate the dirt from the valuables." Alex looked from Mac to Cor. "And we need to work fast." He looked from man to man again. "Right?"

Mac and Cor looked at each other and performed a mutual shrug. Mac was secretly proud of Alex's command of the situation. He eyed the diamond screen that protected Delaney's rear window.

"Let's cut that off and use it as a filter." He pointed at the screen. The others looked at it dubiously.

"Not exactly fine," Cor pointed out. He volunteered that there was a roll of finer mesh in the bed of his work truck.

"Ok. Let's use that," Alex agreed. "But let's step it up."

The trio set up a primitive sieve and with Alex using a shovel and the other two shaking the large square of mesh, they began to sift the dirt and debris. It was slow going. Mac pointed out the obvious.

"This is too slow and we've barely started drilling." He looked at Delaney and raised his thick, black eyebrows. Delaney shrugged getting the point.

"Let's keep drilling," he urged. The others agreed and moved the screen away from the hole. Cor revved up the bit, lowered the tip, and resumed drilling. Immediately, there were more and more shiny, glittering objects randomly scattered through the dirt. Everyone noticed the phenomenon, but no one made a move. The ratio of shiny stuff to dirt was easily three to two and then became four to one.

"Holy shit," Alex exclaimed as a mound of glitter grew and grew. The others stared wide-eyed. The ratio became ten to one. And, then, fifty to one. They were recovering pure treasure. Every twist of the drilling bit brought an unbelievable amount of glittering stuff up to the surface. There could have been damage wrought by the bit, but none of the three was thinking that way. Alex stared and thought that the pile now looked like one of the chests in that Disney attraction with the pirates. There was a background of gold sprinkled with red, green, blue and white stones gleaming. Alex also thought, we did it. He looked at Mac and Cor. They were both slack-jawed. Mac must have sensed Alex's scrutiny for he stepped forward.

"Hold it. Hold it," he said slashing across his throat with the flat of his right hand. Cor cut the motor. "Let's see what we have." The trio simultaneously approached the mound.

"Holy shit," Alex said again as he got a better look at what they had recovered. There was a small hill of mostly gold coins, what Alex assumed were cut rubies and emeralds, gold jewelry such as necklaces, bracelets, and chains, pearls both free and mounted, and quantities of silver. Alex looked at his partners. "We fucking did it!" He smiled broadly and embraced first Mac and then smelly Cor. Everyone was grinning when Cor spoke up.

"We aven't finished digging," he pointed out. The others looked at him somewhat confused. Mac shrugged like what the hell are you talking about? "Listen," Delaney said, "the dig ain't done until we pull oop nothing boot daht." Mac's brow went up and his lips compressed.

"Until nothing but dirt?" Alex asked.

"Swoot ah said," the Irishman confirmed. He nodded vigorously. He approached the drilling controls again. He looked at the other two and cocked his head inquiringly. Alex gave a thumbs up and Mac pumped a fist. Delaney restarted the diesel engine, which sputtered and caught and roared back to life. Delaney repositioned the tip of the drill bit and directed it back in to the   ever-deepening hole.

It didn't take long for the hump of treasure to double in size and still it kept on growing. Now there was a continuous revelation of gold coins, both single and in stuck together lumps. There were even some stacks of gold coins so stuck together that they formed rough rods of gold. Alex, whose first emotion was elation, grew worried. There was such a quantity of valuables that he began to doubt his eyes. Could this just be bullshit? he questioned.

Another half hour later and the drill bit began to pull up "nothing boot daht" as Delaney had described. Alex didn't know about the others, but he was definitely not disappointed. His amateur estimate of the worth of the pile they had amassed was more than ten million dollars, perhaps more than fifteen million. He looked at Mac as Delaney stopped the engine. Mac approached the huge pile of wealth. It reminded him of the WWII black and white pictures he had seen as a boy. The Nazis had robbed their Jewish prisoners and warehoused an amassment of watches, jewelry, furs, gold teeth and anything else that was valuable. It had frightened him at the time. Now, looking at the mess of treasure and dirt, he was excited, as he had never been since robbing the Houston Savings and Loan. He was practically tumescent.

Delaney stared in disbelief at the produce of his labors. As he was operating the drill, he hadn't had time to process what was actually being accomplished. Now, in the post drilling quiet, he followed Mac and drew near to the unfamiliar mass of valuable objects. He knelt beside the pile and dug both hands into it. He lifted a double handful and then let the pieces dribble one by one back to the apex.

"Fooking hay," he exclaimed. Mac knelt beside him and started to pick up individual pieces. He examined each one and dropped it. He couldn't think of anything to say. He was overcome with awe at the display before him.

"What do you think?" Alex asked of the two kneeling figures before him. He had his hands on his hips. "I mean how much? How much do you think this is worth?" Mac waited for Cor and Cor waited for Mac. They realized what they were doing and so both spoke up at the same time.

"Eighty to a hundred," Mac said as Cor opined, "Hoondred to hoondred fitty." They looked at each other and shrugged. "Whatever," Mac said, "it's big." Alex looked from one to the other.

"Really? Cause I was thinking ten to fifteen million. But, what the hell, I have no idea." He brushed his hair back with both hands. "You really think it's that much?" He looked at each man in challenge.

"Just look at the gold," Mac said, "the gold alone." Alex saw his point. There was a boatload of gold coins.

"Ok, but conservatively, let's go with, what, eighty? Agree with that?" Alex looked to the others for consensus.

"Too low," Cor grumbled, "but ok. Les load up and git oota here." Mac agreed.

"Cor's right," he said " on both points. Let's load this stuff and move on to the next phase." Alex and Mac nodded assent.

It took the three of them almost two hours to load the two cars and the truck with every item of value they could remove from the accumulated dirt. Both car trunks were full and all available space in their passenger compartments was filled with treasure. Every free space on Cor's truck was stuffed with recovered items. The three vehicles, on sagging springs, headed west to a seaside slurry pond identified by Mac.

It took the little convoy an hour to reach the slurry pond. It was serendipity that the recent rain not only increased the depth of the pond, but also diluted the contents to a soupy consistency. Mac backed his car into position and then directed the other two into similarly advantageous spots.

The three men grouped and looked at the large seaside pond.

"What's the plan?" Alex asked. This was Mac's area of expertise.

"We need to empty our rides and toss it all into the pond. See how cloudy the slurry is? Make sure everything we dug up is covered by that cloudy shit." The trio got to work. There weren't really any suitable tools that could be used in the situation. They used their hands.

Alex grabbed handfuls and tossed them in to the center of the pond. It did not take long for painful cramps to set in. He found that the muscles in his hands, fatigued already from loading the car, just couldn't take any more physical activity. He beat the locked fingers against his thighs to try and loosen them. They didn't respond.

"Mac, got any water? I'm cramping." He held up his claw-like hands. Mac shook his head.

"Sorry, Alex, coffee and rum. Not good for hydrating, I'm afraid. Cor, got any water?"

"Ta cooler was full. Lemme check." He had a big yellow and red Igloo cooler strapped to the bed of the drilling truck. He pushed the button that dispensed the contents. Warm water ran out. "Got water, boot's warm," he told Alex. Alex tried to give him a thumbs up, but the gesture was impossible with his cramps. He just walked up, knelt below the spigot, and directed the warm water into his mouth. He pushed the button with his cramped thumb. He drank all he could and then went back to help his fellow workers.

It took them an hour of hard work to transfer all the treasure to the pond and, then, another hour to clean up the pieces they had dropped in the muddy pond border. They all knew not to leave any sign behind. Mac walked a circuit of the pond, testing the view from various perspectives. When he was satisfied that they had left no visible evidence of the treasure he urged the others to check their vehicles one more time before they left. Alex, in fact, discovered two stones that had rolled under the front passenger seat. He had to ask Mac to pick them up since his hands were still cramping. Mac tossed them into the pond. They all started their engines and headed back to Porlamar to discuss their next step.

They congregated at Mac's restaurant. Beers were drained with enthusiasm.

"We've got to get that shit out of the pond and to the site in the next couple of hours," Mac urged. He knew more than anyone that so many things could go wrong.

"Ok," Alex agreed, "let's get the catamaran and start pumping." He looked at Cor for agreement. The Irishman shrugged signaling he had no idea what was right at this point.

"Little problem," Mac said and the other two snapped to attention.

"What?" Alex asked. At this point he was in no mood for glitches.

"There's too much shit in the pond for my cat to carry. We're gonna need a second cat." Alex felt like slamming his beer bottle on the plastic table. He regained control.

"Ok. Where are we going to get that?" he asked.

"Well, I know a guy," Mac said. "His name's Manny Velez. I'll call him." Mac pulled out his phone and dialed Velez. Alex realized from the half of the conversation that he could hear that Mac more than just knew Velez. They seemed to be close friends. It only took Mac a minute to convince Velez to meet them at the slurry pond. "Ok," Mac said, "Manny can be there in half an hour. Finish your beers. Anybody need to eat?" Both men signaled no. If Alex were asked, he would have admitted that he was too excited to eat. He gulped his beer, burped, and rose from his seat and then sat slowly.

"Mac, how long to recover and do the salting?" he asked. Mac thought it over.

"With two pumps, I'd say an hour to recover, twenty to thirty minutes travel time, and then, maybe, ten to twenty minutes to drop. That's with no complications. Like we discussed, we have to wait for dark to do the salting, though."

"Ok, can we hold up for ten minutes? Let me get Florida going." Mac and Cor agreed. Alex used Mac's computer to send Davis an email containing the information the French and McDonald would need. He asked for confirmation within the next ten minutes.

Jim Davis received Alex's email and, a credit to his intelligence, realized that things were starting to move and required action. He dialed McDonald's number in Florida and was relieved to hear the Florida drawl. He gave McDonald a location pinpointed by latitude and longitude, a name, and a contact number. McDonald, for his part, asked the lawyer to wait while he pulled out the relevant charts. He studied for a few minutes and then picked up his phone. He told Davis that he had a good man, a Dutch captain, named Wilhelm (Wim) Kuyper 500 miles from the area Davis had identified. He would contact Kuyper in Aruba as soon as he broke off with Davis, confirm the arrangements and the timetable, and send Davis an email. Davis agreed. He then called the number Chuck Murtaugh had given him. He had been told it was for the Cultural Attaché at the French Embassy in Washington. The woman's name was Michelle Lovinger. He provided her with the same information that he had given McDonald. She understood and, more importantly, she understood the urgency. She promised to let the proper French officials know what was happening so they could do their part. Davis composed a brief response for Alex, promised more info to come, and clicked Send.

Michelle Lovinger passed Davis' information on to Jean Gerard at the Ministry of Antiquities in Paris. Gerard was momentarily confused as he read the lat and long. These are familiar, he thought. Why? He brought up a spreadsheet of the latest reports. There were fifty-three. Some had the names of ships, some had locations specified by GPS coordinates, and some had both. He scanned the list. There it was. The *Comte de Toulouse* renamed the *Little Ranger*. Identified as a wreck off of the coast of Venezuela. Arrangements made with the Venezuelan government to take over recovery operations and nothing of interest to recover.

Alex got the confirming email on his phone and was happy with the message. He gave a thumbs up to Mac and Cor. "Let's go," Alex said. He desperately wanted to finish the next two phases of his plan. Then success would depend on others.

JJ Wilson, Renee Rideau, and Dr. Braga had been even more confused when they received late word that an American salvage recovery vessel would be arriving on site and all cooperation was to be afforded them. Their work had been progressing nicely. The French heavy lift vessel had identified the requirements for safely raising the *Little Ranger*. The French crew had been busy over the last few days fabricating thick and wide canvas slings and rigging up the hooks and chains that would be needed for the raising exercise. In the mean time, the *Little Ranger* had been allowed to rest quietly; no swimmers, no divers, and no small boats circling.

"What do you suppose this is about?" Dr. Braga asked pointing at his copy of the French government's email. He directed the question at Wilson, Rideau or both. Rideau, running a thick hand through her sweaty blonde hair, shrugged her fat shoulders and pointed at the laptop. The two French had already translated the email into English for Braga.

"Perhaps zis is a mistake," she giggled unattractively. Because Braga spoke only a little French, the trio had agreed to use English for their communications. Braga shook his head but said nothing.

"JJ, what do you think?" Braga asked. He was looking for an analysis, not wishful thinking. Wilson rubbed his small hand through his wiry hair. Braga wondered if this were a French thing.

"Maybe the people at the Department of Antiquities have done a research. Maybe zay have found zomezing we missed? I vill ask for a, *comment dit-on*, a clarification?"

Alex, Cor, and Mac had piled into Mac's car and driven to the mooring where Mac kept his catamaran. Mac gave directions as covers were removed, equipment was made ready, and engine pre-checks were performed. Alex felt that he was being of little use, so he concentrated on lending muscle where he could. The catamaran was made ready and they motored at slow speed in the direction of the slurry pond. When they arrived, Manny Velez wasn't there yet so cigarettes were passed around as Mac shut down the motors and relaxed in his chair. Alex stretched out luxuriously on a clear part of the deck boards feeling tendons and ligaments pop as he did so. Cor smoked lugubriously and gazed out to sea. Alex sat up as the sound of an approaching motor came to him.

Manny Velez arrived and the two catamaran captains exchanged greetings. Mac introduced Alex as Alex realized that Velez and Delaney were already acquainted. Mac invited Manny aboard his cat and the three men sat facing Mac.

Mac said, "Manny, this pump is going to be a little different from those others we've teamed on." Velez leaned forward as Mac told him what was at the bottom of the slurry pond. He briefly explained the back-story and concluded with, "So your share will be five hundred." Velez frowned, not sure that he had understood all the facts correctly.

"That's ok," Manny said, "but kind of cheap, ain't it?"

"Five hundred thousand," Alex clarified realizing the confusion, "dollars." Manny's eyebrows would have disappeared into his hairline if that were possible. He grinned broadly showing a mouthful of bad teeth.

"Sorry," he said, "very generous." The others could see that he was calculating the impact of that amount on his life. "Very generous," he choked and his eyes filled with tears. It was Mac who broke the awkwardness.

"Ok, then, let's start pumping. We've got about ninety minutes of daylight left."

Alex stayed on Mac's cat and Cor joined Manny. The concept was simple. The pumps sucked the slurry pond's contents into fiberglass tanks on the catamarans. This included small debris such as rocks and plant matter. Occasionally the hoses would clog and have to be cleared. Mac had no illusions that they would be able to recover every last trinket that he and Alex and Cor had sunk in the pond, but he expected that they could get back more than ninety percent especially using two pumps.

The recovery pumps were placed strategically at opposite ends of the pond, the pump motors were started, and the slurry began to flow. Manny Velez spotted the problem immediately. He signaled for Mac to kill his engine.

"We got to use the nozzles," he called to Mac. "Lower the depth, get these two in there, and suck the bottom." Mac nodded agreement. He pulled Alex close.

"Put on those," he indicated at pair of knee high rubber boots. "You and Cor have to go in and direct the

347

suction by hand. Be careful. These motors suck good.
Understand? Any questions?"

"What nozzles was he talking about?"

"This," Mac answered and held up a wide-mouthed
plastic nozzle that he fitted to the end of the suction hose.
"Alex, be careful," he cautioned, "she sucks like a
motherfucker."

Mac and Manny instructed Alex and Cor how to place
the nozzles upward at first so that the liquid level in the pond
was reduced. Then they were to slowly advance toward the
center of the pond, swinging the now downward facing
nozzles in short arcs just above the bottom mud of the pond
and being careful not to tramp their boots on areas that hadn't
been covered. The new process was going to double Mac's
original time estimate, especially since Alex and Cor were
unfamiliar with the equipment.

Thirty minutes in to the sweeping procedure, Alex got
careless and lost one of Mac's boots to the suction. He shed
the other boot and was much more careful after that. It was
almost dark when he and Cor met in the middle of the pond.
He was exhausted and could see that Cor was sweating so
much that he must have been dehydrating.

"That's it," he called to Mac waving his arms over his
head. He wasn't really sure that they had recovered all that
they could have, but he was sure that they were spent. Mac
cut his motor and Manny followed suit.

"I think that's it," Alex shouted still holding his nozzle
down in the mud. "I think we got most of it. Whoever drains
next is gonna be surprised when they get a few trinkets."
Mac laughed though he realized that the men in the pond
were tired beyond reason and that the comment was not that
funny.

"Ok," Mac shouted, "let's wrap it up. Manny, turn on
your lights. Let's have a beer and some sandwiches. Then
we'll move up to the wreck. Agreed?" He peered through the

348

gloom for confirmation. Velez gave him a thumbs up. Now it was too dark to see what the men in the pond were doing. There was not much to see as Alex and Cor were holding the nozzles high over their heads and moving one post-holing step at a time toward the edge of the pond. They walked out, Alex barefoot and Cor with his boots still on.

Mac clapped his hands in approval as the two stepped into the dual lights of the cats. They were muddy beyond belief and limping both, but their heads were held high. Mac called Manny over and the four of them had a brief celebration.

"Do you guys think we got most?" he asked of Alex and Cor. They looked tiredly at each other and smiled.

"We goot moost," Cor said and nodded his head wildly. Alex was too tired to argue, but he wondered. Mac told Manny to shut down the lights and get ready to move out. Delaney and Alex took a quick rinsing dip in the sea.

The two catamarans followed a course that would take them off the beach at Playa Madrid.

Dusk had fallen by the time the two cats arrived offshore. Alex could make out the small cluster of vehicles and campers now being used by the French and Rinni Braga. Alex wondered if they were actually sleeping there. He doubted it. Mac and Manny had the engines idling.

"How do we do this?" Alex asked. The big French ship blocked the sky to the north. Alex spoke loud enough for Manny to hear.

"Fast, but clean. We don't need to hit the *Little Ranger*," he said. "We just need to hit around her." Alex thought he could see Velez nodding, but it was pretty dark.

"Ok," Manny said, "let's finish it." The two cats were moved into position. Mac was south of where they estimated the wreck to be and Manny was north. The fiberglass tanks were mounted such that they pivoted on steel pins that were fitted into steel bushings at either end. This way each tank could be rotated so that the top hemisphere was turned down and their hatches could be opened emptying their contents into the water.

As the cats were slowed Alex and Cor rotated and opened the tanks. The cats were barely drifting forward as first there was the sound of liquid pouring into the sea and then splashing as more solid objects fell into the water. Alex in Mac's cat and Cor in Manny's were tasked with reaching into the tanks and scouring the insides to ensure that they were totally emptied.

"Good," Alex said to Mac when all he could feel was the smooth fiberglass of the tank's interior walls. Mac steered the cat in a slow turn back the way they had come. Manny turned the other cat similarly when Cor had given the signal.

Braga, Rideau, and Wilson had driven back to their hotel after receiving the government's message. Wilson had, in fact, emailed for clarification. Almost immediately Wilson got his response from a certain Monsieur Jean Gerard of the Ministry of Antiquities. The message was pointed: the original message was clear, no clarification necessary. Rideau and Wilson, bureaucrats to the bone, felt chastised and would question no further. Braga, the outsider and hired hand, went along. So, it was no surprise that, when the French recovery vessel's crew contacted the experts and told them that their had been some unidentified activity in the vicinity of the *Little Ranger*, no alarm was raised. Night vision glasses had revealed two vessels cruising the site and then leaving. Wilson lied and said that they knew all about it and that there was nothing to be concerned about.

After securing Manny's catamaran, all four men rode with Mac to the mooring and Mac's car. Mac would give Manny a ride back later. They headed to Mac's place for food and drink. Sonia had food warming for them, grilled fish tacos, and cold beer. They were all tired, but especially Alex and Cor. After a few gulps of cold beer, Alex wanted to lean back and close his eyes. But there was more to do. He pulled out his phone and excused himself from the group. Instead of texting, he decided to call Davis.

"Jim Davis, Contracts and Corporate," Davis answered the call. Alex identified himself.

"Mr. Browning. It's so good to speak with you. Fantastic, in fact." He stopped talking, as a professional should, so that he could listen. Alex explained that there was a high urgency to what he was about to say.

"The Florida guy has got to get his guy moving," Alex said, "I mean right now. Make that call. I'll hold on." Davis contacted McDonald on another line and, trying to keep the desperation out of his voice, asked the salvage man if the ship was under way from Aruba.

"Pretty sure," McDonald said, "but let me check. Hold on." There was silence on the line as McDonald made another call. Kuyper confirmed to McDonald that they were under way at cruising speed headed southeast to Margarita. McDonald told him to get his ass in gear and returned to Davis' call.

"My man is on his way. He'll be there in around five hours. That work?" Davis did some quick math.

"He'll be there before dawn, in that case. Can they work in the dark?"

"They can set up in the dark," McDonald affirmed. "By the time they make contact and introduce themselves it'll be light."

When dawn broke over Playa Madrid, the bay presented, to the casual observer, a peaceful sight. The large naval recovery vessel rested at anchor her large deck cranes outlined against the lightening sky. The dark shadow of the *Little Ranger* looked serene just below the water's surface. And the newly arrived *Lovely Jugs*, a fifty-foot barge out of Aruba, lay white and shining in the morning light.

The French crew called in the identity of the *Lovely Jugs* as soon as there was enough light to read her name. Although they were French Navy, the crew of the recovery vessel was not military; they were mostly scientists and technicians. Anything out of the ordinary spooked them.

"Well, look at that," Kuyper said aboard the *Lovely Jugs*. "She's a big bastard, ain't she?" he asked rhetorically. His four crewmen (actually one was a woman) looked up at the looming hulk of the converted French destroyer. Her gray hull appeared black in the dawn light. "Ok, let's get everything ready. We got to clean the site and do no harm to the shipwreck." The quartet got busy performing a well-rehearsed choreography of selecting, moving, and connecting equipment.

"Dive is ready," announced Kim Touw, a tall blonde with long tanned legs and striking blue eyes. She spoke with the casualness of someone performing a repeated routine.

"Good show, Kim," Kuyper said. "How're the detectors coming along?" he asked of the two crewmen setting up the sensors.

"Five minutes," said Albert at twenty-eight the senior crewman. Kuyper huffed.

"Make it three," Kuyper chided. He knew the equipment better than any of his crew and was intimately familiar with the setup times.

"Yes, captain," Albert fired back. The two men doubled their efforts.

352

By the time full dawn had arrived on Wednesday, the salvage team was already in the water. They gathered treasure immediately while Kuyper radioed the heavy-lift vessel and the Braga-Wilson-Rideau team onshore.

Fernando Bautiste had received some disturbing news late Tuesday. He was still in his office as reports of civil unrest continued to come in over the secure police channels. Sergeant Lopez, sweating profusely, was also working late in support of his boss. He had discovered something strange in the registry of the Colonel's computer. Lopez had set up all the office computers so that applications were required to use the registry. An application had been installed and was not using the registry. Lopez didn't recognize the software so he investigated. What he found alarmed him.

"Colonel," he said entering Bautiste's office, "something odd." Bautiste dropped his pen and rubbed his eyes.

"What's odd, Lopez?" He wasn't a big fan of techno-mumble and was tired.

"Someone has installed a software on your computer. And I think this software sent your email archives somewhere." Lopez was prepared to clarify for his boss using the office's whiteboard. Instead, Bautiste just grabbed for his keyboard and began typing. He let out an impressive string of epithets that made Lopez back away as his worst fear was confirmed. His accounts were empty.

"Who did this?" he demanded of the Sergeant.

"I don't know yet, *mi Colonel*," Lopez said. "I have just begun to investigate." He was stammering and Bautiste recognized this. He forced himself to calm down.

"When will you know?" Bautiste asked calmly. Then he thought of a better question. "When did this happen?"

"Monday, the eleventh," Lopez said. Then he had a panicky thought. "Unless," he gulped, "unless the intruder had a way to spoof the date." Bautiste looked red and frustrated.

"Is that possible?" he hissed.

"I," Lopez was sweating freely, "I don't... I'm not sure," he said. "I don't think so."

"Find out," Bautiste ordered, "and dismissed." He reached for his phone.

The Hammer was having a late night beer and enjoying some pornography on his computer when the phone rang. Caller ID said it was Bautiste, so he zipped himself up and answered the call.

"*Jefe*," he said, "*que paso?*"

"Have you checked your accounts lately?" Bautiste asked. The Hammer's heart began to beat ferociously. He reached for his computer. His heart stopped beating and sank. He let out a string of expletives himself, though his string was more imaginative than that of his boss earlier.

"*Mi dinero*," he exclaimed. "*Todo*." He was furious and Bautiste sympathized.

"All of mine too, *amigo*," Bautiste offered. He knew that the Hammer would realize that this meant ten times the loss he had suffered. "We are working on finding out who did this. Then there will be work for you." There was an ominous silence on the other end.

"I will be ready," was the chilling response. And then the connection was broken.

Tuesday night into Wednesday morning there were numerous riots in various Venezuelan cities. Clearly the populace was not and had not been happy with the status quo. The people wanted change.

CHAPTER SIXTEEN—Conflict

Colonel Bautiste shook with fury. Money was not something to collect. Money was something that you used to pave the road to the future. Bautiste's money was all gone. So was all that the Hammer had amassed. The total was, he estimated, over eleven million dollars. He got himself under control and called Sergeant Lopez into his office.

"You need to find out something for us," he ordered the fat underling. "How did this software thing become installed in my office? That is something that can be discovered?" He stared down the Sergeant.

"Yes, *mi Colonel*," Lopez said with a confidence that he didn't feel, "the virus can be tracked." Lopez knew two things: the date of the installation and the scope of the data that had been output. He set to work. He didn't think that there wasn't a chance in hell that he could find out anything of interest.

Alex and Mac arrived at Playa Madrid early on Wednesday. Alex found it exhilarating that the plan he had set in motion with several emails had resulted in divers and salvage crews prowling the *Little Ranger* wreck site.

"Look at that," Alex said with some amazement in his voice. "That's all going to the French government." Mac watched as the divers handed mesh bags bulging with sparkling contents to the crew on the deck of the *Lovely Jugs*. Bag after bag.

"So are you counting on the French to what? Evaluate what we dug up?" Alex didn't know it, but there was a French official already on the salvage boat inventorying each bag and tagging it.

"Right. We thought it was a good idea that they would do the final evaluation. I'm not worried, much," Alex said squinting at the activity in the bay. He had a hard time making out what was going on out there. That meant that he had no idea that the crew of the *Lovely Jugs* were repeatedly astonished as the contents of each mesh bag was transferred.

"Incroyable!" Walter LeClerc exclaimed aboard the *Lovely Jugs*. He was the chief scientist for the French government and charged with validating the recovery. Kuyper had invited him aboard. The reason for his surprise was that, as each load of gold and silver was raised to the deck for evaluation, the evaluation of each load incremented the entire total by orders of magnitude. Walter had no idea of the proportional deal the government had made with the Browning Group. "This is a fortune!" Walter said to the barely listening crew as they just stared. *"Mon Dieu!"* he continued. "Look at the quality!" The seawater had cleaned all the dirt and mud from the silver, gold and jewels and they glinted in the morning sunlight. The treasure was more impressive now than when Alex, Mac and Cor had first laid eyes on it.

For their part, the Dutch crew of the *Jugs* was made up of seasoned salvage specialists. They had all recovered treasure. They could pretty much, each one, estimate the value of a haul within five percent although none of them were historians or numismatists or jewelers. To a man (woman), the crew guessed that they had brought up a hundred million dollars worth of precious materiel. And they were not even half done.

"Make one more pass through this area," Kuyper ordered his divers, "and then we'll move west. Kim, you are in charge." Kuyper's plan was to have the divers sweep the area in a counterclockwise fashion. He wanted his people to circle the *Little Ranger* in an expanding halo gathering as they went.

Alex and Mac were joined by Dr. Braga, Wilson and Renee Rideau around nine o'clock. It was Braga who spoke first.

"Alejandro, what is going on?" Alex explained what he could. He pointed out the people on the *Lovely Jugs* and, based on supposition, what they were doing.

"See the bags they're handing up from the water?" Alex asked. Rinni nodded. "See how each bag bulges?" Rinni nodded again. "Well, that's what the salvage company is bringing up from the *Little Ranger*."

"But," Braga protested, "we have already determined that there is nothing out there but the burned wreck and, perhaps, some, what, some historical artifacts?"

"Well, I'm sorry to tell you this, Rinni, but you determined wrong," Alex said.

"No, Alejandro, I did not," Braga said patiently. "Would you like to tell me what is going on?" He gazed serenely into Alex's icy blue eyes.

"No, Rinni. I would not. Just enjoy the show."

"*Mi Colonel*," Lopez called, "I have found something." Bautiste jumped up from his desk and made his way hurriedly to the outer office. Since the discovery that the contents of all of his accounts had disappeared, he had worried that all was lost forever.

"What is it, Lopez?"

"Look at this," the Sergeant said. He pointed at the computer monitor. Bautiste was impatient with technology.

"What is it, Lopez?" he emphasized with an implied threat. The Sergeant swallowed, but the lump in his throat remained. He found it difficult to speak.

"It is," Lopez attempted to clear his throat, "a small fact that I have discovered." He continued to stare at the monitor. Bautiste approached and looked more closely. He studied the display. He was not a stupid man.

"The size of the information, yes?" Bautiste pointed at the information displayed on the screen.

"That's it," Lopez confirmed. "The mass of the data matches the mass of your archived emails. Someone has gathered all your old emails and downloaded them. Your current emails, too." Lopez felt more confident now. He stood tall and looked Bautiste in the eye. "What were they after? That's the key question." Bautiste looked out of the window reflecting.

"Right," he said distracted. "That's a fucking question. The other question is who did this? And I know a couple of ladies who might have the answers."

At Playa Madrid, the salvage work progressed to the location where Mac had salted his catamaran load. The original divers had been spelled by other crew members from the *Jugs* and the pace had picked up for awhile. Mac couldn't believe how long the recovery was taking.

"Is there more here than we dropped?" Mac asked. Alex laughed.

"It just seems that way. Remember, they're collecting two boatloads by hand. It's going to be slow. And," Alex added, "I checked the process. After they finish with their first sweeps, they're going to go back over every area using sensors. Maybe twice." Mac shook his head.

Bautiste's phone rang just as he was ready to order the arrests of Elise and Erin. He picked up.

"Bautiste here," he announced. The caller was a low-level underling, Juan Quintero, whom he had assigned to keep an eye on whatever was going on around the *Little Ranger*. Bautiste had forgotten all about the assignment.

"Colonel, excuse me for bothering you. I don't know if this is important or not. It seems important, but I am a humble policeman who cannot judge the magnitude of such things with a confidence of accuracy. I..."

"What the hell is it, Quintero?" Bautiste virtually screamed into his receiver. He immediately regretted yelling because this seemed to have hit the policeman's reset button.

"Excuse me, Colonel," said a clearly rattled employee as he started all over again. "I think this is important, but I don't know because I am a humble..."

"Fuck!" Bautiste exploded. "What is it, you mumbling ass?" Clearly, Bautiste had reached his limit. The silence on the other end of the connection was prolonged. Bautiste wondered if the connection had been dropped. "Quintero?"

"Colonel, they are recovering much things at the wreck site." The policeman waited for the response. Bautiste tried to absorb this statement.

"What are you talking about? The site has already been declared absent of anything of value. What are they recovering?"

"Something has changed, Colonel," Quintero pressed on. "There are divers in the water and they are pulling up much what looks like gold. What should I do?" Bautiste's initial reaction was to have his man stop the activity. He knew that was impossible. Venezuela had handed all rights over to France so that only France could stop the activity. Fuck, he thought.

"Quintero, do nothing. Just keep an eye on the situation. Keep me informed." He broke off with Playa Madrid and connected with the Hammer.

"Something is going on at Playa Madrid," he said. "Get up there and check it out. Also, I want you to have the women, Diaz and Rosen, picked up. Use whatever excuse you want. Hold them for my questioning. Something is going on. Understood?" *El Martillo* affirmed that he indeed understood.

The Hammer called Corporal James Ayala. The corporal was confused by the call, but sufficiently intimidated.

"Sergeant," he said with warmth that he didn't feel, "what can I do for you?" The Hammer had faith in Ayala's ability, but doubted his resolve.

"Corporal, I need you to take care of two important matters." He described the situation at Playa Madrid and the need to detain Diaz and Rosen for questioning.

"I understand, Sergeant." The Corporal was sweating through his shirt.

Connie Browning was anxious for news. She had called Jo, but Jo had heard nothing. She called her uncle, but he had been either in meetings or teaching his classes. When she finally reached him he assured her there were no messages on his cell phone.

"Have you tried the lawyer?" Terry asked. "What's his name? Davis?"

"Jim Davis," Connie confirmed. "I tried him earlier, Uncle Terry. I'll try him again. He should know something. I'll call you back. Love you." Terry said he loved her, too.

Sarah connected Connie with the law firm's administrative assistant, Thea Anitis, a Greek beauty. She had platinum blonde hair and a flawless olive complexion. She hadn't been hired for her looks, though. She had two outstanding talents that the firm prized: she had an encyclopedic knowledge of all the firm's current cases and she was a stone wall when it came to an outsider trying to gain access to a busy lawyer.

"I'm sure he'll take my call," Connie argued realizing that this was a bad approach. "Maybe I should mention that my company, The Browning Group, is doing a million dollars worth of business with your firm." Anitis, of course, already knew this. She also knew that Davis and Connie had been out socially. She decided to give Connie a break.

"Connie, he's in a meeting until twelve or so. But I can tell you that the salvage firm in Florida sent a ship to Venezuela from Aruba. We know that it arrived and has started the salvage. It looks like everything is going fine. From the reports we've received. Shall I have him call you when he's free?" Anitis finished.

"That's great news," Connie said, "and, yes, please ask him to call. He has my number. Thank you so much." Connie hung up and then relayed the news to her uncle and sister.

Despite Thea Anitis' assurances that everything was going fine, Wim Kuyper and Walter LeClerc were in a quandary. The size of the recovery should have delighted both men, but both men were disturbed. This was not right. The amount of treasure brought aboard so far could not have gone unnoticed in this location for all those years. Kuyper suspected salting and he tasked diver Kim Touw, in Dutch, to report anything else unusual that she might notice. Salting was not unknown and Kuyper was aware that the French were unchallenged claimants to the salvage. The salvage was being handed over to the French so there should be no problems from the salvage company's point of view. It was just weird to the Dutch captain that so much gold, so many precious gems were all being gathered from this one spot. No doubt there had been bigger salvages throughout history and in different parts of the world, but Kuyper hadn't been a part of those.

Walter LeClerc toyed with his bushy mustache as he watched the parade of mesh bags continue unabated. The replacement divers had themselves been replaced. LeClerc had caught Kuyper's eye and the big Dutchman had merely shrugged. LeClerc now had a new concern: security. He was responsible for more wealth than he could ever have imagined. He had pleaded with the French navy to send more help and had been assured that a small contingent of Marines was on their way from Martinique. LeClerc was not appeased. He received a radio call from the captain of the heavy-lift ship. They spoke in French.

"A Venezuelan policeman is telling me that the salvage may be illegal. Is there some doubt?" The French captain, a man named Gerand, was no nonsense career military and he hated having all these science types on his ship.

"No, Captain. There is no doubt. The recovered items belong to the French government. That is by maritime law, the release by the Venezuelan government and by the contract between our government and the salvagers." The Captain hadn't liked the Venezuelan policeman.

"Good. I will tell him to fuck off." Captain Gerand was happy.

Sergeant Lopez had had a huge stroke of good luck that was very bad luck for Alex Browning. The Sergeant, working on a hunch, had examined Bautiste's communications stored on the archive server. He had started with the texts and emails from a month ago and painstakingly examined each one. There was one from Alex Browning received on March 12 that was strange. The size attribute showed that it was larger than the email client reported. Lopez performed a hex dump of the file and examined the results. He found the embedded virus. Now he knew the answer to one of the Colonel's questions: Alex Browning. He picked up the phone.

Alex and Mac were tired of watching the slow pace of the recovery process.

"I'm going back to the hotel," Alex said. "It's getting too hot to stand around here." Mac nodded and started to rise from the sand where he had been watching the proceedings.

"Good idea. I'm going to head back to the restaurant and help Sonia get ready for lunch. Call me if you need to. Hell, call me if you get *any* news." They parted and went their separate ways.

Alex caught up with Erin at the hotel. She gave him a big hug and kiss.

"So how's it going out there?" she asked. "Any problems?" She had been researching salvage operations worldwide. To her, it was fascinating.

"Mac and I watched from the shore," Alex explained. "There wasn't a lot that we could determine from the beach, but it looked like the salvage operation was going great." He poured himself a glass of ice water. "The Florida guy, McDonald, seems to know what he's doing. The Dutch guy is cleaning up everything Cor and Mac dropped. From what I could tell," he amended.

"Did you know that the largest recovery ever accomplished was worth half a billion dollars?" Alex sipped his water.

"Sure, I knew that," he said to her disappointment. "The *Black Swan*, right?"   She brightened a little.

"Well, that was just a made up name," she said. "Made up by the salvage guys. They claimed that they didn't know the identity of the wreck."

"Yeah, I think you're right," he said and then there was a knock on the hotel room door.

Alex had felt helpless as Erin was arrested. It was unclear what the charges were and the arresting officers were bullying in their demeanor and simply unprofessional in their conduct. Alex tried demanding paperwork and a named authority under whose orders they were acting. The officers merely shoved him aside with smirks and laughter. They led Erin away and wouldn't say where they were taking her. Alex, frustrated and angry, called the one person he could think of that might have answers.

"Bautiste, you asshole," Alex shouted in to the phone, "What the fuck do you think you're doing?" Bautiste wasn't at all put off by Alex's outburst. The fat Sergeant Lopez had informed him that Alex's email had been the carrier of a virus. That virus had resulted in all of the Colonel's emails being uploaded.

"Señor Browning, such language," he admonished. "Your girlfriend is being much more polite, I assure you." Bautiste was infuriatingly reasonable in his tone. "But you have questions, yes? Perhaps you could *email* them to me." At that point, Alex knew that he had been found out.

"So," he said calmly this time, "you found out about the money?" He was fishing to see what Bautiste knew. He waited for Bautiste's response.

"Yes, I found out about my goddamn money!" Alex could hear Bautiste struggle to regain his self-control. "So did Sergeant Garcia," Bautiste added much more calmly. "Now, you fucking thief," Bautiste growled, "give us our money back. Or else." This pissed Alex off.

"Give Erin back and I'll think about it," Alex said with a flippant tone that he didn't feel. There was a silence on the other end and then a sophomoric response.

"Give our money back and then the woman will be returned. Without harm." That really pushed Alex over the line.

"Fuck you!" he shouted and broke the connection. He reached for his laptop. He remembered something from a couple of years ago. A young Army recruit named Manning had uploaded a large amount of classified data to a whistleblower website named WikiLeaks. The owner of the website, some Australian guy as Alex recalled, had steadfastly rebuffed all attempts to squelch the dissemination of the secret data. There was little that the Army or the US government could do. Alex had been both appalled and impressed. He contacted his daughter requesting information. Jo sent him a step-by-step set of detailed instructions on how to upload to the website.

He zipped all of Bautiste's email and text message content and uploaded it to WikiLeaks. He assumed that so much data would take quite a while to appear on the Internet for everyone to see. He was wrong.

Jaime Hernandez was a Major General in the National Police and Colonel Bautiste's boss. Hernandez had been a very close friend of Hugo Chavez and was privately mortified at the unrest in the streets since the great man's death. Maduro, as the chosen successor, had been pressuring the Major General to regain control of the populace. Maduro wanted a peaceful election.

Hernandez had put out the order that every uniformed officer that could be spared should be pulled from current duty and loaned to him to patrol the major cities. Hernandez wanted a show of force everywhere. All of his subordinates responded by reassigning all men and women performing non-essential duties. Nueva Esparta had stood out because Bautiste has assigned no one to the effort. Hernandez had ordered a report on the situation in Nueva Esparta. He thought that maybe there was some extraordinary circumstance on Margarita Island that required every man and woman working there to remain on duty. In the mean time, the reports on the situation in the streets were more and more dire.

After Alex completed his uploading task, he realized that Bautiste didn't seem at all that concerned about the email theft. This confused him until he had time to consider. Then the answer was obvious. Bautiste was concerned about his millions, not his reputation. Alex had hoped that if he held the data hostage, Bautiste would be intimidated and would back down. Alex was upset. He just didn't know what to do. In the movies, you walked up to the Colonel and beat him until he agreed to call some underling. Through puffed lips, he would instruct the subordinate to release the girl and ask no questions. He and Erin would be reunited, music would play, and they would fly off with Bautiste bound and gagged in his office.

Alex forgot about the movies and applied his brain to the practical problem of Erin. In his world, she would not be in any real physical danger. Villains might attempt to terrify their captives, but certain lines would never be crossed. The consequences were just too unthinkable. Alex's best course of action, he reasoned, was to enlist Mac's help and pressure Bautiste with threats of notifying Venezuelan officials and diplomatic authorities, specifically the U.S. Embassy although Alex honestly admitted to himself that he had no idea how they could help, or even if they would help.

At Playa Madrid Kuyper was astonished. To his knowledge no salvage had recovered more than a half billion American dollars in value. By his estimate, the recovery made so far on the *Little Ranger* had already surpassed that. His imagination was driving his estimation it would turn out, but he was not far off. Aboard the converted French destroyer, the crew of scientists was finally getting a chance to examine the recovered gold and jewels and silver. Several of the scientists were expert in placing valuation on items from the eighteenth century. The other members of the team deferred to these experts as they catalogued and tagged each piece. The number the French government was most interested in was $100 million. According to the salvage agreement, this would place $90 million in the French coffers. The valuation went on into Wednesday afternoon.

Alex assumed that the several gigabytes of data he had uploaded would be stuffed onto some WikiLeaks server until an employee of the site got a chance to examine the contents. Alex was very wrong.

Sarah Gilbert had been working for WikiLeaks for only three months. She had been attracted to the web site's stated mission when an Army private, PFC Bradley Manning, had been identified as the person responsible for storing classified military and diplomatic data on an unclassified site, WikiLeaks. Sarah was against war and the military and wanted all such organizations exposed for the bullies she believed they were. She noticed that a medium-sized quantity of data had been uploaded and all of the data came from the same server. She sat down at her monitor and began to rapidly organize the content. An hour later, she called her boss over to show him what she had.

Erin had been seated alone in a room that had one window placed high and covered with a thick wire grate. The chair was gray metal with a poorly padded back and seat. The walls were painted an unattractive shade of green reminiscent of a bodily fluid. The time had passed slowly and she tried to reason that this was an attempt at intimidation.

368

She knew that she was in a government building, but wasn't sure what the building was used for. She tried to focus on her belief that the police wouldn't physically harm her. They were the police, after all.

Elise Diaz, seated in a similar chair in a similar room, had no such beliefs. She had heard stories of police corruption and brutality all her life. She knew that she had one card to play and that she needed to play it well. Fernando Bautiste was deathly afraid of her ex-husband drug lord, Daniel. Daniel had been living in Belgium for the last two years, but Elise knew that he kept tabs on what was happening on Margarita. During the time that Daniel and Elise lived in Caracas and, subsequently, on Margarita Island, he had run a small drug empire ruthlessly. His few interactions with the National Police in general and Fernando Bautiste in particular were defiant and full of threats, threats that Daniel, on occasion, fulfilled. One night Bautiste realized that Daniel could mean business. As Major Bautiste was leaving a late night meeting, three men approached him. The men appeared to be having a good time, laughing and clapping each other on the back. As they passed Bautiste, the Major was hit with a Taser between the shoulder blades. He regained consciousness in an alley and had been severely beaten. A packet of cocaine had been pinned to the lapel of his uniform, a signal from Daniel to back off. He backed off and stayed away from the drug dealer after that. Elise was sure that Fernando carried a memory of that beating.

Sarah Gilbert and her boss, Tomas Friedmann, spent an hour looking through the emails and text files that the web site had received. Since PFC Manning's upload and the subsequent publicity, WikiLeaks had received a constant stream of alleged whistleblower uploads. This content was different, however. The most notable difference was the name Hugo Chavez both as recipient and originator of electronic messages.

"It looks like this Bautiste and Chavez were buddies. Stupid of Bautiste and Chavez to be so mean, though," Friedmann noted. He was referring to emails that mocked the Venezuelan poor, the devout, and the clergy.

"All of those groups were staunch supporters of Chavez when he was alive, I'm pretty sure." Friedmann shook his head in regret. "Stupid," he repeated. "Anything else?"

"Looks like this guy Bautiste was involved in some graft and corruption," Sarah pointed out. "Maybe some drug activity on the side." Friedmann nodded his agreement.

"Good job, Sarah. Do we have any idea who pushed this to us?"

"No," she said, "but it looks like it came from a Latin America server. Could be Venezuela or not. I can't tell. Should I post it?" She was asking if she should make the data public.

"Why not? It's going to drive a lot of traffic. Good for business." She tapped a few keys and the world had access to Bautiste's emails and bank information.

Included in the worldwide audience was an unknown data analyst working for the National Security Agency in Hawaii. He devoured the contents of WikiLeaks' latest post. This is great, Edward Snowden thought to himself. This is what I should do.

Fernando Bautiste coldly welcomed *El Martillo* into his office.

"You have picked up the women?" he asked. He had calmed down somewhat and now felt that he had regained the upper hand with the American.

"*Si*," was the answer. The Hammer didn't care about the two women. They had nothing to offer him. He was feeling the sting of the missing fortune and he had to trust his superior officer to set things right.

"And? Anything to report?" the Colonel asked impatiently.

"Your friend, Diaz, says she knows nothing and, if you attempt to harm her, she will let her ex-husband know and there will be, what did she call it? Consequences." Sergeant Garcia shrugged. He didn't know about the Bautiste and Daniel Diaz history.

Bautiste wasn't happy with the turn the conversation had taken so he asked, "What about the girlfriend? What does she know?"

"She might know something, but she is terrified. She's not going to say anything." Garcia sounded sure. Bautiste wasn't convinced.

"Why not try *el martillo*?" Bautiste asked. "It seems like a good time for it and, anyway, we are leaving this place as soon as our money is returned." It had been a long time since Garcia had last used *el martillo*. He grew excited at he prospect.

"I agree. I will use it." He grinned.

"Good. But let the Diaz woman go. She knows nothing and I don't like her threats. Understood?"

"I understand, *mi Colonel*." Almost immediately after Garcia had left, Bautiste's office phone rang.

"Bautiste," he answered gruffly. He wasn't in the mood to handle his routine duties.

"Colonel Bautiste," the caller said with authority. Bautiste stood straighter in his office.

"General Hernandez," Bautiste said deferentially. "Forgive my discourtesy. My Sergeant is away from his desk and the call rang straight through. As usual, I am very busy with this civilian protest thing." Hernandez interrupted.

"Bautiste, are you at your computer?" Bautiste sat down at his desk and logged on as he answered.

"Yes, General. I am logged in right now. I was just going over some reports."

"Reports," Hernandez repeated. "Yes," he paused. "Bautiste have you ever heard of a WikiLeaks web site?" Bautiste was confused by the question expecting Hernandez to be upset over Bautiste's failure to supply manpower to the capitol. He decided that this call was about something else. He relaxed a little.

"Yes, General," he said reaching for a cigar. "I believe I have heard of it, although I must admit, I have never visited it." He leaned back and lit his cigar. As he puffed, the General spoke.

"Perhaps you should visit it now." There was something in the officer's tone that chilled Bautiste on a visceral level. He put down the cigar and pulled his keyboard close.

"Right now, *mi General*," he said no longer relaxed.

He had told the General the truth. He had never visited the site before. The WikiLeaks home page was organized according to recency of articles. Each article had a headline describing its contents in magazine or newspaper fashion. There was a stylized logo of an hourglass wherein the top section was a globe dripping something into the lower section. Older content was archived along the left side as well as a hyperlink list of the world's countries in alphabetical order. But it was the very first article that made Bautiste's heart stop. The headline read: "Venezuelan Politicians and National Police Officials In Corruption Scandal?" Bautiste

372

quickly scanned the announcement. It was dated that day and read:

"Today WikiLeaks released the very private personal and official emails and text files belonging to a high-ranking member of Venezuela's National Police. This data is significant because it reveals the dark side of an uncaring government that publicly purported to care. The attitude of the leaders (including the much revered and late Hugo Chavez) toward the people is shown to be more than just apathy. The devoted followers are openly mocked. More, the data released suggests a level of corruption and an amassing of wealth, presumably at the public's expense, rarely revealed."

Fuck, Bautiste thought. What's going on?

"Mi General," he began and struggled to gain control of his cracking voice.

"Have you clicked the link?" Hernandez asked with a patience that frightened Bautiste even more. He looked around for a hyperlink to click and then realized that the headline itself was a link. He clicked it.

What the Colonel saw next filled him with despair and anger.

"Who, who did this?" he asked the General. He was staring at list after list of nicely catalogued links sorted by date and then subject. They were links to his emails, he realized. Sarah Gilbert and Tomas Friedmann had done an admirable job. Bautiste had difficulty breathing. He ignored whatever the General was saying and skimmed the contents. Jesus Christ, he thought, my name, Garcia, even *El Comandante*. This was a disaster!

"Colonel? Are you there?"

"Yes, General," but there was no life in his voice, "I am here."

"I want to see you in my office here in Caracas tomorrow morning. Maduro himself will be here with many questions. And, Colonel?"

"Yes, General?"

"Have no thought of running. I have already given the order to Sergeants Lopez and Garcia to detain you." Hernandez broke the connection.

Bautiste was stunned as he continued to scan the contents of what he recognized as his own computer. He remembered what Lopez had said about Alex Browning's email as being the carrier of the virus. Could that American have been responsible for this too?

Elise Diaz was at first thrilled when her jailers told her she was free to go. Then she was suspicious.

"I'm free?" she stammered. "Why? What did I do?"

"Just go, bitch," the smelly jailer ordered. "Stop asking foolish questions." He scratched his groin and licked his lips. He felt that one had gotten away. Elise picked up her bag and walked out into the walls of the green-painted hall. She followed the direction indicated by the jailer. She emerged into the afternoon sunshine of the Porlamar afternoon. She was surprised that everything seemed to have gone on as normal while she was locked up and frightened for her future. She headed home.

Erin was staring at the bare walls when the jailer entered the room without preamble.

"Get up, bitch," he ordered. She stood, afraid of what was coming next.

The jailer led her out into the same hall that Elise had traversed not five minutes before. He indicated a left turn up some stairs and Erin went that way. When Erin arrived at the end of the rise she entered a room. There was a man she recognized. She recalled the night in her apartment when they tried to drown her with a soaking towel. This was also the man who been in their hotel room before Alex's second trip to Miami.

"Sit down, bitch," Sergeant Garcia said.

Brother Terry and his fellows sat down to a room full of snacks and beer. The television was broadcasting the local news, but would soon be tuned to the channel that would carry the La Salle versus Boise State as a First Four play-in game in the West Region. The entire La Salle community was electric with anticipation. La Salle hadn't been in a tournament game in quite a while and every one knew the odds of a win by the small Philadelphia university. The Brothers were gathered around the 42-inch LED television with anticipation. This year had been a long time coming. The younger Brothers really didn't understand how significant this game was. The La Salle basketball team hadn't had a meaningful victory in the Tournament since 1969 when they made the Tournament and lost to Columbia at the University of Maryland court, Cole Field House. This game was to be played in Dayton, Ohio and the winner would, seeded a 13, travel to Kansas City, Missouri to play the number four seed next, Kansas State University, on Friday. La Salle was pegged as an underdog to Boise State.

Alex, with Mac's help, devised a plan that involved threatening Bautiste and the National Police with legal action. Mac knew a local attorney who would help. The attorney, Guillermo Sanchez, insisted on being called Bill and insisted that he would take no pay. Sanchez explained that, under the Venezuelan legal system, the National Police had the authority to detain indefinitely someone if that person was suspected of planning to do harm to themselves or others.

"So, our job," Bill said, "is to present a case that shows that Miss Rosen has no plans to harm anyone and that to continue her detention is unlawful and subject to litigation."

"Sounds straight forward," Alex said. "How long does something like that take?"

"If a judge orders a hearing and agrees to sign an order, she can be out tonight."

"Do you know a judge who will do that?"

"Of course, and she is a good friend of mine." Alex relaxed for the first time that day.

Fernando Bautiste had no intention of flying to Caracas in the morning. He did intend to make life miserable for Alex Browning. He picked up the phone and put out an arrest bulletin for the American and a hold on his passport. That would prevent Alex from leaving any Venezuelan port, airport, or bus terminal with a foreign destination. Busses didn't really present an option on Margarita Island. Where the fuck is he? wondered Bautiste. He wanted to dismember the American piece by body piece until he screamed how the Colonel's money would be returned.

The Colonel wasn't yet defeated. He had over two million American dollars stashed in cash at his opulent house and would use all of it, if he had to, to escape the Venezuelan borders. He had had enough of his mother country. Two million in cash was not an insignificant amount nor was it an insignificant volume. It was, in fact, a large suitcase full of currency.

By late Wednesday night, all La Salle fans nationwide were going crazy. In Dayton, Ohio, the Explorers trailed early, as was expected, but good and fast guard play brought La Salle within striking distance of the at-large Boise State

376

Broncos before half time. More hard fought guard play put La Salle up by eight at half time and the Explorers never had to look back. The guards kept up an assault for which BSU had no answer. The Broncos used a switching defense in the second half in a valiant effort to make up the half time deficit. La Salle's offense and defensive scheme set a pace that confused and disorganized the Broncos.

The La Salle religious community cheered and roared as they watched the game's progress on the forty-two inch flat screen television. As the time wore on it was obvious that La Salle would win. Boise State had no answer for La Salle's backcourt play and the result was a foregone conclusion. The conversation in the community room turned to the Kansas State-La Salle matchup that would occur on Friday. Kansas State would be heavily favored.

Major General Hernandez was extremely agitated. He not only had to deal with that piece of shit, Bautiste, but there were riots breaking out in all of the major cities. He knew that he didn't have a big enough force to deal with this size of an uprising. The people, especially the young people, were angry and feeling betrayed. Hernandez had to admit that they had a point. Chavez's government had neglected their demographic. The university students and their contemporaries were immensely dissatisfied with the status quo. The Chavez government was widely recognized as anti-intellectual and anti-business. The upcoming Maduro government was expected to be exactly the same.

By Wednesday night the Venezuelan government had declared a full crackdown on assembly nationwide. The riots would only grow worse as the internal dissatisfaction went from protest groups to angry, destructive mobs.

CHAPTER SEVENTEEN—Loss

Thursday morning, news of the crackdown had spread all over the country. But what also spread was news that WikiLeaks had posted damning evidence of the government's corruption and duplicity when it came to caring for and about the poor. Social media, especially a program called WhatsApp, was used to organize even more demonstrations and protests as the WikiLeaks links were passed from person to person.

Sergeant Garcia cared little about all of this. He had left Erin overnight bound to a chair in the basement room. He ordered a Corporal to keep an eye on her. He went off to a bar in the rough part of Porlamar, got drunk, got into several fights, got a prostitute, got arrested and got released in the morning. As he sobered up, he considered his ever-shrinking options. Whenever he was faced with difficult prospects the Hammer resorted to violence as an outlet and as a solution. He was not stupid though.

He frowned as he examined the papers in front of him. The accounting was from a bank in Lithuania. The balance was a little over a million euros. This was the first overseas account Garcia had set up when he had initially realized that his activities on behalf of his superiors might lead to trouble, trouble which his senior officers might not be able to make disappear. Garcia reasoned that he should have cash at hand, travel papers in another name and country, and access to a large retirement sum in the event he had to flee. He was sure that no one, not even Bautiste, had any inkling that he had been able to amass that amount. The largest part of his savings was, in fact, the result of theft, several thefts in fact. As a young policeman authorized to enter private homes and encouraged to intimidate, Garcia often took whatever valuables he found as "evidence." He converted these objects to cash and moved the cash overseas. Later, as his reputation for physical violence preceded him, he found that his targets were often more than willing to pay him whatever he wanted to forego a beating. Thus, he was able to skip the step of converting goods to cash and could simply send his bribes overseas. His bank in Lithuania paid a healthy rate of return on the foreign cash and, twenty years later, Garcia was wealthy. He also declined all the bank's efforts to have him switch over to paperless communication.

Though wealthy, Garcia had lived simply. Unmarried with no family, his only responsibility was to his job and himself. His colleagues, including his bosses, considered him, he knew, a brainless brute who blindly followed orders. He had realized a long time ago that this assessment gave him certain advantages around the workplace. He could eschew office politics with no consequences, he could ignore all office social activities with no pressure, and he could treat everyone at work as rudely as he wanted with no repercussions. Since his "skills" were, though not unique, hardly embraced by other officers on the force, Garcia was the specialist called on when pain was to be inflicted.

Garcia went to his desk and unlocked the center drawer. He pushed an inset button on the left side of the drawer and this action was rewarded with a soft click. He pushed a thumbnail along the side of the drawer's bottom and lifted the bottom and placed it on the desktop. He then lifted out a Costa Rican passport in the name of Juan Herdez. The passport's photo was of Garcia. The Sergeant also lifted out matching credit cards and a Costa Rican driver's license. He thumbed the credit cards feeling the embossed numbers. They were courtesy of American banks. Twenty years ago, Garcia had no idea how to set up such accounts nor how to procure false documentation, but daily contact with thieves, forgers, and con men had given the Sergeant an education unavailable anywhere else, except maybe prison.

Garcia replaced the cards and passport and then covered them with the drawer bottom. Seeing them again had helped him make a decision. He needed to flee Venezuela and no later than tomorrow. He had made his escape plans years ago and they included his documents, cash, and a property he had purchased nine years ago. It was a large home surrounded by high walls located on the north side of Tehran, Iran. It had a pool and quarters for servants. He judged that with Iran's isolation in the international community he would be safe there from Western law enforcement. All that was left was for Juan Herdez to make airline arrangements.

Alex was alone and felt alone in the empty hotel room. He was exhausted and knew that he needed to sleep. Sleep wouldn't come though. He couldn't get anyone at the National Police to answer his inquiries about Erin. Every path he attempted through the bureaucracy was blocked and every line of questioning he pursued was rebuffed. Mac's lawyer friend, Sanchez, reported that he also had made no progress in ascertaining Erin's well being. The most that he had been able to determine was that she was still in custody. Sanchez, when pressed, told Alex that it was unusual and disturbing that his usual police sources were not forthcoming with information. He took it as a bad sign and told Alex so. Still, he promised to continue his inquiries.

Alex, for his part, had never before realized how important transparency and freedom had been in his life as a U.S. citizen. Now, living under a system of curtains and lip service, he felt frustrated and impotent. To distract himself, he opened his laptop and checked his messages. There were three new ones. One was from Jim Davis, the Philadelphia lawyer representing the Browning Group.

Davis reported that the salvage process taking place less than twenty miles from Alex's hotel was going great and would wrap up on the morning of the twenty-first of March. The initial estimates, Davis was happy to convey, were that the recovery would be in excess of two hundred million dollars. Unnecessarily, Davis reminded Alex that based on the negotiated percentages this would mean a hundred million dollar return for the Browning Group. Alex saw the math but couldn't absorb the final figure. He was happy that everyone who had helped would get rich. He noted that Terry, Connie, and Jo were on distribution.

The second email was from his brother. It was an exuberant report celebrating La Salle's basketball win over Boise State University. Alex smiled and shook his head. He was happy for his brother but couldn't have cared less.

The third was from Joanne and was similar to the second. She was sending love and the news that La Salle had won and would play Kansas State on Friday.

Alex sent replies to the messages from his daughter and brother and closed the laptop. He had to consider the ramifications of his new wealth. Davis would need authorization and direction to pay Mac and Cor and anyone else that was owed as soon as the French paid the Browning Group.

Alex drafted, polished, reviewed, and polished again his reply to the lawyer and, when he was finally satisfied, hit Send. Only then did Alex slide open the glass door to the balcony and go outside and sit down. Immediately, he realized he was in the mood for the crutch of a cigarette. He got up and went inside to retrieve cigarettes and matches. The activity of smoking helped him think, Alex convinced himself as he lit up. In fact, the nicotine relaxed him and that did help him think more clearly. The sky was beginning to lighten.

What Alex wanted to think about now was how to get the hell out of Venezuela. He had plastic, but lacked cash. He had given all the cash he had left from the trip to the casino to Sanchez, the lawyer. He could borrow the cash from Mac, maybe. He was pretty sure that Bautiste would have the Porlamar airport watched. That meant he couldn't fly off the Island. Escape by sea was still possible, but would have to be done clandestinely. Again, Alex would need Mac's help. He felt that he had already drawn the big man too far into his own troubles. The smoke from Alex's cigarette drifted toward the tops of the near by tall palm trees.

Bautiste didn't know it, but, like Sergeant Garcia and Alex, he was also considering how he could flee Margarita Island. Like his Sergeant, he had a stash of cash. He did not, however, have the false passport and credit cards that the Sergeant had been prudent enough to acquire. His idea was to somehow leave Venezuela and to use false credentials to enter another country. He was fairly certain he could accomplish this. Once he was far enough away from the reach of Major General Hernandez, he could then concentrate on the American and how to get his fortune back. He fantasized that his future encounter with the American would involve a great deal of pain while the questioning was taking place. He wished that he could rely on the expertise of the Hammer to be available, but he knew that this was impossible. He also knew that such men and such talents were to be found in every corner of the world and could be hired for a price. He had no doubt that when the time was right, the American would talk.

Bautiste's more pressing concern was how Major General Hernandez would react when he realized that the Colonel was not going to show up in Caracas that morning. Bautiste had no illusions that an arrest warrant wouldn't be issued. He also knew that the flow down would take time. That kind of warrant would be questioned and requests for clarification would be passed up more than once. National Police colonels weren't routinely taken into custody. So he might have until tonight or even tomorrow to grab a flight from Porlamar headed east, maybe to Grenada, maybe to Barbados. Trinidad was another possibility. In any event, he would be gone. He had another problem, however,

The WikiLeaks story would soon spread and, as a major character in the scandal, his name and maybe even his face would be widely reported. He couldn't move about freely if reporters seeking comment constantly hounded him. There was no way to refute the story. It was true. The only hope Bautiste knew was what every person who found themselves as unwanted pieces of a major news story hoped for: a larger story would break and replace the personally embarrassing news in the media. Bautiste also knew that such an occurrence would be serendipitous and couldn't be counted on. Bautiste paced his office considering his options.

Later around noon in the Eastern Time Zone of the United States, millions of basketball fans gathered around their televisions and computers to follow the tip-offs of the initial games of Thursday's NCAA men's basketball tournament. Philadelphia fans and the La Salle faithful were no exceptions.

Alex finished another cigarette as he made a decision. He had been struggling between asking Mac for two thousand dollars in cash that he estimated he would need to run and asking Elise for the money. He felt that he already owed Mac more than he could ever repay. So he had decided to ask Elise. He had no doubt, based on the email from Jim Davis, that he would be able to pay her back plus any amount of interest she wanted. He called her at her home.

"Elise?" he asked when someone answered his call.

"Alex," she said, "it is not good to hear from you. It is dangerous for me. I was in jail yesterday. I was so afraid. You shouldn't call me. It's bad for me. What do you want?" Alex was taken aback and thrown off his message since this wasn't the greeting he had expected.

"I just wanted to see how you were doing," he improvised. "How are you?" He realized that he really wanted to know.

"How am I? How am I?" she sounded shrill. "I am afraid of my good friend Fernando, that's how I am. I am afraid to go back to jail, that's how I am." There was silence and Alex realized she wanted him to respond.

"I'm sorry, Elise, I really am. I wish that there was something that I could do." He was sincere.

"I don't care about your sorry," she said now sounding tired. "I have to go. Good luck, Alex," and she disconnected. Well, that went well, Alex thought grimly to himself as he turned off his phone. He had a thought. He had never used the capability before, and had all but forgotten that it was a possibility, but he reached for his leather cardholder. His Visa card had an international number on the back and he called it to enquire about a cash advance. The representative was friendly and helpful and cheerfully conveyed that the transaction would be exorbitantly costly. Alex decided to do it anyway. He had the representative explain (twice) the steps involved in collecting a credit card cash advance. He had no doubt that he would pay back the loan early or be dead before the first payment was due. He set out for the nearest bank to claim the cash.

That morning Major General Hernandez was reviewing the reports of demonstrations in major population centers. More than one report contained details of protestor fatalities. The fatalities in all of the cases were attributed to failure to comply with lawful orders and/or attempts to interfere with or harm officers engaged in lawful conduct of their duties. There was not a lot of concern about the fatalities. Student demonstrators, especially, received little sympathy from the general populace. They were considered to be spoiled children of middle class climbers who should have been studying or working part time jobs to pay for University fees rather than marching and yelling in the streets. Screw them was the prevailing public opinion. The University students should stay home was Hernandez's opinion.

"Excuse me, General," his adjutant interrupted his reverie.

"What is it, Esteban?" Esteban Uribe was an eager young officer whose family was well connected to the Venezuelan power structure. Hernandez considered him a sycophant with no backbone.

"The Colonel has not reported as ordered," Uribe pointed out. Hernandez was confused and Uribe could see it. "Colonel," Uribe consulted his notes, "Bautiste. You ordered him to appear this morning," Uribe reminded the General. Hernandez remembered the order and glanced at his watch.

"You are right, Esteban. Call the Colonel and find out what excuse he has." Hernandez recalled that last night he was concerned with the WikiLeaks posting. This morning, however, the protests had his full attention. WikiLeaks was a distant second on his radar.

"Immediately, *mi General*," Uribe answered and reached for the phone.

Erin's body was stiff and sore from sitting all night. When one of her jailers arrived with something to eat and drink, she was not only grateful for the repast but also for the human contact. She had tried to engage the young officer in conversation, but he was having none of it. The eggs were undercooked and the bread was a little stale, but the coffee was good and she was famished anyway. She asked for the chance to stand and walk around and the young man was agreeable. She was amazed that her butt was numb enough to hamper her ability to ambulate. The tingling in her backside was almost pleasurable as she, at first, limped around the room and then began to walk more normally.

"Thank you," she said rubbing her glutes and kneading out the lack of circulation. Her activity could have been construed as flirtatious, but the young jailer paid no attention. She stretched out her hamstrings and calves, bending deep at the waist. She was beginning to feel much better.

"Has anyone been asking for me?" The young man ignored her and busied himself with cleaning up after her breakfast. "Maybe an American?" she prodded. "A lawyer? Someone?" she persisted. He cleared away her detritus and then returned to have her sit down and be restrained. He left her the way he had first found her.

The lunchtime games on the East Coast of the United States were Valparaiso versus Michigan State followed almost immediately by Bucknell versus Butler. Neither game would usually be compelling but this was THE tournament. The Brothers of the La Salle University faculty found seats around the television.

Alex had taken a two thousand dollar cash advance on his Visa card. The denominations were in Bolivars and created quite a wad of paper. Alex stuffed his pockets and walked back to the hotel glancing about him as he progressed. He attained his hotel room safely and stashed the cash in the room safe that already held his electric razor charging cord. He had no reason for safely storing his cord. He had reasoned with Erin that there was no other use for the safe.

While he was dealing with the bank, he had considered how he might use his newly attained cash. He expected that he could pay some boat captain to transport Erin and him to safety. He just hadn't worked out the details yet. As he had learned over the last three weeks, when he needed help making a plan, call Mac.

"Yeah?" Mac answered gruffly.

"Got a minute?" Mac recognized Alex's voice. He was happy to hear from   the American.

386

"Sure. What's up?" Alex brought Magrew up to date on the happenings since they had last been together omitting the recovery valuation since Alex was still not convinced that it was accurate.

"Mac, I feel like when I collect Erin, we need to get out of here. I mean escape. Bautiste knows what I did and he's gonna want his pound of flesh. Do you know of a way we can get a boat out to another country? I can pay." Mac didn't have to think about it.

"Sure. This is an island. There are lots of boats. You'll need cash to pay though. By the way, don't you already know a guy with the right kind of boat?" Alex couldn't understand what Mac was talking about and he told him so.

"Your fisherman buddy on the North shore? What was his name? You know who I mean? You told me about him. A guy with a ponytail?" Alex realized who he meant.

"Luis Ramirez," Alex said. "Right. I forgot all about him. He was great. Great family. We shared a couple of meals and some good times." Alex tried to think if he had some contact information. "I don't think I have his cell number, but I think I know who does." Alex was remembering the two young reporters and the group's day trip to the wreck site. "You're right. He knows guys with those fast smuggling boats. Thanks, Mac. You saved my butt again."

"You're welcome and be careful, huh? Venezuelans can be focused when it comes to getting revenge."

Alex told Mac that he appreciated the warning and he would be very careful. Alex's next call was to Ramon Goncalvez, the young newspaper reporter.

"Ramon? It's Alex Browning. Do you remember me?"

"Alex, yes, of course I remember you. How are you? Julia is right here, too."

"That's great. Tell her I said hello." He could hear Ramon talking to Julia away from the phone's microphone.

"She says hello back to you, Alex. I'm putting you on Speaker. What do you need? How we can help?" Alex was touched by his obvious sincerity.

"Ramon. Julia, do you remember Luis Ramirez, the fisherman who fed us breakfast on the sand? We took him steaks and grilled them on the beach that afternoon. Remember him and his family?"

"I do," it was Julia's voice. "That was a great day. We were working a story of trafficking."

"Right," Alex agreed, "that was a great day. Any chance either of you got and kept Ramirez's contact information? I'd like to get in touch with Luis and make him a proposition." There was long pause at the other end. "Ramon? Julia?"

"Yes, sorry Alex. Julia went to get her notes. Alex, does your proposition have to do with all of the unrest in the civilian population?" Ramon decided to rephrase his question. "What I'm asking, Alex, is are you attempting to leave the country? To escape the riots? Do you feel unsafe?" It was clear to Alex that Goncalvez had allowed himself to slip into reporter mode.

"Look, Ramon, I appreciate that you have a job to do, but you can interview me another time. Ok? Right now it's important that I get in touch with Luis Ramirez. Luis Ramirez?" There was a short silence.

"I'm sorry, Alex. You are right. But can I interview you later? That would be great. Here's Julia." Julia apparently moved closer to the microphone. She announced her presence and gave Alex Ramirez's address and phone number. They said their good-byes.

Alex tried Luis' number and one of his children answered. A comical round of Is your father there?/Yes

388

ensued until an adult took the phone away. It was a neighbor's wife who was watching the children while Luis and his wife and some of the older offspring were out on the boat pulling in the catch of the day. Alex explained that he would call again later.

At La Salle, the Brothers who didn't have afternoon classes were gathered around the flat screen television, drinking beer and snacking. There were chicken wings, potato skins, and pizza and sour cream, ranch and bleu cheese dressings as dips. Everyone compared their bracket results so far and most had every game right. The only mild upset, a nine over an eight, was Wichita State beating Pittsburgh. Brother Terry swept in late having finished up his morning classes and then attending a working lunch and a President's meeting. He grabbed a cold glass of beer and settled into an overstuffed chair. He pulled out his Blackberry, something he hadn't been able to attend to since early that morning. He had seventeen new emails and six new voicemails. What the hell is going on he thought to himself. He brought up the voicemails first. Three were from Connie, two from Jo, and one from the young lawyer, Davis.

Brother Terry was sitting down as he listened to the news from Connie. Her first voicemail simply referenced "the email" and asked what did he think, "woo-hoo". The second was more excited and had a more insistent, "call me". The third was just like the second.

Jo's voicemails were similar to Connie's except more teasing in nature, asking "who wants to be a millionaire?"

The voicemail from the lawyer was cryptic. It congratulated him, offered legal counsel through the firm, and asked what he thought of the email.

Terry turned his attention to his emails. He left his beer untouched. He thumbed the appropriate buttons on his Blackberry as he scrolled through his emails. Because he was wired that way, he went through his Inbox and deleted the emails that were selling things. There were twelve of these. Of the remaining five, two were bills, two were from Connie, and one was from Jim Davis. He accessed the one from Davis and was glad that he was sitting as he read the news. One hundred million dollars for the Browning group. As a minority owner, Terry realized he was wealthy. The "rules" dictated that technically he couldn't be wealthy. A vow was, after all, a vow. He would have to re-assign his shares in the Browning Group. Easy come, easy go he joked with himself.

"What's so funny?" It was Brother Roderick.

"I was a millionaire. For a short time."

"Good for you. Your beer's getting warm," Roderick point out and he moved on.

Everyone else's attention was on the East regional game between 14 seed Davidson and 3 seed Marquette. It was a battle.

Connie and Jo had agreed to take a late lunch at a downtown Philly sports bar, the City Tap House over by the University of Pennsylvania campus. Paul Tanner joined them and all three had their brackets pulled up on their smart phones. Of course, they were interested in the games playing out on the numerous big screens, but they were more excited about the email from Jim Davis. Tanner was obviously skeptical.

"But how do you know it's for real?" Tanner kept pointing out. "Davis could have made a mistake. I mean I wouldn't get excited until I saw the money in my bank account. Don't you think?"

"Paul, we're not stupid," Jo countered. "We're not going to go out on a big spending spree just because of an email. Right, Connie?"

390

There was mischief in Joanne's eyes.

"Right, Sis. I only plan on maxing out <u>two</u> of my credit cards. I'm not crazy." Tanner's look in her direction indicated that he disagreed with her self-assessment. Joanne laughed.

"Good plan," she said. "Count me in." She sipped her beer and eyed Tanner. He stared back at her and then got it.

"Ok, you one percenters," he said. "You two can pay for lunch." They all laughed and turned their attention back to the games. Bracket pride was on the line.

Alex got through to Luis on his second try. The fisherman sounded glad to hear from the American.

"*Hola, Alejandro*," he said and Alex could picture the ponytail swinging back and forth. Alex explained what had happened and why he needed Luis' help. Luis, for his part, seemed to appreciate the gravity of the situation and asked Alex for more time so he could formulate a plan. Alex assured Luis that time was short.

"I have a thousand dollars, *amigo*, if that will help." Luis was clearly affronted.

"Money? Money? Between friends? I can't accept your money, *Alejandro*." He sounded sad and Alex was embarrassed and at a loss as to how to repair the damage. Then the wily fisherman gave Alex what he was looking for.

"But, my oldest son wants to marry his *novia*. He could accept your money as a wedding gift." Alex smiled broadly into the phone. You got me again, you sonofabitch, he thought.

"Consider it done, Luis. Please work up a plan, *amigo*. I'm going to try to get Erin loose by tonight and we'll be ready to go tomorrow. Is that ok?"

"That is fast, *amigo*. I'll see what I can do. How can I get in touch with you?" Alex passed on his contact information. "I'll call you back when I have details."

Terry was watching the last of the Thursday games. They had started late and would end even later, but he had no Friday morning class so he could sleep in. The final games were Missouri vs. Colorado State, Akron vs. VCU, Harvard vs. New Mexico, and Syracuse vs. Montana. The Syracuse and VCU victories were blowouts. Colorado State won fairly easily. The Harvard game was the most competitive. Terry was surrounded in the darkened room by the other March Madness aficionados of the community. Groans or cheers went up as the games went on depending on how someone had filled out their bracket.

Erin had been confined to her room for over twelve hours. She wanted more than anything else to take a long hot shower. She had been permitted to use the bathroom, but had had no contact with anyone except a young policeman with bad teeth. She was exhausted from twelve hours of tension. Not knowing what the immediate future held proved to be a grinding proposition. She began to wish that Alex would appear, but, for the ninth or tenth time that day, pushed the wish back down to the hopeless place where it had originated. She had promised herself that she wouldn't be weak and she saw herself as loyal to Alex and all his friends. She just felt so damned uncomfortable.

Late Thursday afternoon at the newspaper Ramon and Julia were extremely busy. Besides the civil unrest that was taking place on the mainland there were reports of a new development. Due to the information posted on WikiLeaks and especially the naming of Colonel Fernando Bautiste, the head law enforcement officer on Margarita Island, a flood of protesters and demonstrators were attempting to book passage on the ferry service from the mainland to Margarita. Apparently a huge demonstration against the National Police in general and Bautiste in particular was organized for Friday. The numbers were expected to be in the thousands.

"What do you think?" Julia asked. "Will it be peaceful? Will it be dangerous? I want to cover it." Ramon smiled at her enthusiasm.

"It will be peaceful and then dangerous," he predicted. "The marchers will march as they always do. When the police show up, some of the marchers will react and provoke them. The police will overreact and then some people will get hurt. It always happens the same way." Ramon shook his head in regret.

"That's awful," Julia said. "We should cover the demonstration. If we expose the violence, maybe we can stop it."

Money, Alex thought, fucking money. People get killed for it, people get killed over it, people kill to get it. It's just fucking money. He rubbed his face and ran both hands through his hair. He considered what he and Mac and Cor had done harmless. There were no victims. It wasn't until Bautiste bullied him about the drugs that he felt compelled to strike back and take Bautiste's money. He smiled at the thought that Bautiste's money was being used to fund the Browning Group, that Sergeant's money too. Alex couldn't remember his name.

Alex's phone buzzed. He didn't recognize the number except that it was local. Alex answered it. It was Guillermo Sanchez, Mac's lawyer friend.

"Señor   Browning?"   Alex

393

acknowledged that it was.

"I am not bothering you? You have a minute?" Alex agreed that he did.

"I think I have found a way to get your lady friend out of custody." Sanchez went on to explain his plan.

"So, what do you think, *Alejandro*?" Alex told him what he thought. He was disappointed.

"I think, Señor Sanchez, that it's not a very original plan. Bribe the guard?" Alex couldn't believe that was a solution being given serious consideration. "How much money would it take to secure Ms. Rosen's release?"

The lawyer went on to describe the difficulty of determining such things and promised to continue to work for Erin's freedom.

Friday morning Erin was just about a beaten woman. She could smell her own body odor and breath. She had been denied access to a shower or even a toothbrush and toothpaste. All she wanted to do was go home and clean up. It was at that point that an angry and frustrated Sergeant Garcia showed up carrying a small cloth bag.

"How are you, *Señorita*?" he asked with a mocking tone. "You need something? You want to walk around a little?" The idea of being able to stand up and stretch her legs was immensely appealing to Erin.

"Yes, please. Let me stand and walk around, please." The Hammer looked like he was considering her request, but then he laughed cruelly.

"You continue to sit," he ordered. "You tell your boyfriend to return my money. You can then go home. Walk and walk." Erin was on the verge of tears.

"I can't. I won't. I can't ask him that." She was pleading. The Hammer slammed his fist on the table. Erin jumped in reaction. The sound was confined to the well-insulated room however. The Hammer leaned in close.

"Show me your hand," he said indicating the left one. Erin was confused and asked him what he said.

"Your hand. Show me." She extended her left hand hesitantly. He reached for it, but she drew it back. He grabbed it insistently.

"Nice," he said. "Manicured, painted nails; you take good care of it." He turned her hand palm upward. He continued to hold her left hand with his right as he reached into his cloth bag with his left. He pulled out a tool with a rounded wooden handle. The tool was a leather worker's awl. He scratched his left cheekbone with the point of the awl as a terrified Erin watched wide-eyed. Erin had no chance to pull away. The tip of the tool penetrated her palm fixing her hand to the surface of the table. She screamed in pain. He slapped her left cheek with his right palm.

"You can ask him and you will ask him," he snarled at her. He pressed the handle of the awl to more deeply drive the tip into the table. She hummed in pain her lips pressed together.

"He will never give it back," she mumbled through her pain and the law enforcement officer slapped her again. She didn't scream this time. She didn't even react. She just stared into his dead eyes. "You can kill me," she said, "he still won't give it back." The Hammer pulled the awl from the table top and back up through her wounded palm. He watched, as she still didn't react. He wondered if she was in shock. He didn't believe she was that tough. He replaced the awl in the cloth bag and retrieved a nine-pound sledgehammer.

"Maybe you are right. Maybe I believe you. Maybe he won't give it back." The Hammer looked at her

395

considering. She looked back at him. She was resigned. "So he will know that if one steals from Garcia, one pays the consequences. I am sorry." Erin was about to ask for what, but the down-swinging arm was her final realization. Her brain was sending signals to the muscles of her mouth and voice box when the sledgehammer impacted with such force that there were no more signals and there never would be.

The La Salle religious community was buzzing with basketball fever on that Friday. The Explorers were heavy underdogs to the fourth seeded Kansas State Wildcats. The game was scheduled to tipoff at 3:10 in front of a KSU friendly crowd in Kansas City.

Alex received the call at 4:00 local time. Señorita Erin Rosen, who had listed him as a contact in case of emergency, passed away in custody at 11:13 A.M. local time. The N.P. offered their sincere condolences and could offer no other information at this time.

"Wait a minute!," Alex shouted into the phone. "What are you talking about? What do you mean? Erin's dead? That can't be. You made a mistake. She wasn't even arrested for anything serious. My, our, lawyer is going to have her released today. He had arranged for a ..." Alex realized he shouldn't say any more. "How could she be dead?"

"Señor, I am sorry. She slipped and hurt her head. A skull fracture, I believe. The report will be made available to you." Alex was stunned and then overcome by an immense grief. His throat thickened and his eyes watered. He couldn't speak.

"Señor? Are you there?"

"I'll be in touch," Alex said flatly and hung up.

The La Salle five were playing well and the La Salle religious community cheered them on even though the team had no idea of the magnitude of support behind them. La Salle jumped out to a commanding first half lead and was ahead 44-26 at halftime, a virtual slaughter that was certain to not hold up over a quality KSU opponent.

Alex was as saddened as he had ever been in his life. He was allowed access to the morgue and was the person who officially identified the remains of Erin Rosen, female, deceased. Despite the disfigurement to the shape of her head, Alex sadly knew it was her. Alex had pressed for details surrounding Erin's death, but the NP were tight-lipped. Alex could tell that the young officer who was the spokesperson for the NP was embarrassed. She tried to maintain an official demeanor, but wasn't experienced enough to pull it off.

"So, Señorita Rosen was alone when she had her, eh, accident?"

"No, she was with an — well, yes, she was alone when the accident happened, as you say."

"So, she was not alone?"

"No, no. She was alone."

"You said that she was with an officer, didn't you?"

"Well, I didn't say that, but she was. With an officer before the accident. Not when the accident happened. That is what you asked, yes?" Alex could see that the young officer was nervous. She had, obviously, never had to handle a case involving death before.

"Who was the officer?"

"Sergeant David Garcia. A fine police officer."

"I've met him. He is an asshole." Alex could see by her reaction that she didn't exactly disagree with him. "Was it really an accident?" Alex watched closely. She considered before she answered.

"No, Señor. I'm sure he killed her. We are all sure." She lowered her eyes.

Now Alex felt more cold-blooded than he had ever felt before. If he could have observed himself from a distance, he wouldn't have recognized the person he was looking at. His mouth was tight and his eyes narrowed reflecting the intense focus he was feeling. His body was tense, he muscles full of adrenaline - ready for action.

The young NP spokesperson had been easy to manipulate. Alex told her he needed to meet the Sergeant face to face and simply hear him admit the truth. She was sympathetic. Against her training, she supplied Alex with the Sergeant's address. Now Alex stood in the shelter of a covered walkway at the Sergeant's apartment complex. As Alex leaned against the stuccoed wall, he looked perfectly in place. He was holding a one liter plastic cup, the kind that was filled with soda and sold by convenience stores. Alex's plastic cup had a plastic lid and a straw protruding from a hole in the plastic lid. Alex didn't sip from the straw. In fact, he held the cup at his side and nowhere near his face.

The cup had once been filled with soda. It was now filled with one liter of high-octane gasoline. Alex waited. He was ready.

Sergeant David Garcia was dressed casually. He had applied cologne to his face and neck and then reached down inside the front of his slacks and wiped his crotch. The killing had satisfied something inside him, but it had also

398

aroused something. Now he was in need of a good meal and the company of an easy woman. He knew where to get both. He exited his apartment, locked the door, and headed for his car. He felt good and barely noticed the man with the soda stepping out of the walkway just behind him.

Garcia did notice that a liquid had been poured on his head. As he began to look for the source, he at first noticed that it was cold. He then noticed that it burned his eyes so much that he had to scrunch them closed against the pain. Then he noticed the smell and he realized he was in trouble.

Alex flicked the cheap butane lighter so that it sparked and then produced a flame. At his arm's full extension, he touched the flame to the Sergeant's shoulder. Alex stepped back and watched in fascination as the man's head was engulfed. The Sergeant's hands flailed reflexively at his flaming skull. Alex watched as the Hammer batted ineffectually and then sat on the concrete sidewalk. Alex guessed that the man was suffocating. He couldn't imagine what it must feel like to gasp for air and then breathe in flames. Alex also didn't care. He wished he had a baseball bat to bash in the fiery skull.

Around dinner time in Philadelphia, the La Salle religious community could talk of nothing else except the Explorers' stunning and surprising win over KSU, 63-61, only the second La Salle win in the tournament since 1955. Next up for the Explorers was Ole Miss on Sunday.

CHAPTER EIGHTEEN—Moves

Alex had, for the first time in his life, killed another person. He tried not to think about it. To assuage his guilt he tried to rekindle the rage he had felt when he learned that Erin was dead, tried to plan his next move. He knew he had to be careful, more careful than he had ever been before. He had considered telling Mac what he had done and asking for help or understanding, but, somehow, some instinct drove him to keep his act to himself. This was one of those times in life when it was best for a person to keep what they knew internal. Maybe in the future Alex would meet someone who shared a similar secret and then there would be a mutual revelation. But, for now, Alex needed to try to put the horrific flames out of his mind and to concentrate on what he should do next. He knew he had to wait for Luis to contact him and that made Alex check that his phone was charged. It was. So, Alex packed his bag, considered leaving Erin's things in the hotel room, thought better of it, and packed her belongings too. Vaguely he thought that perhaps Luis would know someone who could benefit from the clothing and personal items. When he was finished, he called down to the front desk to have his bill readied and a taxi summoned.

Ramon Goncalvez and Julia Martinez covered the demonstration in Porlamar. It was non-violent and sparsely attended. Apparently, the NP in Caracas were able to prevent most of the protesters from boarding the ferry and, apparently, the citizens of Porlamar were more interested in dancing and drinking on a Friday night than in protesting. Ramon and Julia split up early. Therefore Ramon wasn't monitoring the police scanners late Friday night, so he wasn't the first to hear the call on the NP frequency. An NP officer was dead and homicide detectives as well as crime scene specialists were needed at the address of an apartment complex. An All Points Bulletin was also issued for the whereabouts of Colonel Fernando Bautiste. The Colonel had gone missing since the early afternoon.

When Ramon read the news on his computer, he called Julia.

"What are you working on?" he asked.

"Some background on the demos and who's involved and why. What's up?"

"It looks like there's trouble in the NP ranks. One of their own is dead and homicide has been called in."

"Interesting, but..."

"I mean here in Porlamar. And Bautiste is missing. They've got everyone looking for him."

"Wow. Do they think they're related?"

"I don't know, but I'm going to look into it. Want to join me?"

"Sure. Count me in. Can you pick me up out front?"

Bautiste's expensive bag raised eyebrows when he checked in to the rundown hotel near the airport. It was the kind of place that hourly workers patronized when the tourist season was in full swing and extra help had to brought in from the mainland. The room rates were cheap, but that wasn't what attracted Bautiste. He liked the anonymity of the place and the fact that they preferred cash.

He had turned off his phone and removed the battery when he left his office. He was aware that he could be tracked otherwise. He had purchased a "minutes/data" phone so that he could make untraceable calls. Sitting in the mildew-y hotel room he considered the risk of briefly activating his phone. He wanted to check his messages. It seemed critical to him to know how much trouble he was in with General Hernandez. He didn't dare turn it on in his room. He would have to go somewhere with multiple entries and exits. He decided on the Mall.

Major General Hernandez was furious. Now, not only was Colonel Bautiste still missing, but also one of his Sergeants was dead. He lifted the report. What was the man's name? Garcia. That was it. He summoned an aide.

"Nothing on Bautiste's cell phone? Are we sure we have the right number?" The young Lieutenant assured the General that they were monitoring the correct phone.

"And what is the latest on this Sergeant? What does the Coroner's office think?" The Lieutenant pulled up a report on his computer's screen and scanned it. He summarized for the General.

"Death was caused by asphyxiation. An accelerant, probably common gasoline, was poured over the Sergeant and ignited. Actually, poured over the Sergeant's head and shoulders. The Coroner hasn't ruled out suicide, but there is nothing that points specifically that way.

"However, there is always the possibility that the Sergeant, as a member of Colonel Bautiste's inner circle, may have been implicated in the WikiLeaks scandal that was recently revealed. Such guilt has driven men to suicide before. Personally, I think that a police officer would not choose such a gruesome method. A police officer usually chooses a bullet." This last was delivered in a manner that made it clear it was the Lieutenant's opinion.

"I hope most police officers choose to live," the General said with a tone that left no doubt that he disapproved of the Lieutenant's previous comments.

"Of course, my General. I meant only to be helpful. In any event, the Coroner is not yet ready to rule homicide or suicide. That is all for   now."

Saturday morning in Philadelphia was clear and cool with a promise of coming warmth. The Brother's dining room was unusually noisy at breakfast with the excited chatter of everyone expressing an opinion on either yesterday's Explorer win or tomorrow's match up with Mississippi, a twelve seed. Mississippi had upset a five-seeded Wisconsin team to advance. Plans were made to grade papers or tests or assignments while watching Saturday's games. Beer and pizza would be available throughout the day.

Alex settled his hotel bill and met the taxi driver outside under the hotel's overhang. He had no idea of Luis' exact address, but, thanks to Julia, knew the general area so he told the driver to head north. He considered calling Luis, but knew that his instructions were to wait for Luis' call.

While they drove, Alex sat back and watched the scenery flow by. He recalled the day at the beach with Ramon and Julia and Erin. Christ, he thought, that was just a little more than a week ago. He remembered the delightful breakfast served by Luis' family and the reciprocated dinner of beef and vegetables cooked over an open fire. His stomach growled and he also remembered that he hadn't eaten yet this day.

"*Señor?*" He got the driver's attention.

"*Si?*"

"Have you eaten yet this morning?"

"*Si, Señor.* Why do you ask?" The driver was a slight man who seemed to have difficulty seeing over the steering wheel.

"I am hungry and I would invite you to join me. Do you know of a good place nearby?"

"*Si, Señor.* There is a very good place on the way north. It has good food and the prices are good. A family runs it from Mexico. Do you like eggs and chorizo?"

"Very much. Please, you will be my guest, yes?" The driver agreed.

The restaurant was unimpressive on the outside, stuccoed blue pastel walls with windows whose trim was obviously painted freehand in a darker blue. Inside it was not much more confidence-inspiring, heavy painted armless wooden chairs around formica-topped pedestal tables. The menu apparently didn't vary — it was painted on a roughly finished wall. Alex smiled; he was charmed.

"So, what are you going to order?" Alex asked the driver whose name was Edgar. They both studied the painted menu. They decided on eggs and cheese-stuffed chiles with chorizo and strong coffee. The eggs turned out to be egg whites and the chiles and chorizo were perfect. The coffee was great and as Alex summoned the server for a refill his phone buzzed. It was Luis.

The Mall was crowded on Saturday morning. There were the usual families browsing and barely shopping since they had no money to spend. Teen boys skateboarded among the families, bothering them but with no consequences from the Mall security. As Bautiste wandered by the stores looking for a suitable location to activate his phone and to make sure that he wasn't being followed, he noticed that some of the shops, especially those selling food, were extremely low on stock. From chocolate ice cream to chicken sandwiches, food products seemed to be in short supply. Bautiste also saw that, of all things, toilet paper was being rationed. Hand-lettered signs advised that only two rolls per purchase was the limit.

The Colonel found a recessed area that led to a closed door posted as authorized access only. He checked the time on his watch, allowed himself a full minute, inserted the battery and turned on his phone. He had over one hundred emails, fifty-seven text messages, and twelve voice mails. He had to make a quick decision so he listed the voice mails first. They were all from General Hernandez and were all between one minute and two minutes in length. He didn't bother listening to any of them. Instead, he brought up his text messages. More than half were from the General and the rest were evenly divided between officials associated with coroner's office and news reporters. He checked his watch and saw that he only had ten seconds remaining. He opened one of the messages from a news reporter. It was a request for comment on the death of Sergeant David Garcia.

Bautiste opened the phone's cover and pulled the battery so that his location could not be traced. So the Hammer is dead? Bautiste doubted it. The Press was imperfect in its accuracy Bautiste knew well. He pulled out his "burner" phone and punched in Garcia's number. The phone went direct to voicemail and Bautiste immediately knew that the Press had it right this time.

General Hernandez' desk phone buzzed and he pushed the button that activated the speaker.

"Hernandez."

"General, you asked to be informed if Colonel Bautiste used his phone."

"Yes."

"Well, he is using it now. We are triangulating his position."

"How long will it take?"

"Two minutes, maybe less. Would you...? Just a minute, General. He has shut down his phone again." There was a side conversation taking place and then the caller

405

returned. "I'm sorry, General. Not enough time. We will continue to track his activity."

"He knows our capabilities so I do not hold much hope. But he may make a mistake. Carry on." The General punched a button on his phone and killed the connection.

The French government was working that Saturday. At least some departments were working. The Bureau of Antiquities was one of those departments and Monsieur Jean Gerard had been evaluating the recovered items as well as he could from the high-definition digital images he had been reviewing on his twenty seven inch computer monitor. He would have a more precise valuation when he could actually hold and weigh and closely examine each object, but for now the photos would have to do.

By the time he was done with all of the pictures, his final tally was two hundred and seventy-seven million dollars. He calculated that they had made, according to the percentages negotiated, more than one hundred seven million dollars for the French government. Jean was proud. It was a lot of money and they still were going to raise and bring the *Little Ranger* home.

He mused that the American company had done well too, by his estimate, one hundred seventy million dollars. *Pas mal,* he thought, *pas mal.* He sat down at his computer and drafted another email to the Philadelphia law firm advising them of his updated estimate.

Jim Davis called Connie and relayed the update and Connie called Jo.

"Hey, Sis. What's up?"

"Busy? You sound distracted."

"Paul's here and we're thinking over what to do with the millions I'm going to have as a partner in the Browning Group. Just kidding. Not about Paul, the other stuff. So, what's up?"

"Jim called and guess what?" The silence dragged on awkwardly. "Jo?"

"I'm here. I'm just not going to guess. What is it?"

"Ok. Jim says the French government updated the estimate and guess what?"

"Stop doing that."

"Sorry. Anyway the new estimate for the Browning Group is $170 million dollars. We're rich, Sis." There was a silence as Joanne was obviously considering the implications. She smiled.

"You're right. You know what T-shirt I'm wearing today? 'God Made Us Sisters. Prozac Made Us Friends'."

"What?"

"Just kidding. It's the 'I Suffer Delusions of Adequacy' one. But, you're right. We're rich. What do you think the Browning Group ought to do with all that mun-nay?" Connie laughed. She loved her sister.

"Well, it isn't up to just us, but I was thinking that it'd be nice if we could do something good with it. Maybe start a Foundation or something. What do you think? I mean it's up to Dad too."

"Sounds great. I always wondered what the hell those Foundations did, by the way. Now I guess I'll find out."

Elise Diaz' phone buzzed just after noon local time. She didn't recognize the Caller ID number so she ignored the call. She was at home that Saturday. She was trying to sort out how she felt. Erin was dead. Fernando's Sergeant, what was his name? was the main suspect. Alex was available again. Did she want to pursue Alex? She had turned her back on him just days ago. Her phone buzzed again. It was the same number. She was annoyed. So she answered it.

"Yes? Who is this?" She recognized the voice immediately.

"Elise, it's me. Are you alone?" It was Fernando.

"Yes," she said cautiously. "Where are you? I didn't recognize the number."

"Don't worry about that. I don't have much time. I have to know. Are you still my friend?" He waited for the answer. And waited.

"I am your friend, Fernando. But Erin is dead. Murdered. It is said by your man. What do you know about it? Am I in danger?"

"Elise, I swear, Garcia had nothing to do with Rosen's death. Did you know that Garcia is dead, too? It's true."

"What? How?"

"He may have killed himself. Poured gasoline all over himself and lit a match. Maybe I'm wrong. Maybe he <u>was</u> feeling guilty about Rosen. Who knows? Anyway, that's all over. We need to talk about the future."

Elise asked what he meant and he explained about the WikiLeaks post. She wasn't surprised, but was confused.

"Fernando, how did someone learn about your, um, activity with *El Comandante* and the others? What happened? How did all of this become public?" Bautiste barely hesitated before he accused Alex.

"Your American friend," he said, "I'm certain he did it. He also stole from me. Me!" Elise could imagine Fernando slamming his palm on something.

408

"Fernando, what did he steal from you? How did he steal?"

"He stole everything I had saved. Millions." Bautiste sounded deflated and defeated which surprised Elise.

"Everything? How? He is really just a retired old man."

"I believe he used a computer trick, like a virus. Anyway I am leaving Margarita and Venezuela. I want you to take over my house and my cars and my boat. I will write it down and send it to my lawyer." He paused to allow her time to react. She had no reaction so he went on. "Will you do it? Will you see that my things are taken care of? I will stay in touch. This Internet news is something I must stay away from for now. Maduro will not be happy with me." He spoke as if Nicholas Maduro were already President of Venezuela.

"I'll help you, Fernando. This is a sad time for Venezuela and us." After she broke the connection, she had the thought: Alex is a millionaire.

Alex was glad to hear from Luis. That man was anything but a simple fisherman, Alex thought. He had arranged for Alex to leave Margarita by fast boat and head for Trinidad and Tobago. He had explained to Alex that the other options were Aruba, Grenada and Martinique. Both Aruba and Martinique were suitable as ultimate destinations for the American, but were risky to try for by boat. Luis offered the possibility of hugging the Venezuelan coast and either making a run for Columbia to the north or Guyana to the south. Luis had recommended against this. The Navy would be patrolling the entire coastline in case Venezuela's enemies might try to take advantage of the political unrest in the country.

Alex had finished up his breakfast and paid the bill. Edgar and he got back in the taxi and Alex gave a destination address supplied by Luis. The driver seemed familiar with

409

the address, but all taxi drivers everywhere acted this way so Alex had a medium level of confidence. As they drove, Alex looked carefully for familiar landmarks. Soon he recognized the turnoff to Luis' beach shack. He pointed it out to the driver and two minutes later he spotted Luis.

"*Hola*, my friend. Are you ready for a little boat ride?" Luis was grinning broadly. Alex gave him a bear hug and held up one finger. He went and paid the driver and gave him a handsome tip. The driver helped him remove the two suitcases from the trunk. He said something to Luis that Alex couldn't quite catch and then drove off.

"Have you got a cold beer for me?" Alex asked. He wanted to relax for a few minutes. "And, what did the driver say?" Luis laughed.

"He said that he understood that he dropped you off on a corner in Porlamar. He won't say anything if anyone asks. And, as for beer, no. No beer for you. You have a long ride ahead of you and most of it over open water. Better to have an empty stomach." Alex thought of the eggs, chorizo, and coffee, but didn't say anything.

"All right," he said, "you're the boss. When do we leave?"

"You leave," Luis emphasized. "That's your ride and your driver over there." Alex had to shade his eyes to see a dark man with a big hat sitting in what looked like a luxury fishing boat. "His name is Ernesto."

"Ok," Alex said, "as I said, you're the boss. That suitcase, by the way, is full of Erin's things. Maybe your wife or one of her friends can use them." Luis looked at the suitcase and then at Alex. He nodded his understanding.

"I am sorry, my friend. I liked your lady. May she have peace." Luis made the sign of the cross and kissed his thumbnail.

"Thank you. If justice brings peace," Alex announced, "she has peace." He pointed with his chin at the fishing boat and Ernesto. "When do I leave?"

Paul Tanner was spending Saturday with Jo. They had planned to ride their bikes along the Schuylkill River Trail that morning, but for a variety of reasons, they kept putting off their start time until it got too late. Jo's conversation with Connie had left them with a topic of conversation over lunch. Jo made chicken sandwiches, but Tanner put the bread aside. He was avoiding carbs for a while at least until he dropped a couple of pounds. He watched his body's metrics as if his life depended on it. In the security business, Tanner knew without being overly dramatic, your life could depend on your fitness.

"You don't mind, do you?" he said indicating the bread. Jo laughed.

"Your girlish figure is just fine, but knock yourself out. I assume a beer is out of the question?" She was challenging him, he knew.

"Not for me, but go ahead. What are they called? Plus sizes?" He laughed and puffed out his cheeks. She threw a balled up paper napkin at him.

"Ass. Do you really think I'd ever need a plus size? But, you did talk me out of that beer. Water, anyone?" Paul raised his hand.

After they had their waters, Paul revisited the question Connie had raised.

"So what does somebody with do with millions of dollars? Were you guys serious about the Foundation idea?"

"I was. I don't know how serious Connie was. What do you think about it? You sound skeptical." Tanner

411

munched his chicken sandwich filling, chicken, pickle, onion and a touch of mayo.

"Well, I'm a capitalist," Tanner said with his mouth full. "If it were up to me, I'd find a way to turn millions into billions." Jo snorted in derision. "Why not? With the money the Browning Group is going to get from the French, you guys could open a company." He filled his mouth again. "With the kind of money the French are talking about, there's no limit to what could be accomplished. I'd rather see your family make more money than start another well-meaning Foundation that gives handouts to people who accomplish nothing."

"What the hell are you talking about?" Jo said laughing.

"Ok, maybe I'm not saying it well. What I mean is that charity, in my view, accomplishes nothing. It only makes the charitable feel good about themselves and makes the receptors feel inferior and dependent. Wouldn't it be better if people, instead of getting free stuff, did something to earn what they got?"

"Like what? Do something like what?"

"Whatever. I don't know. Whatever their talent or capability was. Everybody can do something. Wouldn't that be good?"

"Well, I disagree. Charity accomplishes a lot. I read recently that it can hurt kids developmentally if they don't have what the other kids have and are made aware of it. It hurts their performance in the classroom, for example. I think the stat is that one in five kids under thirteen in this city live in poverty."

"Ok. I'm not going to argue with stats. But if a school kid is aware that he or she has less than a classmate, it seems to me that the school kid would be motivated to find out how to get something more? I mean, really, doesn't just about every school kid have less than some other kid in class? That's how kids learn that there are differences and

412

how kids get motivated to make themselves better. Getting a handout is not motivating. That's all I'm saying." He picked at the crumbs of his lunch.

"Ok. I see your point. But I think charity can make a huge difference in a poor person's life."

"Ok," he agreed. "But, back to the money. What does Connie want to do?"

With Elise's agreement to handle his affairs on Margarita Island, Fernando was ready to leave. He had shaved his facial hair and close cropped his hair. He sat in a rental car with the engine running out near the airport. He had been studying the activity around Porlamar's airport looking for any sign of something unusual. Everything looked normal.

Bautiste drew a 9 mm pistol from the nylon shoulder holster he was wearing and checked that it's magazine was fully loaded. He chambered a round, returned the weapon to the holster, turned off the engine, and opened the car door. The heat of the day smacked him and he began to sweat immediately. He looked casually around and walked to the rear of the vehicle. He unlocked and opened the trunk, pulled out and shouldered a soft bag, slammed the trunk lid and relocked it.

Instead of heading toward the commercial terminal, Bautiste turned right toward the private aviation hangars. He pulled out his throw away phone and thumbed in a number. The call was answered immediately.

"*Hola?*"

"It's me. I'm here. Everything looks ok out here. How is it in there?" He was in touch with the pilot he had contracted, Tony Villafranca.

"Everything looks normal in here. Come on in. The flight plan is filed, the plane is fueled, and…. Hold it. NP Captain and two cops just walked in. They are looking around. Are they looking for you? Is there a problem?"

"No problem. I am going to have to take you into my confidence. Can I trust you to be discreet?"

"I don't know what you mean? You have trusted me already."

"You're right. Listen. There are certain political enemies on the mainland who are hoping to blame their failings on me," Fernando lied. "You know about all of the riots and demonstrations, of course. But they have also put out stories about me on the Web. They say I am dishonest and have stolen from the people. I have not done any of this. These policemen are probably there to arrest me if they can. Are they still looking around?"

"They have finished. They are leaving," said Villafranca giving the all clear.

"Good. I'm coming in. Get ready to leave as soon as possible." Bautiste moved to his right toward the glass double doors. He entered the air-conditioned interior and looked around. Satisfied, he moved toward the pilots' lounge to meet up with Tony.

"*Señor*," a voice called from behind. "A moment, please." Bautiste turned slowly to see if the voice was addressing him. He saw the Captain and his subordinates and realized that they had tricked him by exiting one door and looping around to come up behind him. He decided not to bluff.

"Yes, how can I help you Captain?"

"I only have some questions." The Captain glanced down at Bautiste's phone. "May I see your papers, please?" Bautiste produced papers in the name of Señor Buenavista, businessman. "Señor Buenavista?" The Captain looked from the ID to Bautiste's face and back. Bautiste was familiar with the police tactic and was not intimidated.

"Yes, Captain."

"And what is your business in this terminal today?" The Captain ran his index finger around the edges of Buenavista's photo.

"I am flying to Martinique on business."

"And what is your business?" The Captain turned the ID over and examined the back, not only looking at it, but also feeling it.

"Import and export."

"You mean smuggling?" The Captain looked up into Bautiste's eyes and the Colonel realized he had been caught.

"No, Captain. Not smuggling. But, if you and your men would join me in private, I will reveal something you all need to know." The Captain was intrigued but did his best to hide it.

"We can step into the office," the Captain indicated a door to Bautiste's left. Bautiste gallantly allowed the Captain to lead the way. The Captain, however, motioned Bautiste to precede the others. Bautiste was counting on this.

He entered the unlocked door and took up a strategic position halfway behind it. As the trio entered the office he discreetly pulled his pistol. He slammed the door as hard as he could to shock and get their attention. They stared at the pistol in his hand. Since this was not a movie, Bautiste didn't launch into a monologue describing what was about to occur or warning them that he was in charge. He simply shot the Captain first and then each policeman. All three were headshots. The three reports were deafening in the office and Bautiste's ears were ringing as he stepped out into the terminal corridor and closed the door. He made his way rapidly toward the pilots' lounge and Tony Villafranca.

Alex had been in nice fishing boats before and knew that the ride could be rough or not depending on the driver and the speed. Ernesto seemed to be devoted to making it as rough as possible. Alex had read about fighter pilots who, when providing orientation flights to a newsperson or a visiting dignitary, foreign or domestic, made a point of having their passenger empty their stomach contents. It was supposed to be an unspoken goal. To Alex, Ernesto was looking for membership in that regurgitation fraternity.

Determined to defeat Ernesto, Alex kept his eggs, tortillas, and chorizo down for as long as he could. After the sixteenth minute, however, he extended his neck over the boat's rear deck and produced an admirable volume of fish food. He scooped seawater and rinsed his lips and chin. He sat back down, realized the boat was still bouncing, was hit with another wave of nausea, and gave up more of his breakfast.

The cycle continued until all that Alex could offer the fish were strands of yellowish phlegm that required explosive expectoration to break them free. He sat back exhausted, hating Ernesto.

"How far to go?" Alex asked weakly.

"Four more hours," Ernesto announced cheerily. "You hungry? You want eat? Have es-kid. Have octopus. Have oysters." Alex groaned, leaned back in the cushioned seat, and closed his eyes.

Bautiste entered the pilots' lounge and spotted Villafranca. He walked toward him and, as he got near, Tony looked up. He wrinkled his brow in confusion. Then his brow raised in surprise.

"Fuck, Ferdie. I hardly recognize you. No hair." He laughed and then cut it off as he noticed Bautiste's expression.

"Tony," Bautiste acknowledged. "I'm ready to go. You ready? We need to go."

"Ready to go," Villafranca announced. "Got my fee?" Bautiste reached into his trousers pocket and produced a fat envelope.

"Here you are, my friend." Bautiste handed over the envelope. Villafranca examined the contents and stuffed the package in his back pocket.

"Let's go," he said. He lifted his own nylon bag from the floor and shouldered it. He led the way through the pilots' lounge toward a glass door leading to the flight line. A security guard smiled and waved them through. The sunlight was excruciating after the dim, cool interior and the two men hurried along the line of parked planes until Villafranca stopped at a white and blue Cessna Skyhawk. He opened the pilot's side door, tossed his bag onto one of the back seats, and got in. Bautiste walked around the single propeller and opened the passenger side door. He also tossed his bag onto a back seat and slid onto the leather copilot's seat. He looked around the cabin and nodded in silent approval at the luxury.

Villafranca hopped onto the pilot's leather seat and began to flip switches and push buttons. The avionics suite came to life and the dual LED maps lit up. Villafranca put on a headset and began talking to the Porlamar Control Tower. He was apparently happy with the response and subsequently started the single engine prop. Bautiste was impressed with the cabin's muffled acoustics.

"Quiet," he said to Villafranca who, wearing the headset, didn't hear anything. The aircraft started to taxi out to the runway. Villafranca noticeably relaxed and motioned to Bautiste to don his own headset which hung on a hook to his

417

right. Bautiste adjusted the ear cups until they were comfortable.

"… so we can talk. But, remember, stay off the radio. Anyone nearby can listen to the radio." Bautiste nodded his understanding at Villafranca.

"How do I know if the radio is on?"

"See that switch?" Villafranca pointed to a large black rotary switch labeled COMM.

"Yeah?"

"If it's set to intercom, that's what we want. Got it? It's safe to talk." Bautiste looked down at the small labels.

"I see. Ok."

Villafranca lined up the nose of the Cessna along the runway. He revved the engine, released the brake, started the takeoff, lifted, and gained altitude. Bautiste was pleased at the easy transition between ground and air and the smoothness of flight. Villafranca banked the plane and settled it on a heading north.

"You are on your way, *amigo*," he said. He settled a pair of Ray-Ban Aviators on his nose and started to hum.

Alex's spine felt as if it had been ground to powder. He continually shifted on his cushioned seat in the rear deck area striving for a comfortable position. He watched as Ernesto stood forward at the controls and expertly shifted his balance, first using one leg and then the other.

"Only one more hour," Ernesto announced. This information encouraged Alex to attempt standing and walking forward. He felt that it might help to get out of the sun even though near the windscreen the airflow was not as significant as in the open. Alex approached Ernesto.

"Have any drinking water?" Ernesto jumped at the sound. He hadn't noticed Alex walking up behind him.

"In there," Ernesto said pointing to a well-disguised mini-fridge behind him and to his right. Alex found cold bottled water and took one, opened it, and drained it. "Feeling better?" He looked at Alex with some concern.

"Some." Alex puffed out his cheeks and exhaled. He gazed out the front windshield. "Did you have to go full out?" Alex squinted at the Venezuelan fisherman.

"I'm sorry, my friend. It was best to get clear as fast as possible. And, unless we had the rods out, it would be suspicious to go slow. Your stomach ok?"

Alex patted his belly. "Better," he admitted, "but now I'm starving." Ernesto laughed.

"There's some dried meat in that cabinet," Ernesto said. "You should just chew it and don't worry about swallowing." Alex found the jerky and took his guide's advice.

The next hour passed uneventfully and Ernesto call Alex's attention to the looming landmass.

"Trinidad," Ernesto said. "I will put you ashore near the biggest hotel. Many tourists. You can just walk in and get a room. No problems."

"No entry visa?" Alex asked. "No trouble?"

"No. It's ok. Show your passport to the desk clerk, pay for your room. The clerk will get your visa for you. You say you arrived by boat. It is very common."

"What will you do?"

"I will go back to Juangriego. No problem for me."

It turned out just as Ernesto had described. Alex simply walked into the hotel's lobby using the beach access and carrying his one bag. The clerk was very helpful and

English was the language of choice for every one of the hotel staff with whom Alex dealt. He took a suite on the top floor and was glad he did. The rooms were cooled by sea breezes coming through the patio doors and the open windows and Alex was grateful for the quiet once he was alone. He sat in a comfortably upholstered chair, got up, paced the room, and considered taking a shower. He noticed the wet bar, found ice, and made himself a gin and tonic. After the first mouthful, his hunger returned and he called room service and ordered a cheeseburger and fries. He sipped his drink and hummed that Jimmy Buffett song as he stripped for a quick shower. As he stepped out of the shower and picked up his drink, he heard the knock on the door. The young room service attendant was cheerful and efficient and Alex gave her a big tip.

Alone again and feeling refreshed, he munched his food and called the hotel operator. He asked the operator to connect him with the airport and made arrangements for a one-stop (Miami) flight to Philadelphia. He then had the hotel operator place an international call to Connie.

"Daddy," she squealed to his delight as soon as she recognized his voice. She started asking a series of rapid-fire questions and, when she realized he wasn't answering, she slowed down and asked if he was all right.

"Tired, baby, so tired. It's been a helluva last three days. I'm coming home."

"When, Daddy? That's great news. What happened? Did you hear about the Browning Group? Jim says we're rich." Alex had to think who Jim was and how Jim would be aware of their financial situation.

"Who's Jim again?" Alex had to ask.

"Jim. Jim Davis. Our lawyer? Here in Philly? Are you Ok, Dad?" Alex could hear the concern in his older daughter's voice. He sipped his drink, but the ice had all melted and watered it down. He spit it back into the glass.

"I'm fine, Con. Just tired. I've got so much to tell you guys. Some stuff I'm not too proud of. Can you and Jo, pick me up tomorrow?"

"Sure, just give me a sec to grab something to write with. Ok, go. What's your flight info?" Alex relayed his departure and arrival times and his Flight numbers.

"Got it?"

"Got it. We're so excited you're coming home. Erin's coming with you, right? It seems like a year since you've been gone."

"Seems even longer to me. I'll tell you about Erin when I see you guys, ok? Rich, huh? I think I could live with rich."

"Well, we've already started arguing about what to do with the money, so don't expect yachts and stuff, ok?" She laughed.

"Ok. Can't wait to see you guys. Love you."

"Love you, too. See you tomorrow. Gonna call Jo now."

Fernando Bautiste enjoyed his flight to Aruba. He knew that Aruba was like all the other Caribbean islands. It was fueled and fed by money, specifically gambling and banking money. Visitors were welcome with open arms, no questions asked, as long as the visitors brought their money and left some of it behind. Bautiste, traveling under the alias of his false documentation, was granted a tourist visa at the small aircraft regional airport. Villafranca turned the Cessna around and flew back to Venezuela. Bautiste arranged for the rental of a villa overlooking the Caribbean Sea and looked forward some quiet time so he could explore his options.

Venezuelan cities were rocked by protests and riots. The general populace was not only enraged over the WikiLeaks reports of corruption and graft, but were also angry at the post-Chavez, pre-Maduro government's inability to manage a steady supply of necessities and staple items such as toilet paper, sugar, cooking oil, and flour. The Maduro political machine had its work cut out.

CHAPTER NINETEEN—Steps Forward

Joanne Browning had set up her web site while she was still in college. At that time it was more of a social page, meant for her fellow software engineers to access her research efforts and her findings and leave comments. Jo often found the comments useful and sometimes hilariously clever. She took great delight in the intelligence of her fellow students. After she graduated and started her company, JB Software Enterprises, she maintained her personal/social site, but also registered a professional site where prospective clients could browse and decide if her services were right for them.

Among Joanne's "services" was that of protecting other web sites against Distributed Denial Of Services (DDOS) attacks, attacks that harvested usernames and passwords (identity theft), and attacks that were purely malicious in nature. The web sites who employed Joanne's services were grateful for her successes and readily paid her fees. The attackers who were rebuffed by Joanne's services were angry and motivated to avenge their defeats.

One such attacker was Zodiac, a Russian hacker located in Novosibirsk, the third largest city in Russia and located in the bleak area of Siberia. Zodiac was talented and fearless, but like most Russian hackers, he needed a dual support system: the Russian mob and strong political protection. Zodiac had a botnet under his control consisting of a thousand slave computers. He had been conducting DDOS attacks against gambling web sites for the last eighteen months. His "business model" was to deny gamblers access to the gambling sites. He would then contact the site and ask for a ransom in return for ceasing the attack. Most sites would pay. The problem arose when an intruder such as Joanne blocked the attack. Joanne had, in fact, thwarted two of Zodiac's attacks on Belize-based gambling sites. This bitch would pay, thought Zodiac.

Alex sobbed over his coffee. He tried to accept that Erin was gone. The voyage from Margarita had been a distraction, but now he couldn't avoid his heartbreak. He kept reviewing his shitty options as he felt the empty hole in his heart. Could he have done more? Should he have done more? He was crushed by the guilt of thinking that, with Mac's help or his lawyer's, he could have brought pressure to bear, enough pressure, somehow the pressure needed to have saved her. Alex's tears blurred his vision. He had to wipe them away with a napkin. He sipped his warm coffee.

He gazed about his hotel room. The appointments, bedspread, curtains, furniture upholstered in cloth or finished in lacquer or both, tile floor partially covered in colorful rugs, were upscale by most of the world's standards. Alex didn't care. His mind was clear after the coffee. He wanted to make a difference in the world now, not be made different by it. He got up and walked to the balcony and drew the curtains. The view was terrific if he were in a mood to enjoy it. Everything had changed in a matter of hours. His future was unmapped, a blank page, a nothingness toward which he had to move with no option. He longed to see his family. He tried to breathe deeply, but the breath caught in his chest in a truncated hiccup. He decided to take a quick shower and head to the airport. He saw no sense in sitting around the hotel room. He could wait out the time just as well at the airport. He searched for and found his pack of cigarettes. Although he had agreed that the room was a non-smoking room, he lit up and sucked the nicotine deep into his lungs.

At WikiLeaks headquarters Sarah Gilbert followed the news out of Venezuela. Colonel Bautiste had disappeared and was a suspect in a triple murder at an airport on some island. He was believed to have fled the country. The reports of shortages and rioting were very disturbing to the

424

outside world.   It was universally accepted that the government was losing control. Reports said that the flood of emigrants who fled the country in 1989 and were now residing in Columbia and Panama, were considering a return to Venezuela to avenge the *Caracazo*, the military response to rioting by the middle class back then. Those middle class businessmen who fled the country depleted Venezuela of professionals such as dentists, doctors, and, most importantly, oil executives who knew how to produce the one commodity that kept the economic engine of Venezuela thumping. Sarah Gilbert knew her history and realized that monumental changes were possible once again in Caracas. Among the news out of Venezuela there was a small story of the possible self-immolation of a police sergeant on some island.

Captain Gerand had sailed into Martinique, supervised the transfer of the *Little Ranger's* bounty to a French Air Force jet, took Kim Touw out to dinner and back to his hotel room where they enjoyed each other's offerings. French Antiquities expert Jean Gerard, embassy attaché Michelle Lovinger, and on-the-scene negotiator Walter LeClerc all read the final valuation after the French Air Force's cargo was off-loaded and handed over to the true experts in Nice on the Cote d'Azur. The experts had been forewarned that the recovery was the most remarkable that any of the field team had ever witnessed. Not only from the sheer volume of treasure, but also from the historical significance of some of the recovered articles. The experts were completely unprepared for what they say when they opened the containers.

The valuation was now official. The *Little Ranger's* bounty was worth over four hundred million American dollars. The French government was delighted. For little effort, they had garnered over one hundred thirty million dollars for the government treasury. And they still had to evaluate the hulk of the wreck that was on its way to Nice. This was more difficult to place a number on since there was no way to guess the worth of the attraction to the public. Jean Gerard, although it was not his area of expertise, envisioned a display of the restored *Little Ranger/Comte de Toulouse*. He secretly believed that he had a talent for theater and his vision included video screens, life-sized manikins, and ALL of the recovered treasure spread about and dramatically lit to best effect. He wanted to get to work on a proposal, but first he had to oversee the transfer of a check for three hundred million dollars to the Philadelphia firm, The Browning Group.

As a participant in the full adventure of the *Little Ranger/Comte de Toulouse* Monsieur Gerard was privy to the email thread initiated by the French Embassy in Caracas. The email was an obvious effort at ass covering combined with a child-like cry for attention. It began by raising the possibility that, because of the ship and treasure recovery, the French could be seen as unfavorably profiting at the expense of Venezuela. And this at a time when the cities were in turmoil and there were shortages of basic goods on the shelves. It ended by a needless assurance that the Embassy staff were prepared to justify each and every action of the French government should questions arise. Gerard smiled when he read it. He could almost hear the opening strains of *La Marseillaise*. There were a number of sarcastic responses from various government departments. Jean Gerard found it all highly amusing.

Working through the Philadelphia lawyer, Mister Davis, Monsieur Gerard performed an electronic funds transfer in the exact amount of Three Hundred Two Million One Hundred Sixty-Three Thousand Four Hundred Seventy-Two Dollars and Thirty-Six Cents. This sum was deposited to the account of The Browning Group. There were a number of French government officials who second-guessed the terms of the arrangement with The Browning Group. Monsieur Gerard was not one of them. He knew that when performing ocean salvage there were no guarantees. He thought the government was lucky this time to have come out ahead.

"You want to see something?" Jim Davis asked when Connie answered his call.

"It's not Willy, the one-eyed..." she started, but Davis' laughter cut her off.

"What a perv," he said, speaking through a smile. "Cut it out. I'm at work. Anyway, what was I asking?"

"You were going to show me something," she helped, "and I'm at work too, just not a corporate slave. Like you," she added gratuitously.

"Well, you weren't a corporate slave until today," he said cryptically.

"What are you talking about?" she took the bait. "I'll never..."

"Hold on. Just log in to The Browning Group's site and check your account balance. Do it for me?" he teased.

"Hang on. Putting you on speaker." He could hear her put the phone down and then the soft clicking of a keyboard. "Holy fuck!" she shouted. "Is that right? Two hundred million?"

"Check again, baby girl," he laughed. He waited while she absorbed the data.

"Holy shit! Three hundred million? How? What the hell?" He laughed. Jim Davis wasn't all that accustomed to handling hundreds of millions of dollars, but he had done it twice before. He enjoyed the thrill once again.

"You're filthy rich, Con, you and your family. The firm will gladly handle your tax problems. I'll see to that. It's a boatload of money. Any idea what you're going to do with it?"

"I've got some ideas," she admitted. "I want to talk to my Dad and sister first, though. You ok?"

"Fine. Excited for your family though. Of course, the firm will make a fair profit, too, you know."

"I have no problem with that, Jim. You earned it." Connie was being truthful. She believed that the young lawyer had done a good job for her family. And, she believed something more.

"I would have done it for free," Davis admitted. "I adore your Dad, sister, and her boyfriend. If that doesn't sound too homoerotic." Connie laughed. "Anyway, the Brownings are set for life, as well as their heirs. By the way, have you heard from your father?"

"Yesterday. He's coming back today. I'm going to pick him up. He sounded so old. I've never heard him like that. Like he had no energy left. Jim?" Davis was a little upset that she sounded upset.

"Yeah, Con?"

"Could you go with me to pick him up? I already emailed Jo, but she's kind of fragile where Dad's concerned. She might break." Davis didn't hesitate.

"When and where?" Connie's heart swelled and her eyes watered.

"Pick me up at four?"

"I'll be there," he said. "And it's not just because you're rich."

"But it helps?" she teased.

"It doesn't hurt."

Fernando Bautiste, traveling under the papers of Felipe Buenavista, was enjoying his time in Aruba. The island was well suited for catering to the desires of tourists who could afford the finer things. There were casinos for

428

gambling, restaurants to address the most discriminating of appetites, and panderers available to handle other appetites. Bautiste was having a good time.

He had consumed a five star dinner, gambled in the casino at Chemin de Fer, and had purchased sex with an under aged Asian girl. Now it was time to consider the future. He had a vague plan. It involved immigrating to Belgium. He wanted to meet with Alex one more time though. But he was in no hurry to leave his leased villa. He was a careful man.

"Hey, Con. What's going on?" Jo Browning was having a pleasant Saturday. She hadn't had a chance to check her email or her website. She had worked out hard with Paul running, lifting, and soaking in a 102-degree hot tub. Her muscles were as relaxed as they had ever been. Although there was still a winter chill in the spring air, Jo had her windows opened. She was longing for warmer weather.

"Picked out a yacht yet?"

"You still fantasizing?"

"Not a fantasy any more, little Sis. I just got a call from Jim. Want to guess on the final number?" Joanne stretched both arms over her head and worked her shoulders. It felt great. She returned the phone to her ear.

"Nope. No guessing. Just tell me." Connie told her. "Wait. What? Say that again." Connie repeated. "Holy shit!"

"That's what I said," Connie laughed. "By the way, did you get my message?"

"No. Crap. I was working out with Paul all morning. I haven't checked anything. What did I miss?"

"Dad's coming home tonight. Jim and I are picking him up. Want to be there?"

"Yeah, of course. What time? Can you guys pick me up? Paul, too? How did he sound?"

Connie answered Jo's questions including her impression that Alex had sounded deflated and, maybe, depressed. His daughters hadn't seen him really unhappy since the period after their Mom died. He had always been upbeat and ready to move on to life's next adventure.

"He said he was just tired and had a ton of stuff to tell us. Some stuff, he said, he wasn't - how did he put it? - proud about. Or something like that. Anyway, we'll find out tonight, right?"

"Right," Jo said. "See you later. Love you."

"Love you, too."

Major General Jaime Hernandez was bone tired. So many events were demanding his attention and each one needed a judicial touch. He delegated where he could. Control of the cities was his top priority as dictated by the government. He also had to resolve the circumstances surrounding the death of Sergeant Garcia. The coroner's office seemed to be in no hurry to release a cause of death. Most aggravating to the General, however, was the disappearance of Colonel Fernando Bautiste. A NP detective had been dispatched to the airport where the Colonel's rental car had been traced. No passengers named Bautiste had boarded any flight yesterday. However, the detective had been able to determine that a passenger matching Bautiste's description and named Felipe Buenavista had departed Porlamar in a private aircraft, destination as yet undetermined. The detective was experienced enough to know that people using assumed identities were much more successful when choosing an alias with their same initials. It had something to do with brain's reaction when signing in or responding to requests for identity. That split second was important. The detective concentrated on the identity of the plane's pilot.

There had also been a report from the airport in Porlamar of a fatal attack on three members of the airport security team. The perpetrator appeared to have escaped. In any event, it was a local matter being handled by the local authorities.

At the international terminal in Trinidad's airport, Alex experienced that the rigamarole of secure travel found everywhere else in the Western world was somewhat more relaxed on this island. He handed over his passport nervous that he had no entry stamp for the country. He had forgotten to ask for one at the hotel. A cheerful airport official noticed the lacuna. He summoned a superior official and pointed out the problem. In the singsong accent of the islands the superior directed his subordinate to take the only sensible course of action. The smiling official left his chair telling Alex to wait. He returned with a new stamp. With great fanfare, he inked the stamp and brought it down on an empty page of Alex's passport. He admired his work briefly and handed the passport back to Alex. Alex looked down and realized that he now had an entry visa. The smiling man asked that Alex once again hand over his passport for the exit visa. Life made simple.

Alex watched the planes arrive and depart. He was struck by the fact that there were no jetways. But, when he thought about it, why did they need them? Rain? Big deal. He recalled the time long ago when he had flown from Phoenix to Rochester, New York in January. No jetways. He had stepped out of the plane onto the stairs wearing only a crew neck sweater and the air seemed to freeze in his lungs. No jetways. He smiled at the memory. It was a long time ago.

His thoughts turned to his daughters as he watched the flight line activity. It seemed like another life ago since he had seen them together. He wanted so much to relax with them and know that they were all safe. He realized that, despite his age, he hadn't really met evil until his time on Margarita Island. Bautiste and his henchmen used their positions of authority to bully and intimidate. They were cowards, really, Alex knew. He checked his watch. Two hours until boarding.

Julia Martinez and Ramon Goncalvez submitted their co-written story following up on the WikiLeaks reports. It was Julia who uncovered a twist. It was Julia who wondered if there could possibly be a tie-in between the alleged corruption and misuse of power by Chavez' close associates, including Colonel Fernando Bautiste, and the ostensible suicide of Bautiste's always present, always faithful Sergeant David Garcia, also known as *El Martillo*, The Hammer. Julia checked all the background material on the Sergeant to see what indicators there might be of character flaws that would lead him to kill himself. There were none that she could find. In fact, the Sergeant seemed to be the antithesis of someone who would commit suicide. By all the evidence Julia could uncover, Sergeant Garcia was a fighter, maybe even a nasty fighter. According to his colleagues, he was Bautiste's enforcer, rumored to often act outside the law. He sometimes received assignments from the Colonel that were never written up in official reports.

"So, he wasn't your ordinary policeman," Julia had told Ramon. "He wasn't exactly dishonest, according to others in the department. But he was reported to have been fiercely loyal to Bautiste. Apparently, he would do anything for the Colonel."

"Speaking of, whatever happened to Bautiste? Any opinion on that from your interviews?" Julia pulled up some notes on her laptop.

"Unofficially, there was an incident involving three security staff members at the airport. They were all shot and killed at almost point blank range and the suspicion is, unofficially, that Bautiste was involved."

"Unofficially involved?" Ramon joked darkly.

"Right. Sorry. News-speak. You know how it is." Julia paused, "Allegedly." Ramon laughed.

"Allegedly," he agreed, using the adverb all reporters in all media used, presumably at the direction of their legal staff. "So, was Bautiste involved?"

"Nobody will say anything on the record, but, since the dead men were not police and just security guards, no one's making a big fuss about it either. It'll probably be filed and forgotten."

"Hmm. Could be another twist to the story."

"Could be, but there's nothing that ties Bautiste to the shootings. No cameras and no forensics. He wasn't on any passenger list either."

The two reporters were summoned to their editor's office. There they were told that the story expanding on WikiLeaks' report would not be published.

"It's a good story and well done," the editor said, "but, at this time, it's the owner's judgment that it would be too inflammatory. Given the riots and all. I have to agree."

The young news people were deflated, but accepted their boss' decision.

Fernando was watching television in his room and having a beer, satisfied and relaxed. The world news was playing and the pretty announcer was emoting to the "trouble in the Middle East". As with all news programs in the age of the 24/7 news cycle, the screen not only had an inset for financial markets and the current weather, but also had a "crawl" informing the watcher of news which was not currently under discussion by the talking heads.

The "crawl" reported that the Venezuelan authorities were searching throughout the Caribbean for Colonel Fernando Bautiste, a missing member of the *Policia Nacional*. The "crawl" moved on to the next story.

Bautiste was no longer relaxed. He was alert and suddenly saddened. His plan had been to stay in Aruba for at least a month, to live quietly, to ponder his options. As a policeman, he knew that the most frustrating and fruitless of all police efforts was the dragnet. Almost one hundred percent of the time the activities of the police produced no results and, in almost all cases, information leading to a capture was provided by a civilian who had a chance encounter and remembered it. He had taken basic precautions against casual recognition: shaved his mustache, buzzed his hair to a close-cropped look. He had taken some sun to tan the skin that had once been covered. He had confidence in his false papers. And yet he had a bad feeling.

He knew that once the police were able to connect Felipe Buenavista with the three dead bodies at the airport, it wouldn't be long before they knew who Buenavista was and where he had gone.

Bautiste reached for the villa's phone.

Alex's flight to Miami was called for boarding. Finally, Alex thought. He shouldered his carry-on and checked the terminal waiting area to be sure he hadn't left anything behind. The pre-boarding consisted of merely checking that each passenger had a valid ticket. Alex was surprised to see that more than one prospective traveller had no ticket. These people were directed to stand to the side.

Alex showed his ticket, the airline employee scanned it with a handheld machine, and waved him through.

Thirty minutes later and there was a bump as the jet went airborne.

Connie and Jim arrived outside Jo's apartment as arranged. Jim was driving his Toyota SUV, which would have ample room for five and whatever luggage Alex might bring. Connie got out and started to walk up the steps to Jo's door when the door opened.

"We were watching for you, Sis. I can't believe how excited I am."

"Me, too. Even though Jim and I had that one evening in Miami, it seems like way longer than a couple of weeks since we saw Dad." Paul Tanner appeared behind Jo and closing the door of the apartment, checked that it was locked.

"Hi, Con," he greeted. "Good to go." The trio joined the lawyer and Davis navigated their way to Philadelphia International Airport. They rode in silence for a while.

"So, Connie, how did your Dad sound?" It was Tanner who asked the question this time. Connie struggled to formulate a precise answer.

"I'll tell you what I told Jo, Paul. Maybe tired, maybe a little defeated. Or depressed. I don't know why I thought that." Connie shrugged. The others were quiet as they absorbed what Connie had said.

"Well, from everything I know about the agreements, the recovery, and the transfer, there was absolutely nothing depressing about the money the Browning Group acquired." Jim spoke as he drove. Surprisingly, it was Tanner who demonstrated an analytical mind.

"What about the treasure itself, Jim?" Tanner paused as he thought. "What if it's tainted somehow? What kind of difference would that make?" The women looked at him

435

expecting him to say more. "Just asking," was all he added. The lawyer considered the ramifications of the issue Tanner had raised.

"It could make a difference to France's claim," he said as he drove. "The agreement between Venezuela and France was for Venezuela to recognize France's ownership of the sunken ship and any artifacts found in the wreck's vicinity." He thought some more. "Paul brings up a good point. If the artifacts, in this case the treasure, weren't somehow originally part of the sunken ship," he risked a glance from the road to see who was listening. They were all listening. "Now it becomes a complex legal issue. Did France know that? What was the original location of the artifacts? Were all parties acting in good faith?" Davis blew out his cheeks. "Like I said, complicated."

"Anyway," he continued, "there's no reason to believe that anything untoward occurred. We'll just have to wait until your Dad gets home to find out the whole story of what happened in Venezuela, agreed?" They all agreed. Tanner felt bad that he had brought it up but kept his feelings to himself.

Alex's flight to Miami was thankfully boring. He slept most of the way even though he had always claimed that he couldn't sleep unless he could stretch out completely. He woke once, unkinked his muscles, checked his chin for drool, and went back to sleep. By the time he arrived in Miami he wasn't sleepy anymore. He didn't feel rested either.

Dealing with the U.S. customs officer was a pleasure this time. He was simply happy to be back on American soil.

"Are you bringing back any souvenirs from Venezuela or," the Officer checked Alex's visa stamps, "Trinidad today?" Alex answered in the negative and had to rack his sleep-addled brain as to why not. He could only think of the jewels and gold, but they were irrelevant to the ICE officer's question. Alex just waited for the next question.

"Nothing? No trinkets, no clothing, no handcrafted goods, no plant life?"

"No, nothing." Alex knew his answer was honest, but he didn't blame the officer for doubting him.

"Any food, plants, animals?" The officer had accepted Alex as legitimate and returned to his list of routine questions, although, somewhere in Washington, a computer screen came to life, logging the fact that Mr. Alexander Browning had re-entered the United States through the Port of Miami.

"No, nothing," Alex answered. The officer seemed satisfied, put Alex's passport into a machine, typed something on the keyboard and said, "Welcome home, Mr. Browning." He handed Alex his passport and called, "Next."

Alex shouldered his carry-on and followed the signs to the domestic terminal for his connecting flight to PHL. He checked the status board and confirmed that his flight was ON TIME. He was tempted to call Jo (might as well spread the calls around), but decided that within hours he would be with his daughters so he let it go. He found his gate and took a seat to wait.

Bautiste made a reservation, first class, in the name of Felipe Buenavista. The flight was from Aruba to Amsterdam with a change in Madrid. He thanked the operator for her help.

He entered the villa's well-appointed master bathroom and gazed skeptically at his reflection. He considered a further modification of his appearance. Maybe hair dye for his stubble? Maybe shaving his skull completely? Maybe a total queen look with mascara, eye shadow, and lipstick? He smiled at the thought. In the macho Caribbean, such an appearance would draw more attention than anything else. He decided that he looked enough not like himself to pass airport inspection. Besides, he wasn't sure that he was even being sought in Aruba and, for another thing, he was sure that, once at the airport, he could fall in with a crowd of tourists and avoid scrutiny that way.

He packed, called the lease company, called for a taxi and locked the front door. Queen Beatrix International Airport was small but modern. Within thirty minutes, Bautiste (Señor Buenavista) was validated as an airline passenger on his way to Amsterdam. As a law enforcement professional, Bautiste inwardly scoffed at the low level of alertness on display. The airport security staff was just short of incompetent according to his observations.

"Monsieur, votre passeport?"

"*Voici.*" Buenavista handed over the fake document. The officer scrutinized the forger's handiwork and Bautiste could see that, by his examination, he was only going through the motions. He had no idea of what exactly to look for, Bautiste could tell, when trying to determine a document's authenticity.

"*Bien.*" The less than astute officer returned Buenavista's passport. He waved the Colonel through to the waiting area and focused his lack of attention on the next passenger.

Bautiste sought out a refreshment stand and purchased a bottle of juice and a pastry. He found a seat with its back to a wall that offered a view of the entire waiting area. He opened his drink and unwrapped his sticky snack. He munched slowly, keeping an eye out for trouble.

At the time Bautiste was enjoying his doughy repast, Alex was boarding his Sunday flight to Philadelphia. He was enjoying the sensation of being under the control of American efficiency.

438

"Welcome aboard, Mister Browning. Seat 23D. Do you need any help?" the smiling attendant asked with cool professionalism.

"No, Ma'am. I'm sure I can find it. Excuse me," he said as he sidled by her in the narrow space. Alex passed through the First Class area and thought to himself that the flight was pretty empty. He continued to move to the rear until he found row 23. Taking his seat, he felt a pang of loneliness, needing to see his daughters and his brother more than ever before. He also felt a need for a Bloody Mary.

It was one of those flights. There was an annoying person in front of him trying to recline her seat. Since Alex was six feet three inches tall, Alex's knees continually thwarted the woman's efforts. She summoned the Flight Attendant to report the problem.

"I can only put my seat back this far. Can you help me?" Alex heard the woman say. The Attendant noticed Alex's knees and looked at Alex. Alex shrugged helplessly.

"It appears to be broken," the Attendant told the woman. "I'll report it when we land. I'm sorry. Would you like a free beverage?" The woman declined the drink. The Attendant asked Alex's row if anyone wanted something to drink. Alex ordered his Bloody Mary. Somewhere ahead a baby was crying.

Alex sipped his drink and read the newspaper, USA Today Sunday Edition, that someone in the row ahead was holding up. Fortunately for Alex the person seemed to be a very slow reader. Alex caught up on the national news, the world news, and was getting to the latest in sports when he realized that March Madness was going on. He realized that it was Saturday's paper, so Thursday's winners would be playing each other. Sunday would see the Friday winners compete. He strained his eyes to see if he could see the La Salle Friday result.

Major General Hernandez received the information late on Sunday afternoon.

"And the pilot's name?"

"Antonio Villafranca. Should I spell it?" the detective asked speaking into the car's police radio. The General spelled it instead. "That's it," the detective confirmed.

"Do you have him in custody, this Villafranca?"

"He's cuffed in the back seat of my car." The General smiled. He liked efficiency.

"Good. Bring him here for questioning." The detective agreed and broke off.

"Finally, some good news," the General said to the roomful of young officers who were hard at work on a Sunday. He summoned one of them. "Get me everything we have on a Señor Antonio Villafranca," the General ordered. He spelled the name. "Send it to my email."

In five minutes the General had his information. He smiled at the young officer's work. Efficiency again. Instead of cramming all of Villafranca's data into the email, the officer had provided a link to an internal police web page. The web page had more links.

The General discovered that Villafranca was a midlevel criminal, a sometimes smuggler, trafficker, and all around bad guy who would apparently do anything as long as there was pay involved. The General was still absorbing the information when he was alerted that the detective had arrived with the suspect, Villafranca.

Bautiste had a first class window seat just behind the galley. He stretched out and watched the apron activity as power and air cables were moved about, luggage carts streamed back and forth threatening to dump at least one overstuffed bag on the tarmac, and skinny black men dropped baggage on a conveyor belt, which loaded them into the belly of the plane.

"Señor Buenavista?" the pretty flight attendant checked her list. "Would you like a pre-flight cocktail?" Bautiste thought about it briefly and ordered a glass of champagne. Might as well celebrate a little he thought. When his drink arrived, he sipped it. When the aircraft began to taxi, he toasted his rapidly darkening window. Shortly, the attendant came around to take dinner orders. Bautiste realized that he was of good appetite. He looked forward to his meal.

The questioning of Villafranca was going well. The criminal was familiar with the police routines and so the conversation was as if it were choreographed. Eventually, Villafranca identified Bautiste as the man he had flown to Aruba. He kept insisting that no names were exchanged, but, eventually, the detectives broke him down.

"Buenavista was his name," the sweaty and trembling pilot told the detectives.

"First name?"

"I don't remember. We were not really friends, you know?"

"First name. Of course, you remember."

"I don't remember." And so it went for thirty minutes or more, the pilot/career criminal claiming that he couldn't remember and the detectives continuing to press. Finally, Villafranca cracked. "It may have started with an 'F', I'm not sure." The detectives stared at him. Neither made a remark. Villafranca seemed intimidated by their silence. "Ok, ok. Francisco or Felipe or Flavio? Felipe, I think. Yes, Felipe."

The detectives gave Villafranca a bad cup of coffee while they checked on his statement. Aruba confirmed that a Felipe Buenavista had arrived the day before. The lease of a villa had been arranged online a few days prior. However, when the Venezuelan authorities requested a hold on Señor Buenavista, they were informed that the man had left the island country and was currently in transit to Amsterdam.

"Bullshit!" exclaimed one of the detectives. "What do we have with Holland?" He was asking about agreements with the Netherlands concerning extradition, hold and return, or nothing. No one seemed to know, so they took a break while the subject was researched.

"Fuck," said a detective reflecting the mood of the team. It turned out that Venezuela had a cooperative agreement with Holland where escaped felons were concerned, but there was no agreement concerning suspects. Buenavista was free to land and then to roam.

Bautiste enjoyed a light meal of tournedos and arugula. He ate his bread liberally slathered in butter and his dessert. He consumed several more glasses of champagne and then surrendered to his alcohol induced stupor and fatigue. When he awoke, the cabin lights were dimmed and a display mapping their progress toward Madrid was on the big screen. It was almost a cartoon, an aircraft depicted in white inching along a predetermined white arc terminating at Madrid's Adolfo Suarez Madrid Barajas Airport. Bautiste watched the animation briefly and then returned to sleep.

He awoke to the sound of soft gongs and gradually brightening lights. It took him a minute to orient himself and when he did he recognized that his mouth was dry and tasted awful. He could only imagine how bad his breath must be. He looked around for a flight attendant who could supply him with bottled water.

Connie, Jo, Paul Tanner, and Jim Davis took seats in the Arrival waiting area. Alex's flight's status was On Time. It was awkward having a four-way conversation because the seats were so far apart. It was Jo who did the analysis.

"These seats are set up as if they expected that people sitting here would have a ton of luggage. Do people waiting for flights usually have luggage?"

"You wouldn't think so," Paul said.

"Maybe the designers were just in 'airport mode' for everything," Jim said.

"What's 'airport mode'? You mean that since it's in an airport, the seats should be far enough apart to allow for suitcases?" Connie laughed. "That's retarded!" Jim Davis laughed.

"Don't you guys have this experience every day: people suck at their jobs? I seem to see this all the time. Don't you?" Davis asked. The others laughed.

"Every damn day," Connie agreed. "For example, I just called my dentist to make an appointment for cleaning and check up. It took the receptionist four tries before she got my name right. And when I got to the appointment, my paperwork was screwed up. She spelled my name wrong after all. B-r-o-n-i-n-g. Is that even a name? Unbelievable." They all laughed and began to exchange their own experiences of incompetence in the workplace.

They were so absorbed in their stories that they were surprised when the jetway's doors were unlocked and passengers began to emerge.

Alex checked his seat and the surrounding area (per the flight attendant's instructions) to make sure he had all of his stuff. He wasn't the kind of person to spread his possessions around in a public place, but he was aware of the possibility of having an item slip out of his pocket.

Satisfied, he shouldered his carry-on careful not to assault passengers standing near by. Alex liked the way American passengers were polite and handled the merge of rows into the center aisle. And it felt good to stand up and stretch his legs. He was waved into the center aisle by a polite woman and joined the flow of passengers heading toward the door and the jetway.

When he neared the end of the jetway, he was able to see his daughters over the heads of the preceding passengers. He waved until he was sure they had seen him. He noticed the young men with his daughters, recognized Paul Tanner and the lawyer, Jim Davis.

"Daddy!" Jo led the charge forward to embrace him and welcome him home.

Bautiste deplaned at Amsterdam's Schiphol Airport to have no one greet him. He claimed his checked bag and hailed a cab. He directed the driver to the Grand Hotel Downtown, a nice modern hotel located not far from the city center.

Bautiste didn't have a reservation, but the hotel staff was accommodating and checked him into a clean, smallish room. Bautiste arranged for a Monday mid-morning wake up call, showered, and got into bed.

CHAPTER TWENTY—Home, But What Now?

"Daddy," Joanne said with obvious delight, "look at you! You're all tanned. Did you lose weight?" She held Alex at arm's length so she could examine him. Connie stepped in embrace her father.

"Welcome home, Dad," she said. "You ok?" Alex's worries and sorrow over the past few days disappeared as he surrendered to the love of his family.

"I'm fine, baby, now that I'm home. What a time, though. I've got so much to tell you guys." He kissed the top of Jo's head as he squeezed Connie tighter. The daughters asked about Erin. Alex said he would tell them later and his tone worried them.

They piled into Davis' SUV, Tanner assuming the front passenger seat. Just being there between his girls was an incredible return to normalcy for Alex. They wanted him to sit on one side or the other so that he would have more legroom, but Alex was where he wanted to be. He was surprised that he was enjoying himself.

"Have either of you had a chance to call Uncle Terry?"

"Not me," said Jo. "I assumed he was wrapped up in the Tournament. La Salle's playing today."

"Holy crap," Davis said from the driver's seat. "I forgot all about it. It's probably over. Anybody know who won?" He glanced at Tanner.

"I don't even know who they're playing," Alex admitted. "I lost track completely." He was shocked that this had happened. "What's been going on?" Paul Tanner leaned in the gap between the front seats.

"How much do you know?"

"Not much," Alex admitted. "Nothing," he clarified.

"Ok. La Salle got chosen for one of the play-in teams. The weird thing was that they were playing against Boise State for a thirteen seed. They won last Wednesday by nine or ten."

"Wow. So now they're a thirteen seed?"

"Right. But, bad news. They had to play a four seed, Kansas State on Friday. And, the game was in Kansas. Anyway, La Salle built up such a first half lead that Kansas State's comeback wasn't enough. So, move on to today against Mississippi. Anybody know what time they played?" Everyone was busy with phones except Davis and Alex.

"Play, you mean," said Jo. "Tip off at eight. Where should we watch it?" Alex had a paroxysm of guilt. He wanted to go to Connie's or Jo's. He wanted to drink and unwind and feel the closeness of his girls. But, he kept his mouth shut.

"Bar or how about my place?" It was Davis. "I've got plenty of beer, a big screen, we can call out for pizza, and you can take your shoes off. What do you say?" He had directed his comments at everyone but his gaze in the rear view mirror was on Connie. Everyone politely waited for everyone else to respond. It was Alex who spoke first.

"That sounds great and thank you for offering, Jim. I could go for a free beer or two," he added. They all laughed and the chatter turned to La Salle's chances against Ole Miss. No one knew how good the Rebels were.

"Anybody know what their seed is?" It was Connie this time. Jo checked it out before anyone else.

"Ooo," she said, "twelve seed. They beat Wisconsin in the first round. Low scoring game." Alex liked the feeling of everything getting back to normal.

"I filled out a bracket when I was in Venezuela," he said. Then he laughed. "I just can't remember which website it was on." Everyone laughed.

Davis' condominium was on the fifth floor of a building overlooking the Schuylkill River. The side facing the river was a glass wall that led out onto a furnished balcony. Alex was given a beer and, taking a long pull on the bottle, unlatched the sliding doors. He walked out and immediately felt the chill that still lingered in the night spring air. He was reminded that he hadn't been in temperatures this cold for four weeks. He approached the low wall of the patio.

"Those lights over there," Davis had slipped up behind him, giving him a slight start, "those are the college boathouses." Alex followed Davis' pointing finger and picked out the lights almost directly across. "One light for each boathouse," Davis said. It was a peaceful sight in the dark. The river picked up each light and reflected it in its shimmering surface.

"Nice view," Alex said. "Must be great to watch the sculling in the morning, huh?"

"Really great. There are singles and crews every morning, summer or winter, rain or shine. Impressive." Alex could imagine sitting up here having coffee. The thought of people having an innocent good time, doing what they loved to do, made him feel guilty. He turned toward the lawyer.

"Can we talk a minute?"

"Sure." Davis was alert to the change in their conversational tone and, as a professional, made an immediate adjustment. "What can I do for you?" He indicated two chairs around a glass-topped table. Alex noticed the circular hole in the center of the glass presumably for an umbrella. He thought that an open umbrella up this high was inviting disaster. He turned his focus to the moment.

"So you're my lawyer, right? I mean lawyer-client privilege and all that." Davis cleared his throat.

"Well, I'm your business lawyer. Do you need a personal lawyer?"

"I'm not sure. Can't I give you a dollar or something like they do in the movies and make you my lawyer? Just for right now?" Davis shifted in his cushioned seat.

"You can. Give me a dollar." Alex checked his cash.

"I have a five. Here." He handed the five-dollar bill over.

"Remember this, though: if you tell me you've done something illegal, I'm obligated to report it. As an officer of the court."

"How do I know if it's illegal until you tell me it is? That's kind of screwed up, right?"

"Right. But, if you're not sure, frame it in a way that doesn't inculpate you."

"Inculpate? Make me involved? Look guilty?" Alex was trying to grasp the rules of this new game.

"Hey you guys," Connie called. "Getting ready for tipoff. You coming in?"

"In a minute, Con," Alex said.

"Be right there, babe," Davis added, and then realized he may have been inappropriate. "Sorry." He directed this last at Alex.

"No problem. You two seem to have hit it off. Is it serious?"

"She's unlike any I've been with." Davis realized he might have said the wrong thing. "I mean, to me, she's special."

"She's special to me, too. She's my little girl. Maybe, one day, you'll know what that means. Anyway, I think I understand what you mean by 'inculpate'". Alex edged up in his cushioned seat.

"Ok. Go." Davis leaned in also.

"Let's say a friend of mine had a chance to own a special object. But the object was in his neighbor's yard, for example. Could he move it, if no one knew, to another location, a location that would give him a right of ownership?"

"Absolutely not," Davis said. His tone was definite.

"Well, how about if the special object wasn't in his neighbor's yard, but in the woods nearby that no one owned. Could he move it then?"

"Not really. Why would he need to move it in that case?" Jim was confused. "I'm not sure I follow." Alex was getting frustrated trying to explain the drilling and the slurry catamarans.

"Ok, how about this. Anything found in the nearby woods would be the property of the Sheriff of Nottingham. But if my friend moves the object from the woods to another location, the object appears to be his. How about then?"

"Does the Sheriff have any idea the object even existed?"

"A hint. Maybe. But no clue where."

"Interesting," Davis mused. "So an argument could be made that the property was never possessed. In the legal sense." He looked frankly at Alex. "So you somehow recovered whatever and moved it?"

"Yes, my friend moved it."

The Zodiac took a long draw on his cigarette and exhaled through his nostrils and mouth. He felt the nicotine buzz and enjoyed it. It took the edge off when he was feeling tense and pressured. This American had stopped his bots and now the gambling site refused to pay.

The first thing was to overcome the block. Send more bots in to the attack. Overwhelm the defense. Make the bastards pay double. Except that the additional bots weren't getting the job done. How was this possible? The Zodiac had to call the Nazi.

The Nazi had made more ransom money performing DDOS attacks than anyone in Russia. His command of a huge botnet made him the man to know when a hacker wanted to perform a DDOS attack and didn't have enough resources. The Zodiac sent him a message explaining his situation and asking for help.

The thing was that, in Russia's hacker society, no hacker could act without protection. Protection took two forms and both were extremely necessary. One had to have political protection. This was gained by bribing local officials. Second, one had to have mob protection. Organized crime in Russia was not that organized, but it was brutal and without a scintilla of humanity. The Nazi had protection and the Zodiac did not. Zodiac was hoping that he could pick up Nazi's protection while enlisting his botnet.

Zodiac's phone rang. There was no recognition of the caller.

"Allo?"

"Piece of shit? You are contacting me? You?" Zodiac was put off balance at first. Then he realized who was calling.

"I am sorry, Nazi. I am sorry. I need your help. I mean, I need your botnet. I need your botnet's help." Zodiac knew he was stammering, but he couldn't help it.

"Yes. You need my help. You need the protection that my *tovarishch* can provide, yes? That is what you need. Tell me I am wrong." Zodiac was sweating, but Nazi had no idea. Zodiac decided to try a bluff.

"You are wrong, brother. You think that your politicians and mafia protection are what I need, but what I really want and need is your botnet." Zodiac paused and Nazi had no response. "So give me what I want, what I need, and fuck off." Zodiac waited. Nazi was surprised.

"There is a reason you do not have the resources you require," Nazi began, "and that is because you are a cheap fucking hacker little bitch. What are you?" the Nazi shouted.

"A cheap hacker little bitch?" Zodiac whimpered.

"No. A cheap fucking hacker little bitch," Nazi corrected. "So you understand?" There was amusement in his voice. "You don't have enough bots. Who you trying to attack?" Zodiac could sense the Nazi was considering his request. He named the well-known gambling site. Gambling sites were sensitive to DDOS attacks and the hacker community knew all of them.

"Is good target. What is problem?" The Nazi didn't let Zodiac answer. He guessed what the problem was. "Someone is blocking your attack, yes? All right. You pay me fifty percent of what you get from gambling site and you can use my bots." Zodiac knew the request was totally unreasonable, but he also knew that he needed more that just bots from the Nazi.

"Ok. Fifty percent," Zodiac agreed. "But, brother, you believe in me, yes? You know I can get paid, yes? You should let me join you." Zodiac's suggestion hung in silence. He was young and impatient, but was smart enough to know that the next one who spoke would lose. The silence went on. And then the Nazi spoke.

"All right. Join me," he said and he broke the connection.

Zodiac opened a bottle of vodka in celebration. He felt sure that his skills were better than anyone on the Nazi's team. As he poured himself a glass, he thought about who had blocked his attack. Usually those who opposed his country's hackers did their best to remain anonymous online. This person was good at hiding his identity. Maybe they worked for one of the Western government agencies that were always trying to have hackers arrested. This pursuit by the West emphasized the need for political protection in Russia. Western governments provided Russian authorities with the identities and locations of hackers and expected the Russians to arrest and prosecute the offenders. In reality, the Russians offered reasons to never go to court as political pressure or even bribes were used to discourage vigorous prosecution. Zodiac was not worried about being found out, but he wanted to know who was thwarting his DDOS attack. He had developed something special for just such a person.

Jim Davis thought he now understood what Alex's concerns were.

"Ok," he said, "so let's see. Party Number One and Party Number Two have an agreement that says whatever Party Number Two finds in this room of One's house belongs to Two. Two just has to clean the room, let's say. But Party Number Three tosses something from another part of the house into the room. So far so good?" Alex agreed. He could see that the lawyer grasped the situation.

"Right. That's about it. One doesn't know what Three did and, of course, Two and Three had a separate agreement."

"Well, the legal issue is that Three basically stole from One whatever was the value of the object added to the room. Two isn't culpable. Two didn't know what Three did. So, One has a case for theft.

"But, as I understand it, One didn't know that the object wasn't originally in the room. So One never made a claim. It's an interesting situation. The only party who knew what happened is Three and I assume Three isn't talking.

"So there's a legal issue. And, of course, there's a moral issue. But it looks like that's where it's going to remain. Am I right?" He gazed across the glass-topped patio table at Alex. Alex thought briefly of Erin.

"You are. That's where it's going to remain. Should we go and watch some basketball?" Alex pushed his chair back and then changed his mind.

"One more thing, Jim," he said resuming his seat.

"Go ahead," the lawyer encouraged.

"I'd like you to form a financial team for the Browning Group. I assume we will need advisors and tax people and accountants and investment types. Can you do that? You'll, of course, have a lead position on that team." Alex almost said 'as my son-in-law', but he knew he would be getting way ahead of things and it wouldn't even be a good joke.

"I can set that up for you. The firm knows some good people. And, may I say, that's a really smart move by you? That amount of money should get the respect it deserves.

"By the way, do you have any idea what you're going to do with it? Connie was talking earlier about setting up a foundation."

"Yeah, I know, but I'm not convinced that's the way to go." Alex was hesitant to go against his daughter, but he had a vague idea of what the money could be used for. And, besides, he thought they should grow the money responsibly.

"What's your idea? By the way, we're missing the first half." They could see the others fist pumping and high-fiving in front of the TV.

"Well, it's admittedly half-baked, but I think I'd like to set up a VC company here on the East Coast. Why should Silicon Valley have all the fun?" He was referring, Davis knew, to a Venture Capital firm.

"Interesting. That would have a good potential for growth. If handled right. I like that better than the Foundation idea. Let me talk to the experts on it and see what they say, ok? It'll be confidential at this point."

"Sounds good. Hey, my brother's here. Let's go in and watch some basketball." Alex had noticed Terry's arrival as he hugged his nieces and shook hands with Tanner.

Alex slid open the glass door and held his arms wide.

"Nice tan," Terry remarked as they hugged. "You lost some weight, too. Right?" Alex rubbed his stomach.

"A little," he admitted. "Some exercise and some stress. I'll tell you all about it later.

"Congrats, by the way on La Salle. Surprised the hell out of me. How about you? Were you expecting this kind of success?" Terry held his palms together and directed his eyes toward the ceiling.

"The power of prayer," he said piously, "plus good guard play." Alex laughed and helped himself to another of Davis' beers. He took a seat to watch a very close first half.

Fernando Bautiste, as Felipe Buenavista, strolled the streets of Amsterdam. His dark skin drew more than a few stares from the locals despite the size of the city. He was enjoying the change in climate from tropical to northern Europe. In spite of the late March date, the weather was still winter-like. Bautiste had purchased a warm coat complete with hood at a very good late-season price. He was planning his future as he walked along. Amsterdam, as a good-sized European city, offered a degree of anonymity. However, his

454

flight could be traced here. Another, more appealing, choice was twenty miles across the border in Belgium. The smallish city of Antwerp was handy to all European capitols and yet was, more or less, a bedroom community. Bautiste found a bookstore and entered.

He browsed the Travel section and found five references for Antwerp and a big pamphlet on Belgium. He paid for all his material and left the store to seek out a cafe.

The cafe's outdoor area was closed and the inside was overheated. He took a seat at a small table and removed his coat. The place was fairly empty at mid-morning and he ordered a coffee. He pulled out his purchases and began to read.

Major General Hernandez was disappointed at having missed Bautiste in Aruba, if in fact it was Bautiste. He decided to have his detectives fly to Aruba with a photo of Bautiste to confirm Villafranca's story and the identity of Buenavista. Another team of detectives was gathering ballistic evidence. If anyone used a service weapon to kill the three guards at the airport, his men should be able to make a ballistic match because all NP service weapons had their ballistic characteristics entered in a database. He decided to close the case on Sergeant Garcia. The coroner listed his cause of death as possible suicide and the man's apartment and office, when searched, revealed that he had a false Costa Rican passport and other forms of identification in the name of Juan Herdez. The General liked things tidy and closing the Garcia case freed manpower for more important investigations. His phone rang.

"Hernandez," he said. His voice reflected his weariness. The population showed no signs of letting up in their protests and demonstrations.

La Salle was ahead at half time, but by only two points. Mississippi's size was, so far, being countered by La Salle's quick guard play. Everyone watching at Davis' condo was mesmerized. Terry and Alex, as the old guys, remembered the last time La Salle had done well in the Tournament. Instead of sixty-eight teams, back then there were only twenty-four. Waiting since the late Sixties for another chance at national recognition had been painful. But, maybe now, the Explorers' time had come.

"Think they can keep this up?" Alex directed the question at his brother. Terry held the cold beer bottle to his forehead.

"I don't know. Mississippi is bound to make adjustments for the second half. Should we change what we're doing? Would you?" Alex's basketball coaching experience consisted of being an assistant coach for Connie's ten and under league and then being head coach of Jo's thirteen and under team. "Coaching" at that level consisted mainly of encouragement and remembering post-game snacks.

"I wouldn't change anything coming out of the locker room. I'd wait to see what Mississippi does to adjust. If their changes were working, then I'd adjust to their adjustments. Plus, I'd make sure I didn't forget the post-game snacks." Alex's delivery was dry. Terry did a double take on this last pronouncement.

"Huh?"

"Just recalling my coaching days. Another beer?"

Zodiac, despite his conversation with Nazi, had grown tired of DDOS forays, identity theft, and data destruction. He had decided that a more direct approach was needed to create a revenue stream that would be reliable. He had initiated contact with a small group of Chinese hackers. He believed there were three of them. He

456

presented his idea to them after one of them pointed out a security hole in the Windows operating system registry software. The exploit depended on an unwary user clicking on a website link. Then the site would allow a hacker to upload a virus that would lock the user's computer data and send the user an email demanding a few hundred dollars to get a software key that would unlock the data. The lock, the email explained, was on a timer. If the user didn't pay in a timely manner, the data would never be unlocked and the hacker would move on to the next victim.

Zodiac was excited about the prospect of having a relatively small amount of money paid over and over as opposed to demanding a huge sum from a wealthy gambling website and the uncertainty of ever getting paid. The concept of putting a time limit on the victim was developed in the late Nineties. It had slowly come to be the model adopted as a useful means of adding pressure. The hacking community didn't want their victims thinking too clearly.

The system turned out to be a winner for the hackers. Victims paid fairly regularly, even law enforcement organizations, which were not especially singled out. They were just chosen randomly, like all the victims, based on email or IP addresses. Police departments, like small businesses or even families, could not afford to lose their data whether they had a large Oracle database or a tiny one based on Microsoft Access. They all paid, or, at least, most of them. When people didn't pay before the time ran out, they never got their data back. It wasn't that the hackers withheld the data in a mean-spirited fashion. The hackers just moved on to the next victim.

A good hacker, meaning one who hustled like a maniac, could make a million dollars in a year. Zodiac wasn't interested in hustling. He always wanted to do things the smart way. So he wrote a script that would spread the locking software as far and as fast as possible. The money had rolled in.

The second half of the La Salle/Ole Miss game was a mirror of the first. Ole Miss stubbornly insisted on trying to impose size and strength on the smaller Explorers. The Explorers used a three-guard line-up to counter the bigger, slower Rebels. It was clear after five minutes that this was going to be a standoff. Alex, despite his fatigue, was riveted by the action.

"This team is great," he declared. "How did they do last year?"

"They were good," Terry said. The brothers were seated next to each other. The younger couples were seated according to their pairings. The couples were devoting most of their attention to each other. "Too young last year, though," Terry said, "seasoned now. The coach did a good job."

"He's not a big name guy, though, is he?"

"It's the La Salle way, Alex. We make the most with the least." Alex smiled, an idea forming.

"Terry, what would you like to see done with all that money? I mean, what would be your number one priority?" He split his attention between the TV and his brother. Terry obviously considered the question seriously. He wanted to watch the hotly contested game, though.

"Let's talk later, Alex. For now, let's watch the game, ok?" Terry gestured toward the television. Alex touched the neck of his beer bottle to the neck of Terry's.

"Great idea, Ter."

The basketball game went on and, if you were a fan of basketball, you appreciated the back and forth, the give and take. By the final two minutes, it appeared as if Mississippi was going to pull off an improbable victory. Foul shots brought La Salle back to even. Finally, on the last play of the game a La Salle guard forced the issue, drove to the basket, arced the ball under the larger defender's outstretched arm and made the winning basket. La Salle fans all over, including the six gathered in Jim Davis' home, jumped up and screamed in sports craziness. La Salle had won by two points and would be in the Sweet Sixteen for the first time since 1955. For their fans, it was unbelievable.

"So who's next?" Alex asked leaning in to Terry's right ear. Terry laughed.

"A little cold-blooded, Alex. Think of all the Ole Miss fans. Don't you want to give them a chance to heal before targeting the next victim?" Terry was smiling broadly. Alex smiled, too.

"I'm not as charitable as you. Now, that the game's over, let's grab a beer and go outside. I want to hear your ideas on what we talked about before." Terry had to think for a second.

"Oh, the money. Sure. Let's go." Terry got up and headed toward Davis' kitchen to get two beers. Alex looked about the room and saw that his two daughters were involved in conversation with the two young men. He headed for the glass patio doors and intersected with Terry.

"Here you go, my brother." Terry extended an opened beer. Alex accepted as they headed for a couple of patio chairs.

They sat in the brisk air and got comfortable and then an uncomfortable silence ensued.

"So," Alex sipped his beer, "what is your number one priority? Where spending the money is concerned. It's part yours, too, you know?"

Terry considered the implications.

"I heard the sum is, like, three hundred million? Is that right?"

"It's even a little more. That's what we've been told by the French government, anyway. So there's a lot to go around." Alex sipped his beer again. "I should say that I've got a couple of ideas, as do the girls." Terry sipped his beer and put the bottle on the table. He looked across the table at his brother.

"Well, I'm not going to stand in the way of the Browning Group's ideas. You guys go ahead and spend or invest or give it away as you see fit. I'll support you." Alex thought before reacting to Terry's statement.

"That's great, but I really want your input. There's a ton of money, Ter. Isn't there something you'd like to see it used for?" Terry did have something in mind. It had been gnawing at him for forty years.

"Ok. I do have an idea. I'll tell it to you, but you have to promise that if it's too stupid or it doesn't fit into your scheme, you'll just forget about it and not think that I'm an idiot." Alex knew his brother better than anyone else. Terry was the furthest thing from an idiot. And, Terry was shrewd where money was concerned. The University's endowment fund was approaching a billion dollars and, although Terry was Provost, he often had good ideas on how to best grow the endowment fund. Terry passed his ideas on to the University President who, in turn, passed them on to the Board. The Board usually accepted with enthusiasm.

"It won't be stupid, Ter! How can the Provost of a major University even think that his advice would be considered stupid? What the fuck?"

"Nice. You used to kiss Mom with that mouth, asshole." Terry smiled and pointed at Alex's lips. "But, anyway, what do you want to know?"

"Actually, I just want to know what you think is a good idea. For the money." Alex looked quizzically at his brother. He thought that his brother look baffled by the question, by the simple question.

"I have an idea, like I said. You'll hate it, but I believe it's a good idea on a lot of levels. It's an investment. It's guaranteed, I believe, to grow. It's reasonably priced from what I can tell. Seller is motivated. Tax advantages..."

"Ok, ok. What is it? What's your idea?"

"Whitewood Hall," Terry announced naming the century-old property located north of Philadelphia in the community of Elkins Park. He studied his brother's face for reaction. Positive or negative, he didn't care. He just wanted to know what Alex thought.

"What's Whitewood Hall again? I know you mentioned it before."

Terry reminded Alex of their previous conversations, and more than just conversations. Alex remembered visiting Terry when he was an undergraduate student. At that time Brother Terry's community lived in Elkins Park. Across the road was a Protestant Seminary, a huge light-gray building set on a large estate. It looked like a District of Columbia government building with stately columns and imposing facade. It was called Whitewood Hall. As Terry spoke, Jim Davis joined the two men on the patio.

"Mind if I join you?" He looked from one brother to the other. It was Alex who gestured to one of Davis' empty chairs.

"We're just discussing high finance," Alex said wryly.

Connie joined the patio group. She pulled a chair up close to Jim and wrapped her arm in his. Alex noticed that, as they listened to Terry talk about the mansion and its estate, the young lawyer affectionately and naturally put his free hand on Connie's arm and gently stroked it. Alex smiled to himself and wondered if Davis was "the one" for Connie. He trusted his daughter's judgment and was not worried (well, maybe a little) at her choice.

461

Jo and Paul Tanner stepped out on the patio, their arms around each other's waist. They walked up and stood silently as the group listened to Terry further describe the hundred-year old estate. Alex watched them as they leaned in to each other. Jo only came up to the security consultant's shoulder, but she gave an aura of strength that was equal to Tanner's. Alex tried to figure out what it was that made his diminutive daughter seem so strong. He realized it wasn't just the muscle definition under her layer of lady fat. That was part of it though. The real reason was her face. Her jaw was set in a way that said, "You don't want to get in my way." Her dark eyes were watchful and missed nothing. Alex was so proud.

"Hey, you guys," Alex said, "Just talking money. Grab a seat."

"Thanks, Dad," Jo said. They pulled a lounge chair close and Paul sat at Jo's feet as she scrunched in to the seat. Terry continued to explain why he thought the pursuit of the Elkins Park property was deserving of attention.

In an Amsterdam cafe Fernando Bautiste scanned and absorbed a myriad of source material on Antwerp. The more he learned the better he felt about being able to avoid attention there. It was close to Holland. It was a quiet city of stately homes and a thriving business district, wide boulevards, and a mix of the historical and the modern. He sipped a very good cup of coffee and nibbled on a piece of chocolate. Antwerp was his place he decided. So now he needed to choose a residence. He considered the Muslim section since his dark skin would blend in. However, and ironically, he despised the intolerance of those people. He chose instead a city section that was described as the destination of expatriates. Now he needed to make some phone calls. He decided to call from the hotel lobby. He paid for his coffee and headed back to his hotel.

"So we're all rich," Terry said gesturing toward his family members. He picked up his beer bottle and shook it. It was empty. Davis volunteered to get him another one. "Of course, I have a vow of poverty, so I'm not allowed to be rich," he joked.

Alex corrected Terry. "We're filthy rich, Ter. There's a big difference." He smiled.

"Dad, can you tell us what happened down there. We only know you wanted that software. Is that where the money came from?" It was Jo asking. She lowered her voice. "Did you steal it?" Alex leaned in toward his younger daughter.

"In a way I did." He watched each person's reaction to this news. By and large, this was a Catholic group. Some were more religious than others he knew. "I absolutely stole the original money from some very bad people."

He explained how they had tricked him into becoming a drug smuggler and how he had cooperated with his friends in Federal law enforcement. They were fascinated at his story. Paul Tanner spoke from his own special perspective.

"It sounds like you made some enemies, sir. You should take precautions. People who lose that much money are going to hold a grudge. They'll even look for some payback." The security expert/bodyguard gestured with his palms up. "I'm just saying."

"I appreciate it, Paul. I can tell you one of the bad guys is dead. I'm not sure what happened to his boss, but I'm not too worried. I doubt he has enough resources left to do me any harm."

"Well, you never know. My experience is that you should be careful until you know you're safe."

"Do you really think Dad's in danger?" Jo asked. Her expression showed her concern. Tanner sought a balance. He didn't want to sound alarmist nor did he want to minimize.

"Probably not," he said honestly. "We'll talk about it later, ok?" Jo had grown to trust Paul's judgment and, even though it was her father's welfare they were talking about, she nodded in silent agreement. She still had a vivid memory of how Tanner had recently handled the would-be mugger.

"Look, you guys," Alex said. "For one thing, stop talking like I'm not here. For another, don't we want to celebrate, a little?" He raised his beer bottle and quickly brought it down. "Jim, do we have something a little more celebratory?" Davis, who had just replenished Terry's beer, considered for a second.

"I think I can come up with something. How about champagne and I think I have some bourbon if you prefer that?" Davis looked around at his guests with his eyebrows raised.

"Champagne sounds great." It was Connie who was first to accept the offer. Alex and Terry both asked for bourbon and Jo agreed with her sister. Tanner said he would stick with beer.

"So Dad," Connie asked while Davis brought the refreshments, "how *did* we become rich? Excuse me, filthy rich?" Alex laughed and decided to concoct the story that would have to hold up for the foreseeable future.

"Well, there was this shipwreck off a Venezuelan beach. The ship's name was the *Little Ranger*, but actually it turned out to be a French ship named the *Comte de Toulouse.*" He realized they were confused and couldn't follow his narrative. He decided to simplify.

"So there's the ship. But there was also this ship's log in a local museum. No one understood the list of names in the ship's log, but Jo solved the puzzle. It turned out there was a message pointing to a lot of pirate loot right there just waiting to be collected. I made a deal with the French to tell them where it was. They agreed. We got very lucky. There was a lot more treasure that anyone imagined." He looked around the table to see if his audience was satisfied. He decided that they looked like they were.

"So all the treasure was pirate gold and jewels and stuff?" It was a great story and Connie loved the romance of it.

"I guess," Alex lied. "You know, I never got to see any of it. The Florida company, that guy McDonald?, and the French recovered everything." He thought for a second. "Maybe there are pictures that they took. I'll have to look into it."

"That is such an amazing story," Jo said. "I mean you read about this stuff all the time, but to have it happen to you... wow." She shrugged, at a loss for words.

"So the Florida company and the French converted all the treasure to cash?" asked Paul Tanner. "Where'd all the millions come from?"

"Well, I think it was the French government that put a value on the recovery, but Jim probably knows better than I do. Jim?" Alex handed the question over to the lawyer.

"That's right," Davis said. "The French had experts on the scene and back home in France to give a running evaluation of the treasure as it was recovered. We, as the Browning Group, had agreed to accept their evaluation. We made a decision to trust the French. Does anyone want an independent audit?" He wondered if any of the family doubted his judgment.

"Hell, no, Jim." It was Alex who spoke up. "We made a shitload of money, sorry girls," he tipped his head toward his daughters and then went on, "so much money that I know it was far more than anyone expected. So I don't care if we could squeeze the French for one or two million more." Alex paused and, although the others thought he was letting his point sink in, he was actually thinking that one or two million was sufficient penance for the life of one Venezuelan Federal

465

policeman who burned to death. "Or even ten million more. I'm satisfied with the deal we made and I think that we should all be satisfied. Ok?" Alex looked to his daughters and brother for affirmation.

As Alex looked for his affirmation, Zodiac discovered who had stopped his DDOS attack on the gambling website. At least he had discovered that the source of the blockage was a single IP address located in Philadelphia, Pennsylvania, USA. He had to bring up a map of the United States to identify the precise latitude and longitude of Philadelphia. Near New York City, he thought wryly, but somewhat naively, always New York. He performed a search of the registries and discovered that the address was assigned to a domain name of JBSoftwareEnterprises.com. He searched the website's ownership and found Joanne Browning owned it. A little more probing and he determined that Joanne was woman, a young woman. He lifted the bottle of vodka, not bothering with a glass, and drank deeply. The bottle was nearly empty. A girl, he thought. He explored the website and found that it was a business that specialized in defending against identity theft, malware, DDOS attacks, and other kinds of computer shenanigans. This Joanne Browning had cost him a lot of money. He was determined that she would pay. Joanne, of course, had no idea of the enemy she had made.

As Felipe Buenavista, Fernando Bautiste sped south on an Antwerp-bound train. He had a comfortable cabin and had purchased a number of periodicals and newspapers from around the world. It was an article he found in the *Wall Street Journal* that enraged him so much that he punched the window of the cabin and, although his punch didn't break it, it caused it to fracture and shatter. His angry scream that accompanied the punch was audible through the walls of the two adjoining cabins. Those passengers alerted the conductors and two of them showed up at Felipe's sliding glass door.

"*Monsieur*, is everything all right?" They noticed the shattered glass of the window and attributed it to something from the outside. "*Monsieur*, I will summon the repairman and we will move you to another car, yes?"

"No. I'm all right. Do you have some tape? We can tape the window." The conductors looked dubious, but radioed for the repairman. He arrived with two thick rolls of tape and proceeded to cover the window's cracks. Buenavista refused to be relocated and the conductors and repairman left.

Felipe Buenavista retrieved the newspaper that had lain ignored on the cabin floor. He reread the article that had infuriated him. A newly formed Philadelphia company had decided to place a bid on a century-old estate located in nearby Elkins Park. The company wanted to use the property as it headquarters.

It wasn't the article that had caused Buenavista to lose control. It was the accompanying photograph. Centered among a group of apparent company executives was the man Felipe/Fernando most hated in this world. Alex Browning, smiling to the camera. In Philadelphia, Pennsylvania, USA.

Epilogue

The place was the northwest coast of the island of Margarita, not far off the coast of Venezuela, on a beach known as Playa Madrid. The time was the 1720s, more than 200 years after Columbus and after two centuries of Caribbean colonization and exploitation along the Spanish Main. A large group of men, maybe thirty in all, representing no identifiable country, sweating in the sun, was busily at work in the rocks and heat west of the beach. An observer would notice that these men spoke little and were working with a common purpose, in the fashion of military units or professionals who knew their task. These men were pirates, not in the romantic sense, but in the sense evoked by modern day Somalia and the Horn of Africa. They were in the last stage of their work when Franz, a young and less-disciplined member of the group, spied a young dog watching them from a distance. Sensing a sporting opportunity and needing a break from their hard labor, the men lured the unsuspecting animal closer with offers of beef from their pockets. The men thought it was great fun to catch, torture, and kill the poor dog. They imitated the dog's whelps and confused cries as they laughingly returned to their work. Franz, they all agreed, was a talented mimic.

Another larger group of men, maybe one hundred in all, led by a boy whose dog they were following witnessed the finale of the torture. These men were Guaiqueria Indians and were not sweating from the heat. They were descendants of the locals who had greeted Christopher Columbus in 1498, receiving the Spaniards with open arms. These simple people had had no suspicion that they would be enslaved due to the super abundance of pearls, which they willingly had shared with their new acquaintances. By the 1720s, however, all Guaiqueria were less naïve. Because a boy in their tribe owned the dog and because retribution went without question, the Indians were unemotional as they massacred the pirates slaying all but one. That pirate was singled out for special treatment since he was the one they actually witnessed applying the final acts to the dog. That pirate was stripped from the waist down, pinned on his stomach across the hard coral of the shore and, after hacking off the left hind leg of the dog and stripping all the flesh from the bone, the still-moist bone was inserted in his rectum and pounded home with wooden clubs. To silence Franz's screams, the same wooden clubs were used to crush his skull. Then all the bodies of the pirates were tossed into the nearby hole where the pirates were working. The dogleg pirate was tossed in last followed by the carcass of the dog.

The Indians held a quick discussion concluding that thirty pirates hadn't arrived from the mainland in the small boats that had been pulled up on the beach below. The Indians, as expert in the water as they were on land, embarked in the small boats to find and attack the largely unmanned ship at anchor offshore. They burned it to the shoreline and sank it after killing the skeleton crew. They then returned to the island.

The beach was clean except for some bloodstains and the pirates' tools and weapons. The Indians recovered whatever was of use and could be easily carried. A leather-bound journal was also recovered and was delivered to the boy, as rough consolation.